D1235616

LOVE IN DEED

GREEN VALLEY LIBRARY BOOK #6

L.B. DUNBAR

WWW.SMARTYPANTSROMANCE.COM

COPYRIGHT

DEDICATION

For John and Pam,
my second parents as a child,
and my only horse barn experience.

* * *

Disclaimer of sorts

If you've ever been in a verbally abusive relationship, you're familiar with the old adage: sticks and stones can break my bones, but names will never hurt me. However, you also might know the saying is hard to live by when you're pushed so far down that your feet are higher than your head. Breaking free of such a relationship can leave deep emotional scars which are so much harder to see than the ones people wear on their bodies. Coping comes in many forms, with addictions being a primary source, but support is out there. Therapy, counseling, groups, friends, family. You are not alone, and you should not bear your burden alone either.
This isn't a story of how a man saves a woman but a tale of how love

reawakens our spirit, opens our soul, and reminds us of our worthiness.

Beverly's story is about the aftereffects of a verbally abusive relationship, and the years it takes her to release what she experienced. Let it go is easier said than done for some. Beverly falls into such a category, but bitterness takes energy. Lots of energy. And it's draining. So, pass the bitter cookie over and nibble on whatever brings you hope instead. I promise, bit by bit, you'll be restored…or maybe you'll just grow older like me and realize life is too short to waste on those who don't matter—like Beverly learned and accepted. Find yourself. Let love in. Just be…

PROLOGUE

SPRING 2009

[Beverly]

"Hello. My name is Beverly, and I'm an alcoholic."

"Hi, Beverly." The chorus of various voices respond to my introduction, and I stare out at the circle of strangers in all sizes and colors looking back at me. I've never had so much attention on me, and I fidget with the skirt covering my weak legs. I sit in a wheelchair today, grateful for the life I could have lost because of a stupid decision.

Are you stupid? Howard would have asked. I'd been stupid over him.

After rubbing my palms down the material of my skirt, sweat remains despite my attempts to dry them.

"Beverly, why don't you tell us what brought you here today?" encourages the sweet, melodic tone of the facilitator. I don't suppose I can give the snarky response that first comes to my tongue.

The probation officer is making me attend.

"I'm here to learn about myself and seek forgiveness for what I've done."

The repentant child—one offering confession and seeking

redemption—is something I've mastered. As a mischievous young-ster, I'd do all sorts of things requiring an apology to my parents, who practiced their own sense of religion. I didn't follow rules very well. As an adult, some rules were unavoidable.

Nameless faces in the circle nod their agreement with my state-ment of contrition. I'm told they will understand what I've done, how I felt, and who I have become. If that's true, I'd like someone in the crowd to tell me who I am because somewhere along the path of my life, I've lost myself.

"Want to tell us a little bit about what happened, Beverly?"

I don't, actually, but I know I have to. It's a requirement of my probation—mandatory participation in regularly scheduled Alco-holics Anonymous (AA) meetings, which I am to attend in their entirety, so no sneaking out early.

"I was in an accident."

I wish that was the extent of my answer, and the short, simple statement would absolve me of my sin. But the hesitant pause and the encouraging brow lift of the chairperson hints that she knows there is more to my story.

"My husband left me." I chew at my dry lips as I leave out how it was years ago. "I'm a single mother." A slight smile curls my lips as the truth of the matter is, I love my child, who has grown into a good-hearted, generous college co-ed. More than anything, she's a ray of sunshine in my life.

I should have been better for her.

I should have done better.

Instead…

"He abandoned us when my daughter was young. It'd been ten years since he left, and I thought I knew where he was. I decided to investigate, but I needed liquid courage before I went after him." A few people chuckle as they understand the reference. I thought an alcoholic drink or two would ease the tension, relieve the heartache, and settle the anger, but it did none of those things. Instead, it fueled something inside me I didn't want to acknowledge. Bitterness rooted so deep I physically shook. Betrayal carved so savagely my blood boiled. Determination so willful it became an entity of its own. And I made a decision I would forever regret.

"He'd left me for another woman. One of many he'd been with over the course of our marriage, and rumor had it they were back in the area. A Pink Pony reunion." *Can you believe they have stripper reunions?* It's actually a thing. When you bare that much of your skin with others, you form an unprecedented bond, I guess. The removal of some woman's clothing and the hands of my husband on her were a vision I didn't want to revisit because that was a *thing* as well. A common occurrence. One I'd ignored, or enabled, or hadn't believed could happen to me. He'd always came back to me with promises that he'd do better, be better. I'd held onto those words of affection and pleas for forgiveness.

Howard had loved me.

But had he?

I wouldn't do something well enough, and the condemning words would spew. He'd step out again, citing it as my fault.

A man to my left shifts in his seat, and his movement hints at his recognition of the name of the local strip bar as well as his familiarity with the reunion, but he says nothing. He isn't allowed to speak. This is my meeting. An introduction of sorts.

"Anyway, I drank…and then drove." The silence that follows my admission fills the room like helium trapped in a balloon. The severity of what I'd done is not lost on this group. Drinking and driving is not only illegal, but it can also be deadly. Fortunately, I did not kill the victim.

"I ran a red light and clipped the back wheel of a motorcycle. He survived." As if the listeners had held their breath, a collective sigh of relief empties into the space, swirling around us like a sympathetic hug.

He'd lived. Huzzah.

I *am* relieved. I did not know him even though I'm told he was a member of a local biker club outside our small community of Green Valley. I'm waiting for the day they want retribution against me for harming one of their own.

It was an accident.

The truth rumbles through me like the tires treading down the mountainous switchbacks near my home. Although I'd driven that stretch of road a hundred times, the red light had snuck up on me. In my quest for Howard, my vision blurred on my surroundings. Then again, the alcohol had impaired my sight…and slowed my reflexes.

"Sending my vehicle into a tailspin, I crashed into a tree." My hand clenches the loose material over my mangled left leg. The one crumbled and crushed. From toes to upper thigh, a cast covers my damaged limb. Rehabilitation. Limited ambulation.

You could walk again.

I didn't deserve to walk. I had nowhere to go. Howard was gone. I was alone. And lonely.

"I damaged the left half of my body. Dislocated shoulder. Broken leg. Broken hip." Another round of gasps, more sporadic, while others wince. I agree with the sounds. Recovering is slow and painful, but the greater struggle is the will to recover. Hannah is my sunshine.

I'm here for you, Momma. Just don't leave me.

Her plea was the small sliver of motivation dragging me off the hospital bed to attempt therapy.

"I'm told I'll regain mobility but never be one hundred percent. I'll…" I can't say the words I should admit.

You'll always have a limp.

I didn't want a limp. I didn't want to be deemed incapable. I didn't want anyone to see me. Internally, I chuckle bitterly with the thought that no one saw me anyway.

I've tried to live my life believing it could always be worse. Someone else always has it sadder. Someone else has it rougher. But over time, I could only take so many layers of sorrow and struggle before the rungs on the ladder of bad circumstances snapped, and I'd tumbled to the ground.

Forced marriage. Miscarriage.

I'd thought that was bad.

Philandering husband. Verbally abusive.

4

Still could be worse.

Abandonment.

The solitude had seemed like a welcome reprieve, only with it came confusion and bitterness and poor decisions.

One drink. Then two a night. A few during the day. Suddenly, I'd lost count, and the only way I could function was with support. Jack Daniel's was my best friend. What can I say? I live in Tennessee.

I'm lost in my thoughts until the chairperson clears her throat, and I look up. She has soft eyes and an encouraging half-smile. Her skin is clear, and her hair is a beautiful blond-brown combination. She looks like my Hannah; probably similar in age to her, too. My girl look a leave from college to watch me. Her fear of losing me turned into her remaining home because she worries about me. Apparently, I can't be trusted to my own devices.

"My daughter has come home to stay with me. We own a farm." Which I can no longer tend. I'll never work those fields again.

We recommend the use of a walker, then graduating to arm crutches and possibly a cane.

"I don't know how long I'll be in the wheelchair." Tears blur my vision of the yellow daisy print skirt over my cast. It's my favorite skirt, and I pair it with my white blouse that has a Peter Pan collar. I used to think it made me look pretty, but I no longer think such a thing. I feel conspicuous and naked before these strangers, these fellow alcoholics.

"My daughter's come home to assist me," I repeat, running out of things to tell the group. I have no idea how long she'll stay—*if she'll stay*—or if one day, she'll abandon me like Howard.

CHAPTER ONE

TEN YEARS LATER: FALL 2019

[Beverly]

At my age, I no longer believe in love at first sight.
The breathtaking, thigh-clenching, blood-rushing sensation of seeing a person for the first time and sharing a moment.

But I am *in lurve* with Tripper Hanes, construction project manager of *Nailed*, a home improvement television show where he and his wife fix up old houses. He's married to the beautifully exotic Virginia Hanes, who masterminds the decorative ensemble of a newly restored house like none other. I should know, as I spend a great deal of my time watching daytime television and do-it-yourself programs.

And I'm currently being interrupted from my favorite show by a sharp rapping on my front door.

"What the...?" I whisper as Tripper makes his introductory announcement: *"Let's nail this one, baby. See what I did there. Nail. Nailed."* Tripper Hanes is the full package: humor, handy, and handsome.

My thoughts wander back to love at first sight. I'd believed in the lie once—such a damn fool—and chased Howard to the very porch where someone now stands. Back then, I was young—just seventeen —and pregnant with Hannah. I'd grown up fast on this farm as a wife and a mother.

"It's demo day," Tripper announces from the flat screen, thankfully breaking up my recollections of Howard, and I smile despite myself. I love the antics of this ginger-bearded man as he tears down walls and builds up homes.

Only, the front door thunderously rumbles in the jamb once again.

"Nobody's home," I mutter as I stare at the television, listening to Tripper call out to his wife a parting, *"Love you, GinGin."* He has a nickname for her, and it's sickeningly sweet. I'd gag a bit except I like them as a couple. Their relationship is something I've never had.

My comfort-cozy rocking chair angles toward the front window, directing my gaze—should I wish to gaze—at the least-traveled road in Green Valley edging my property. The television set sits off in the corner. Hours of my day are spent in this chair because moving about my house is difficult at best.

You could walk again, doctors said.

I can walk; I'm just choosing not to, just as I'm *not* answering the rambling front door.

"Go away," I mumble as my eyes remain on the television screen. Tripper rushes at a brick wall, hoping he's loosened the concrete cutout enough so the section will fall from the impact, but the barrier doesn't budge and he bounces back with enough force to knock his hard hat off his head. I wince as if I can feel the thud of his body, both against the solid structure and then collapsing on the wooden floor.

My door rumbles once more.

"What in tarnation?" Slapping my hand on the armrest, I feel my irritation growing. *Patience is a virtue*, my mother used to tell me, so I figure I can outlast the rabble-rousing of an intruder on my porch. Since my wayward husband's disappearance and the unfortunate accident, I've spent most of my days sitting here. Waiting.

Waiting on a man who isn't going to return.

Waiting on a miracle for the homestead he left behind.

Waiting on my daughter to be the next to exit.

Eventually, the porch intruder will get the hint.

"Tripper, honey, can you move that wall over there and this doorframe here?" The sweet Southern drawl of Virginia Hanes draws me back to the television set briefly before another powerful knock on the upper portion of the Dutch door interrupts my viewing once again. My eyes drift to the door panel where a large mass with broad shoulders is outlined behind the etched glass. Judging from the stature, I'm surmising whoever's knocking on my door is a stout man.

Maybe he's a bill collector. The thought makes me plant my feet on the floor, stilling my chair and attempting to scoot it backward a few inches (which would be nearly impossible for me to do).

Lord knows, we owe on this property.

With my disability and Hannah working two jobs to provide the essentials for us, it's been ten years of debt. My beautiful girl grew up too fast, just like me. Thankfully, it wasn't *exactly* like me. At least she wasn't pregnant by a worthless man.

We all become victims of our circumstances at some point.

As firm knuckles tap the glass panel one more time, my attention snaps back to the gentleman outside. *Is he a gentleman?* His head lowers as he pauses from the incessant knocking. One hand lands on his hip, and I hold my breath as if the sound of exhaling could expose my position and redouble his efforts.

"Howard?" The deep masculine timbre, boisterous like a lumberjack bellowing, sends a shiver up my spine. *Must be a bill collector as no one seeks out Howard.* His gambling debtors. His philandering girlfriends. They'd called after his disappearance but had tapered off over the years.

"Howard, you in there?" The man pauses another beat and then paces to the porch railing, staring out at the property. It's October, and the front pasture needs mowing. His broad back to the bay window gives me better access to view him, and my head tips,

9

drawing lines across a leather harness strapped over his shoulders and crisscrossing between his shoulder blades.

Is that a holster? Is he carrying a gun? Have the Iron Wraiths come for their revenge? It's been a decade of solitude without a glance from the motorcycle men living nearby.

It was an accident.

My eyes flick to the television set as Tripper and Virginia stand with their arms around one another, making some joke I can't hear through the blood rushing in my ears.

What does it take for a man to love a woman like he does?

Abruptly, the stranger turns back toward the house, narrowing his eyes at the window even though the glass is thinly veiled by sheer curtains. My breath catches. For a moment, I wonder if he can feel my gaze. Does he know I'm looking at him? If I rock backward, the movement will give me away, and if I try to stand, I'll definitely draw attention to myself, so I hold still like a deer in the forest sensing the approach of a threat. He can't possibly see me because I'm too far back from the glass. Like an animal inside a cage at the zoo, I'm hiding in the shadows, hoping he'll go away.

Nothing to see here. Keep moving.

He steps toward the window. One large stomp forward. Then he shields his eyes with a palm at his brow and rests the edge of his hand against the glass.

"I see you," he states.

For some reason, my eyes leap to Tripper on the screen, about to reveal a finished kitchen. If only *he* could see me and help me out by getting rid of this poser on my porch. *I'm ridiculous.* What I should be is frightened. I should scream, but who would hear me? I'm alone in this big house with acres of distance to the next property.

If a person screams with no one around to hear it, is there really a sound?

"Go away," I bellow toward the window. "Howard isn't here."

A pause passes as he observes me, and I look back at him. If I were to romanticize the moment, I'd be certain our eyes lock, but they don't, and I'm no romantic.

"Beverly?"

My throat clogs. *How could he know my name?* "What do you want?" My voice comes out a screech like an owl. *Who are you?*

"I'm looking for Bev." No one except family calls me Bev. Ever. Nicknames are stupid.

"Then why did you ask for Howard?" I yell. He retracts his hand from the window and shakes his head.

"I'm looking for Howard's wife." *Howard's wife.* After all these years, it's strange to hear the label, and it proves this man doesn't really know me or us. Howard's been gone for seventeen years. Disappeared.

"Howard isn't here, but...but I have a gun." I reach for the nearest large object and hold it up, aiming it toward the window as though I intend to shoot.

A deep chuckle ripples through the glass. "That's the oddest shaped gun I've ever seen, and you're holding it wrong." He chuckles a second time. "It looks like a baseball bat."

Darn it. He's observant albeit incorrect. The large needle used for chunky yarn knitting is one of Hannah's attempts to find me a hobby. Chunky knit—it's all the rage. Hannah's encouraging me to make blankets. I'm not very good at it.

"Bet my swing is better than yours." He laughs at his baseball joke and holds up his left arm. Ignoring his guffawing, my eyes trace the outline of his appendage, thinner and leaner than the opposite one. A glint flashes from the metal in his hand.

He has a gun.

He definitely has a gun!

"Go away," I shout again, sitting up straighter, finding boldness I don't feel. "If you're with the Wraiths, I apologize. If you're a bill collector, we don't have any money." My daughter has taken over our finances. I won't consider selling. I don't want to leave, but I can't answer why.

Waiting.

So much waiting.

"I don't know who the Wraiths are, and I'm not here collecting

11

on a debt." He pauses again, lowering his hand with the gun and lifting his other hand to shield his eye for the window. "Well, not exactly."

I don't have the slightest idea what he means. All I do know is I want him off my porch.

"We don't have anything of value," I holler, finding it strangely comical that we are caterwauling at each other through double panes of glass. What I stated is the truth, though. All the pretty items women would have received from a wedding—china, crystal, silver—I don't own. "Being pregnant out of wedlock does not garner a girl a trousseau," my mother told me after I'd informed her of my impending nuptials and motherhood. Real love, I'd told my parents. A dream come true.

What a nightmare in reality.

"That isn't true." His voice is deep, sergeant worthy, and it takes me a moment to realize he means items of value and not my nightmare. He pulls back from the window, facing the front property, twisting his neck to survey the land with a slow sweeping crane of his head. Then he spins for the window, curling his forefinger and thumb around an eye like a monocular, observing me once again. "Everything of value is within my line of sight."

My skin prickles like a sleeping limb fighting to awaken, and I have so many dormant body parts left restless and yearning for too long. It's longer than I care to remember since I've been with a man. And something in what he said and how he said it in that too-loud lumberjack voice makes me shiver.

My eyes flick to the television set just as Tripper kisses his wife's temple. Then my sight lowers to my left leg, thinner than the right, withered like a wilted tomato vine. *No man is going to be interested in me.* The thought pisses me off. Even my own husband wasn't interested after the first few years.

"You were never going to be enough for me, Beverly," Howard had said.

"Leave my porch," I squawk, my ire growing. I hold the knitting needle higher as if I'll javelin throw it at him if he comes closer, which is preposterous as he's behind the barrier of the window.

Or am I the one barred inside?

"I think I'm getting off on the wrong foot here," he mutters loud enough I can still make out the depth of his voice through the window.

"Is that a joke?" I hiss. *Wrong foot?* Is he implying how I can't effectively use mine?

You'll walk again.

Doctors. All liars. I'd been vain enough back at thirty-five to consider a limp a weakness, but at almost forty-five, I couldn't care less. No one sees me anyway.

My eyes narrow at the stranger as the weight of his glare presses back at me. He's taking me in, assessing me. No one has really looked at me—*seen me*—in years. People either consider me old and senile or they feel sorry for me. Moreover, they pity Hannah—stuck with an invalid, homebound mother—as if her plight has been worse than mine. I snort.

"Beverly, may I please come in? Or maybe you could step out?" he questions. "I have a proposal for you."

The man on the porch pulls back from the window once more and hangs his head when I don't respond. A hand scrubs over his face while the other dangles at his side. My eyes squint, and when I twist my head for a better view, I realize he isn't holding a gun. The metal glint coming from his hand, or rather where a hand should be, is a two-pronged claw like a small garden utensil used for raking. Some kind of material wraps up his arm and over his elbow, then tucks under the edge of his T-shirt. The straps I assumed were a gun holster are the supports for a prosthetic arm.

My shoulders slump a bit. *Oh my.*

While there's nothing this man could propose that I want to hear, staring at his arm causes all kinds of sensations to conflict in me. My heart races behind my ribs in a way I've never felt. *Maybe I'm having a heart attack.* My stomach twirls like a whirligig. Lowering the knitting needle, I reach for my arm crutches and slowly raise myself from the rocker, pulled by an almost magnetic force to an unsuspecting metal object. Like attracts like, my father-in-law used to say, and even though I don't know him and it's preposterous, I sense a familiarity with the porch invader.

After all this time, maneuvering around my living room is still awkward and clumsy at best, and ridiculously robotic. My crutches are the kind that cuff around my forearms; however, it's been nearly ten years, and Hannah prefers to push me in a wheelchair. Her long strides are constantly in a rush compared to my slow hobble. Plus, I sit most of the day, so my legs don't work the way they did before the accident. Not to mention, my left leg lags due to the hip injury.

Sweating and out of breath once I reach the entry, I fumble with the latch for the upper half of the old Dutch door. I struggle to hold the knitting needle in my other hand as a precautionary weapon in case I come to my senses about opening the door to a stranger.

Only I drop the giant stick.

Cheeseoncrackers.

I bend at the waist, the foot of each arm brace slipping behind me on the hardwood flooring. If I don't counterbalance myself some-how, I'll fall over, and falling would be mortifying. I've slipped up enough in this life. I don't need witnesses.

"Are you all right in there? Do you need some help?" The concern in this stranger's thunderous voice rattles me even more.

"I don't need anything," I holler, but my voice cracks as I wiggle my fingers for the fallen knitting needle, before finally reaching it and slamming it on the floor one time in my irritation.

I don't need anything I reiterate, because I've always taken care of myself—myself and Hannah. Well, at least until the accident.

My arm crutches slide free and clatter to the entryway wood, so I use the ledge in the middle of the door as leverage to right myself. My mobility is awkward as the large knitting utensil remains in one hand, bulky under my palm. I refuse to stand without this potential weapon even though the power of his voice suggests this man could do more harm to me than I'd ever do to him.

Shakily stable against the door, I finally release the catch and swing the upper half inward. I nearly smack myself in the head with the wood barrier and snake around it, keeping my hand with the needle on the edge of the upper partition as my other hand reaches forward for the lower half. My body is weak, and I hate the sensation. I'm standing, but my legs tremble uncontrollably. A heavy exhale empties my lungs.

"What do you want?" I growl, out of breath from the exertion.

Then I look up.

My breath hitches at the sight.

Before me stands a man with the most scrutinizing brown eyes, like soil after a rainstorm, rich and earthy. His cheeks are molded clay, etched and chiseled, and his hair is solid silver cropped close to his skull. He appears shaven, but it's not even noon and it's already growing back to pepper his chin with sprinkles of chrome and ink coloring.

Would he think it odd if I rubbed my hand over his jaw? Is it soft or prickly? Would it tickle or scratch?

He's tall, and while one bicep bulges with thick muscle and veins running up his forearm, the wrapped arm is mechanical with a metal claw on the end. It's neither here nor there to me. He looks imposing, intense, and impossibly good looking.

And that love at first sight thing—breathtaking, thigh-clenching, and blood-rushing—could be happening again, if only he was a television star instead of reality because I no longer believe in love.

CHAPTER TWO

[Jedd]

B efore me stands a woman who looks years beyond her age.
Beverly?

If my quick calculations are correct, it has been twenty-five years since I've seen Beverly Townsen, and she shouldn't look as old as she does, which makes me kind of an ass for judging her. If I was a gambling man, I'd place all my bets on her no-good husband, Howard, for her weary appearance. Howard Townsen and I were not friends. Let me repeat: we'd never been friends, and I'd felt sorry for his wife long before our first encounter.

It had been right before I'd left Green Valley, and I'd seen her in the Piggly Wiggly with that asshat Howard.

She was young and beautiful with light brown hair, sun bleached and streaked, and these incredibly sharp gray eyes. She was the kind of beauty you changed all your plans in life for. My airway clogged as she turned to smile at me; I was a stranger to her, but I was familiar with who she was—and I realized Howard Townsen had taken a bride much younger than him.

"Quit lollygagging, woman. You don't need ice cream. You're fat enough as it is." I should have taken him out right there between the ice cream and tator tots for speaking to her in such a manner. My eyes scanned down her slim body, and there wasn't one ounce of fat on her. She was tall and lean. Actually, she looked too thin—all angles and bones. Then I noticed a small bump in her lower belly. A toddler already held her hand.

"The ice cream isn't for me," she explained, her eyes shifting to me as she smoothed a hand over the slight swell of her abdomen. "My sister's coming for dinner."

Howard stiffened. "We don't need the likes of her at our table."

Beverly flinched as if Howard had struck her. I'd be worried for her physical safety if I didn't already know Howard was a wimp. She swallowed and looked up at her husband. "Please don't speak of her like that."

He huffed. "Woman, I'll speak of her however I damn well please." With that, he walked away, and her shoulders sank but not before she snagged a container of something-chunky-chocolate from the freezer and placed it in the shopping cart. Then she tilted her face in my direction and winked. Her eyes gleamed as if we shared a secret, and it took all my willpower not to walk up to her and ask her to run away with me.

Oh, the foolish thoughts of a young man.

The woman before me looked nothing like that girl. Her face was stitched with sorrow. The fine lines near her eyes were rivers of misery, and the fierce set of her mouth suggested discomfort. Her eyes, however, still held a spark of mischief. Whether she meant to set me passionately on fire or scorch me to smithereens, I had yet to determine.

"What do you want?" she snaps through gritted teeth, holding the upper half of the door open while clutching her bat-like object. *That was an assault weapon?* If she thought she'd bludgeon me over the head or stab me in the eye with that thing, she had another thing coming. Not to mention, she didn't look strong enough to hold herself upright, let alone strike someone with a thick stick.

"That's some serious weapon you have there," I tease, nodding toward her hand.

"I'll have you know I can wield a mean blanket with this stick." She was one hundred percent serious as she spoke, but then I looked at those eyes—*that spark*—and I couldn't help myself. I laughed. She blinked, balking at the sound as if it was the strangest noise she'd ever heard. It might have been, as I'd lost some hearing in my ear from the accident and I couldn't monitor the volume of my own guffawing.

"Well, I imagine it's the meanest blanket that's ever been wielded."

When she continues to stare up at me, my chuckling slowly dies. I clear my throat, recollecting my mission.

"So Vernon Grady—"

"You don't need to yell. I'm lame, not deaf."

Blinking at her abrupt interruption, I stare at her. *She's what?* "I...I'm sorry. I can't always hear myself." I twirl the claw around my left ear. "I have severe hearing loss on this side." I'm hoping the swirling metal contraption clarifies things without her thinking I'm crazy, but I look like I'm making the international sign for *cuckoo*. I feel a little nuts for what I'm about to propose.

"What happened to you?" She juts her chin in the direction of my left half. There's a certain tone to the way people ask this question. One is rude. Another is sympathetic. Beverly falls somewhere in between, and giving her the benefit of the doubt, I call her curious despite the edge to her acidic tone.

"Accident."

She waits on more explanation, but that's all she's getting from me today.

"So, as I was saying, Vernon Grady mentioned your land." I pause, choking on the words. *Your land.* "Is that better?" I point at my lips, implying the volume, and her eyes fixate on them. As I continue to speak, she isn't taking her gaze from the movement of my mouth, and it's doing funny things to my chest. My heart's skittering. My breath's quickening. "I understand you own all this property, and I'm looking for land."

She blinks up at me. "We aren't for sale," she brusquely barks, defensive as a wild dog.

"I'm not looking to buy. I'm looking to lease. I'm a horse breeder, and this looks like as good a place as any to raise them. You have space, and—"

"Vernon sent you. Are you an investor? A gambler?"

My mouth pops open, but I'm not ready for full disclosure. "No, ma'am," I state instead.

"I've told him time and again we aren't selling. We don't need his help."

Vernon warned me against using his name as a lead into my proposal, but I needed to start somewhere, and I can't start with the truth. Being as he's one of my oldest friends and one of only a few contacts in the area, I name dropped.

I'm distracted for a moment by her flaring eyes, which break from my mouth to roam up and down my body. Those steely gray beauties stroke down my center like a thick paintbrush coating a fence, or maybe that's her way of sizing me up before she cuts me open and dissects me—which is more so how she's glaring at me. There's an edge to her, and I sense it in both her body language and the sharpness of her tongue. Either way, a shiver slithers over my sternum. There's a juxtaposition between the cutting bite of her tone and the hungry gleam in her eye, and it makes me wonder what her mouth tastes like. Acidic? Bitter? Sweet?

Focus.

"I'm not looking to buy. As I said, I want to rent."

Beverly sighs. She's holding the lip of the door like a life preserver. Her arm trembles as if it takes all her strength to grip the barrier. Or maybe she's just holding back from punching me.

Wonder what her knuckles would feel like...dragging down my chest?

I shake away the thought.

"You okay, honey?" I saw her approach the door and then lower behind it. I should ask her about it, but I don't.

Her brows raise, and then her eyes narrow. "Don't you 'honey' me. Just spit out what you want so I can tell you to get lost. Tripper's waiting on me."

Tripper? Has she moved on since Howard left? Does she have a second husband? Vernon didn't mention anything.

Her sharp speech surprises me. With her hair pulled back into a tight knot near the nape of her neck, her face looks severe, stern even, and too serious for someone still relatively young. She's angles and edges from what I can see of her body as the sweatshirt she wears slips from her shoulder. The devious spark in those eyes doesn't match the rest of her.

"I'm looking for an exchange—"

"Exchange?" She bristles at the word, attempting to stand taller, but her elbow collapses, and she sags forward. She's tall, if I remember correctly, but she's slumping to one side so it's hard to gauge her height. "I'm not selling my body like Hank's girls."

Whoa, filly, settle down. I freeze. Funny she should mention Hank—Hank Weller—as he's next on my list of people to visit, but I forget him for a second. My eyes are the only part of me moving as I scan the parts of her body I can see. The slope of her neck. The edge of her collarbone. The tip of her shoulder. She's slight in build, but it's hard to tell what kind of rack she has from her oversized shirt. I'd bet her tits are smallish because she's so thin, but none of that matters since I'm not here for her body like she suggests.

You sure about that, cowboy?

I'm adamant. I need the land, not the lady.

"Hank doesn't sell women," I defend, supporting his efforts as a strip club owner instead of arguing my case.

"His women sell their bodies for show," she retorts.

"They aren't prostitutes," I huff, not interested in defending the merits of Hank's business. "They strip."

"People see their nakedness," she admonishes.

And that's a bad thing? Is she one of those religious types, prejudiced against everyone?

Focus, Flemming.

"Look, I'm not here to argue the machinations of the stripping industry. I'd like to discuss an exchange. I work this land, raise horses, and you allow me a place to live." This woman's property is my aim. Pissing her off isn't about to win me any favors and I need a favor from her, but her head snaps back like one of those bobblehead toys.

"This isn't a hotel."

"That's not what—"

"And there's nothing in that list for me." Her head twists like a curious owl as if it took a second to calculate what I said, and now that she's processed it, she's hooting her opinion. "Now, if you'll excuse me, Tripper is—"

"I'd like to make myself a room in the barn," I interject, not caring to hear about her Tripper. *Is he her roommate? Her lover? Do they live together?* I've placed my hooked hand on the upper half of the door before she slams it in my face, and she startles at the movement, staring at my claw. I ignore the expression on her face. With my arm reaching into the house and her body leaning against the lower half of the door, we stand in close proximity. Her face is near my own, eyes searching eyes as her chest depresses with her exhale. The air brushes my lips. My hand reaches out for a wayward hair of hers, and I brush it back, not thinking before I act.

"What that…?" Her hand slaps at the back of mine, and I freeze, a statue positioned to touch something I'll never touch.

"You can't just…" She swats again, like a mosquito annoys her, pushing at my wrist which begins to retract.

What was I thinking? I wasn't thinking. I shouldn't have touched her like that, but now that I have, I can't erase the sensation. My arm tingles—both of them—which is just…strange.

"This is the hashtag-me-too era, buddy." She smacks the back of my hand as it lowers for the door between us as if she's killing a pesky bug. "You can't just reach out and touch someone."

I stare at her moving mouth, but I'm not making out all the words. I want to trace those lips despite the rejection spewing out of them.

"I wasn't suggesting we rip off our clothes," I retort. I just wanted to know if her skin is as soft as it looks up close.

"You need permission first." Did she mean touching her or ripping off her clothes?

I clear my throat, remembering the directive at hand.

"I apologize. That was...I don't know where that came from. I just want the use of the land. I can offer to fix up whatever you need around here, free of charge. It won't cost you a thing to have me living here."

"Except my barn and the fields." Her voice cracks as though she's admonishing me, both of us still stuck that I touched her. She narrows those flaming steel eyes. "And how will you work with that thing?" She nods at my arm. *My, she's unpleasant and fiery.* I pause, taking a deep breath to remind myself some people are just ignorant. Others are plain mean. Beverly again falls in between. She's guarded, very guarded, and I don't really fault her. I usually get a quick read on people, but I'm struggling with Beverly.

"It will work just like any other arm. It holds. It grabs. It squeezes." My eyes drop to those breasts I can't discern but imagine exist under the oversized material. Her body quivers a second under my gaze, and my eyes pop up to meet hers.

Maybe I shouldn't want this woman's property.

Maybe there is somewhere else.

I shake my head. *No, this is the land. It has to be here.*

My sight drifts in the direction of the listing barn. "I'd be getting the short end of the stick if I stay. I'll need to rebuild that thing before it collapses," I assess. "Looks like an old hen house behind it. Then there's the land. I'll need a practice ring, and those back fields could be used for grazing. So don't you worry about 'my thing.' I'll have you know I'm plenty strong in all the places I need to be."

She waves her giant needle at me, and thankfully, I've stepped out of her reach. "Your stick will need to be stronger than mine." Her eyes spark again, and if I didn't know any better, I'd think she was teasing me.

I have a stick for you, honey. The sarcasm whispers through my mind, but a false smile remains plastered on my lips.

"Where's Howard?" I ask instead, driving the proverbial knife a little deeper. I've already been informed Howard disappeared years ago. Good thing to know or else he'd be the first person I sought. Running away doesn't surprise me about him. He was a coward at his core. I'll add it to the long list of infractions I already hold against him. Beverly bristles at his name, and her knuckles turn white on the door's edge.

Interesting.

She's definitely holding herself back from punching me in the kisser.

Wonder what would happen if I leaned forward and kissed her?

She'd slap me for certain this time, but my goodness, am I distracted by her.

It's been too long since you've been laid, old man.

"Howard isn't here," she hisses. "I am." I recognize the fight in Beverly. The push and pull of holding her own yet needing to be held, and by the way she's gripping that door, I want to relieve her fingers, clasp them with my own, and tell her I'm here for her.

See? The kind of woman you change your plans for.

Goddammit, focus.

"Maybe I should speak with your Tripper? Or your daughter?" Vernon mentioned one. I remember the toddler holding Beverly's hand.

"Speak with me about what?" I turn to find the spitting image of Beverly from twenty-something years ago looking up at me from the yard. I didn't hear her come up the gravel drive—hazard of being hard of hearing and apparently my attention on her mother.

"You stay away from my daughter," Beverly growls, mama bear claws at the ready as she points her wooden knitting utensil at me as though she's about to knit me into something.

"Momma," the girl warns, and I can't take my eyes off the younger version of Beverly, complete with light brown, almost blond hair, and eyes the same shape as her mother's. She's stunning in a young and beautiful way, but I'm not into women twenty years my junior. *No, daddy-issue role-playing here, thank you.*

"Hi, I'm Jedd. Jedd Flemming," I offer. Holding out my hand, I realize I never officially introduced myself to Beverly. Then again, I worried she'd know the name, and I wouldn't have been able to share half my sentences with her.

She'd throw you off the porch if she knew your real intentions.

Beverly's daughter steps up the risers and shakes my hand while her eyes drift to my left arm. I've grown accustomed to the swift drive-by of stares. The ones where people glance, look away, then drift back. Eventually, they fight to keep their eyes focused anywhere but on me.

"I'm Hannah."

"Nice to meet you." I turn back to Beverly, watching her face morph into shuttered eyes and steaming cheeks as I hold her daughter's hand. The lines near her eyes etch deeper. Her lips flatten, and her face turns bright pink.

"Jedd Flemming, our barn isn't open for your stick, and neither is my daughter," Beverly snaps, teeth gnashing like a rabid animal.

"Momma!" the girl shrieks.

"Now, get off my porch before I skewer your ass with this thing." She releases the partition, waving the knitting needle in my direction like she intends to spear me... and then, she disappears.

"Momma!" Hannah screeches, racing around me and attempting to open the barrier that her mother has disappeared behind. With her mother wedged behind the door, Hannah struggles. "Momma, scoot back a bit. Reach for your crutches."

I peer over Hannah's hunched back to see a set of arm-cuff crutches sprawled beyond Beverly's reach.

"What the…?" Was this what she meant when she called herself lame? What *happened* to her? Did Howard do this? My insides rumble.

I'll kill him.

Then, all questions are shaken from my thoughts as a stone of sympathy sinks in my stomach. "Let me help." I step forward, ready to move Hannah out of my way when Beverly shouts from behind the door.

"We don't need your kind of help. Go away."

My kind of help? I can't see her, but the edge in her tone brooks no argument.

"Please," her daughter drones, turning cloudy eyes to me. Embarrassed by her mother's sharp words, she's begging me to walk away.

I'm not the gambler Beverly accused me of, but I'd bet on a horse race she's mortified by her collapse. I remember the struggle and know the feeling all too well.

Meeting Hannah's worrisome eyes, I hold up both hands in surrender. Taking a step back, I feel helpless and hopeless, but also a strange kinship with Beverly Townsen. She's hurting, and it's more than physical.

Fall seven times. Get up eight. It's an old Japanese proverb, and one I accepted early on.

How many times has Beverly fallen?

"Okay," I acquiesce, accepting their desire for privacy. "You think about my offer, Bee," I holler over Hannah, not caring if my voice is too loud. I want her to hear me. "Sleep on my proposal. Knit a blanket for that sleep and maybe one for me as I'll need it when I put my stick in your barn."

With that, I nod at Hannah and hop off their porch.

Beverly will change her mind. She has to. This land needs me.

And so might she.

CHAPTER THREE

[Beverly]

"Good Lord, Momma, what was that all about?" Hannah's face remains flushed as the man—Jedd Flemming—excuses himself.

"He interrupted Tripper and Virginia," I say by way of an explanation.

"That's one big truck," Hannah mumbles, ignoring me as the roar of an engine alerts us of his exit. She turns her attention back to me.

"As long as his stick doesn't match," I mutter. That man had me all kinds of flustered. He *touched* me, but then I noticed the look in his eyes when he saw my daughter. Instantly, I thought *he wants her*, and my mama bear claws sprang. Emotion took over, my body gave out, and I collapsed to the floor like a cripple.

"Crippled is a crippling word, Beverly," my younger sister Naomi would admonish in her somber, sweet tone, trying to flip the coin to good. Life dealt her a toilet-flush hand of cards as well, so I

don't know how she can be chipper most days, but she's a tree hugger and I write her attitude off to that.

Hannah has maneuvered herself around the front door as I've scooted back a few feet. Although I reach for each of the arm braces, I don't have the strength to pull myself upward, and Hannah assists me.

"Momma, you know you shouldn't be moving about the house without me," she scolds. "And you shouldn't open the door for a stranger. Who knows what could have happened?" Her voice fades as she easily lifts me under my arms. Her reprimanding tone rivals a displeased parent. When did she become an authority? It's a rhetorical question I don't need to answer.

Since the accident, Hannah and I have practically traded places. Previously, I was the single head of household, and now she's the sole provider. At first, I needed her to assist me with everything, and it's a humbling and humiliating position to be in as a still-young woman when your barely adult child has to care for you in all manners. Somehow, the power shift remained. I'm the constantly-errant toddler doing what I shouldn't and getting caught.

Like the time I took Hannah's old Cadillac and collided with a car owned by one of those Winston boys in the church parking lot.

Or the time I drove to the Piggly Wiggly for chunky chocolate ice cream, and Sara Stokes had to drive me home.

I wasn't allowed to drive after the accident. I'd lost my license, and with my condition—lacking controlled use of my legs—I really am a hazard on the road.

Not as bad as I was the night of the accident, though. Never that bad again.

Still, sometimes a woman needs to get to church for a little prayer or the grocer for some sinful ice cream.

Each time I escape, Hannah finds a new hiding place for her car keys.

"We hope you live a happy, healthy life in your new home. Until next time on Nailed.*"* My eyes glance at the television set and the fading credits of my program. Oh, Tripper.

"Where's the chair?" Hannah asks, searching the living room after settling me in my rocker, but she doesn't mean this chair. She means my wheelchair. *That* chair and I are old friends, and Hannah prefers I use it. It makes it easier for her. However, not one to do as I'm told, I use the braces to get around the house instead.

My forehead bears a sheen of sweat from the energy exerted to hold myself upright and spar with Jedd Flemming. He hadn't introduced himself to me, I recall, but something about the name rings familiar.

"What were you doing standing without your crutches?" Hannah asks, disapproval still evident in her tone as she looks down at me. With her hands on her hip, she almost looks like my mother.

It isn't that I can't stand. It just takes considerable effort to get upright, and then once I'm in the position, I need support. Movement takes determination, and no matter what I do, the limp persists.

"You need exercise and practice," the physical therapist had said.

"She needs me," Hannah had rebuked. Somewhere along the way, it became the truth. Our family stratosphere shifted. She was no longer the quiet, shy child who hid behind me, but a force of patience and resilience. She's the one constant in my universe. My sunshine, despite her employment decisions.

"Are you just getting in from *work*?" It's midmorning, and the word tastes bitter on my tongue. I'm caught on a double-edged sword between hating what my daughter does and needing the money she makes doing it.

"Momma," she states, ignoring my admonishing question and waiting on an answer to hers. I can't say I understand why I tried to stand up to Jedd, literally facing off with him at the door, but the moment he saw Hannah, my energy gave out. Something snapped in me, and it was more than the protective nature as her mother. My chest swelled. My belly dropped. And down I went with emotions I don't wish to admit.

Jealousy. And fear.

"Who was that might be a better question..." Hannah asks, peering up at the window and our vacant drive. The position allows

me to observe my daughter. Such a beautiful woman. I love her for her patient grace while her pretty features frighten me.

A man could fall in love with her. She'll leave me.

My quiet, shy girl sang in the choir when she was younger. Her beautiful melodic voice was heaven, and she'd behaved as she should've because she's a good girl at heart. Then she became someone else, showing off her body, and it's my fault. As Howard said, always my fault.

It's your fault I seek pleasure with others, his voice whispers in my head.

"Has he seen you naked?" I blurt, more irritated than I should be. Lots of men have seen her practically naked. My daughter is a stripper, and I hate her job at the Pink Pony. Is it that she removes her clothes for desperate men? Not really. I'll never admit I'm a little envious. Men want her. But the deep-seated issue is she removes her clothes because she thinks it's the only means to provide for us and take care of me. Typically, I banish thoughts of my daughter's chosen employment. Since my absentee husband met some floozy there and ran off with her, denial sleeps with acceptance. But I'm focused on Jedd. He's probably seen handfuls of naked women, and my daughter being at the top of that list sets my blood boiling.

"I'd remember him if he came into the club." She dismisses my jab as she often does. Her response drives the resentful knife deeper. My daughter isn't blind. She recognizes a handsome man when she sees one, which he is.

"Are you attracted to him?" The question eats at my soul. My stomach churns with concern and a twinge of emotions I hate to admit I hold against my child. When her eyes close, I recognize the look. It's her give-me-patience-Lord look.

"He's nice looking for an older guy."

"He wasn't *that* old," I defend, curious why I'm suddenly defending him.

"No, he wasn't, Momma, but he isn't my type." She sighs, exasperated with me.

"What's that supposed to mean? He is extremely good looking."

Now I'm really off my rocker, trying to argue my daughter into attraction with a man twice her age.

"Oh, so you noticed?" She lifts a perfectly arched eyebrow at me, and my face heats.

"I don't know what you're talking about," I snap, swiping at invisible lint on my pants. Pants which are old, outdated, and a color I hate, but Hannah got them for me, and she works hard for us, *for me*.

"It's okay, you know." Hannah's voice softens. "You can look. You could even fall in love again." Is her comment willful hope that she can stop taking care of me or wistful desperation for love to happen for her?

My head jolts up at my daughter's words, and I wave a dismissive hand. We both know that's a lie stronger than a double shot of espresso. "That will never happen." In hindsight, I'm not certain I've ever been in first love for there to be a second chance. Oh, I'd believed all kinds of things about Howard. *He'd love me forever. He'd make it good for me. He'd take care of us.* An iron skillet of reality upside the head had finally made me see the light and realize Howard's true nature.

He loved women—all kinds of women—just not the one labeled his wife.

Howard was critical of the female body. Had some quirks and tics about positions. He couldn't possibly have been stepping out. Yet he had been, plain as the weeds in my garden. There'd been rumors about him for years, but I hadn't wanted to believe them. Scotia had tried to warn me while Naomi had pitied me. Both my sisters' attitudes had upset me terribly.

While I slaved on my man's land, he'd been out playing the field, and like a pea being shucked, I'd snapped one night.

Flipped a wig.

Derailed.

Pick your cliché for the madness that had consumed me as I drank myself silly…and then drove.

I twaught I saw a pudty cat. That night, like a hunter on the

prowl, I'd been determined to kick that pussy's ass right after I stran-
gled Howard. Only there was no confrontation; there'd been a
collision.

And my life had spiraled off course once again.

"Get me to my room," I bark at Hannah, frustrated by talk of love
and the possibility of Jedd Flemming being attracted to my daughter.
It isn't her fault I'm in this position, but I take out my emotions on
her. "And take a shower. You smell like smoke and cheap men."

Hannah shakes her head, tugging at my hands to help me stand
and then supporting me to my room because the wheelchair's stored
there. I lean on her as I always do, and my chest pinches. She really
is the best slice of my dysfunctional life, and I send up a silent prayer
for forgiveness for treating her like she's burnt crust.

* * *

My room is the former dining room of our traditional farmhouse.
Since the stairs are difficult for me, I've been reduced to this location
between the living room and kitchen. Hannah thought it best I
remain on a single level. With tight spaces for heating and cooling
purposes, the house was a nightmare to maneuver in a wheelchair.
We had too much furniture in most areas. Since the accident, the first
floor looks more like a minimalist moved in. A detached garage is
out back behind the house with the hay barn across the drive. From
my room, I have a clear view of the old structure and the gravel drive
leading up to it.

Rehab Dad airs on the television in my room. The smaller set
balances on an old nightstand. The burly man rehabbing homes isn't
as humorous as Tripper Hanes, but he's clever in his own way. With
a thick beard and a gruff Georgian accent, he's good looking in a
manner opposite Tripper. I like the rugged look, which makes me
reconsider Jedd Flemming, withdrawing my attention from Rehab
Dad Duncan to gaze at the barn.

The building looks dilapidated and lists to one side like my body.
Worn strips of red paint and a weathered gray roof give the appear-

ance of abandonment. Bales of hay for feed used to fill that barn near to the top, a sign of prosperity and dedication. Now, it stands empty and worthless.

Left behind.

"Horses?" I mutter aloud. "What do I know about horses?" When I'd first moved here, a house that had been in the Townsen family for generations, I'd cared surprisingly little for weather conditions and growing anything from scratch. But I'd quickly learned to care under the tutelage of Howard's father, Ewell.

Ewell was a coarse man, crotchety and stern, but an excellent mentor. He was kind in an unusual manner, and I took comfort in his grouchy ways. He seemed to get me on some level. Perhaps our sarcasm drew us together. Perhaps he felt sorry for me and the way Howard had treated me. We didn't discuss emotional things or my marriage, so I've never known why he took a liking to me. Through his teachings, I developed an understanding of the soil and raising chickens. When Hannah began to look into colleges, I discovered the study of agriculture was actually a degree. Soil science. Horticulture. Food production. Everyday labors were an actual course of study, and I could have graduated in something similar had I ever gone to university.

"A woman's place is in the home," my mother had sermonized. *"Making babies and bread as God intended."* Only Mother wasn't quite so God-loving of her offspring when I'd created the baby before having the breadwinning husband.

As a child, I'd blocked out my mother's preaching on most days, which often lead to my getting in trouble. I was only one rung above my sister Naomi on Satan's ladder down to hell. Naomi had done the unmentionable as well, and the timing coincided with a terrible family tragedy. Mother and Daddy couldn't separate the two, and they considered Naomi a real-life Jezebel and thought God had cursed *them* for her sin. At least I'd dated Howard a time or two before I slept with him, if you call a diner meeting and a cup of coffee a date. The first night we were together, I got pregnant. That's sex education 101—it only takes once.

Howard married me because his father made him do it.

"You'll get nothing if you don't claim that baby," Ewell had warned his only child.

"Horses," I scoff again.

Of course, I didn't know anything about raising chickens back when I had them. Or children. Hannah had been a blessing, and I was grateful for her existence. Howard clearly hadn't been. He hadn't been attentive. Or loving. Or patient. *Love is patient. Love is kind.* Quick to criticize, he had a comment about everything I'd done or said or wore or cooked or cleaned or tried in the bedroom. I'd tried to please him, I really had, but in the end, I wasn't enough.

He wasn't enough for you either, my abandoned heart whispers.

Jedd continues to haunt my thoughts, as does my reaction to him. My heart pattered. My mouth dried. My hands grew clammy. He was so intense with those penetrating eyes and his sharp jaw, yet I was strangely curious about his salt-n-pepper stubble and full lips. *How might they taste and feel against mine?* That was when I knew I was in trouble because I hadn't had the urge to kiss someone in over ten years, let alone a strange someone.

Jedd saw my weakness, too. *Could there be anything more embarrassing than falling on my ass?* But it wasn't just my physical difficulty he observed.

I turn to face the old full-length oval mirror resting on solid oak feet. It's an antique that once belonged to Howard's mother, whom I never met. In the reflection, my hair is severely pulled back like an ancient schoolmarm, slightly greasy and grayed. My angular face is sallow and sordid in color. The once-called-exotic eyes staring back at me have lost all luster. My fingers retrace the path he made, brushing back my hair. The phantom touch remains. Then negative thoughts crash.

He'd never want to kiss someone like me.

"What do I care?" I snap, smoothing a hand over the loose skin under said eyes, drawing down the bags and noticing more wrinkles in the corners. Releasing my face, I quickly turn away from my reflection to stare out the window again at the decrepit building across the drive.

I'm just like that faded structure. Right before everyone's eyes yet no one notices me.

I sigh.

"It doesn't take much to turn something old into something new again," Rehab Dad states in the background. He's fixing up a post-Civil War home in Georgia, and it's turning out lovely, but my concentration drifts.

Horses. Four-legged creatures roaming this land. Metaphorically, I've become a four-legged creature with gangly and angular movements like a newborn filly. What would it feel like to run again, the liberation of laughing in the sunshine with the wind blowing in my hair? Visions of chasing Hannah as a child flitter through my memory. The hay billowing in the breeze. The smell of earth and the pride of growth. The sense of accomplishment in keeping this farm afloat.

Could something in Jedd's proposition benefit us?

The question has been niggling at me all afternoon.

Could a bargain with him relieve Hannah?

The thought saddens me. I hear the shower turn off on the upper level, and a lump forms in my throat. *Why did I say what I said to her?* She works hard, even if I don't like her place of employment. My daughter's been here too long, trapped just like me, and while I don't want to suffer alone in my misery, she's too young to continue beside me. At least one of us should be freed.

I should tell Hannah about Jedd's suggestion.

"You never know the things you'll find when you tear down an old wall," Rehab Dad states, lifting his mallet to demo old plaster. *"But the unknown never holds me back."*

Hannah's feet patter down the stairs, and the fear of losing her holds me hostage. I decide to keep silent about Jedd's proposal, dismissing the possibility of change, and get lost in my second favorite home improvement program.

CHAPTER FOUR

[Jedd]

The Pink Pony is just what one would expect in a strip club: dark corners, a haze of smoke, and bright highlighter-pink lights over a dim stage, plus ladies disrobing. A carousel pony on a pole takes center stage. It's the day after my failed attempt to bargain with Beverly Townsen, and I'm here to see Hank Weller, not the naked girls. I've had my share of buckle bunnies over the years—groupie sorts for rodeos—but quickly burned out on the disconnect with women only wanting one thing with a cowboy warrior.

As I sit at the bar, vaguely recognizing the song with an 80s beat, I can see the legs of a girl in the reflection of the mirror mostly crowded with liquor bottles opposite me. I lower my eyes. I don't need to see something I shouldn't see. These girls are young enough to be my offspring.

"What's up, man?" Hank's cheerful greeting breaks into my thoughts. At nearly thirty, he has a twinkle in his eye along with a sly smile.

"Hey." A week ago, I came to this club to inquire after my missing brother, my reason for returning to Green Valley after a twenty-year hiatus. Boone is...different. When he'd stopped answering my calls, I'd worried, but not overly. When my sister had called me, the panic in her voice told me it was time to return. Vernon knew Boone frequented the Pony, and he recommended I come here for information. Tonight, I have other questions.

"What do you know about Beverly Townsen?" I question, my curiosity getting the best of me.

"I know her daughter works for me, so she's off-limits." His warning is clear, but that isn't what registers. *Her daughter works here?* No wonder her momma was nasty about the stripping industry. I hold nothing against stripping, but I can see how a mother might not want it as her daughter's chosen profession.

"Why didn't you tell me before?" I ask.

"You weren't asking." Hank isn't wrong. When I'd first come to the Pink Pony at Vernon's suggestion, we discussed my missing brother. It wasn't up to Hank to hand over a list of the girls he employed.

"Crap." I really got off on the wrong foot with Beverly, and that idiom makes me think of her feet. She collapsed before me. Her daughter mentioned crutches. "Did she recently hurt herself? Beverly, I mean, not the girl." *Hannah was her name, right?*

"You sweet on Mrs. Townsen?" Hank teases. The nomenclature is a reminder that Beverly is married, or was, to one of my nemeses.

"If I was, I wouldn't be sharing that information with you before mentioning it to her, but I'm curious about the Townsen land."

Hank's brows rise. "I don't pass out information for free." He nods at my glass, which is almost empty. He gave me a freebie the other night when I mentioned my time in the service. A beer on the house for my dedication to our country. Tonight, he's not so generous with either the alcohol or the information.

"She's about your age, isn't she?" Hank hints. Uncertain of the insinuation, I'm quickly learning he's a business shark, but does that mean he's a matchmaker as well? I doubt it, even if parading barely-clad woman constitutes his income.

"Her land?" I question again, tipping a brow at my only interest in Beverly.

"It's not for sale," he states, crossing his arms as if defending his answer or the Townsens. His expression turns serious as his eyes focus behind me. "I've been trying to help them for years."

His eyes soften a bit, and I wonder about the story behind him hiring Hannah. Without forking over more money than I care to spend on liquor, I don't think I'll get any details.

"I'll give you fair warning, new friend. Beverly is one tough woman. She had to be with old Howard, and her daughter's even tougher." Hank's eyes leap up to the stage again, and I stiffen, nervous Hannah might be the next act. Her naked body is not something I want to observe. "If you're just looking for land, I could recommend a few other places."

"I want that property," I interject, my indoor voice probably louder than it needs to be. Between the ringing in one ear and the thumping bass in the other, I've spoken with a passion I haven't felt since before viewing the property. *It's been too long*, my heart sings.

"Hmm." He shakes his head as if he's all-knowing, and he might be as he is familiar with my brother. Changing the subject, he brings up my younger sibling. "Anything on Boone?"

I'm sensing this establishment's owner might have looked out for him a time or two. I shake my head. Nothing's turning up on him, and nothing's making sense about his disappearance. *Where are you?*

"If you have a mystery, I'd suggest an introduction to Cletus Winston. He knows everything about everyone in this town. Perhaps he knows something."

"Cletus Winston? Don't know the name."

Hank eyes me suspiciously. "Winston? His mother was an Oliver. You said you were from around here."

Oliver? "Bethany Oliver?"

Hank slowly smiles as recognition dawns. "She married and then divorced Darrell Winston, an Iron Wraith." A what? The name sounds like a motorcycle gang.

"Cletus is her third son." There's pride in Hank's speaking of this man, and I assume they are friends.

"I'll look him up," I mention, although I don't know that I will.

"He's easy enough to find. He owns Winston Brothers Auto Shop."

I nod in gratitude for the information, and then we fall silent for a moment as Hank watches the goings-on behind me. I refuse to lift my head, suddenly worried I'll see something of Hannah Townsen I shouldn't. A naked peek of her slender body is only going to remind me of her mother when she was younger, and I don't need the reminder.

I'm here for the land, not the lady.

Still, my thoughts keep returning to Beverly. The way she looked at me was a toss-up between wanting to scoop out my innards and lick up my sternum. Either way, the image of her hands on me has been doing things to me for the past twenty-four hours.

"Whatever you want to know about Beverly, you could always just ask Hannah. Although I don't think she'll be so forthcoming in passing out particulars about her momma, either." Another clear warning. "She's protective of her."

The statement rings with pity and sympathy, both of which I surmise tough Beverly Townsen would hate. I called her Bee as I was leaving because the name is fitting. Her tongue stings like the pesky pollinator. *Wonder what else it could do?*

The thumping bass behind me abruptly ends, and a hesitant, sporadic clap applauds the performance. Hank's brows scowl as he stands to his full height. He nods at something, or more likely some-one, and I take another sip of my beer. A nice cold one in a chilled glass is a luxury I never take for granted. I rap my knuckles on the bar for Hank's attention.

"Let me close out."

"You got it," Hank says, but he doesn't move from his position. I lay a twenty on the bar top and spin on the stool when my knees nearly collide with long legs in a short pink kimono. My gaze drags up the bare skin, over the silky hem, and collides with familiar eyes.

"Hannah?"

"Hey. Mr. Flemming, right? Is there some place we can talk?" Her hand comes to my shoulders as she leans toward my right ear. Instantly, I glance at Hank who straightens even taller behind the bar. A dark expression covers his otherwise friendly face.

"I'm not interested," I say to Hank, while addressing Hannah. This has all kinds of trouble written on it, and I don't need what this girl is offering. Raising my right hand to remove hers from my shoulder, I'm a little surprised she's touched me as Hank has a strict no-touching on the premises policy.

"Not for that," she scoffs, pulling back repulsed. Her eyes leap to my prosthetic. I should be offended, but I'm not. It's a force of nature to stare. My skin is pretty thick. "It's about my mother."

My head swings back to Hannah, and Hank lowers his elbows to the bar.

"Eavesdropping much?" Hannah asks him in a snappy tone, which surprises me as he is her boss.

"Damn stubborn," Hank mutters, pressing off the wooden counter and stepping a few paces away. With his back to us, pretending he's busy with his computer cash register, I return my attention to Hannah.

"I'm listening." I'm more than listening. I'm twitching with anticipation.

"Can we meet somewhere? Too many ears here." Hannah inclines her head toward Hank. "How about Daisy's Nut House?"

* * *

A half hour later, I'm sitting across from Hannah in the Valley's famous donut shop. It's more of a diner, but its claim to fame is these delicious donuts which I've eaten one too many of in the past week. Daisy Payton, the owner, hasn't recognized me. Too many years have passed since I've last been in Green Valley, and I've changed quite a bit—most noticeably, my arm. Still, she's friendly with a smile and a polite word.

"Let me know if you need anything." Looking like Michelle Obama, and dressed nearly as professional, she's not working the tables as a waitress but present as the business owner.

She recognizes Hannah and asks about her mother.

"Momma's the same as always. Taking it day by day."

Daisy nods in sympathy. While I wait for Hannah's attention, I take a bite of the pumpkin spiced delight before me.

"You tell your momma I'm thinking of her," Daisy says, closing out their conversation.

"Always," Hannah says, smiling sweetly at the diner owner. As Daisy walks away, I notice a group of men in leather vests and bandana skullcaps off in the corner. The Iron Wraiths, perhaps. Is this who Hank was referencing? Too often, veterans like me are sucked into groups like them, looking for solidarity and brotherhood, filled with disappointment after returning Stateside. I have nothing against finding your people, but the looks of some of these men concern me.

"Momma mentioned you tried to proposition her," Hannah starts, drawing my attention back to her.

"I did not—"

"She didn't tell me all the particulars, so I'd like to hear what you have to offer."

My head tilts in question. The cautious look in Hannah's eyes is similar to her mother's, and she glances down at the table to avoid meeting my gaze.

"Does your momma know you're talking to me?"

"I'm my own person, Mr. Flemming. I'd like to know what your interest is in our land."

"I'm told it's not for sale."

"Momma mentioned you didn't want to buy it." Her brows lift, surprised and concerned.

"Interesting. What else did she tell you?"

"You had a proposal. Our land for the use of raising horses.

You'd build a room in the barn and do repairs around our place." Hannah pauses before adding, "And Momma tells me everything. We don't keep secrets." There's more to what she's saying, but I don't question it.

"I'm interested in negotiating a percentage of the profits, once I have the horses and begin breeding. I have a silent partner who is fronting some of the money I'll need for supplies. Lumber. Feed. Equipment." My investor friend wishes to remain anonymous for his own reasons, but we mapped out a detailed business plan. He wants me to breed horses. Rodeo horses, specifically. It's going to cost a pretty penny, but in one year, the return on investment could be huge. It's not that I need the finances—I'm set through military disability and award winnings over the years—but I want this new adventure. A nomad by nature, I've been itching for stability in the past year. I need a purpose.

"I can offer you ten percent for the use of your land."

"Ten percent?" Hannah's voice squeaks again. "No deal." She shifts on the booth seat and reaches for her purse, telling me with her body language that she's finished with this conversation.

"Look, I just want to raise horses," I say, my voice coming out desperate, which is how I feel. I'm this close to getting what I've always wanted, so if I let this girl slip out of the booth, it could be the end for me.

"Why?"

How do I explain to her how I grew up around these creatures and always felt an affinity for them? How do I explain that a special ops program with horses kept me in the military when I didn't think there was any reason to come home? How do I tell her all the ways horses have saved my life after my injury?

"I'd be good at this," I begin, taking a deep breath. "Ever want to do something just because you know you'd be good at it?"

Hannah lowers her head, and I wonder what she's thinking. Is she good at stripping? Is that why she does it? Does she get some kind of personal fulfillment out of it? Or is there something else she knows she could do, be better at, but just hasn't gotten the chance?

"Who's the investor?" Distrustful eyes eventually meet mine.

"I'm not at liberty to say." The deal moved rather quickly from the first proposition. Most of my partner's business is a mystery, and it baffles me, but it's his life.

"Hank?" Hannah questions. *Is he the local investor?* This is the second time his name has been thrown out as a financier type. When I don't immediately reply, she states again, "No deal." Her purse makes it to her shoulder, and her legs swing out of the booth.

"Listen." I reach for her wrist to stop her. Her eyes narrow in on the possessive touch, and I remove my fingers. "I'll swear on the graves of honorable men that this deal is solid and doesn't involve Hank." *What's her hang-up with him anyway?* "I wouldn't be risking myself for something I didn't believe in, and I'm very committed to this venture. I know you don't know me, so I'm asking for blind faith here. I can even offer a contract. Look, your land needs me as much as I need it." I pause and glance toward the darkened window along our booth. "Have you ever been down on your luck?"

Hannah meets my gaze in the reflection of the late-night window, questioning if I'm earnest in my asking. After a second of silence, she answers me. "I wouldn't be stripping if I wasn't short on it. There's nothing wrong with the job, though. It pays good money."

"Sometimes we gotta do what we gotta do," I state. It's a philosophy I believe in, so much so I've lived my life accordingly, but lately, my luck has run a little dry. "When opportunity knocks, we can't ignore the door."

"Unless that opportunity is a wolf in sheep's clothing." Hannah's shrewd comment turns both our heads so we face one another again.

"I'll give you fifteen percent. I'm guessing those fields haven't yielded anything in a few years." The upkeep necessary for the number of acres the Townsens own hasn't been done. This offer comes out of my portion as I have no leeway with my partner's commitment.

"Twenty-five. And I couldn't work the land and take care of Momma," she counteroffers with the additional explanation. "We couldn't afford to pay someone either."

"What happened to your mom? Where's Howard?" Howard always was a loser. I don't know why I asked for him upon crossing his porch. Maybe force of habit. Maybe reenacting the past.

I'll kick your ass, you fucking pansy, for breaking her heart.

"Someone hasn't already told you?" Bright eyes widen at me, and she gives me only half a second to reply before continuing. "If we knew where *he* was, we might not be in this predicament. Momma could use her legs, and I'd be…"

"Free?" I suggest, tipping up a brow.

"Don't make assumptions, Mr. Flemming." She hitches her bag on her shoulder, but I'm not letting her leave without giving this offer a good effort.

"Fifteen," I interject. "It's all I can spare. I'll need to build a stable and a training ring, but you have a lot of land. It's double what I remember. We can even plant a portion if you'd like, but I'll need some of the space for grazing."

"We used to yield hay and raise chickens." That explains the large barn and a low building off to the side, empty and dirty from years of disuse, but it doesn't explain how the Townsen homestead is twice the size with no return on investment. "We've only produced a few tomatoes the past few years for the local farmers' market…" Hannah's voice drifts off again, and I imagine anything they grew wasn't enough to support them, thus leading to Hannah's employment at the Pink Pony.

"How long has your mother been in those braces?"

"I'm not discussing my mother's condition with you. It was an accident," Hannah states before clamping her lips as if she's already offered too much. It's one of those moments when I wonder if she's trying more to convince herself or me.

"I imagine things have been tough."

Hannah narrows those sharp eyes at me as if I've stated the obvious. "Assumptions again, Mr. Flemming," Hannah warns. I suppose she knows a thing or two about being judged, as do I.

"Help me understand then."

Her lips pinch, and her head slowly twists from side to side.

Hank warned me. *Hannah's sort of the martyr type. A stripper with a heart of gold.*

"Actually, you'd be helping me." I wiggle my prosthetic arm, taking a new approach with this girl. "I need this. I need the work." *I need that land.*

"Fifteen," Hannah reiterates, failing at the art of negotiation. She should have countered with twenty which is the highest I could risk. "I don't know what that means, but I intend to investigate horse breeding." She definitively nods with her threat, but I smile.

"You seem like a smart girl, Hannah, so I'd expect nothing less."

My compliment startles her, and her face pinkens before she finally escapes from the booth. Standing tall next to the table, she looks down in my direction but not directly at me.

"I'll get Momma to agree."

CHAPTER FIVE

[Jedd]

The next day, I pay an overdue visit to my sister. We've become a bit estranged over the years. After all that happened, she felt it best to walk away from the family and head off to college in Nashville. I didn't blame her, but the slow unravelling of our sibling thread stung. I suppose I'd done the same thing, though, when Hasting cut me out, and I went off to the military.

Janice always was the smarter of the two of us, and Momma wanted her daughter to have a career before a family. Unfortunately for Janice, her career ruined her aspirations for a family. She divorced after only a few years, rising to the top as a fierce divorce attorney. Eventually, she went into property law and contracts, and gave up the large office overlooking the Tennessee River in Knoxville to open an office in Merryville, just outside Green Valley. Julius & Caesar was founded with an eclectic mix of family law and real estate contracts. Her partner, Ramirez Caesar, had been her divorce attorney.

"You need a lawyer for injury?" A male voice with a heavy Hispanic accent addresses me as I enter Janice's office. The room is small with only one chair and an oversized desk. With thick black hair and deep-set eyes, he looks like a doe in headlights, but something tells me there's more to this man as he scrubs a hand down his tie.

"Nah, it was a long time ago, and I don't suppose suing the United States military for my stupidity would work."

He stands upright, slants his hand for his forehead, and addresses me with a salute. "A soldier. Thank you for your service, sir." He holds the position, stiff and salutary, but I can't get a read on him. *Is he mocking me?*

"Quit saluting him." The smoky sound of my sister's voice turns my head, and I notice her standing in the hallway entry. She looks so much like our momma, and my breath catches for a moment. Ebony hair pulled back in a loose twist. Bright blue eyes behind thick horn-rimmed eyeglasses. Bright red lips that purse as she addresses the man behind the desk. "Where's Sandy?"

The man drops his hand from his salute and shakes his head. Janice sighs.

"Not another one," she mutters.

"What can I say?" His accent falters, lessening a bit.

"What you can say is *I'll keep it in my pants*. That's the sixth assistant in as many months."

"It's only been three in eight months," he corrects.

"Ram," she groans, and I realize the man acting as desk clerk is really her partner.

"Jan," he whines and then winks at me. "Office romance."

"Office nightmare. You know you're one secretary away from a lawsuit for sexual harassment."

"Who's harassing? She was using all this." Waving his hand, he gestures down his body. His accent is completely removed, and his voice thickens. He's certainly confident and a bit conceited. Must serve him well in a courtroom.

Janice snorts. "I doubt it." Breaking eye contact with her partner, she turns to me and nods for me to follow her. Without a word of greeting, I do.

We enter her office, which holds more oversized furniture but is clear of any clutter minus a computer and a file cabinet.

"Jedd." She states my name, motioning to a chair across from her as she takes the seat behind her desk. It's too formal for a sibling reunion, and I don't like it.

"Janice," I mock as she scoots her rolling desk chair forward.

"It took you long enough to come see me. What's it been, almost three months?" Her calculations might not be wrong, but her snippy tone sets me off.

"I'd have been here sooner had I known things were this bad for Boone."

Janice sighs and removes her glasses, pinching the bridge of her nose. "Really, Jedd? You would have given it all up and returned here to save him?"

"I sent him money," I remind her, disheartened that she would question my sibling loyalty. I did what I could for him.

"Money is not what he needed."

"I didn't know that." On the rare times I'd spoken with my younger brother, he hadn't mentioned the urgency of his issues. With my momma and Hasting dead, Boone was alone in the house, but Janice checked on him. He never told me he was in trouble, though I knew he still played cards. His father's secret weapon in a game. He never inherited the land, after all. Hasting placed the wrong bet—putting his chips on his son—and then throwing down the deed to the farmstead, thinking he couldn't lose.

He lost.

"He has issues," Janice snaps. For years, she's wanted to move my brother to an independent living facility, one where he would be among others needing support and supervision. Janice couldn't take him in because Boone refused to go with her. Considered high functioning, we'd allowed him to remain in the house as long as he stayed in the Valley. But now, he was gone.

"Why now?" Janice asks. "Why did you come home now?"

"Because you called me. Telling me Boone was missing."

Her eyes narrow. "What do you really want?" The question doesn't startle me.

"I want the land back."

"It's tied up. I've told you that." My sister could be disbarred for what I know but shouldn't.

"I'm working something out. I've made a deal."

Janice huffs as she falls back in her chair. "Just like Hasting. A deal. A bargain. A scheme." Her voice rises. "I wonder where Boone got the idea to gamble."

"I recall you once appreciated my deals." I'd failed to protect my sister a hundred times until it all fell apart, and she'd allowed me one final confrontation.

Stay away from my sister. The threat had been idle. The man's fate had already been sealed.

Janice had wised up because of her heartbreak. She'd returned to college in Nashville, changed her major to law, and here she sits.

Her head tilts to the side, dismissing what I've said. "It was all so long ago."

We sit in silence only a second before I say, "Tell me what you can about Boone."

"He refused to move and was often absent when I tried to visit, but this time was different. I just knew he was gone. Things haven't been good. The house is in squalor. His conditions rustic. When I finally called you, he wasn't there, and the evidence proves he hadn't been."

"What evidence?"

"Empty cabinets. No dirty dishes. Nothing really out of place. Well, as best you can tell with the mess."

I didn't need to ask about horses. They'd been sold to pay off debts. The land lacked tending. The current owner must have covered the taxes, but the property just sat there. No one tried to evict Boone, which hadn't make sense until I returned to Green Valley. Still, there was one piece of the puzzle missing.

"Why didn't he call me?" I question of my older sister.

"Would you have answered?" She knows I always returned calls when I could. *Eventually*. The past year had been…difficult.

"I'm here now." I state the obvious because I can't change the past. If I could, I'd do so many things differently. Fought Hasting for the farm. Taken care of Boone. Not reached for an electrical wire.

"Finally lose a competition?"

When I finished with the Army, discharge due to injury, I was lost until I'd heard of Professional Armed Forces Rodeo Association, or PAFRA. I found a sponsor and entered every competition I could. *The one-armed warrior rides a bucking bronco.* Though it was quite a spectacle, it was a profitable one that resulted in a celebrity status of sorts. The notoriety of both a warrior and a cowboy was heady. Only, years of banging random woman and bucking on the back of a bronco had taken their toll. I was looking for an excuse to settle down, but I just hadn't found the right place to settle.

Then Boone disappeared, and an idea sprang to life.

"I never lose," I tease my older sibling. She should remember well the competitive spirit we each had, racing horses over our land, chasing each other on tractors, or fighting over chicken legs at the supper table. Our momma had been a good cook. Janice's drive to be the best makes her a good lawyer. My ambition kept me away too long.

"Look, I'm working on something on the old Townsen homestead and—"

"You know you need to stay away from there," Janice hisses, interrupting me as she sits forward in her seat.

"Why? Howard's long gone." My eyes narrow at my sister.

"Jedd," she warns. "Don't be stupid."

"I'm not being stupid." Famous last words before I act foolish. "She needs me."

"Who?" Janice's brows crease.

"Beverly." I mumble her name under my breath.

"What did you do?" Janice hisses, familiar with Beverly's name.

"Nothing. I worked out a deal, like I said."

"Jedd," she warns again, but I dismiss her with a wave of my hand. Her eyes catch on the metal attachment. "How are you?" she adds as an afterthought.

"You know me. Fall down seven times. Get up eight." Janice stares at me as if she isn't familiar with the Japanese proverb.

"You need to stay away from that farm," she commands, the threat lacking.

"I have it under control. I'm more worried about Boone. Do you suspect foul play?" Lord knows he owes many players. The wrong hand. Slip of a card. People took advantage of him without his father as protector. I don't know that Boone had much left to lose, other than his life.

"I'm not sure. I suppose anyone associated with him might have considered no one would miss him if he was taken out, but there are plenty of people keeping up with Boone's whereabouts." Vernon Grady was one of them until Boone somehow gave him the slip. Boone's ridiculously large size couldn't be missed, and his presence was also well-known at a few haunts like the Pink Pony. So while anyone looking for him might have noticed his schedule, Boone no longer following the pattern would have been noticed by the places he frequented. Daisy's Nut House. The Pink Pony. The Watershed.

I'd already interviewed the waitress at Daisy's, and I'd spoken with Hank. I also interviewed the newest bartender at my current haunt, but he'd only started working this fall, so he wasn't familiar with my brother.

"And you contacted the sheriff?" I'd been to the sheriff's office when I first arrived in town, but that Jackson James character took small-time county protection to a new level of assholery. Maybe Janice would have better luck as an attorney dealing with local law enforcement.

"I have. He promised to look into it again, but the place is rundown, so it's hard to say if there was a struggle or not."

Taking out my brother would have caused a scuffle as he is rather big. Solid and broad like his father, he was already as large as I was when he was fifteen and I was twenty. I imagine he still had height to grow and weight to gain, given he was only an adolescent when I'd left.

"What did he find?" I ask Janice, who looks back at me, puzzled by the question. "What did the sheriff find when he looked at the house?"

"I don't understand. I just told you, it was a mess."

That's not what I'm asking and decide I need to do my own investigation. It's time to steel myself to the memories and return to the old farmhouse.

CHAPTER SIX

[Beverly]

"Hannah," I bellow as I watch a silver pickup truck pull up the gravel drive and park next to the barn. My eyes don't leave the large vehicle as the owner slides out the driver's side. I recognize his build before he even turns for the house. Broad back. Thick thighs. Nice butt. How do men get backsides like that? Two well-formed globes of perfection.

I'm seated in my room, rocking in my chair, hopefully hidden by the sheers hanging over the three windows facing the dilapidated building. The bed of his truck holds a pile of two-by-fours. My blood sort of white-water rapids through me, and a cold shiver ripples up my spine. My breathing hastens.

He's here. He's really here.

"Hannah," I call out again, watching as Jedd Flemming enters our barn, seeming to make himself at home.

My eyes briefly flick to Tripper Hanes on my television set, watching him hammer studs as he frames a new wall during a renovation project. There's just something about a construction project…

My eyes travel back to the live man lugging a few boards at a time over his right shoulder and bracing the stack with the attachment on his left. *That ass.* Two moons draw my attention to the tight khaki-colored work pants. The muscles of his back expand with the effort of balancing the studs on his shoulder, and his gray tee tightens. He adjusts the weight, and something in me pulses to life.

"What, Momma?" Hannah says from behind me, scaring the bejesus out of me. My hand clutches at my throat.

"Sweet butter on biscuits," I hiss, startled. Taking a deep breath, I search for the reason I called her name as I watch Jedd walk toward the barn. Has anyone ever made the motion that incredibly irresistible to observe? The power in those thighs. The tightening of his backside. The pinch to his spine.

"Momma?" Hannah questions, and I clear my throat.

"That man is not pitching his tent in our barn," I stammer, unable to draw my eyes from the structure where he's disappeared.

Where'd he go? my heart whispers, although I know the answer. I'm acting a fool over him, but my breath hitches in relief when he reappears to collect more wood from his truck. He disappears again, and I can't remove my eyes from the open door. My breathing is doing this teasing tango where it holds when Jedd slips into the hollow of the wooden structure and then catches once he reappears in the brightness of the fall day.

"It's fifteen percent," Hannah states.

No, he's one hundred and ten percent, I think. Then I realize what she means.

"What did you do?" I turn to her, eyes widened in surprise. The sheepish look on her face is one I haven't seen since she was ten and wore my high heels to play dress-up. She stumbled, and the heel broke off a pair of shoes I hadn't worn in years.

"He's going to rent the space for fifteen percent of his profits once he's up and breeding horses."

Aghast, I stare at her. *What is she saying?* I heard the words, but I can't believe my ears.

"He can't live here," I bellow.

"He isn't," she clarifies. "He's living in the barn."

My eyes remain wide, unable to blink. "Why would you do this?"

For a moment, I can't read the expression on my daughter's face, and then she steels her emotions. "Because we could use the money."

My mouth falls open. Then shuts. Opens again. Snaps closed. Money has been a constant struggle for us. We've gone with less. We've scrimped. We haven't saved, and it's an argument I don't wish to have with my daughter as I haven't been a contributor to our finances. I've grown a few tomatoes for the local farmers' market, but it hardly pays for a week's worth of groceries.

"We agreed we wouldn't take handouts." Whether we actually made a verbal agreement or not, pride on both our sides has kept us from asking for any means of support over the years.

"It's not a handout. He's using our land, and he's going to pay for it."

"With money we won't see until he begins breeding or whatever scam he plans to participate in. Gambling implies just that—a gamble. Fifteen percent means nothing to me." I pause, taking a deep breath before I whine. "I don't trust him. We don't need anyone else out here. We're doing well enough, right?"

"We're perfect, Momma, just as we've always been, but this might be good for us." She tries to assure me, but a trace of concern scribbles over her expression.

"Hannah, you can never count on a man's word. Trust *me* on that."

She shakes her head in response. "I need to get to work."

I snort. "Try to keep your clothes on." I don't know why I say it. It's the very opposite of what she does.

"If he makes the money I believe he can, then I could possibly quit the Pink Pony." *Well played.* This argument should solidify the decision. Wanting her away from that place has been a goal since the moment she took the job. What if some old man waltzes in and steals her heart like her father did to some young, unsuspecting thing? Is that Jedd's intention? I try to vigorously erase the thought.

Still, a stranger living in our barn—a strange man, for that matter —with my young daughter in the house doesn't seem right. It just doesn't seem appropriate.

My eyes draw back to his movements—unloading wood from his truck. A peek in my peripheral shows Tripper Hanes doing nearly the same action.

What kind of surreal, alternate universe am I living in?

"He's promising us, Momma."

"Men make promises all the time, sunshine. It's in their nature, just as it's in their nature to break them." It's a cruel lesson in male psychology, and one my girl has learned through her father's disappearance and her lack of relationships in the past decade.

Hannah looks out the window and sighs, then lowers her voice. "It's fifteen percent."

I don't know the first thing about return on investment or percentages on net worth. I just know we won't see the money. Howard wasn't only a cheater, he was also a liar and a weasel, especially when it came to finances.

"Money makes men rich in foolishness," my mother used to say in her judgmental tone.

"He plans to raise horses and work the land to turn a profit. That's an honest day's labor right there."

"How?" I bite. "The man only has one arm." I shouldn't be judging. Lord knows, I'm in no position to.

"Don't be cruel, Momma. He has two, only one's different from the other, and he seems more than capable to me."

So capable. Jedd Flemming is a rugged man, as witnessed from the tight tee and fitted pants he wears. Did I notice his behind while watching him through the window during that first meeting? I don't think I paid his backside any mind, but I should have given it more inspection. A backside that fine is just asking for trouble, as is this man by moving into my barn.

Jedd stops his steps, exiting the structure. His gaze falls to the house, and I sit up straighter. My heart races, and my fingers tighten on my throat.

Can he see us watching him? Does he notice me? Do I look as decrepit as that old barn he's entering?

The thought forces me back into my rocker. I don't want him noticing me. I don't want him *anything*-ing me.

When I glance at the television and see Tripper and his wife laughing at something, my heart pinches.

I turn back to Jedd, his face still pointed in the direction of the house. His head tilts, his face questioning, as if he's trying to peer through the sheer curtains but can't quite make out our figures.

"Step back, Hannah," I demand. "He'll know we're watching him."

Hannah shakes her head like she's ridding her mind of a thought. "I'm not watching him, Momma." She turns her gaze to me, and the weight presses on the side of my face, but I can't draw my vision from Jedd.

"Momma," she whispers, and I turn at the soft question in her voice. Her eyes scan my face. Does she fear she'll look like me one day? Those bright eyes will dim, and lines will form in the corners. Will they be rivers formed from tears, or will she eventually find laughter? Does she wonder if her lips will match mine, permanently curled downward? Can my girl still smile? Will her hair go gray too young as mine did? Will the stress of her life turn her into someone lonely and lost?

I blink back the tears fighting for release. I won't cry. Nothing left to cry over. It's all gone.

"Do you fancy him?" my daughter asks, and I choke on the question.

"What...? I...of course not. Don't be silly. I'm sure he'd be more interested in the likes of you."

"What's that supposed to mean?" Hannah asks, brows rising in surprise.

"I'm sure I don't need to explain the birds and the bees to you.

Men like him only want young things and only want one thing from those young things. I don't think he should stay here," I sneer, recognizing the pulse at my neck and the thump of my heart. My daughter is a pretty girl, and this older man could be attracted to her for all the wrong reasons. Young girls go for older men to solve their daddy issues.

"He's sleeping in the barn," Hannah counters, her voice deepening in displeasure. Ticking off points on her fingers, she continues, "We don't need to feed him. He'll rebuild at his expense or hire what he can't do himself. The back field will be plowed and prepped for spring planting."

I snort in response, but my eyes return to Jedd's movement. Into the barn. Out in the yard. My observation traces down his perspiring spine to the waist of his pants where his shirt has untucked. My fingers curl on the armrest of the rocker as my eyes outline the fine globes accentuated by those smooth pants. My mouth goes dry.

What is it about this man? *Why am I suddenly lusting after him?*

I can't. That's the bottom line. I can't anything him. Under fifteen percent and tight pants and a perfect backside is still a man with empty words.

My eyes fall blindly on the reality television program. The only man a girl can count on is the fictional kind. I force my attention away from the barn, but my eyes seem to have a will of their own.

"We can't have a stranger living in our barn," I huff. Jedd stops, turning in his tracks with a pile of lumber on his shoulder as if he heard me, which is impossible on two counts: the panes of glass and his lack of hearing. Still, he stills, and his eyes narrow on the house as if he knows I'm watching him, I'm talking about him, and I don't agree with this arrangement.

"Too late. He's moving in." Hannah definitively nods, dismissing my opinion as Jedd swings back around. She leans down to kiss my cheek and then exits my room, but I remain transfixed.

Suddenly, reality is more fascinating than television.

My eyes continue the cat and mouse game of watching Jedd disappear and then reappear. I don't know how much time transpires, but eventually, the bed of his truck is empty. Still, I hold my breath as if the barn is a giant octopus, swallowing him whole. I fear he might disappear forever like Howard did, which is the silliest thought I've had in a decade. I don't need Jedd. *We* don't need Jedd. There will be no attachment to him.

But then, Jedd appears at the open barn door and gives a single wave toward the house, and I smile in spite of myself.

* * *

After a week of waking to the sound of hammering and the tension of growing curiosity, I decide to see for myself what's happening in my barn. Jedd has spent his nights in the dark space, or at least I think he has since his truck doesn't leave in the evenings. However, he disappears for a portion of every morning, and it's the perfect time to investigate as Hannah is still sleeping from her late-night shift.

My decision to cross the drive involves a choice. Either I struggle to wheel myself over the rough terrain or I use the forearm crutches to tread carefully across the uneven surface.

Hannah believes the wheelchair is more stable for my unstable condition, but today, I'm feeling rebellious like the mischievous person I once was. I opt for the arm supports although my legs quake from disuse. Determination rattles me, but like a foal learning to stand, I decide I *will* make it across the drive and back before Jedd returns from his mystery morning machinations.

It's slow going as my left leg lags behind my dominant right. Like a three-legged creature, I develop a strange rhythm with each step and drag movement.

Left *behind*. Left *behind*. Left *behind*.

It's my greatest fear and my current reality.

By the time I've made it to the barn, sweat trickles down my back and my hair is plastered to my forehead. I can't brush it back without leaning against something to support my strained body, so the locks cling to the edge of my face. I consider I've made a terrible mistake when I reach the barn door and realize I'll need to grapple with the heaviness of the wood on a rusty track. Placing both hands on the edge of the thick barrier, I force it to the side with renewed energy and almost face-plant when the door easily glides open.

Did Jedd oil this old thing?

I've faithfully listened to Jedd work for days, not being able to witness the progress hidden within the barn. Although I still get my daily dose of *Nailed* and *Rehab Dad,* watching him is better than any reality television. My attention has rarely waned from this project, which I've privately dubbed *The Jedd Juncture.* I no longer sit in the front room, gazing at the television. Rather, I find myself in the brighter light of my bedroom, glancing up at every opportunity from my favorite programs. I don't know how I missed him fixing this vital mechanism or how he did it.

When I ponder Jedd—his arm and his ability—I'm astonished at all it appears he *can* do. The hammering is constant. He's building something out here. Construction. Progress. And I'm so curious. I've convinced myself that I'd walk in on a hodge-podge of misangled two-by-fours and crookedly hung plywood, but instead, I find a symmetrical structure in place. Working my way to the corner Jedd has sanctioned off, I peer inside where he's missing a door. A camp cot with a sleeping bag over it and a single pillow rest against one wall with a crate as a makeshift nightstand beside it. A camping lantern sits on the crate along with two books. There's some sort of bag under the cot of military grade material in dark, sand-colored canvas. A trunk rests at the end of the bed. Though it's clean and comfortable looking, it doesn't appear very homey.

I realize as I scan the room that there is no electricity or heat. The nights are dropping in temperature. *How does he stay warm out here?* My eyes catch on another crate with canned goods and a few dry food packages. A case of water sits next to it. Mice would have a field day with the easy-to-chew food boxes, and I wonder for the first time in a week what Jedd's been doing for meals.

You haven't been very kindly, Beverly Townsen, my conscience scolds.

I hobble over to the makeshift bed and allow myself a seat.

Goldilocks is gonna get caught.

I just need to rest for a second, but my curiosity holds me in place. I reach for the books on Jedd's crate-stand. *Taming of the Shrew. Hamlet.* Shakespeare? My brows lift at the unexpectedness of his reading selection. One is a comedy of errors and assumptions. The other, a prodigal son returned to right the sins of his father's brother. Interesting selection for light, nightly reading.

I return the books to their place, hoping I have the angle of their original position correct. My vision travels the room, not yet ready to leave Jedd's abode. Having removed the arm cuffs when I sat, I scoot to the end of his bed and open the trunk. Inside is a pile of what looks like extra-large belt buckles and some placards. Pulling one forward, I read the engraving: World Champion Rodeo. Professional Armed Forces Rodeo Association. Bucking Bronc Champion. Jedd—

A rustling in the hayloft above draws my attention. It's more than the sound of a trapped bird's wings flapping or a small creature scampering for cover in hay because there's no longer any hay up there.

"Hello," I call out. My palms anxiously sweat. I lunge to the side and drop the buckle on top of the other trophies inside the trunk. Hastily, I knock the lid to close the storage unit, which gives off a loud clack, and I reach for my arm crutches. Slipping my forearms into the cuffs, I position the metal legs to hoist myself upright. I haven't had this much motivation to move in years, and an unfamiliar thrill rustles through me as I hustle to remove myself before I'm caught where I shouldn't be. Once righted, the shifting of boards above me creaks once again.

"Hello?" I say, not quite as loudly as before. If something large and possibly human is within the confines of this barn, I won't be able to outrun him. I lurch forward, hoping to make my way across the dirt-packed flooring of Jedd's room. My crutches make circular divots in the fine grain, and I use my foot to swish at the evidence. I'm almost to the entrance of his space when a panel of sorts fills the opening, and I pause.

"Well," Jedd says as I squeak at the sudden barrier, and he glances around it. "Seems I've finally trapped my mouse."

I haven't been face to face with Jedd since our initial meeting. The whisper of his touch tickles over my cheek again. The hard lines on his face give him a stern expression, and I'd worry he is seriously angry if his dark eyes weren't twinkling.

"What mouse?" I choke, struggling to find my voice as his eyes roam down my body. I swallow and attempt to stand taller, but there's no hiding my condition from him. He can't ignore the crutches around my forearms or the way I lean into them for support. I don't go out in public with them, but still, there's something about the way Jedd is looking at me. My eyes travel to his arm.

Does he understand what I've been through?

"Someone's been stealing my food," he states, interrupting my thoughts. "Finally got around to getting a door and a lock for my little corner of heaven."

I snort at the thought of this dirty barn being celestial, and then I realize what he said.

"Someone's stealing your supper?"

"Yep. Although I don't know why you'd want it?" His eyes land on my hands, which are clearly empty as is his accusation.

"Of course, I don't need your food. Don't be ridiculous. My sister takes me to the Piggly Wiggly once a week. My kitchen is stocked." I speak rather sharply, and guilt riddles me as I realize, once again, I haven't been a generous hostess. This man is living out of a crate with powdered potatoes and canned beans, and I have a kitchen filled with fresh food that I hardly use.

"Maybe you're trying to run me off? But a giant mouse making off with some macaroni and cheese every morning isn't enough to frighten me. All the same, I'm tightening up security." He winks as if the barn is some exclusive resort rather than an out-in-the-open space with easy access. "You want to tell me what you're doing in my room if you aren't the thieving rodent?"

"I..." No reason to lie. I've been caught crutches-handed, which Jedd scans once again. The funny thing is, the skim of his eyes down my arms feels like a soft caress. Like his bare knuckles might travel over the underside of my forearm. "I was curious."

"That killed the cat." One brow tweaks up as he stares back at me with deep, midnight eyes that question my intentions. "Maybe I should get one to scare away the mouse and unwarranted guests."

"I'm not afraid of a little cat," I huff.

"Not afraid of a little pussy myself," Jedd says, and my mouth gapes at the crudeness of his comment. His face holds firm, but mine heats, and a rush of prickling pinkness creeps up my neck. I'm ready to reproach him for his boldness, but he steps aside to set the new door against the outside frame of his room. When he crosses back into view, he's blocking my exit, and his eyes traverse his room, landing on the trunk.

"Find anything of interest?" he questions.

"Nope. Nothing here I'd ever want," I state, meeting his gaze. My fingers curl over the handle of the crutches, turning white as I lie.

"Yeah, I doubt it." He smirks, crossing his arms as if he's reading me. We glare at each other in silence for a moment. "I'm surprised Tripper hasn't done more work around here for you."

I blink. "Tripper?" I blink again.

"Yeah, you said the other day you needed to get back to Tripper, and I just thought your man should be a little handier around your place."

"My man?" I mutter, still staring at him.

"Tripper is the name of your fella, right?"

"Riiiiiight. Tripper." My man, Tripper Hanes, elite handyman of a reality television show. He's my man. I bite the inside of my cheek to prevent my laughter.

"On that note, I wanted to apologize again for the other day. Hashtag me too. I shouldn't have touched you without your permission. You were right. And I apologize too because you have a guy." Jedd nods, his apology finished, but I list forward, shocked that he's apologizing and surprised he thinks I have a *boyfriend*.

"Let me help you." Jedd easily reaches out for me, but I withdraw from his touch, my eyes drawn to the claw on his wrist.

"I have it," I snap although I don't. My heart hammers in my chest, a mix of emotions.

I don't want him to be sorry he touched me.

He won't touch me again.

I don't want him to touch me again.

But I do.

My arms are quaking, and my legs tremble. My upper body strength is lacking, and it's another reason I hardly use the crutches. *I need to exercise more.* And I'm still fighting the chuckle that he thinks I have a man. Wonder what he'd think if I told him *Rehab Dad* Duncan was more my age.

"I'm headed back to the house," I say as if going to the house by way of his room inside the barn is a route.

Jedd steps aside, releasing a huff as I start my journey past him.

"If you want to know something about me, all you need to do is ask." His tone holds more invitation than warning, and the rushing within me settles a bit. I shouldn't have been snooping through his things. As I continue forward, I hear the dirt scuffle behind me.

"I said, I got it," I mutter over my shoulder, noticing Jedd following me.

"I'd like to walk you back all the same." My heated veins warm a little more. When was the last time a man walked with me? When was the last time anyone walked with me? I expect Jedd to grow agitated with my slow, dragging pace, to exhale in irritation and decide to turn back for another day of solitary work, but he saunters beside me as if the day has more than twenty-four hours. As our elbows almost brush, it's strange to have another person this close to me.

We travel in silence for a few minutes, but it seems as though it's taking a millennium to cross the gravel. My eyes eventually focus on the meager collection of tomato plants on the back steps. Another of Hannah's Momma-needs-a-hobby idea. At one point, I had a beautiful garden full of daisies, black-eyed Susans, coneflowers, bee balm, and butterfly weed. They attracted so many butterflies native to the area: Monarch, Tiger Swallowtail, and even the Eastern

Tailed-Blue Cupido, less seen but one of my favorites. The garden was a luxury Ewell had allowed me. I'd save seeds from one year to the next, doubling and then tripling the size of my plot. I'd even experimented with cross pollination, which was difficult. I'd once had bees. Nature's pollinators. I sigh with the memory. The garden's gone to weeds, and the bees were set free. I can't work the dirt as I once did.

The tomatoes are in pots, but lately, the hungry night critters steal my efforts. When I see the withering stalks with the slowly disappearing vegetables, I consider how much I hate tomatoes after ten years. I miss my flowers, and for some reason, this makes me blurt, "I suppose you could come to supper in the house."

I don't look at Jedd as I extend the invitation, too afraid to see the rejection in his eyes. Why would he want to eat in the house other than to have a hot, home-cooked meal? Why am I considering it more than a peace offering?

"I promised I wouldn't impose."

"I wouldn't ask if it was an imposition." How is it imposing? He needs to eat. I need to eat. It's not a date. A date would imply conversation and preparation, and I'm not *tion*-ing anything, so imposition this is not. It's dinner. Just dinner.

"I don't cook much, but I won't kill you." I can't remember the last time I truly cooked any meal, much less one for a man. Hannah usually makes us something, and we eat early to accommodate her schedule, or she preps foods that can be eaten cold: sandwiches, salads, leftover fried chicken. We also have a generous gifting from the outreach community, giving us a freezer full of tuna casserole and meatloaf.

"Death by dinner." Jedd chuckles. "Didn't die from an electrical shock, so I don't think a little meatloaf can hurt me." When he holds up his left arm, the sunshine reflects off the metal end. Puzzled, my expression prompts him to continue. "Was in the military for years, and no enemy could take me down. But I worked construction to help rebuild a town in the Middle East, and like a dumbass, I reached for an electrical wire. They tell me I was dead for five minutes.

When I came back to life, I was missing an arm." He chuckles, but there isn't much humor in what he's just told me. "I don't like to claim wounded warrior status, as I wasn't hurt it in combat, but people like to make assumptions."

"And you let them think what they will?"

"Ain't nobody's damn business what happened to me. I'm not afraid to share the story if people ask, but it seems like such a foolish mistake to admit. And most people don't ask. They just assume. Veteran. Wounded soldier."

My brows pinch as I stare at his arm, really taking in the mechanics of it and the shoulder holster keeping it attached to his body.

"Is it heavy?"

"You get used to the weight."

"Does it hurt?"

Jedd wiggles his arm and snaps the metal tongs together. "It gets itchy in the heat, but so do lots of body parts. You get used to it, too."

"Do you miss it?" My lips clamp together after I ask such a question. Of course, he misses his arm. It's rude that I asked, and the furrow to his forehead tells me so, but I turn my shame back on him by glaring. He said I could ask about anything I wanted to know, but I've crossed a line here. Jedd's head turns to the left, his hands coming to his hips.

"You're something, Bee." He shakes his head, and my brow pinches at the nickname.

"Do you have to wear it?" The question equally surprises him, and I realize my lack of social interaction has reduced my interrogation filter. I'm about to tell him he doesn't have to answer me when he speaks.

"No, but sometimes it freaks people out when I don't have it on. If I showed up here with only one arm, you might not take me seriously. Seeing two arms makes it easier to believe I can do all I say I can."

"What makes you think I take you seriously, arms or no arms?"

Jedd looks at me for another second, and then his lip curls up in the corner. "You're teasing me, aren't you, honey?" The other corner curves, and suddenly, Jedd Flemming is smiling at me, and it changes everything. The stern edges of his face soften, pinching his cheeks and squinting his eyes as if the sunshine blinds him. Only he's the one blinding me. His teeth are white and straight and his lips a deep red, and I'm curious once again what that mouth would feel like against mine.

Curiosity killed the cat.

The man said he isn't afraid of a little…

I can't repeat the term. It's embarrassing to admit how much the innuendo affected me. How my…nether region…pulsed, and an errant sensation filled me. His mouth. My…

"You're turning fire engine red there, Bee. Whatcha thinking about?"

"It's Beverly. Bev. Er. Lee," I emphasize, ignoring his question. There's no way on this green planet I can tell him my thoughts. Then another thought occurs. No one's ever given me a nickname. It's very…Tripper Hanes. Jedd's hand comes forward, hesitating, and I hold still. Even my breath gets caught in my throat before his fingers cautiously cup my chin. His thumb extends upward, and he rubs my lower lip. *My, he takes liberties.* I should admonish him, I should scold him, but I can't find the words as his eyes follow the line of the thick pad tracing over my pouting mouth.

"Nah, you're a bee, like the pollinator." Jedd snorts before making a buzzing nose and moving his hand away from my mouth and through the air like the hyper insect. "You're full of sting, Bev-er-lee, but you don't fool me. Your tongue is sharp, but it's only words. Nothing long-lasting. Sticks and stones and stuff." Instantly, I think of Howard. Only words. Thousands of insulting words. I step back from Jedd, giving us some much-needed space.

"Bee stings can be deadly," I snap. "I'm allergic." The pollinators' potential can be just like words that cut deep, very deep. A metaphor isn't unwarranted. I've been stung by many a bee, and the itching, throbbing aftereffects lasted for days. A strong reminder that while the initial pain lasts a second, a sting lingers long after the offender is gone. Just like words. Hurtful words. And mean men.

"Really?" Those midnight eyes widen in concern.

I hate that I can't lie. "No, not really."

Jedd chuckles. "Teasing me again." He pauses another second and then tilts his head. "Having a sense of humor is good. I like that. I'll figure you out yet, Bee."

He wants to figure me out? What's to figure out? A lump forms in my throat.

"I admire you, you know?" *He admires me?* "You've been able to keep this place. With all that you've been through, all your daughter has done, you still have your land, and that's something. It's admirable."

Admiration. No, no, *no.* Determination maybe. Dedication possibly. But admiration is not what we have here.

"So dinner?" he interjects on my *-tion* list. "Will Tripper be joining us?"

"Tripper." I bite the inside of my cheek. People think what they want, he just said, because they don't ask. "Not tonight. We eat at six."

We've been standing outside by my back steps. Jedd's eyes haven't lingered on my crutches, and over the course of time, I've become less and less conscious of them. *What are we even talking about?* I'm lost again in Jedd's smile, and he's looking at me as though I'm a drooling idiot, which is how I feel.

Will he touch me again? I might not complain.

"So..."

"Oh..." We speak at the same time, and I stand a little taller, ready to dismiss him. I've had an overdose of Jedd's junk—I mean, *The Jedd Juncture*—and I need a commercial break from that smile that makes me feel warm and fuzzy when I don't warm and *fuzzilate*.

"You go..." we say in unison, and now I blush. This *is* silly.

"I was going to say see you at six." I nod, dismissing Jedd, but he holds firm a second.

"I was going to ask what interests you. You said there was nothing of interest in my room, but what does interest you?"

My eyes leap to the outline of where a garden once stood. Where weeds are more predominant than flowers. Taking a long minute, I realize I don't know where my interests lay. Where did they go? What do I like to do?

Momma, you need a hobby. Something to keep your mind active if your body can't be.

"I fucking hate tomatoes," I blurt, and Jedd's eyes widen, his lids blinking once before his lips curve again.

"Okayyy…" He waits. I waffle. I have no idea why I said that other than it's the truth. I'm sick of tomatoes.

My eyes meet Jedd's. *Oh Lordy, that is not a good idea.* The gleam to them is like a beacon, calling me to say all the naughty thoughts in my head, curse the things in my heart, and strip bare the truths I've been holding deep inside for a long time.

It's not like he asked you to rip off your clothes. I might if he asks.

"I don't have any interests," I snap, suddenly irritated with his asking.

Jedd nods, pursing his lips. "Okay, Bee. You have until six to think on it."

What? "What?"

"See you at six, and I want one thing of interest. Dinner conversation." He tips his head as if he's wearing a cowboy hat and turns for the barn.

Conversation? No *tion*-ing, my brain screams. Discussion or otherwise.

And definitely no admiration.

CHAPTER SEVEN

[Jedd]

Grady's Seed and Soil was just outside Green Valley proper and one of the only places around for farm and feed supplies. As a frequent visitor when I was a teenager, Vernon Grady and I had struck up your typical farmer-kid friendship. Backroad driving. Empty field partying. Late-night shenanigans. And neither of our daddies spared the rod at our unruly behavior. But where Vernon's father had visions of his oldest son taking over the family business, my stepfather had other plans.

"What do you mean you're giving everything to Boone?" At twenty years old, I'd stared at the man I called Father. When my mother married Hasting, I was four and Janice six. We'd been encouraged to consider him our daddy as we didn't know any other man to give the honor, but when Boone was born, everything changed.

"He's my son." Hasting had stated of his then fifteen-year-old offspring—his biological son with my mother.

"But I'm the one taking care of everything." My life plans had included his land because the land wanted me. The farm. The horses. I'd be damned if I worked *for* my little brother. I'd worked hard—as hard as Hasting—to keep things running smoothly on his family's legacy. The future was mapped out. Breeding. Therapy. Hasting Horse Farm was his pride and joy, next to Boone, apparently, and Boone didn't care one horse's ass for the animals or the land.

"Mama?" I'd questioned. Turning to her had been my downfall. Our mother would always side with Hasting, and Hasting snapped.

"Why you looking at her, boy? Your mama ain't going to help you here".

Hasting and I had been rivaling for a while. He'd thought I was trying to one-up him with my new ideas about horse rearing and rodeo possibilities. He also couldn't use the belt as much when I grew bigger than him. His words lashed just as hard some days, but I developed a thick skin to leather straps and verbal slaps. He was delicate on his own son, though, spoiling him, and this turn of fate was my breaking point.

I was out. Out of Green Valley. Out of the mountains.

I ran off for the military.

"Well, look what the cat dragged in," Vernon stated when I'd arrived at his store some twenty plus years after leaving Green Valley, and we picked up right where we'd left off.

"Shower," I announce as I enter his office in the upper levels of the supersized store featuring farm equipment, feed supply, and a garden center. As I don't have running water in Beverly's barn, Vernon's been allowing me to use his office bathroom. An outdoor shower is on order to rectify the plumbing situation.

"Evenin', Jedd," Vernon states, reminding me I'm not using my manners. I'm running late. The eldest Grady is your typical mountain man, complete with thick beard and belly and a different colored flannel shirt for each day of the week. He loves the small-town community of nearby Green Valley and the large home he owns up on the ridge. He's done his daddy proud with the family business, and he's been a good friend.

"Evenin'," I offer as an afterthought apology for my rush.

"Hold up," he calls after me as I breeze by him with my shower kit, a towel, and a bag holding a clean change of clothes. I stop, not having time to hang out as I usually do. He holds out a beer to me, but I shake my head, so he questions, "What gives?"

"Got dinner tonight with Beverly."

Vernon pauses in handing me the beverage. "Dinner?" His eyes widen, but his jaw tightens. "With Beverly Townsen?"

My eyes narrow as I take in the strange expression on Vernon's face. I should ask him about Tripper, Beverly's man. Who is he, and why haven't I seen him come around?

"Hot date?" Vernon teases.

Is it a date? I don't think so. Beverly is clearly repulsed by me, staring at my arm as though it will harm her and retracting from my touch as though pestered by an annoying insect. Still. I wouldn't mind calling it a date. Wouldn't mind having dinner with someone. It's been a long time of eating alone and meager meals.

"Nah. It's not a date. I'm working her for the land." I pause with what I've said as the expression on Vernon's face turns to ash. "I mean, I'm just there for the land. Nothing more."

Vernon clears this throat. "You know Beverly's good people despite what people say. She's had it rough, Jedd, so don't be laying on your charm, thinking she's one of your buckle bunnies. Howard did a number on her, and it's made her hard."

I know what he's saying even though I might disagree. Beverly's tough on the outside—like armor used for protection. If nothing can penetrate it, nothing can hurt her. I recognize the defensive mechanism because I've used it myself a time or two. But underneath, Beverly is a fragile woman who I'd bet was once soft and tender. A woman willing to love until a man like Howard got a hold of her. He'd ruined her.

"I'm just warning you not to hurt her." Vernon stands from his desk chair.

"You threatening me?" I tease, but there's an edge to my tone, not liking the implication.

"You're full of deals, Jedd. Don't make her a bargain." My brows pinch. Hasting had the gambling problem, not me.

"If you weren't one of my best friends, I might be offended." I'm not joking anymore. Is he comparing me to Hasting?

"As your best friend, I'm saying tread lightly."

"Don't you worry about Beverly," I state, defensive once again. "I'm not looking to plow anything but her back field." I pause, letting that sink in before I change the subject. "Hear anything about Boone?" It's like my brother vanished into thin air, and I need to remember he's the reason I came back in the first place. I owe my sister a call. We need more information. I've been to the old house, but it's vacant and slightly disheveled. *How did things get so bad?* I don't understand what's been going on back here, but I blame Hasting. He's the one who lost it all. He's the one who gambled it all away. If he'd only given it all to me as I'd thought would happen…

But no.

I can't think of Hasting and Boone right now. I have dinner with Beverly. The non-date dinner date.

* * *

I arrive at eighteen hundred hours with nothing in hand. *Dammit.* I should have brought flowers or a bottle of wine. It's been a long time since I'd done dinner with a lady, and I've lost my touch. Empty-handed, I stand on her back porch and knock.

Hannah answers the door, and I'm a little surprised by her presence.

"Mr. Flemming," she states rather formally as she steps back and allows me entrance. Beverly is already seated at the table wearing a white blouse with some kind of collar that makes her look like a schoolgirl instead of a woman in her forties.

"I didn't expect you this evening," I address Hannah. "What a pleasant surprise." Hannah nods at me and then points at a seat.

"Dinner's ready. I called in late when Momma told me about

inviting you to supper. I usually do the cooking as Momma really shouldn't be using the oven."

My eyes flip to Beverly who keeps hers focused on the empty plate before her.

"Momma mentioned you might be joining her for dinner from now on. We didn't know you were living on macaroni and cheese. That's not enough sustenance for a man working as hard as you do. I apologize I didn't have more advanced notice of this evening. I typically prepare meals ahead of time if I need to work the dinner shift. I have a second job at the Front Porch, the steakhouse in town."

Hannah works two jobs? She's a busy woman. As directed by Hannah, I take a seat next to Beverly while Hannah sits across from me.

"Beverly," I state, feeling an uncertain tension in the air.

"I thought you might not be coming," she mutters. Her eyes shift quickly from her plate and then back to the stoneware, her voice remaining low. Her tone holds something short of expectancy with a dash of relief, and I grin.

"I wouldn't miss it," I whisper. Hannah sets a meatloaf on the table, and I almost chuckle at the irony. She says a quick prayer of gratitude, and I bow my head, giving an extra thank you to a higher being for allowing me this meal with these two women. Beverly reaches for the serving utensils, but Hannah's reach is faster, and she serves me first.

"I got it, Momma," she states, and I watch as Beverly retracts her hands like a disappointed child. A glass of sweet tea already sits on the table by my plate, and I take a sip, my mouth suddenly dry.

"Beverly, thought any more on what I asked earlier?" I'm not good at chit-chat, but I'm equally horrible at silence.

"What was that?" Hannah asks before Beverly can speak.

"I asked your momma what she has interest in."

"Momma likes to knit and grow tomatoes."

Beverly keeps her head lowered, not answering me and not correcting her daughter.

"Beverly says she hates tomatoes," I say on her behalf but

suddenly feel uncomfortable speaking about her as if she isn't sitting at this table.

Hannah looks up at her mother. "Momma loves tomatoes. They're award-winning, and she sells out at every farmers' market. After she couldn't garden any longer, tomatoes in pots was the next best solution."

"You gardened?" I ask Beverly. Her mouth opens, but Hannah interjects.

"Momma loved gardening. She could grow anything. A real green thumb, but then…" Her voice drifts, leaving off the rest of the story.

"You like flowers?" I question, but it's really a confirmation. Again, Hannah answers.

"Momma's favorite were daisies but really anything that attracted butterflies tickled her. There's an actual plant called a butterfly bush. Did you know that, Mr. Flemming? It lives up to its name, calling to butterflies like some kind of siren," she explains.

"Buddleia davidii," Beverly mutters, closing her lids as if she can see the plant in her mind's eye.

"It was the most beautiful purple color, remember, Momma?" Hannah asks, but Beverly doesn't need to answer. The small grin on her closed-off face tells me everything.

"What other plants do you like, Bee?"

"Bee?" Hannah's face wrinkles. "Beverly," she corrects, but her mother's eyes have opened and the grin on her face grows. I don't understand what's happening here. The same snarky woman who greeted me over a week ago and the one who snooped in my room earlier is absent. In her place is this meek, quiet woman seated next to me.

"We used to grow the most beautiful sunflowers." Beverly finally answers for herself, and I watch as her face morphs from pride to sadness. She closed down as fast as she opened up, and her eyes snap over to her child. "I apologize, but I find I'm not very hungry this evening. If you'll excuse me, I'd like to retire early."

Beverly's hardly touched her meatloaf. Who retires at six thirteen in the evening? She reaches toward the floor, lifts her forearm crutches, and works her arms into the cuffs.

"Momma, I told you, you should have sat in your chair. It would be easier for you." Hannah immediately stands to assist her mother as do I, and for the first time, Beverly looks at me. Her eyes plead with mine.

"Please, don't help me." The normal bite and bark of her tone is absent, and hollowness remains. My hand lingers between my body and hers—my hook hand—and not for the first time, I wonder if Beverly is afraid of it. It seems preposterous to consider she's nervous of a mechanical hand as she has her own assistive device, yet there are so many things I don't understand about Beverly Townsen.

"Please don't let me interrupt. Finish this delicious meatloaf my daughter prepared for you, Mr. Flemming. It was wonderful having you join us this evening. Feel free to come to supper anytime." The emptiness of her tone laced with her finest manners troubles me. *Who is this woman?* Remaining standing, I exert my own manners as a woman excuses herself from the dinner table, and I watch in frustration as Hannah hovers behind her mother down the hall.

I should excuse myself, but I don't. I wait until Hannah returns to the kitchen.

"Has it been difficult? All these years just the two of you?" I soften my tone, knowing I'm balancing on a precipice that's none of my business, but I feel a kinship with Hannah Townsen, fearing she's worked hard as a child to please her parent, who might not have been grateful for all she gave up.

Hannah lifts her head, and with conviction, she states, "I'm all Momma has."

I've learned that isn't exactly true as Beverly's sister, Naomi Winters—a local librarian—took her to the Piggly Wiggly during the week.

"What about Naomi?"

Hannah straightens at the mention of her aunt. "Aunt Naomi's been as dedicated as she could be, but Momma is very private. She's always felt guilty for shunning her younger sister when she was in need. Momma didn't want to be a burden to her. To either of her sisters." Hannah's lips twist as if she's told me more than she intended.

"Sisters?"

"Momma's older sister is Scotia Simmons."

My brows raise in surprise. The Simmons family were Valley royalty like the Donners and the Olivers.

"Any relation to Karl Simmons?" He was the only child, the golden child, of old Mr. and Mrs. Simmons, and a few years older than me in school. His mother often referred to him as their miracle baby.

"His widow," Hannah clarifies.

"What happened to him?" I ask like a church-going gossip.

"He was murdered. Mistaken identity."

Oh my. "I'm sorry for your loss," I offer, but Hannah dismissively snorts at the sentiment about her uncle. "What about Scotia? She couldn't have helped your momma?"

"Financially, Scotia could have done all kinds of things, but Momma and she haven't always gotten along, and Momma would have refused charity from her sister, had she offered." Hannah's mouth twists again as though locking her lips has been difficult. She quickly tries to rectify. "But Momma doesn't want charity."

How is helping a sibling charity?

I should ask Hannah about Beverly's beau. Where is this mystery man? Why isn't he helping her? But I don't want the daughter to think I'm prying too deeply into the mother's affairs. It's none of my business if she has a man. A lackluster, surprisingly absent man.

There's so much I suddenly want to know about Beverly. So many pieces to a puzzle that don't fit, but I don't continue interrogating Hannah. I thank her for dinner and see myself out.

CHAPTER EIGHT

[Beverly]

"Bev, do you think you'll ever love again?" my sister Naomi questions as we sit in a booth at Daisy's Nut House. It's been a few days since that disastrous first dinner with Jedd, and I've decided to break my cycle of ogling him from the window, especially as I can't really see the progress he's making inside the barn. I haven't ventured over to spy or snoop like I did the other morning, choosing instead to remain on my side of the yard. Still, I am curious, but I'm even more curious what has made my sister ask such a question. I sputter tea all over myself, and the spray rivals a hose pressurized by a thumb for maximum water coverage. Continuing to sputter-cough, I try to respond.

"Would I *what?*" I'm not looking at her as I reach for paper napkins in the metal dispenser on the table and then struggle to dab the large stains mercilessly spreading on my white blouse with a Peter Pan collar. It's one of my best shirts. I haven't bought anything new for myself in years, allowing Hannah to make all my clothing decisions and purchases in the last decade. I don't want her wasting her hard-earned money, and I don't feel right asking for personal items I don't need. I don't go anywhere other than to church on Sunday and my outings with Naomi on Wednesdays, so anything more than casual attire isn't a necessity. I've had this blouse forever, and I wanted to look a little nicer today for no particular reason, so I snap at my sister, "You made me ruin my shirt."

"That shirt needs to be ruined," she bites. My head pops up, and I widen my eyes at her retort. My sister never talks back to me, and she never insults me, or anyone for that matter.

"What makes you say such a thing?"

"That blouse isn't flattering on you."

Just when I think I can't open my eyes any wider, I try. "I meant why would you ask me about love?"

She shrugs, looking out the window toward the parking lot, and I stare back at her. My sister has gray-white hair in wild waves down to her breasts. It's gorgeous, and so is she; she's just been misunderstood in this community. We both have. She hasn't dated. Ever. After one night with a young man when she was twenty-one, she gave up on the opposite sex. *Oh, the irony.* Her heart broke in a million fragments, but she's put herself back together as a new person. She's very different from when we were teenagers. She was the reckless one while I was the one with stars in my eyes. Unintentionally mischievous—objects in the toilet, overflowing a bathroom sink, artwork on the back of a couch—I wasn't a risk-taker like Naomi had been. Or like our brother Jebediah. I was just…creatively curious.

"Did something happen? Did you meet someone?" My forehead wrinkles. I'd be so envious in a non-threatening way if she did, but I'd also be overwhelming happy for her. She deserves someone. "Who is he?"

"Remember the night Jebediah died?" Her voice lowers as she sits up straighter, clasping her hands before her on the tabletop, and my eyes narrow. My sister shoulders unhealthy guilt over a situation she had no control over. Our brother was a menace, spurring the ire of our parents and the wrath of their sermonizing. Their condescending nature chipped at each of their children, some more than others, and I hate when Naomi lumps herself with what happened to Jebediah.

It was an accident. The words filter through my thoughts, attached to multiple circumstances.

"Do you remember Nathan Ryder? I've recently seen him."

"What?" I choke again and then listen as my sister recounts all that's been happening in her life over the past month. Reunited. Reacquainted. Renewed feelings.

"Did you sleep with him again?" I admonish, although I'm not admonishing. Actually, I might be a little proud of my sister if she gave in and experimented with someone after all this time. What would it be like, I wonder, as it's been almost as long for me. The feel of tender hands on my body. The whisper of sweet words in my ear. The nip of teeth at the juncture of my shoulder. For years, I thought I missed Howard until I realized it wasn't Howard. It was intimacy. On the rare occasions Howard expressed it as a husband would to his wife, I fell into a rabbit hole of overwhelming sentiment for a man who could not reciprocate the feelings.

"No," Naomi whispers, as if ashamed that she hadn't, or maybe ashamed because she wishes she had. "I just … I like him, but then I told him about Jebediah—"

"Stop blaming Jebediah for everything that happened to you. You didn't hold the bottle before he drove." My voice falters. Jebediah's decisions were his own. Even if I wasn't with him that night, I can sympathize with his plight. A desperate need to drown oneself. A deep desire to numb the pain. A stupid decision to drive. I'd made the same unforgivable choice. Only I'd survived my disaster—if survival is what you can call my existence—while Jebediah perished in his.

Naomi and I were about to embark on an old argument, one she and I had agreed to respectfully disagree on years ago.

"He made his own choices," I state, implying Jebediah. "Besides, Nathan's the one who walked out on you so quickly. Did he ever explain why he didn't call?" Being left behind seems to be a Winters' woman curse as Nathan Ryder ditched my sister after he got what he wanted from her, just as Howard abandoned me with a child and a farm, and Karl Simmons stepped out on Scotia.

Naomi feeds me some malarkey about Nathan forgetting a phone number and roaming the Southern coast and *blah, blah, blah*. Men always have enlarged excuses instead of generous gumption.

"That's a cop-out. You deserve to know the reason. In fact, you deserve it right now." I'm growing more agitated the longer I listen to my sister's story and Nathan's paltry palliation.

She deserves the truth.

She deserves an explanation.

A storm brews within me with each consideration, but I'm no longer certain I'm talking about my sister.

"You're the one who's all 'girl power' and 'go goddess', yet you still choose to blame yourself, and you need to stop. Quit faulting yourself for everything related to that night." I exhale as I rant. The storm swirls to a full-on tempest. "Maybe you should have slept with him again."

"Beverly!" Naomi's shocked retort startles us both.

"Well, it's one way to get over a man." *Is it?* Am I listening to what I'm saying? Is sleeping with someone else the way to cure the pain and pining over someone who is never coming back? No, the answer is a resounding no. I'd been close to that position, too close, and it would not have eased my aches.

"You could have slept with him to keep him, but then again, what do I know? All the sex in the world didn't keep Howard home with me." It's true. I'd given myself to Howard too many times in too many ways, and it was embarrassing to admit. I hate him for what he did to me and how he made me feel, but I hate myself more for allowing it. I take a deep breath before I continue as I'm dangerously close to admitting things I don't want to admit to another human being, even my sister. "Then again, Nathan is older, and maybe he has that erectile dysfunction thing you so often see advertised on television, and his penis doesn't work like it sh—"

"It works just fine," she interjects, holding up a hand to stop me and flushing deep red.

What can I say? I watch a lot of television. That's where I learn these things.

"How would you know if you haven't slept with him?" I can't fight the grin slowly curling my lips. What has my sister been up to with this man? Then I have another curious thought. "So he hasn't called in three days?"

She nods.

"And you think he's ghosting you again?" Another word I've learned from television—*ghosting*. The act of ending a relationship quite suddenly and without communicating an explanation.

Howard Townsen ghosted me.

"You need to go after him instead." It was my best advice and my worst advice. I'd gone after Howard on a whim. Vernon Grady had told me he'd seen Howard in the area with a girl from the Pink Pony. Just when I thought I'd pulled myself back together, this news had broken me all over again. And then I broke myself by making a poor decision. Almost as poor as deciding to chase Howard in the first place. Almost. All I'd wanted was an answer. It was no longer a matter of what had *I* done wrong, but why had *Howard* done what he did?

"You need closure, Naomi." I speak as if I'm talking about myself. "You need to confront him and get your answers, so you can let him go. So you don't spiral into believing something about your-self that isn't true. If he walks away, let it rest on him, not you, but at least you'll have said your piece. You can't allow him a free pass."

I'd never said my piece with Howard. I was never able to face him and tell him how much he'd hurt me or how much I truly despised him. I've held onto my disgust for my husband and my desire for a justification for nearly two decades. And I am exhausted. At what point do I let him go? No, *not him*, the idea of him, the concept of a philandering husband and absentee father. When can I release Howard from my head and my heart so I can be whole?

"I'm not allowing Nathan a pass." Naomi interrupts my thoughts.

85

And then, she smacks the table with her hand, and I jump on the booth bench, thankful I'm not sipping tea or even holding the cup. "You're right."

"I usually am," I mutter sarcastically. But am I? Have I been right in how I've handled my own desertion by Howard? How I've allowed Hannah to assist me? My thoughts flip back to the night Jedd joined us for dinner. Hannah didn't let me speak, and it's the first time I noticed I wasn't speaking up for myself. Not wanting to cause a scene with her in front of a stranger, I allowed it to happen. I thought it best to excuse myself and disappear into my room as I've done on too many occasions to avoid confrontation with her. But I'm the mother. When did she overtake me?

I'm giving sage advice to my sister to take what she needs and fight for vindication, but I'm not certain I've done the same for myself. I have all the answers to the questions of when, and how, and why.

What I need to answer is what do I plan to do about it?

* * *

In my determination to take back a little control, I go to the extreme the next time Jedd joins us for dinner.

"Jedd, what's the schedule with the land?" Hannah asks, expressing interest in the future. She could have been anything she wanted. The world was hers that first year of college, and then I had the accident. Me. My fault. She came home to help…and stayed.

Who is to blame there? Howard's voice niggles in my head.

"I've actually got someone in mind to work the fields. Just need to get that old tractor running." Everything has gone to rust at this old place, and there are no funds to invest in new equipment. I'm surprised how dedicated Jedd has been to *The Jedd Juncture*. He's worked tirelessly in the barn, and I'm taken aback at his assessment of our old equipment and progression in seeking assistance. "I've worked out a trade with Vernon Grady about the tractor."

Vernon Grady? *Oh, hell no.*

"Another exchange?" I snort, my tone acidic. This man is full of wheeling and dealing, and while I'm impressed with his determination, I'm still unsure of his intentions.

"Vernon Grady," Hannah's voice interjects, raising an octave as her eyes shift to me, but I ignore her attention.

"Momma, you remember Vernon Grady, right?"

"How can I forget him?" My tone cuts.

"We've used Mr. Grady's services in the past. What kind of trade are you hoping to bargain with him?" Hannah's voice remains cheerful, hopeful even. She'd grown attached to the big man who'd haul her over his shoulder like a bale of hay and toss her in a pile of it at his supply store. As a child, Hannah enjoyed their seasonal displays with Vernon's three young sons, especially Grizzly. Ewell took us there often enough, allowing me to occasionally purchase flower seeds or starter plants. I always wanted more—more seeds, more flowers, just more—but Ewell said patience was the good Lord's promise to a farmer.

Life is sweeter when it grows from the hard work of your hands and results as the fruits of your land.

Thoughts of Ewell make me miss him.

"We aren't bargaining with Vernon." My tone brooks no argument to my opinion on the subject—*that's final*.

"Well," Jedd begins, ignoring me and turning to my daughter, "I've known Vernon since way back, and we'll figure something out."

"Oh, and how do you know him?" Hannah asks. Over time, Hannah had stars in her eyes over a man who was kinder to her than her daddy.

"He'd been my best friend growing up in these parts." I ignore the mention of him growing up in the area because I'm too focused on Vernon.

"We will not be indebted to Mr. Grady."

"Why not?" Jedd asks.

"Because I said so," I snap, smacking the table while I scold him like a child, exerting my authority. This is my farm. This is my land.

Jedd's eyes narrow, and his jaw sets. I read his expression. He is not asking for my permission.

"Vernon will assist me in fixing the tractor," he states, ignoring me once again and directing his statement to Hannah, who hesitantly looks from him to me and back to him.

"Unless your Tripper wants to help?" Jedd mutters, but his inability to speak quietly makes the statement loud enough for Hannah to hear.

"Who's—" Hannah begins, but I hold up a hand, halting her question. *Not this. Not now.* I'm in no mood to laugh, and I'm not addressing the Tripper issue.

"Last I checked, I'm still the owner of this property," I interject, ignoring his suggestion that a reality personality fix my tractor. Although I can't say with confidence my statement is exactly true. The deed is still in Howard's name as far as I know, having been passed to him upon the death of his father the year before Howard left. My hand slams on the table once again, causing the utensils to jump and clatter. "And I say no to Vernon."

"Momma," Hannah hisses under her breath as her eyes shift to her plate.

"Give me one good reason Vernon isn't allowed to help," Jedd questions.

"Because I—" I'm about to repeat *because I said so* because I cannot admit the real truth to him, or Hannah, or anyone. My shame will go to the grave with me.

"Not good enough," Jedd cuts me off before I can finish, raising his hand to emphasize his disinterest in any concern I may offer. He pauses for a millisecond before addressing my daughter. "Hannah, what do you think?"

My heart leaps to my throat, nearly choking off my airways as heat rushes my cheeks. How dare he ignore me and continue to speak to her? "She has no opinion on the manner."

"Oh." Jedd sits taller in his seat. "Like she has no say in her life because she's too busy taking care of you?"

The collective gasp of Hannah and myself fills the kitchen and echoes into the silence which follows.

"You're out of line, Mr. Flemming," Hannah states softly without much warning in her tone, but she's stealing my thoughts all the same, and this pisses me off even more. How dare she have the same thoughts as me? My body hums with irritation, and if I had the wherewithal to stand, I'd lean across this table and smack Jedd.

"No, I'm crossing the unspeakable line. I've watched you work night and day in this house, Hannah, and then go out and work two jobs. You can't possibly believe this is enough for yourself. You're almost thirty. Don't you want more?" His questioning sympathy for my daughter eats at the core of concerns that keep me awake at night. Does she want more? Has she given too much of herself to me? Has she lost too much time?

"Not that it's any of your business, *Mr.* Flemming," I retort, the anger in me building to lava pouring over a volcano lip. It's my turn to speak, my turn to talk over my daughter. "Of course, she wants more. We both wanted more for her. She's as smart as a whip and talented with her pretty voice, but who the hell do you think you are asking such things?"

The confidence in Jedd's expression tells me he knows exactly who he is.

"A better question is, who are you, Beverly Townsen? You're all shut up in this house, hardly going anywhere. You could do so much more yourself. You could *be* so much more."

"Mr. Flemming, that just isn't true. Momma isn't capable of—"

"She's more than capable, Hannah. With a little more practice, your momma could move about this farm just fine. You're too young for this. You need to get out and find some fun. Live your life." His voice rises with each declaration as does the bile in my throat. We're spiraling out of control around my supper table.

"Momma can't do things for herself, Mr. Flemming. She needs me."

"She doesn't," Jedd calmly states, the volume loud while a vein strains in his neck, and the truth in both their statements hits me like a sucker punch to the gut.

Flabbergasted, I fall back in my chair.

Hannah believes I'm not able-bodied. Suddenly, I recall years of her *telling* me I can't—can't use the stove, can't clean the house, can't reach the washer, can't work the soil—and then doing those things for me. She took control. Maybe unintentionally on her part, but I've allowed it to happen, and eventually, she stepped over me, just as Howard did. What I cannot do is allow this to continue.

I turn to Hannah. "I see what you're doing. You're turning this on me. I'm the incapable one. I'm the stupid one, and by offering our land to him, you've secured things for yourself. You *want* him, but a man like him will not replace your daddy. *He* left you. He abandoned *us*. Men cannot be trusted."

Hannah stares at me as though I've struck her, something I've never done. Her mouth hangs open, and her face turns red while tears well in her eyes.

Jedd's words rang equally as stunting. I've conditioned myself to believe Hannah is correct in her assessment—*I can't*. She has replaced Howard in her condemnation of my abilities. My accident has given her a good reason to enable my behavior instead of enforce rehabilitation. I couldn't do anything for myself, so I accepted her doing things for me. I've given her the power to crush my control. But Jedd's the stranger here—the porch intruder, the barn invader—and we don't need him telling us how our life is or how to live it.

I turn on Jedd next. "And you, thinking you can smooth talk your way onto my land, maybe into my daughter's bed by giving her all your attention. I will not let you near her, trying to manipulate her by asking her opinion, feeding her pretty lines of promises to fix things and plant fields. You're just like Howard, manipulating young girls with promises you won't keep."

Jedd's hand hammers on the table, forcing the silverware to collide with the plates. We glare at one another. He's angry, angry enough to maim, and I've no doubt he's done so in the military, but I don't care. My body vibrates with hatred and disappointment and disgust. *In myself.*

"Get. Out."

Hannah looks over at me with terror in her eyes. "Momma, he can't leave."

"Don't you 'Momma' me." My voice drips, the venom of my words salivating in my mouth. I point between the two of them. "You want each other?" I question, looking from one to the other. "Well, my daughter, who takes her clothes off so men can gawk, will not call the shots in this house. You don't want him to leave?" I direct to Hannah. "You don't want him to run off like your daddy did? If you think fucking this man will keep him here, you won't do it under *my* roof."

Hannah's face is ashen, mortified by what I've said, and I admit I don't even recognize my own voice. Self-loathing possesses me as I'm hit with the ugly truth of being used by a man, manipulated by my offspring, and called to task by an outsider.

"Apologize to your daughter," Jedd commands, his voice terrifyingly calm as his hand fists on the table.

I don't react.

I'm tired of apologizing.

I'm tired of asking for forgiveness. From Howard, it was always for what I didn't do, say, or think as he wished.

I'm tired of offering a continuous apology to my child for an accident—*it was an accident, an unforgiveable, despicable crime*—that threw both our lives off course.

I'm tired of praying for redemption when I've suffered enough.

When will *I'm sorry* be enough?

I glare at Jedd in defiance. How dare he come into our lives, into our home, and make us question ourselves? But I don't have time to continue my list of curses against this stranger with murderous midnight eyes and a jaw edged in justice. He pushes back his chair and kicks at the leg of mine. My hands clutch the seat, daring him with my eyes to do his worst damage. I'm not afraid he'll hit me. His body language does not suggest he'd use the power of his stature to cause me harm, but he's looking to square off with me, and I'm itching to fight. If I thought I'd get away with it, I'd throw a swing, wanting a good punch at the smirk on his face, and the firmness of his chest, and the appeal of his physique. Because despite our faulty bodies, my body is drawn to his in a way I can't explain and don't wish to define. I desire him when it's the last thing I should desire, especially with the fire flaming from each of our eyes.

Within a second of heavy breathing and smoke practically coming out of our nostrils, Jedd scoops me into his arms, lifting me from the kitchen chair and pressing me into his very capable chest.

"What the hell do you think you're doing?" I demand. "Put me down."

"Mr. Flemming," Hannah calls after him as he turns for the kitchen door and maneuvers the knob to open it. Within seconds, we are outside in the crisp, fall night air, and Jedd calls over his shoulder.

"Just giving your momma some fresh air to cool down."

"I don't need to cool down," I scream. "I will not cool down!"

"You need to settle," he tells me, and while I am overheated— between my temper and the closeness of his body—I yell at him once again.

"Do not tell me what to do!" The power of my lungs surprises me as I holler into the night, thankful only a moment later when I realize I'm angled at the left side of Jedd's body, aimed at the ear he can hardly hear in. My voice cracks as the bellow echoes through the empty air. It feels good; it feels damn good to scream at the top of my lungs.

Do not tell me what to do.

I'm firing up to add, "*Don't tell me what I can't do, either,*" when my body is free-falling. Jedd has released me, and for less than a second, I'm weightless until I hit ice-cold water, and my body's submerged in the frigid liquid.

I'm too stunned to speak, and the second scream lodges in my throat. I sputter. I choke. But I do not respond to my new surroundings.

"Mr. Flemming…" Hannah stammers, catching up to us on the side of the barn. "Momma," she shrieks, stepping forward, taking in my new position inside a deep tub full of rainwater. Her head twists from me to Jedd and back. As she speaks to him, her eyes widen on me. She reaches for my hands. "Mr. Flemming, she didn't mean it. She's just hurting. She's upset."

"Don't defend her," Jedd states, stepping between my daughter and the tub. His dark eyes laser focus on me as I shiver, clothes soaked to my skin, and the cold seeping deeper.

What did I say?

What have I done?

"What your momma suggested was reprehensible, and I will not listen to anyone, momma or not, speak to her child like that, insinuating you have impure thoughts of me and suggesting I'd reciprocate such notions. I'll ask you again, Beverly Townsen, just who do you think you are?"

I glare up at him, my lip trembling and my body quivering. I'd laugh, but there isn't anything funny about what he's said. This— swimming in a tub of rain for the pure enjoyment of it—was the kind of mischief I'd get myself into when I was a teen. But now, in my condition, and with what Jedd has accused of me, after I've thrown accusations at both him and my daughter, *this* goes on the list of things I'll be needing to ask forgiveness for.

I don't respond to him, but I sense my daughter fighting to get around him, his solid mass holding firm as a barrier between me and her. Jedd's and my eyes are locked on one another, drilling holes into each other, disembodying each of us more than we are already disembodied.

"Why would you do this?" my daughter shrieks.

"Because she needed to cool off." His eyes continue to glare at me, ice forming in them that rivals the temperature of the water around me.

"I hate you, Jedd Flemming," I yell, cupping my palm and using it to force water upward, splattering his flannel shirt. He doesn't flinch, but Hannah shrieks a second time.

"Yeah, well, you're no Georgia peach, Beverly Townsen. God gave you two legs, which you still have." He shakes his arm at me to emphasize his point. "And you're squandering the ability you do have and draining this girl in the meantime."

"You have it all wrong, Mr. Flemming," Hannah murmurs behind him, losing her fight to get around him. She looks at me, her drenched mother, sitting in a trough of water, and all I can see is pity in her eyes.

"What am I going to do with you?" those eyes read.

"What do you want me to do with her, Pa?" Howard whined.

"Marry her," Ewell demanded. A pity proposal. Howard had never loved me.

"I don't have it wrong," Jedd corrects. "I see you, Bee. And that tongue of yours sure can sting. That's one thing you're capable of, but you're also very capable of being more than a pesky pollinator." I'd laugh at his alliteration if I wasn't so angry with him, angrier than I've ever been in my life, maybe even angrier than the night I went after Howard.

"You see nothing, *Mr. Flemming*," I screech, pushing more water in his direction and watching him hold firm as the drops settle on his shirt. He doesn't budge.

"I see more than you realize, but maybe that's it. You aren't looking anymore, Bee, and what you need is a good, long look at yourself."

I slap the water around me like a petulant child, allowing the heavy droplets to jump in the air and then cascade back to the tub. My body numbs under the cold temperature, but for the first time in a long time, I feel. I feel the heat of my anger, the beat of my heart, and the rightness in his words. I do need to look at myself, but I'm afraid—afraid of what I'll see, and even more afraid that I'm not going to like the result.

CHAPTER NINE

[Beverly]

Jedd has his arm around Hannah's waist, gently walking her backward toward the house. He leaves me sitting in the tub to fend for myself and makes certain Hannah doesn't help. Or maybe he's making sure I don't get in my own way by enabling her to assist me.

I grip the edges of the metal container, finding I don't have the strength to press myself upward. Between the lacking physical ability and the cold settling into my bones, I am not going be able to lift my own body, so I sort of roll out of the tub, like a giant fish flipping over the edge, and land with a thump on the hard, dirt-packed ground. I'm wet...and dirty. All I keep thinking about is how humiliating it is going to be to crawl to the house.

I hate Jedd Flemming.

I hate him more than Howard, yet, at the same time, I admire him. This sick dichotomy is what keeps abused women with their abusers, but Jedd isn't abusing me. I'm mad. Flaming mad. Ready-to-dismember-him mad. But not because he'd been exceptionally cruel by throwing me in a bin of frigid water, but because he'd been cruel enough to force me to face myself.

I am not happy. I have not been happy for years.

But it runs deeper than admitting my failing emotion.

I didn't know *how* to be happy.

Would better use of my legs make me content? Would the ability to work my land bring satisfaction? Or is it something greater than just physical exhiliration? I have no idea, just as I can't answer Jedd about my personal interests. When was the last time I'd done something for me, something I wanted to do?

Before the accident?

Before Howard left?

Before I even came to this farm?

I can't remember.

With shaky limbs, I press up to three—hands and one knee. My left leg stiffens, the knee refusing to bend, and like a foal learning to stand within moments of birth, I struggle forward. My left side lags.

Left *behind*. Left *behind*. Left *behind*.

Only, I don't feel as empty as I have. I don't feel deserted, but rather entranced. I'm crawling toward something. Toward something bigger than my legs. Bigger than me. Straight ahead is the house. My house. The place I live and own and need to take better care of.

Straight ahead. *Straight* ahead. *Straight* ahead.

A new motto chants through my epiphany, pulling me forward and not allowing me to look back. I've spent so much time and energy on the past, waiting—so much waiting—for answers. Answers that I'll never get. Would any of them matter?

Howard cheated on me.

Would there be any explanation in the world that could take away the pain of discovering he broke his vows to love and honor?

No, no there wouldn't.

Howard abandoned us.

Would there be any justification for him deserting his child and dismantling our family unit?

Nope again.

While I want answers, what would they give me? Words. They would just be words, not redemption, or retribution, or any other - *tion.* Only words.

I crawl a few more painstakingly slow paces before I sense something on my lower back. I catch my breath when I see feet at my side, and for the briefest of moments, I wonder how I missed Jedd returning to help me. Until I glance over my shoulder to find a giant of a man who is not Jedd. I twist at the waist, falling on my backside, which is already bruised from slipping out of the tub. Scrambling back on all fours, I awkwardly crab-crawl away from the beast before me who slowly shakes his head.

No, no, no, the vigorous head motion seems to say, and dark, dark eyes peer through bushy long hair surrounding his face with a mop of a beard hanging off his chin. He stands to his full height but holds up his hands in surrender.

"Who are you?" I ask, but he continues to turn his head, slowing as he lowers a hesitant hand for his lips, tapping them with two fingers, either for my silence or emphasizing his.

Hannah and I have lived on this desolate farm for a long time without a neighbor. The nearest house to be seen in the distance, the old Crawford estate, is much farther than it appears. Ewell warned us never to go there. Something about the youngest son not being right in the head. Howard obtained the place in a poker game. *Men and their cards.* Despite all that, I've never been frightened to live out here until this moment. I flip to my front and crawl as best I can, three-legged and stiff-kneed. I should scream. I should call for help, but I can't. My throat is paralyzed as all my concentration goes to moving forward.

Straight ahead. Straight ahead.

An arm circles my waist, lugging me upward like I weigh nothing more than half a bale of hay. My throat remains clogged, but I attempt a scream. What comes out is a hoarse rasp weakly croaking for help. My hands fist, then pound at his thick arm, which is the size of a small tree trunk. My leg kicks, only one working as the cold has settled in the other. Eventually, my heel jerks, knocking into the heavy leather of the long coat covering his shin. My foot then connects with a thick boot, making no headway in deterring this bear-man. In an attempt to scream again, I take a deep breath, inhaling his wretched scent—ripe like a dead animal and unwashed body—and my nose wrinkles in disgust.

"Put me down," I crow, my voice still not strong enough to imitate my ire. Fear chokes me, but my body still reacts—punching, kicking, squirming.

And then I'm set down on my porch steps.

As my hands fall to the wood, catching myself before I face plant on the risers, I twist at the waist, spinning to face my…attacker. No, not my attacker, my savior…my guardian angel.

"What do you want?" My throat is rough as if from disuse as adrenaline settles into the question. I'm shaking uncontrollably from a mixture of cold and shock. His eyes shift from side to side, darting to me without looking directly at me and then away. I inch up the back steps, one cautious movement at a time while he remains stationary a few feet from the base stair.

"Shoo," I hiss, but he remains still. If his mouth moved in response, I'd never see it under the thick beard. There's no hint of a sound from him when I kick forward as if brushing him away from me.

"Shoo," I repeat like he's a raccoon come for my tomato plants. I knock into a pot as I climb, keeping my eyes on him, but wave a hand forward as if I could sweep him away.

"Get out of here," I yell louder, exerting power I don't feel as I threaten this stranger three times my size. He takes one step back, eyes lowered to the ground as if bowing to me. Then another. And then another, and finally, he pivots, walking down the path to the overgrown fields. There's nowhere to hide him, if he's hiding, and no way to determine where he came from in that direction. He'll walk for a long while before he reaches woods if he's a homeless man hanging among the trees.

Should I be afraid of a homeless man in the woods so close to my home?

I should.

But I'm stumped by his actions, and the realization of where I sit and how I got here without harm.

I should be afraid of him, but I'm more frightened to open the back door and face my daughter.

* * *

Hannah sits at the kitchen table, her eyes puffy and red-rimmed from crying. Her finger draws an invisible image on the tabletop. It's evident in the expression on her face that I've broken my daughter's heart, and it's not the first time. While she unwittingly gave up her dream of college and life thereafter, it has been my fault she fell onto the path where her life has led—nowhere but home. I'm certain her decision not to return to college or pursue a career was disheartening but perhaps not as equivalent to the level of pain I've caused her from my words tonight.

And while I want to tell my child to grow a thick skin against the heartbreaks of this life, I bite my tongue instead because I don't want to be the cause of more heartache for her.

She glances upward as I make my way through the back door, balancing hand-over-hand on objects as my cold, underused legs tremble. She makes no attempt to stand and help me, and for the first time, I'm glad. I don't snap at her for support, but focus on myself, watching where I place my hands to round the counter and then lunge for a chair. My clothes are no longer a waterfall of droplets but more a drip-and-drop of residual rainwater. Hannah sits up straighter in her seat as if she intends to reach out for me, and it takes all her strength to refrain from the action.

I don't want her help.

When I finally sit, Hannah lowers her eyes to the table and

resumes her invisible drawing. An apology from me will never be enough for what I've done, so I don't say anything. Silence ticks between us.

"Is that what you really think of me, Momma? Do you think I'm a watered-down hooker?"

"I didn't say that." My voice returns to its typical edge, and I take a deep breath. "I did not say you were a woman of the night."

"But you think I am, don't you, Momma? You think I'm selling my body for the pleasure of men?"

"I think…" I take another deep inhale. "I think you've sold yourself short. You're so much better than this. So much more than what you do. You've given up your education, put a career on hold, and stripping has turned into your life's course when it shouldn't have."

Hannah's bright eyes widen as she stares back at me. "You needed me, Momma."

"I did, sunshine, but I didn't mean to take over your life and become your responsibility."

"You know I don't feel that way," she states, but the undercurrent to her soft voice tells me my daughter has had to convince herself of such sentiment. I'm the parent. She's the child. It was my honor and obligation to raise her, and I did it as any parent should—selflessly. But at some point, I became selfish, and I let her take the lead on duty and dedication.

"I think you don't know how to feel because all you've thought of for too long is me, and I'm in the same position. I've only thought of myself without regard for you. There's guilt—layers upon layers of guilt—because I should have pushed you more. The same mother who was adamant you go off to school should have been adamant you return."

"It might be too late. I'm almost thirty." Hannah sighs.

"I'm going to hope it's never too late, honey. For anything." I want to believe what I say, but it's going to be difficult. It's going to take a new mindset. There have been so many adjustments in my life, and I don't adjust well. "And I'm going to start by hoping I'm not too late to apologize for what I said earlier."

Hannah's shoulders fall, and her gaze drifts to the kitchen sink. "Do you really think I'd sleep with Jedd? He's like…Howard's age." A shiver of disgust filters through her tone, distantly calling her father by his name as though he's an acquaintance instead of the man who produced her.

"Some girls have daddy issues and do that kind of thing." For a half a second, I realize I watch too much daytime television. However, I do not lust over any of the talk show drama like I worship home improvement shows. "I don't think you'd do anything of the sort, unless you are attracted to an older man, which I'm not saying is wrong, I just…" I pause, taking in the singular wave to my daughter's hair, the color and shine a natural blend of blond and chestnut streaks. She's so beautiful, and men of all ages would be attracted to her. "I'm not sure I know anything about you anymore."

"Me either," she mutters, staring down at her thumbnail on the table. She stops her drawing and flattens her palm.

"I'd like to get to know you," I say, lowering my voice.

"I'm a stripper at the Pink Pony who also works as a hostess at the Front Porch." Her tone turns colder and sarcastic, which isn't like my girl.

"I mean, I want to know more about you than those two things, which don't define who you are."

"You make me feel like they do." Another brick of guilt stacks on my wall. "I take care of you, Momma. Don't you think I've done a good job?" Her questioning tone is full of hesitation, frustration, and a bit of fear.

"An excellent job," I say. My voice falters as tears prickle my eyes because this is how my daughter sees herself—as my caregiver. "But there's more than job titles to you."

I pause and lick my lips. "Speaking of jobs, I don't have one, but I need to get one."

"You can't work, Momma." Her voice returns to her typical softness, and I hear the undercurrent clear as sunshine. She's telling me in her tempered voice who I am, enabling me, and I have believed her because of the sweet octaves in that tone. My daughter has turned me into Pavlov's dog a bit, salivating while she insults me in a voice meant to soothe and show she cares. She does care, but this isn't right. This isn't how it's supposed to be.

"I *can* work," I state, sitting up a little straighter. For a second, a vision of Jedd filters through my head. Hannah was correct. Jedd has two arms; they just appear different from each other. "I don't know what I'll do, or how I'll do it, but I'll do something." Now, I just need to repeat that mantra about a million more times until I believe it, but the point is to let my child know it's time for her to loosen the reins. Time to be who she needs to be so I can discover who I am… without her.

"Momma," Hannah drones in disbelief, and I acknowledge that we will respectfully disagree just as we disagree about my wheelchair, my crutches, my capabilities, and her employment. "What about your hobbies?"

"I hate tomatoes," I admit. "And I don't knit very well."

"You knit just fine, and you love your tomatoes."

"I don't want to do fine," I state, my voice rising a little in irritation. "And my interest in tomatoes has waned." Happiness might be found in never seeing a tomato again.

A weak grin curls Hannah's tight mouth, loosening the tension a little.

"I wouldn't sleep with him or any other man out of some sense of abandonment. I'm smarter than that," she states, returning us to the initial issue.

"You are the smartest girl I know, sunshine." I reiterate what I'd often said when she was a child. "And again, I'm sorry I said what I said."

"You're still upset I'm stripping, though, aren't you?" This is one of our oldest arguments. I turned into my mother, damning my own daughter. When I learned the truth from the local gossips at church— who shouldn't even know who's who at the nearby strip joint—I was more hurt than upset at the fact Hannah lied. I thought she was off to Payton Mill each evening when she was really working nights removing her clothes. And all because of me.

"I can't say I'm pleased with your line of work, but I understand your reasons for such employment." While I disapproved of her showing her private goods to a bunch of drunk-ass men, she did it for the money. "I take the fault for it. I know you did it for us. For me."

"Momma, what if it isn't about you? What if, for once, something I do really isn't about you?"

I blink, startled by the thought. Is my daughter stripping because she likes it? Does she find pleasure in removing her clothes and baring her bits? Dancing was Hannah's justification for her current position. "*It's just dancing, Momma,*" she'd argued. If I condemned dancing, I've really become my mother.

"I hadn't thought of that. You're old enough to decide what to do with your body, and you can do with your body what you please, as long as this...*this dancing*...still pleases you."

Hannah shrugs, and it isn't an answer. Instead, she states, "The audience doesn't get to see the goods." She sighs, as if reading my thoughts and knowing she's explained to me a thousand times how all her private parts—the nips and tucks—are covered. Still, enough skin is showing that the imagination for the rest of her need not go far. "I can't say it's pleasing to be exposed in front of strangers, but I don't mind the attention or the tips, and the dancing..." Her voice drifts.

In my head, the skimpy, fuchsia Pink Pony underthings do not equate to a sweet blush-colored leotard and matching ballet slippers, but we'll just have to agree to disagree. We had other battles to wage.

"Do what you want. I'm just suggesting stripping for a living might not be the best course of action. You're better than that and so much smarter than it, too." I'm not suggesting strippers are dumb, but Hannah could be contributing to society in a more productive manner. I suppose if she really wanted to dance, there's a new dance studio in town Naomi told me about. Stripped is its name. She could apply there for a job.

"Stripping's worked for me so far, though," she states. "But I'll consider what you've said." Conviction lacks in her tone.

I nod, acknowledging I accept what she's said. Stripping has worked so far, but it's only gotten us so far, and we've reached the point of far enough. Maybe it really isn't about me. Maybe she enjoys it. Maybe it is her life's passion. I brush away the thought.

I don't know what the next steps should be, but they need to be my steps, on the two feet God gave me, as Jedd so blatantly reminded me. Which reminds me…

"Where's Jedd?"

"He went out the front door after leading me back to the house."

I recall Jedd's arms around her, moving her away from me. "Did he hurt you?" I question, my voice cautious and concerned.

She shakes her head.

"Was he mean to you?"

She shakes again, but I have a feeling ole Jedd Flemming did his fair share of scolding my daughter.

"What did he say to you?"

Hannah twists her lips, and her gaze drifts to the sink again. "He told me I could be so much more if I wasn't under your feet."

I want to be angry. I want to rant and curse and say Jedd Flemming needs to mind his own damn business, but I can't quite muster the necessary ire. I'm not certain Jedd Flemming is entirely wrong in his assessment, albeit a bit intrusive, opinionated, and out of place with his advice. He reminds me of my older sister Scotia in this manner.

"You were right, Momma. He shouldn't be here. He needs to leave. We don't need him. We'll find another way. We always have."

We have…and it's involved my daughter taking off *most* of her clothes and working night shifts to wait on others. My girl is good at taking care of others, but it's time for her to take care of only herself.

"I think…" A lump forms in my throat, and I struggle to swallow. The admission I'm about to make clogs the passageway, but I press forward. *Straight ahead*. "I think…Mr. Flemming should stay."

"Why?" Hannah's brows pinch to the point a crease forms between them.

"Because we do need him, and who knows? Maybe, for once, a man will keep his promises." I don't rightly believe that, but a strange sense of calm blankets me with the possibility, especially when I factor in the stranger who helped me in the yard. He didn't hurt me. He helped me. "By the way, you haven't seen any unfamiliar faces around here lately, have you?"

"Unfamiliar faces?" Hannah questions. "No one ever travels out this far." She states the obvious, but still, this unknown man traveled near enough.

"No. Big man, looks like a human grizzly with wild hair." I motion with my hands, exaggerating the width of his locks. "The size of Sasquatch."

"Momma." Hannah chuckles. "There's no such thing." She eyes me like she's worried I've taken too many meds. I used to do that to dull the pain in my legs and my heart. I snicker, recalling all the times I tried to convince her the noise under the bed, the bump in the dark, or the rustle in the field was not a monster. Maybe there was no monster, but perhaps an angel in disguise. When I think on it, I realize Hannah and I have been darn lucky living out here, a little off the beaten path of Green Valley proper.

"You let me know if you do notice anything, all right? In the meantime, I don't think having Jedd here will hurt as long as he stays on his side of the yard." I wink, and Hannah's smile grows a little bit before she sobers.

"Are you okay after what he did?" She thinks on it a second. "He really should go."

Throwing me in a tub of icy water when he knows my lack of mobility does make Jedd seem rather mean, but then again, he didn't do anything to me I didn't need. Fresh air and a freezing bath calmed me down. Ironically, I do feel...*better*. Better than I have in a long time.

My next admission is another difficult confession to swallow.

"I may have deserved what he did. That doesn't mean I won't be plotting ways to get my revenge." I grin, and for a moment, I feel like my old self. The one who mischievously did things out of good old-fashioned curiosity *and fun* without meaning any intentional harm. I rub my hands together as though I have an evil plan, and the smile that spreads across my daughter's face reminds me of the ones she used to give me as a child. For a flash, she's my baby girl again, and I'm her momma, making her laugh as if there's no other care in the world. And for just that moment, all feels like it's been put back to rights.

CHAPTER TEN

[Jedd]

I *should not have done what I did.*

I'm mentally beating myself as I sit at The Watershed, a hole-in-the-wall bar on the river running through Merryville. I needed some space and ended up here where the tall, wooden booth seats are reminiscent of old European pubs. The place is loud but not overwhelming. It's just enough to cloud my restless thoughts as I sit at the long bar.

"Need another?" the young bartender asks. The spitting image of his father, it's clear the young man behind the bar is Vernon's son.

"Thanks, Kodi. I think I'm all set." I tip the glass before me, signaling the remainder of my swill. Kodi is short for Kodiak. His mama was obsessed with bears when she named her three boys: Grizzly, Kodiak, and Kermode. Vernon jokes he's relieved he never had twins. Abigail might have named them Polar and Panda. Considering his mama's a severe alcoholic, Kodiak's position as a bartender seems a bit ironic.

The twenty-something with dark bushy hair nods in silence after I decline another beer, and I sit alone with my plaguing thoughts.

I shouldn't have tossed her in the tub.

I'd like to think she asked for it. My momma would have made me bite a bar of Dial soap for using such language and slinging false accusations at a family member, and not the fragrance-free white bar but the old gold bar that had a strong aftertaste. I couldn't very well wash out Beverly's mouth, though, but her words made me feel dirty. I'd never entertained her daughter in my thoughts. I've only had Beverly on the brain. Not to mention, she shouldn't have insinuated her child would be attracted to an old man like me. Not that I consider myself old, but I could be her daddy, and I don't go for that kind of hookup.

You want to blank *this man.*

My spine quivers as I recall Beverly's words. I don't have a problem using that four-letter word for all kinds of references but not in reference to Hannah Townsen. On the other hand, for Beverly, I need to reconsider it. I won't lie to myself and diminish the fact that I've been entertaining that word with her in my mind. Something about her spunk and spirit girds my loins, and they want to be girding her, and I'm not trying to be silly. I'm serious. Each night, I'm wrestling thoughts of Beverly and then wrestling said loins for relief.

Shaky fingers scrub at my forehead. I have got to get myself under control with this woman.

I know Beverly. I *see* her, like I said. She's so buried under insecurity and sensitivity that she strikes out to protect herself. If she lashes first, the recoil won't hurt. If she stings, she can't be stung. It's all a defense mechanism, and one I recognize well. Hell, that was me when I woke up and first learned I'd lost my arm. I struggled with feeling lopsided, incomplete, and unwhole. But eventually, I had to let those self-conscious thoughts go before they ate me alive, so I know. I *know*.

Beverly also has abandonment issues. Men cannot be trusted, she said. *Howard—what a coward and an idiot. Fucking idiotard.* If she can push people away, it prevents anyone from getting close. Only, her daughter already is close. Too close. She's put up with her mother for ten years. Striking out at Hannah makes sense while, at the same time, it doesn't. We often hurt those closest to us because they're the only ones who can really hurt us in return.

Human beings sure are fucked-up creatures sometimes.

Which is why I prefer horses to men. I've been trying to get my partner to commit to purchasing two thoroughbreds since late fall is one of the better times for buying a horse. I'm interested in a set of Quarter Horses I found near Nashville. The barn isn't winterized, and I don't have a stable per se, but now is the time to buy.

I continue scrubbing at my forehead. I have so much to do and shouldn't be wasting time sitting here staring into a nearly empty stein of beer and dissecting Beverly's behavior.

"Keep scrubbing like that and you'll wear off the skin." A deep voice next to me chuckles. "Only two things make a man rub his forehead like that. Troubles *with* women or troubles caused *by* them."

I turn my head to face my barstool neighbor and find a man similar to my age, stature, and status in the gray hair department.

"Adam should have run from Eve in that garden." I chuckle without humor.

"Nah, he couldn't help himself. She was too tempting." He huffs, shaking his head like we understand each other.

"Nathan Ryder," he says, offering his hand.

"Jedd Flemming."

We sit in silence for a moment, eyes mindlessly watching a sport's recap on the television above the wall of liquors. Fun fact: Rodeo is the official sport of Wyoming, and I miss the show.

"What brings you out tonight?" I finally ask, feeling the awkward quiet between us linger for too long. I've been known to start a conversation with a stranger and end it with a new friend.

"Waiting on my girl to close tonight. She's a local librarian. Also had another fight with my seventeen-year-old daughter, so I thought I could use a beer to cool me down before I see Naomi."

Naomi? Not a typical name for the area.

"Your girl wouldn't happen to be Naomi Winters, would she?"

The hackles rise on my bar neighbor, and his body shifts, angling toward me. "She certainly is." His tone hints of possession.

My lips curl, and I nod. "You aren't going to believe this, but my troubling woman is her sister, Beverly."

Nathan's expression shifts, and he lets out a low chuckle. "Oh man, I've heard she's a piece of work."

"More like a work in progress," I mutter. Nathan's eyes spark like he understands what I mean.

"You from around here?" he asks.

"Newly returned to town. Been away a long time."

"We're two peas in a pod, man, as I'm newly back in town after a long hiatus as well. Been back about two years."

"Only two months," I offer. I can't gauge his age, so I have to ask about high school graduation dates, confirming we went to school at roughly the same time but were not in the same grade.

"My older brother is Todd Ryder."

"Small world." I snort, as I know Todd and his best friend, who now goes by Big Poppy, very well.

"He works The Fugitive, off 129 in North Carolina."

I laugh again. "Oh, I'm familiar." The Fugitive is a biker refuge along the famous Tail of the Dragon, a twelve-mile strip of road with snake-ish curves and slithering dips. Mainly a bar, there's a small motel attached to the side of The Fugitive, owned and operated by Big Poppy and managed by Todd.

"Been there recently?" Nathan inquires.

"About two months back. When I first returned to the area." I explain how I'd been overseas and then out in the Western states.

"What brings you back home, soldier?" he teases.

"Family."

His lips pinch, and he nods once again. "Always does, doesn't it?" This reminds me that I still have no word on Boone, and my sister hasn't returned my last call.

I learn Nathan's in construction work, working for Monroe & Sons, a builder in Green Valley.

"Ever build a stable before?" I inquire. "Do you contract on the side?"

"Haven't ever considered it, but we can talk." Suddenly, an ear-splitting alarm sounds, and even with severe hearing loss in my left ear, I don't miss the ring tone.

"What was that?" I chuckle, nodding at Nathan's phone, which was the source of noise.

"My alarm. Time's up for me. Need to get to my girl."

"Enjoy," I say, lifting my glass which still has a thin layer of liquid at the bottom.

"Here." Nathan scribbles his number on the napkin and hands it to me. "Let's talk about your stable."

He pats my right shoulder and excuses himself after I offer my pleasure in meeting him. Kodiak returns before me.

"It ain't any of my business which way you swing, Jedd, but my dad didn't mention you were gay."

What the...? "What the hell you talking about?"

"That man gave you his number on a napkin and then mentioned a stable. Isn't that code for something?"

I stare at Kodiak, his question earnest. "No, kid. It's called getting help with a construction project."

His eyes light up. "I like building things."

My lips twist as I consider him. His physique is large and hefty like his dad. "Ever build a barn before?"

He laughs at the question. "Jedd, I was raised on barn raisings. Remember Grady Seed and Soil?" He points at himself. I had another kid in mind to help with the extra hands I need around Beverly's land, but I can see Kodiak is eager for this work.

"Okay, Kodi. I'm gonna write my number on a napkin, which doesn't mean I'm trying to pick you up, nor does it mean I have the hots for you, even if you look as cuddly as a *widdle bear*." His eyes roll at the reference to his name, and his cheeks pinken.

"Jedd." He sighs. "Give me your phone. I'll just put my number in it."

Now, why didn't I think of that? Maybe I am older than I thought.

While The Watershed was a good distraction, I realize an hour later that I need to face the music—or rather, the buzz of Beverly.

The house is dark as I stand in the gravel drive at the side of the old farmhouse. I'm torn between tossing pebbles at Beverly's window and staring at it like a love-sick stalker. Why did Romeo decide to climb the trellis? Horny. That's what drove him up a building to Juliet's balcony. Me, on the other hand, I'm conflicted, caught between serenading her with an apology and storming the house to demand she apologize to me.

As I stare at the blackened window, my thoughts turn to Hannah and how often she's mentioned her mother needs her. Is she trying to convince me or herself? And what has this meant for Beverly? Beverly has so much potential she could reach if her daughter didn't smother her with well-intended but misplaced kindness.

The thought sends a shiver down my spine again.

Good Lord, have I had it all wrong?

Did I misinterpret Beverly's actions or her daughter's reactions? Have I assumed Hannah was the disadvantaged one when in all actuality Beverly's been enabled? My chest clenches, and my stomach feels as if a boulder's been dropped in the pit.

Did I misread the situation here?

CHAPTER ELEVEN

[Beverly]

I wake the next day feeling mentally drained but physically refreshed as I glance at the folded wheelchair leaning against the wall. I'd be a fool to dismiss it entirely as I know my limits, but I need to walk. I'm going to grow frustrated, and I'm going to tire easily, but I'm going to do this on my own two feet with a little assistance from my crutches.

As I clip-clop my way down the hall like a toddler in those first stages of walking, I decide to give my tomato plants a final check. In these last days of October, I'd be lucky to get any fruit off the vines. As I fumble with the back door and survey the pots in a regimental lineup down the staircase, I notice something lying on the second step. I hobble down the risers, cautious as I go, surpassing the stair and then turning back for it once on level ground.

A single sunflower rests on the wooden slat. The daisy-like petals are a luscious golden color with a saucer-sized center of deep brown. Almost ready to seed, it's perfect and precious, and it reminds me of when I used to grow such a beautiful thing. There isn't a scent so much as a texture in the unique flower, and I draw the round face to my nose and drag the tip over the rugged middle.

A smile grows on my lips as I glance down and notice a small square scrap on the stair. On first inspection, I think it's garbage blown up on the step, but upon reaching forward, I see it's a piece of cardboard, one inch by one inch, like the inner flap on the top of a dry food package. Turning it over, I note I'm correct in my assessment. It's the inside of a macaroni and cheese box. Flipping the square back over, I notice a giant letter B fills as much of the space as possible. My lips continue to curl in confusion and sudden amusement.

Did someone leave this flower for me?

Did someone place this scrap next to it to signal this gift is mine?

Where did the macaroni and cheese box come from?

Instantly, my eyes roam across the gravel drive to the closed door of the barn. Jedd's truck is missing, and I question if he ever returned from wherever he went last evening. Only briefly do I consider if he'll ever come back because something tells me Jedd will return. Glancing at the flower, I wonder if he's already been here.

The week after Halloween brings more changes for me. I learn my sister has been the target of young hooligans in the area. Nathan Ryder came to her rescue, and the two of them are an official couple. *It's about time.* Not to mention—but not because of Nathan—my sister has made some adjustments to her typical attire in conjunction with her blossoming love. The changes haven't gone unnoticed by me, and so we break from our normal visit to the Piggly Wiggly when I ask Naomi if she'll take me to The Beauty Mark, the local hair salon.

I can't remember the last time I had my hair "done," and I must admit there is no greater pleasure than having someone else wash your hair. The girl who works on mine is new and young, and I didn't catch her name. I'm lost to the boisterous conversation of Hazel Cumberstone and Mabel Murphy—the Hester twins—as the shampooer massages my scalp.

Hazel and Mabel are around forty-ish and best friends with my sister Scotia. Us Winters sisters were not born and bred in Green Valley like these women. We came from a small armpit of a community called Cedar Gap. I didn't have to go to high school in Green Valley to recognize Hazel and Mabel peaked at that time and have held onto their rung of the local popularity ladder well into adulthood.

"Can you believe it?" Hazel states loudly, her Tennessee drawl on full display. I miss the follow-up as the technician rinses my hair.

Helping me sit up from the wash sink, I hear Mabel's reply. "And after all this time." She sighs, clutching at her neck only to discover she's missing her pearls.

I glance over at Naomi, who meets my eyes across the beauty salon, reading my concern that they're discussing Naomi and her new relationship status. She shakes her head, dismissing my thoughts. Naomi and I were once close even though our brother, Jebediah, was in the middle of us in birth order. We had secret looks and knowing glances. I've missed those moments between us.

I'm escorted to a chair, and a protective drape is tossed over my clothing. The girl runs her fingers through my damp strands and tugs on the ends.

"May I suggest a change?" She holds up the ends so I can view them in the mirror. "These ends are split, and the weight of your hair is holding down a natural wave." She releases my hair and turns her hand sideways, just under my chin. "If I cut your hair to here, the curl would relax, and your hair would make the young girls jealous."

My brows crease in the reflection. This woman could qualify as a young girl, so I have no idea what she's referencing.

"Oh Beverly, honey, I didn't recognize you," Mabel states from somewhere to my left. She wouldn't recognize me as it's been a while since she's come to visit. At first, well-meaning folk came often to the farm. Casseroles. Volunteers. But time moved on while we stood still, and the visiting occurred less often. I'd have been sad at the loss of these women if I'd considered them friends, but I don't.

"You should do as she suggests, sweetheart," Hazel bellows from somewhere in the salon. "Trixie is a miracle worker. And shorter hair could make you look younger."

"Why does she want to look younger?" Mabel inquires of her sister, not directly insulting me, but more a question of pride. "I'm happy to be the age I am. Embrace your forties. Love yourself." Mabel sits straighter in her seat, but the girl working on her color job forces her head back at an angle so she can continue painting the roots underneath.

"Forty is a good look on you, sister," Hazel rectifies. "I just mean…" Her voice lowers as if she intends to whisper, but the hushed tone travels the salon. "You look so much older than you are. Sort of on-the-shelf, if you take my meaning. Spinsterish." The -ish hisses as Mabel nods in agreement.

"Hold still, Miss Mabel," the color technician warns, and Mabel stops rocking. I'm ready to retort that I don't care how young or old I look until I glance up at myself and see the long grayish locks, wet and weighted against my face.

"It'd be real pretty on you, Miss Beverly. We could even whiten it. Highlight the gray. That's so popular."

"Speaking of gray…" Hazel's disembodied voice travels to me once again, and I assume she's getting her nails done at the manicure table in the corner. "I heard there's a silver fox living on your farm."

"Oh, I haven't seen such an anim—"

"She means that hot hunk of a man with silver hair building in your barn," Mabel conspiratorially whispers.

"Jedd?" I question, and immediately close my eyes, knowing I've just given these women fuel for the interrogation fires.

"Jeeeeeeed," Hazel drawls from her corner.

"Jedd," Mabel repeats on a short, sharp, one-syllable breath. "What a rugged name. Jedd. Jedd. *Jedd*." Her repetition and breathiness is faintly sexual, and I draw in a breath. Naomi rarely shares library gossip, but she's admitted the sisters are voracious romance readers and have shared a risqué poem or two during Thursday Night Poetry readings.

My sister clears her throat to my right, suppressing a chuckle. She's been flipping through a magazine, though I'm certain she isn't reading.

"Yes, well, he's—"

"Speaking of rugged. Your new man is quite delicious, Miss Naomi." Without turning my head, I know my sister's blushing at Hazel's mention of Nathan.

"Thank you," Naomi hesitates, and my lips curl. I'm happy for my sister. Deep down inside, love is my wish for anyone, even if I don't believe it will ever exist for me.

"Speaking of delicious men, have y'all seen Billy Winston lately?" Hazel mutters, rather loud for all to hear, along with accompanied sound effects. "Mmm…mmm…mmm. He is eye candy."

Mabel clucks at her sister. "Now, Hazel, your cougar is showing. And what about Jasper?" Jasper and Hazel were high school sweethearts as seems to be the norm for many in the older set of Green Valley. He hasn't aged how one would expect of the former homecoming king.

"Actually, Billy is only a few years younger than us, sister, and eye candy implies I'm only savoring by sight. There's nothing wrong with inspecting what's fine in the world."

"Well, speaking of fine, what about Jethro Winston?" Mabel waves her hand in front of her face, fanning the false heat. These women have no shame. "Fatherhood dost become him." The thirtyish father of three has always been extremely good looking.

"Bethany Winston knew how to birth beautiful babies," Hazel adds, and the room falls into a reflective silence at the mention of a beloved woman from the community. My eyes seek Naomi, as Bethany was also a librarian at the public library and one of her best friends. "May she rest in peace, of course," Hazel tacks on to her ministrations.

"Rest in peace," Mabel agrees, nodding once again. Mabel is a widow to a war hero, so her prayer is more empathetic. The color technician grows frustrated and forcibly holds Mabel's head to finish the final touches of color at the nape of her neck.

While this conversation has been plummeting, my hair girl has been tapping on her phone. I'm ready to comment on the youth of this country and their electronic addiction when she reaches forward and shows me an image on her screen.

"I could make your hair look like this. You have the face for it, and the white would be so pretty with your eyes."

I glance up at myself, squinting to see what she sees. My eyes are a grayish color, similar to my hair. When I was young, boys considered them exotic. I didn't even know what that meant until Howard.

"The way you look at me," he'd said. I shiver with the memory. Then I think of Jedd.

Jedd. Jedd. *Jedd.*

How do my eyes appear to him? What do they say when I look into his?

"Take it off," I whisper, and the technician leans forward.

"Pardon me?"

"I mean, cut it as you wish. Color it too. I don't care what it looks like." But it's a lie. I wouldn't be here if I didn't want a drastic change to myself, beginning with my hair.

"I promise, you're going to look even prettier than you already are, Miss Beverly." I turn to glance back at the girl, narrowing my eyes in disbelief at her kind compliment. Her body crosses in front of mine as she sets her phone on the stand with scissors, combs, and a hair dryer. As she steps back, Mabel Murphy catches my eye.

"Beautiful, like you're meant to be, Beverly," she says, holding my gaze for a second. I want to tell her she's full of malarkey, but I hold my tongue and face the mirror, taking a deep breath. When the hair tech chops off the initial chunk, I already feel a little freer, the beginnings of the old me returning.

CHAPTER TWELVE

[Beverly]

"*I love taking something old and giving it a new purpose,*" Virginia Hanes mentions in this rerun of *Nailed* where she hunts antique shops for just the right item to complete her decorative genius. Tripper follows her with a fake chicken attached to a headpiece on his head.

My fingers brush through my hair once again. I haven't been able to stop touching the new style. Mabel was correct; the girl at The Beauty Mark is a miracle worker. My hair feels lighter, whiter, and I'm proud of how it turned out: with a subtle wave and easy upkeep. Not to mention, no more tight buns at the nape of my neck. The loose waves frame my face, softening the sharp edges. The color is more bright white than frosted like my sister Naomi's, but our hair hints at sisterhood, despite a difference in length.

"What about these, GinGin?" Tripper asks his wife, holding up an unidentifiable item that looks strangely sexual. Virginia rolls her eyes and shakes her head at her husband, who turns his backside to

the cameraman and smacks his own tush with the heart-shaped paddle. I flinch in response and then giggle. It couldn't have hurt him, but I'm imagining all sorts of inappropriate things with the old utensil and some bare skin. I blush and sweep my fingers up my neck and into my hair again.

Thinking of bare skin, I haven't seen Jedd since he dropped my backside in a tub of rainwater. I've been vigilant about watching out for him, but he hasn't returned to the main house for supper. This also means he hasn't offered an apology for throwing me in the tub. Perhaps the single flower was his plea for forgiveness, and it was rather sweet. I've had time to reflect on what I said to my daughter and what I implied to this stranger living in my barn. It isn't as if I haven't had years to think on my attitude or actions, but something about these past few days has made me continually reflective.

What do I want out of life? I'm only forty-five, and while I feel ancient, this isn't the end for me. What happened to the girl with dreams? I can answer that with one word: Howard. Without giving him undue credit, living with Howard did open a door for me, one I did not expect. Motherhood was the greatest gift. Raising my child has been a pleasure, but she's grown and should be on her own, so what's next? I've given up a decade of my life, decaying under emotions about a worthless man and the state of my health.

"I ain't dead yet," Ewell used to say. *"You can have it all when I go, but not before."*

I'm not dead yet either, despite how I feel inside. Then I think of Jedd. Something about that man lights a fire in me, sparks my curiosity, and has turned me into a regular stalker watching for him out my window. It's a new form of unhealthy behavior, yet I can't seem to pull myself away. I've watched him take the few short steps to the barn from his truck. I've observed the use of his prosthetic arm and the unparalleled strength of his opposite bicep. I've sought out his silhouette in the shadows of the night, and I've smiled to myself when he's caught me and waved. Only he hasn't waved in days, because I haven't seen a glimpse of him.

I glance back at my television set as the final refurbished rooms are presented to the homeowners of *Nailed*. Suddenly, a caravan of vehicles comes down my drive, passing the house for the first pasture. I'm quick to rise from my rocking chair to check out the ruckus—well, as quick as I can be—and reach for my arm braces to help me out to the yard.

It's early morning, and Hannah is still sleeping from her late-night shift at the Pink Pony. We haven't encountered each other much over the past few days, and when we do, we keep quietly to ourselves. I'd like to think all is forgiven, but I know some wounds cut deep, and while the lashes were only words spoken from my mouth, my sensitive girl took them to heart. I'd have done the same thing. Howard was full of ridicule and disrespect, and I learned early on to keep my head down unless he lifted my chin for my attention. His father was equally an irritant, but a little less demeaning. Grouchy Ewell at least tried to increase my knowledge of farm living and offered me a plot for the pleasure of gardening.

Memories of Ewell filter through my head as I struggle down the back steps. *Ka-thunk. Ka-thunk. Ka-thunk*, I hear until I reach gravel. It's even slower going over the pebbly dirt surface, and I concentrate on where I place my crutches as I hear the opening and closing of vehicle doors and the rise of voices calling out to one another.

"Bee?" I stop in my tracks, raising my head to find Jedd a few paces ahead of me. His metallic hand holds a baseball cap while his fingers scrape over his short hair. I hate to admit he's a vision. That rugged skin. Those deep-set eyes. The questioning grin.

A silver fox, Hazel called him.

"Do you still hate me?" he asks, his voice hesitant as his eyes shift to my feet and then back to my face. I should hate him. I should still be angry, but strangely, I'm so relieved to see him standing before me that I forget why I'm mad.

"You are kind of an ass," I snark, but the bite in my tone is lacking.

"You like my ass, though, honey, don't you?" he teases back. Thankfully, he has no idea how much I've checked him out. I don't even complain that he calls me honey, strangely liking the way he uses the endearment on me. He steps closer, and our eyes dance. His hand lifts, pauses and then withdraws, and I swallow a lump of confusion. Was he planning to touch me? Brush back my fresh hair, perhaps.

"What's all this racket?" I snap, the familiar edge tasting sour on my tongue as I dismiss his rejection. I inhale, holding myself still as I balance on the crutches.

"It's a barn raising." Jedd's eyes sparkle like pinpricks of starlight in a midnight sky, excitement ringing in his voice. He twists the baseball cap in his hand and then returns it to his head. A smile grows on his face, softening the hard lines. It's almost infectious, but I steady my resolve, holding on to my anger with him.

"Who said you could build a barn on my lot?" Did we talk about this? What's wrong with the existing barn? I glance over at the building that has weathered decades and seasons but looks old and unloved. The paint's peeling. The roof sags. "I thought you were repairing this one."

"I made a room for myself, but I don't trust the structure for horses. Besides, we don't need a gambrel-style roof on a stable. It's too much extra space above the animals."

It makes sense, but still... "I don't recall giving permission for another building on my land."

"You did give permission when you said I could stay." His eyes drift to the dirt and then upward to my face. "I can still stay, right, Bee?"

It's a surprising question, considering he's already got a load of people scrambling around the field and tossing around lumber. But equally surprising is the question itself. He's asking if he can stay. He doesn't want to leave. Of course, he has a reason to be here. He's using my property for his project. *The Jedd Juncture.*

Surprising me again, he steps closer, his broad stature filling my space. His hand cups the side of my face so quickly and startlingly that I don't flinch at his touch. His thumb brushes back and forth over my cheek. His eyes search mine, and the intensity is too much. I look away.

"Don't matter," he teases. "Because even if you told me to go, I wouldn't leave." My eyes shoot back to his, narrowing at the statement.

"Go," I mutter, lacking the muster to argue with him.

Instead, he leans closer, brushing his nose along my cheek. I'm slack-jawed and stock-still at the liberties this man takes as he nears my ear.

"No," he whispers, blowing softly at the shell.

"Get out of here," I say, but the breathless rasp does nothing to defend the command.

"Not leaving," he mutters, his nose tracing the shell.

"Step away from me." My tone reaches a level I don't recognize, and Jedd stills. He pulls back, meeting my eyes before he drops his hand.

"I'd never hurt you, Bee. Tell me you aren't afraid of me."

Afraid of him? He scares the crap out of me but not in the ways he's thinking. He'd never physically cause me harm, of that I have no doubt. But my heart patters something fierce at his nearness, and my mouth goes dry. I might die of a heart attack or xerostomia, which I learned on television is a dry-mouth condition.

I ignore his question.

"Don't suppose I can kick you out now that you have half a forest of wood lying in my field."

"Now, Bee, don't you be teasing me about laying my wood in your pasture." He chuckles, stepping back to put more distance between us. Is he…flirting with me? He can't be. He's only trying to break the tension wound tight between us. However, my skin tingles without his touch, or perhaps it's a reaction to his touch.

Do I like his touch?

I don't want his touch.

GAH! I'm all over the place with this man.

A slow smile graces his mouth, and my eyes follow the curve. I lick my lips, no longer dry in the mouth but near foaming with hunger. He watches the movement, and his lips slowly part. His chest drags in a breath, and I find myself leaning forward until a loud slam from a truck door startles us apart. I pitch forward with the flinching start, and Jedd catches me by my upper arms. His smile deepens, and small lines by his eyes hint at something *almost* happening.

Was he going to kiss me?

"Jedd?" someone calls out in a deep male voice, and Jedd twists toward the sound before turning back to me.

"I have one more thing to say about the other night, and then I'm letting it go. Don't ever compare me to Howard." His eyes narrow. "And never doubt who's turning my head. My eyes are only focused in one direction." He pauses, emphasizing the glare he's giving me.

I swallow, uncertain of what to say or if I can even speak.

"Now, come meet everyone," he suggests, positioning his hand around my back but keeping some distance between us until I move forward and catch the foot of the crutch on a stone. His arm quickly wraps around my lower back, hand flattening on my belly. We hold still for a second, breathing in the proximity of each other as he steadies me. Warm air hits my exposed neck, and I tilt just the slightest bit as if offering him more skin. My heart races, but it's from the nearness of him and not from the near fall. I inhale as if I'm taking a stabilizing breath when all I'm really doing is drowning in the fragrance of him. Fresh fields. Cut wood. All man. He smells good.

Then his foot slips between mine, rousing me from my thoughts. His inner thigh brushes mine, and with the slight bend of his knee, he nudges me forward.

"I got it," I grit, winded from his support, his hands on me, and his scent. He doesn't release me but holds our position until I bend to him. We take one step like a three-legged creature as if we're joined at the hip, and I nervously chuckle at the awkwardness as the old idiom has new clarity.

"I know you got it, honey," he states, and the confidence dripping from his voice tickles my ear. The rugged sound is like rumpled sheets and early mornings, and I turn to him to see his eyes are on my hair.

"I like this new look." His hand travels up my back and fingers slip along the nape, delving upward and combing through the shorter locks. His fingers fist in a gentle tug, and *oh my*…my body reacts— breathtaking, thigh-clenching, blood-rushing—which seems to be a trend when I'm around him. His Adam's apple bobs as he clears his throat, and I lick my lips again, wanting to lick his skin and feel the prickle of that stubble along my tongue.

What is wrong with me? I hate this man.

His fingers release my hair and lower for my hip.

"We should head to the field," he says, his voice as rough as the gravel at our feet.

"You need to lay that wood." My eyes leap to his, and he laughs, a good loud guffaw that tips him at the waist.

"Aww, Bee, you are something."

With that, he nudges me forward. His fingers dig into my side just above my hip as he guides me—not pushing me, not forcing me, just supporting me, as if we can take all the time I need.

As we near the gathering of men, I notice a variety of ages among them. One man could be a relative of Jedd's with his mostly gray hair, trimmed short but not as short as Jedd. When he turns to face me, I see there really isn't a resemblance other than their stature. With thick stubble of salt and pepper and steel eyes, there's something striking about the other man's appearance, but his smile softens the potential sharpness, giving him a mischievous look.

Another man walks over, and instantly, I note he must be related to the first. They look almost identical in facial features minus the solid whiteness of the second man's hair. Their eyes match in steel intensity, but the first gentleman is more playful than the other, who appears cautious.

"Beverly, meet Nathan Ryder and his brother, Todd." *Nathan Ryder.* He's leaner than his brother, and his smile grows with our introduction. He's a wolf in sheep's clothing as far as that grin goes because he's the wayward man who slept with my sister and broke her heart. He disappeared without a call even though he promised her. Seems a common theme among the men Naomi and I attract. However, now he's her man.

"Nathan." I address him curtly, eyeing him with my best *I know who you are* and *I know what you've done* glare and adding in a dose of *I will maim you if you hurt her again* for good measure. Nathan chuckles, a hearty deep sound that makes my tummy rumble. He is exceptionally good looking. Softer in some ways compared to the ruggedness of Jedd, but still just as masculine.

"This is my brother, Todd. We call him Toad." Todd knocks his brother on the back of the head like they are children instead of adults past forty. He reaches forward to shake my hand as well, grinning with a curt head nod. All the while, I notice Jedd maintains a possessive hand on my back, lingering as if he's prepared to catch me if I start to lilt. His leg is outside mine, but his hip rests near me. If I thought about it too hard, we might look like a couple standing so close to one another, but we aren't anything of the sort.

You'd like to be, wouldn't you? my heart murmurs, but thoughts of coupling slam to a halt when I see Vernon Grady.

"Beverly," he states, a million other things lingering within my name. I want to look away, but I glare at him instead just as I did with Nathan. He had been a friend, and then he was gone like all the other men in my life. Unreliable—which isn't exactly true—but the sting lingers that Vernon disappeared from our lives. He had his own issues, though, his own family, and my eyes flip to the three young men beside him.

"Vernon." He nods to acknowledge me and then turns to the boys in the field.

"Grizz, Kodi, Kerr. Y'all remember Mrs. Townsen, right?" If Vernon had kicked the crutches out from underneath me, I'd be less surprised than with the formality and label with which he addresses me. Seeing his sons, however, brings warmth to my insides. These boys occasionally came over and ran wild on my land. Each boy looks like his father in his own right, but mostly, it's their size that marks them as his kin. Of course, there's a hint of their mother as well in each of their eyes.

They greet me with awkward hugs, hesitating around the crutches, which prevent me from embracing them in return. If I lift my arms, I'd be holding onto them for dear life, and they'd have to pass me from brother to brother, which just doesn't sound right. So I tap a few pats on their sides as they reach in for me before stepping back.

The last man is pointed out instead of introduced directly to me.

"That's Big Poppy," Jedd says, and I swallow back some air as the man turns to face me. He looks so much like the mystery man who helped me the night of the tub incident, but it couldn't be, could it? The man has the same wild shaggy hair and thick bushy beard along with a large stature. The difference is my guardian angel wore a filthy long overcoat, making him look bulky compared to the more solid and slightly buff physique of Big Poppy. He tips his chin in silent acknowledgement from his position halfway across the field and then he turns back to eyeing the land.

"Well, I guess I better let y'all get to it," I state, filling in the sudden silence as the Grady boys don't know where to look, and Vernon stares directly at me. Nathan and Todd excuse themselves and walk back to a truck full of wood studs. There's no sense in trying to argue with Jedd. A building's going up on my land. I turn, and Jedd shifts with me, following me as I hike myself back down the drive.

"Beverly—" He begins as he scratches at the back of his neck, but I cut him off with, "I wanted to thank you for the flower."

Jedd grins, cautious and curious. "Umm...while I probably should have sent you flowers as a way of apology, I didn't."

I stop, and Jedd takes a step before me.

"The sunflower on the back porch?" I prompt, thinking he might have simply forgotten such a small gesture.

"I'd like to take credit, but I don't know what you're talking about." He looks puzzled as he glances back at the house as if he's considering again that he should have sent me something because he's definitely being honest in that he did not place a flower on my back steps. "Seems you have a secret admirer or maybe it was your Tripper fella."

Right, Tripper. I bite my lip, holding back a giggle.

Jedd shifts his muscular body in my direction again and stares at me, taking a long moment to look at my hair and my eyes, then travel down my nose and land on my lips.

"What're you looking at?" I snap, feeling stripped naked before him. My hair blows in the fall breeze, and my neck feels the whisper of the next season approaching. I shiver with the wind, but it's really his appraisal causing the tremble.

"Just looking at you, Bee. Only you."

CHAPTER THIRTEEN

[Beverly]

W hen life gives you lemons, you make lemonade, only I don't have any lemons, and a barn raising calls for lemonade. Staring into the fridge, I notice a gallon of apple cider, and I turn for the oven, deciding cookies and cider will be the best I can offer these men. It isn't nearly enough. A barn raising is a party of sorts, and my mother raised me right, instilling a need for beverages when unsolicited visitors arrive. Being unsolicited, I shouldn't offer Jedd and his friends anything, but a trickle of excitement runs down my spine.

When the stove beeps, signaling the necessary temperature, I hear the patter of heavy feet stomping down the stairs, reminding me of Hannah as a child when she knew I was baking a treat. My daughter stands just inside the kitchen, arms crossed, hair rumpled, with a scowl on her face.

"Momma, what are you doing?"

"We've got men raising a barn in our yard, and they need refreshments. I'm making cookies."

"Momma, you can—"

The glare I give my daughter could melt a candle without a wick. I turn away from her as I hold the countertop and reach for the flour canister. She crosses the kitchen and leans her hip into the counter. With a thick sigh, she swipes a hand through her long hair, and I note her pajamas out the corner of my eye—a short pair of shorts and a sweatshirt.

Where did my baby girl in princess nightgowns go?

"Let me help you," she offers, and I want to dismiss her, but a glance at her expression tells me she's sincere in her attempt to work *with* me and not take over. We make cookies like we haven't done in over fifteen years. Working side by side, we measure the ingredients, then roll the dough for sugary goodness in a variety of shapes. A Christmas tree. A pumpkin. The letter H.

"I'd forgotten we had these," I mutter as my voice cracks with memories of long-gone holidays and birthdays.

"Yeah." Hannah softly chuckles. "We should go through some of the old stuff in here," she states, noting the kitchen is a catchall of unnecessary items. She places the first trays in the oven, then looks out the back door, spying on the builders in the field as we wait the nine minutes of baking time.

"Who's out there?" she asks, hands cupping her eyes at the window in order to see better. I list off the men, but when I get to Grizzly Grady, her head snaps up. "Grizz?" Her attention returns to the window. "I haven't seen him in years."

Her dreamy faraway voice tells me something was once there for her regarding Grizzly. Does she still fancy him? Does she have a crush on someone? Does she ever go on dates? Has she given her heart to anyone?

"You should go say hello," I suggest as her forehead rests on the glass pane, but she turns to me once again.

"I'm a mess," she states, fingering her locks with one hand while looking down and tugging the hem of her sleep-sweatshirt. "Plus,

I'm not even dressed." Her eyes leap to the clock on the stove. "I have the lunch shift at the Front Porch today, so I need to shower." The timer beeps on the cookies, and Hannah removes the two pans. Waiting the allotted time for cooling, she places the first dozen on the cooling rack. Then I spoon out another batch, and she sets the cookie sheets in the oven. Her eyes catch again on the clock.

"Go shower," I say, sensing her need to prepare for work. "I got this."

Her mouth opens, then closes, clamping her lips to prevent any unnecessary protests. "Are you sure?"

"I can do this," I confidently state, but I'm not so certain when the buzzer beeps, and I struggle with the oven door, my braces knocking against the hot surface. I should have removed the crutches and balanced against the counter for support. As I lift the tray one-handed, my arm trembles, and I nearly miss the stovetop. I'm not as fortunate with the second batch, and the cookies slide from the pan, littering the floor.

"Dagnabbit," I curse, allowing the oven door to slam shut and hearing a chuckle behind me. I turn to see Jedd standing inside the back door.

"Did you just say *dagnabbit*?" He laughs harder.

"Who let you in the house?" I snap, then take a calming breath, closing my eyes. It isn't Jedd's fault I dropped these cookies.

"Kerr cut his hand, and I was wondering if you had any bandages." My lids pop open, and his expression tells me he doesn't want to ask me for anything, but the boy is bleeding.

"In the bathroom upstairs, but Hannah's showering."

Jedd nods, taking in the mess on my floor.

"Smells delicious," he states as I lower for the scraps. Most of the cookies cracked from the impact with the wood flooring. Jedd crouches beside me, picking up the pieces and setting them on the counter.

"They were for you and your friends, but..." Obviously, I dropped the set. Feeling slightly incapable and a bit embarrassed, I look up to see Jedd staring at me, his brows pinched.

131

"What?" I bark. His puzzling gaze makes my skin heat.

"You doing something nice for me, Bee?" he teases in that rough voice of his.

"Not if you're going to make a big deal of it," I state, a trace of my edginess outlining the words.

"Five second rule," he says with a tip of his chin and a growing smile. "I want all the pieces."

"Well, they need to cool and then be frosted, and I'll..." The words fade as I glance back at him.

"What?" he asks, reading something in my face. "What's wrong?" He cups my face with one hand, holding his palm to my jaw as his fingers brush my cheek. The tender touch startles me, but I don't move, melting into the heat like the cookies lying flat on the pan. He keeps touching me, and I should push him away, but I don't.

"I don't know how I'll carry these out to you boys." My voice drops quieter. I hadn't considered carrying a tray and using my crutches over the gravel. Jedd slowly smiles, his eyes meeting mine. He guides me to stand, slipping his hand around the back of my neck.

"I'll carry 'em for you, Bee. I'll carry anything you need." My brows pinch with the shift in his tone, rumpled sheets and grogginess returns. He tugs me forward, and his lips brush my forehead. I stiffen under his hold and pull back, glaring at him.

What the...what was that for?

"They aren't ready yet," I note, keeping my voice steady even as the rest of me trembles in confusion. Jedd stands close, too close again, and I inhale the fresh air and cut wood fragrance of him.

"When you're ready then. I'm not going anywhere." There's so much I could read into what he says, so much danger in the false promise and threat of hope. His thumb strokes the side of my neck, and I shake my head, ridding thoughts of him meaning more. He drops his hand and pulls a phone from his back pocket. "Give me your number. Then I'll text you mine so you can call me when everything is ready."

I swallow back an awkward lump in my throat. "I don't actually know my number."

"How do you not know your number?" he teases, and I glance over at the house phone on the wall.

"Well, I don't call myself," I say, falling back into bitter, snappish tones with the reminder of all I don't know. "I give out Hannah's number for everything." She tried to teach me how to use the bells and whistles of a smartphone, insisting the landline wasn't safe enough, but I grew frustrated with the technology. She demands I keep the cell phone near me at all times, but it's an old flip phone. I miss the landline. The phone remains, but the service is off. "I don't think my phone accepts texts."

Jedd chuckles again, and Hannah enters the room wearing a robe and a towel on her head. Just then, there's a light knock on the back door before it opens without being answered.

"Jedd, how we doing on a Band...*Hannah*?" Grizzly Grady's thick voice croaks as he takes in my daughter, whose mouth gapes open at the large man with a trimmed beard and wide blue eyes filling our back door.

"Grizzly," she chokes, but it comes out a crackle of surprise as she tugs the top of her robe together with one hand and then swipes at the towel on her head. "I... it's been... ohmygod." She turns for the hall, and the stampede of feet rushing up the staircase to the second floor echoes back to us.

"Well, uhm..." A flustered Grizzly brushes his fingers through his mop of hair and turns toward us. "Jedd, bandages?"

"Right," he says, and he removes his hand from mine. When did he grab my hand, and why do I miss the warmth? He steps back, and I point at a drawer near the sink.

"There might be some in the junk drawer."

When Jedd steps toward the drawer, making himself at home in my kitchen, he looks like he might belong here. He pulls out a box of adhesives and then a pad of paper. Rustling through the pens, rubber bands, and metal clips, he finds a pencil and scribbles something on the pad. He sets the pencil back in the drawer, picks up the box of bandages, and crosses the kitchen. I remain where I've been the entire time, near the stove, but focus on the paper on the counter until Jedd gets to the back door. He pauses and turns back to me.

"For all the broken pieces, Bee. Call me when you're ready." He gives me a long stare before tugging the door closed behind him, and I'm left with another whispered warning that he means something other than cookies.

CHAPTER FOURTEEN

[Jedd]

Beverly finally calls me, and I cross the yard for a gallon of cider, a mismatched collection of mugs, and some sloppily iced cookies shaped like a pine tree, a squash, and a capital H.

"It's a pumpkin," she corrects. "I'm out of practice," she clarifies on the frosting job, but my mouth waters all the same. I can't remember the last time I had homemade cookies. Hell, I can't remember the last time someone did anything so sweet for me, and whether she admits it or not, she did this as a peace offering to me and the guys.

"They look delicious, Bee. The boys will love them." I pause, glancing at the serving tray. "Where are the broken ones?"

"Oh, I didn't think you were serious. I didn't frost them. They're in that container." A circular, plastic butter tub holds the broken cookies separate from the rest.

"I told you I want all the pieces," I remind her, and she shyly grins. I'll take every scrap of her she's willing to give, and something tells me Beverly is willing or at least wanting. *Wanting* more than what she has, more than who she is, and maybe even wanting me.

"Come outside with me so the boys can thank you properly and you can see our progress."

She doesn't argue but reaches for her arm crutches and stands from her seat at the table. She is getting better at maneuvering with them. She only needed more practice. She watches me as my claw hooks the tray, and my other hand grabs the opposite edge. The wheels spin, questioning my ability, and I'm ready to remind her I'm building a barn, but she doesn't comment. Instead, she just follows me.

My fingers twitch as I carry the tray, the desire to touch her greater than the force of a magnet. I want to draw her close again, run my fingers through her hair, and inhale her scent. Vanilla and heat is her fragrance today. Her skin is addicting. She's a smooth plank compared to my sandpaper touch, but she still has rough edges and potential splinters that need sanding.

"How are you paying these men for their time? You have endless funds or something?" *Or something*, I think as she interrupts my thoughts of caressing her neck. I decide to tell her the partial truth.

"I'm paying them with a couple of cases of beer and some pizzas." I chuckle, but Beverly stumbles. "You okay?" I'll be ditching this tray if I think she'll fall over. She's shaky at best as she walks, robotic and stiff. *Just out of practice*, I remind myself, but she's improving.

"Yeah, I just...I don't drink, so that's a surprising payment." Her face lowers toward the dirt at our feet.

"You don't drink? Like ever?" She doesn't go out, but I assumed she drank an occasional glass of wine at home, but then I realize that's insensitive. Maybe she's on medication that shouldn't mix with alcohol, or maybe she isn't much of a drinker.

"The accident," she starts and abruptly stops. Was she hit by a drunk driver? Goddamn asshole, does he or she know what they did to her?

"I was drunk, and I drove. I could have killed a man or myself. I vowed never to drink again."

I stop walking, stunned. *What caused her to drink and drive?* It's a question I don't ask. In fact, I take too long to respond as we've reached the edge of the construction. Kodiak sees me first, dropping his hammer to come assist me.

"Cookies." He grins like an eager child instead of a twenty-something adult. He pops a cookie into his mouth before he takes the tray from me and groans in pleasure. Beverly chuckles, and the sound surprises me. Rich. Deep. Heat rushes her cheeks despite the cool November air. Her grin is lopsided but genuine, and I want to frame this image of her in my memory. Actually, I want to kiss her, and the thought stumps me again.

I've gone from wanting this land to wanting this woman.

"What do you say?" I nod at Kodiak, dismissing my eager lips and ogling Beverly to remind him of his manners.

"'Ank 'ew," Kodiak mutters around a mouthful of cookie like a kid instead of a grown-up. He nods as he spins away, and I turn to Beverly. A strange desire to hold her envelops me. I want to pull her close and tell her it's okay. We all make mistakes in life. We all bleed, and then we heal.

Instead, I swallow a lump in my throat and dismiss what she told me. "I think it's about to get as ugly as starved cannibals finding prey," I tease.

"It isn't much." A piece of hair blows across her face. The wayward tendril softens the sternness of her face, and not for the first time do I think Beverly could do with a little disheveling. She was wound too tight when her hair was bound, and her clothing wasn't quite right for her shape. Her new haircut and color are surprisingly attractive. The white is so bright but fresh. Today, she wears new jeans and a thick sweater, and there's a spark to her eyes as she stands in the sunshine and looks out over the land. The peaceful look reminds me of when she told me about her flowers.

"Come up with any interests yet?"

"Excuse me?" She rouses from her thoughts.

"Interests. Think of something?"

"Oh, not yet." She squints as she looks off into the distance, and I follow her line of sight. Down this path, the trail narrows but leads to another house, another farmstead, one that no longer exists. It's been swallowed into the Townsen property.

"Whatcha thinking about then?"

Beverly shakes her head and turns to me. "I was just recalling how when I first moved here, I thought it was a dream come true. All this land, this space, freedom to roam, but then it became a prison. I slaved on this property for Ewell and Howard. Then Ewell died, and Howard left. After the accident, it felt like solitary confinement, and I forgot how much I enjoyed the openness." It's the most honest thing Beverly's said to me minus the drunk driving admission, and I'm taken aback. *All the pieces*, I decide. Eventually, we'll have a complete cookie, one whole and crisp with smooth, decorative frosting, but for now, I'll take the crumbs she gives me.

* * *

Continuing with the surprises, Beverly also made up a pot of chili, which the boys devoured. We'd finished all the foundation work, and Beverly chuckled when she noted the stable building would take more than a day with six ornery men taking breaks to eat her treats.

By nightfall, I'm exhausted from a day's labor but rejuvenated with hope for the future. The prospect for Quarter Horses is coming along, and I have the go-ahead from my partner to purchase. The reality of my dream is taking shape even if I don't own this land.

Hasting, I curse. What a fucking idiot. How do you lose your family's land? Then again, Hasting had issues, gambling being one of them, and then he used his son who didn't understand the repercussions of a big man's game—*poker*. Boone liked card games, and Hasting used fifty-two pick up to teach Boone all kinds of stuff, but mainly how to cheat at high stakes. After decades of owning his family's land, he squandered it on five cards, and I vow again that one day, I'll reclaim what should have been mine, despite not being blood.

I'm thinking these thoughts as I work the makeshift shower I designed in the barn. Running a hose to another corner of the large open space, I linked the rubber tube over a metal rod and hooked it in place with an S-hook. A showerhead on a pull string does the trick. An old wood pallet works as a base and keeps my feet from the dirt ground. It's rustic and cold as ice cream on the tongue, but I'm clean. I'm tired of hiking over to Grady's office for a wash, and while I don't love a cool shower, it works on a night full of memories like this one.

Boone. My kid brother was never a worker but a slacker, or so I thought until I realized he wasn't quite like the rest of us. Boone could weasel his way out of hard labor like a mouse slipping through a hole the size of a pencil. He was equally as squeaky, going on and on if he was told to participate and stalling long enough for the day to end without much production from him. Mother babied him, and she was never as soft on Janice or me. I didn't hate Boone. I understood he needed special treatment.

No son of mine isn't right in the head, Hasting would say. *He'll grow to be a man and own this land*. I didn't stick around to watch it *not* happen as Hasting had predicted.

As I stand under a cold spray, hosing myself off, I'm reminded of being in the military and looking for any escape from things lost in this godforsaken Valley, which I loved in my heart but felt cheated from because of blood. The cool water pelts at my skin, and I absorb the shock of it. I circle it over my hair, allowing the shampoo to slither down my skin. I've removed my arm, so suds glide down my body as my hand holds the string to release the water from the hose. Liquid combined with soap splatters on my makeshift flooring when I hear a gasp.

A camp light rests on a nail jutting out of an old barn beam, illuminating me. Releasing the pull, I scrub at my face to clear my vision and see Beverly outlined just inside the barn.

"Bee." My voice chokes as my hand lowers down my chest and

cups myself, covering what I can. I twist at the waist, giving her my backside instead, while fighting the smile crossing my lips. She's getting an eyeful either way. "Bee, honey, whatcha doing?"

"I…" Her voice quickly falters, and incoherent stuttering follows. I crane my neck, looking over my shoulder as best I can.

"Want to join me?" I tease, finding I can't seem to help myself when she's around. Flirting with her comes naturally. I like how she reacts—flustered and shocked—but also not mistaking my meaning and fighting a knowing grin when the innuendo clicks.

"I…" I can't hear her at this angle, so I spin to give her my better ear, noticing she's closer than I expected, or I wouldn't have heard her initial gasp. Risky little bee, buzzing closer, she eventually comes within the edge of the dim light of my lamp.

"I can't hear you, honey." I release myself to point at my ear and chuckle when she turns her head away a little too late. I'm certain she's seen the full package.

"I thought you might be cold this evening. The weather is shifting, so I brought you a blanket." I can't reach for the threadbare towel I use to dry myself without releasing the goods once again. Her head remains to the side as if the most fascinating object is parallel my position.

I want to be the most fascinating being in her view.

"Beverly," I snap, and her head twists in my direction. Her eyes meet mine and hold, but there's only so long the staring game works before someone grows uncomfortable. I won't break, but she does. Her eyes roam down my sternum, across hairs I can't contain to the hand fighting off a growing erection. With the way she's looking at me, my body can't help but react, and I want to react in so many ways. I want to step off this plank and cross to her, cup her face and take her mouth. I want her to drop to her knees and use that mouth on me.

It's been a long time, man.

I grew tired of the one-night stands. Chicks getting their rocks off with an injured soldier. Buckle bunnies hoping to find their own bucking bronco from the rodeo circuit.

Beverly stares back at me, holding the blanket wrapped over a forearm as she balances on one brace.

"It's the blanket you told me to knit for you."

Without thinking, I step off the wet platform and into the dirt. The grit sticks to the pads of my feet and squishes through my toes, but my focus is on her.

"It must be Christmas." My voice lowers. "You've given me so many gifts today."

"I'm not very good at knitting." Her eyes drop to my feet, and I wiggle my toes. A grin struggles on her lips, and once again, I want to take her mouth with mine. She's a ripe peach ready to be devoured.

"Another non-interest interest?" I tease.

She shrugs. This woman needs more than a hobby. She needs a passion project, a labor of love. Hell, she needs *love* period, passion without question, and I want to give it to her. I want her to know what it's like to be desired. My hand involuntarily reaches forward, eager for her skin, but she sets the blanket over it to prevent me from touching her. She shifts her eyes upward for the roofline. I'm naked as the day before this woman, and she's refusing to look at me.

"What would interest you, Bee?" My voice rumbles in my throat, struggling to keep from barking an order. *Look at me!*

"Soap," she blurts.

"Soap?" I chuckle.

"Yes."

"Soap?" I repeat.

"Yes, I believe soap would interest me."

"Soap," I tease, wondering if the interest comes from watching it caress my body.

"Soapmaking," she suggests.

Soapmaking, echoes in my head, parroting her, only I'm no longer questioning the suggestion. Soapmaking is a science, like baking and cooking, growing flowers and testing soil. Is Beverly a scientist? "Bee, do you like to make things?"

"What do you mean?"

Her tomatoes come to mind. "Do you like to grow things from scratch? Create something with your hands?" *Don't think of her hands*, I warn. Especially with how close I stand to her, holding only a folded blanket before my naked body. I shiver with the thought of her hands on my skin, warming up the coolness rippling down my spine and the heat lingering lower.

"I guess so."

"Bee, be confident. Yes or no."

"Yes." She sighs, her voice still hesitant. "Yes, okay?" Better but still not a firm answer.

"Soapmaking," I repeat again, and an idea brews. "Beverly?" The sound of her name draws her attention back to me. Her eyes release from the nothingness above us and land on mine. I flip the blanket over my damp shoulder, knowing it covers my front but only barely, and then I cup her neck, pulling her toward me to kiss her cheek. "Thank you for the blanket."

She pulls back abruptly, her mouth gaping, but no words assault me. I'm making progress.

I can't wait to nestle into the thick knit knowing she made it for me, and I'm hopeful her scent lingers on it. My dick leaps behind the covering. Having Bee's blanket over me might not be a good idea after all because I'm only going to envision her over me and me slipping into her.

She nods, still not speaking, and hobbles away from me.

"Hey, Bee, what happened to my cookie crumbs?"

She pauses and turns back to me, her body in shadow in the dark. "I left the container on the back steps. I thought you took it."

I shake my head. "I never saw it." *Why didn't she bring them to me like she brought me the blanket?*

"Good night, Jedd." Her voice drifts to me through the darkness.

"Night, Bee," I whisper, still naked but warmed all over as I press her blanket to my chest and inhale. *Sunshine and honey*. It's going to be a long night.

CHAPTER FIFTEEN

[Beverly]

I hadn't seen Jedd all the next day, which was a good thing as I was still working through my embarrassment at catching him in his makeshift shower. His physique is unparalleled to any living, breathing male I've ever seen. Despite the missing limb, Jedd is solid muscle. His chest. His thighs. His... Heat covers my cheeks when I consider what I saw. Even when I told myself not to look, it was the first thing I did. I couldn't help myself. I'm drawn to him on a level I don't understand.

I purposely avoid sitting in my bedroom, fighting the temptation to peer out the window at the barn building progress or any other thing that might involve Jedd working as hard as he does. I feel guilty about the missing cookie pieces, and think I should have made him more treats. I didn't find the container on the back steps this morning, but two sunflowers sit in its place. Jedd told me he hadn't taken the butter tub. He also admitted he hadn't left the flower the other day, so I can't ignore the suspicion I suddenly have as to who the cookie-thief-slash-flower-giver is.

I scan the yard through the front window, but I don't have any hints as to where my secret admirer could be or where he came from; all I know is he's out there. Feeling generous and a little tickled by the flower offerings, I'd left a sealed container with an extra helping of dinner on the steps after Hannah went to work. A Post-it note on the returned container held a single initial: B. It's funny how I've always been Beverly. I've never been a fan of nicknames. Thought the reduction in a given name seemed like an insult. But being called Bee by Jedd, and now the singular letter B by this stranger, doesn't feel so much like diminishing me, but more like a forbidden secret. Something private between me and the name giver. Jedd sees me as sharp and stinging but persistent, like the pollinator. The hidden homeless man sees me as something singular and unique. All the same, the new names suggest a new me.

Willing my eyes back to Tripper and Virginia Hanes in a rerun of *Nailed*, my thoughts cannot be contained. I stare at the couple I greatly admire for their devotion to one another and their dedication to hard work. Tripper isn't just some man who stepped in front of the camera for five seconds in miraculously clean attire. His boots are scuffed. His shirts show sweat stains. Hats often cover his head. Yet he is a reality star.

"I'm living a dream," I mutter as my eyes drift back to the front window. A real man who works hard is out there, hammering together a barn. He has scuffed boots, sweat-laden tees, and the occasional ball cap, and *he* is the real deal, not some fantasy on my television set.

"Love you, GinGin," Tripper calls out as he takes the Hanes' crew of children home after a pizza dinner with their mother. Virginia then speaks about family and loving her children, but having to work late into the night to make the home they've designed just right for others. My eyes gaze around the living room, taking in the three walls and the large bay window. *Has this ever been a home?*

It's my house. I live here. I raised Hannah here, but inside these walls is so much heartbreak.

I close my eyes and hear Ewell and his son fighting. I smell the cheap perfume on Howard after another night of stepping out on me. I feel the presence of a man and slowly open my eyes to find Jedd just inside the entrance of the living room.

"Sweet butter on a biscuit," I mutter. "Have you no respect for personal property, letting yourself in my home at your will?" My heart leaps, and my fingers spread over my chest.

"You shouldn't leave the door unlocked," he says, his eyes fixed on my television. "Besides, I called out your name."

Silence passes only a second before he speaks.

"Tripper *Hanes*?" Jedd's expression morphs from watching the program to agitated wonder. "*Tripper* Hanes." His eyes snap to mine as he crosses to the television set and stands in front of it, his back to the screen. His hand rests on his hip with the ball cap dangling off his claw, and he hisses at me. "You let me believe Tripper was a real man. Your man."

"Get out of the way," I snap, the familiar fight in me returning as he blocks the screen. I don't really need to see the remainder of this show. I've seen it before; I've watched it too many times, in fact. Yet Jedd standing before it, learning my secret obsession, pisses me off.

He takes a step forward, his wide stance making more of a door than a window, and I sigh in defeat.

"I never said he was my man. You just assumed that."

"You didn't deny it," he states, irritation filling his tone.

"You're the one who mentioned assumptions." My mouth hangs open, ready to say more, and then catching my tone, I clamp my lips shut.

Jedd huffs, dismissing his words thrown back at him. "Why?"

"Why what?" I retort although I know what he's asking.

"Why fool me?"

I...*don't know* why I didn't correct him.

Was it foolish to pretend I had a beau? Yes, it was.

145

Was it interesting to watch his expression when he mentioned Tripper? It also was.

Suddenly, Jedd is in my space, which is becoming a habit of his like entering my home unannounced. He balances over me, his arms like fence posts on either side of me as he sets his hands on the armrests. The chair tips, and Jedd's eyes widen.

"Is this a rocking chair?"

I nod in response, glancing up at him like a petulant child and then dragging my eyes away as he's too close.

Wood shavings. Fresh air. All male.

"Oh, the things I could do with this seat," he mutters, his voice that sleepy rumble sound, and I risk another gaze at his face. Big mistake. Those dark eyes. That crooked smirk. "Don't you dare look at me like that when I'm upset with you."

My eyes widen at the roughness of his words, which contain a chuckle.

"Upset with me? What did I do?" I snark, but a grin graces my lips, and I bite the corner hard, fighting against the curve.

"You little vixen," he mumbles. Lowering his body, he slips to his forearms as he kneels on one knee, wedging his chest between my legs. He's trapped me in the cushioned seat, and my hand comes to his chest.

"I…can't." I don't know what I'm saying I can't do. *Kiss him?* Why can't I?

"Oh, because of Tripper?" Jedd mocks. He tips his head to motion over his shoulder. "Is he watching us?" I humorlessly snort. Turning back to me, he reaches for the edge of my hair with his fingers, pinching the tips. His eyes watch the motion. His face is only inches from mine, and my hand on his chest pauses. Fingers caress flannel. His heart beats underneath.

"Bee, why do you have such a tough shell?" he questions without looking at me, his Southern drawl deep.

I shrug. He waits.

"It's not a shell. I'm just cautious. I don't…" *trust anyone*, I think as he answers for me.

"Trust anyone."

"I don't need anybody anyway," I reply, watching my fingers spread on his flannel-covered chest, pressing at the soft fabric barrier to a firm chest.

"Everybody needs someone."

"Men are all hot air."

"Howard was hot air," Jedd retorts. "I'm just hot."

Shaking my head, I can't help the smile growing on my lips. He's ridiculous but not wrong. Heat permeates through his shirt, warming me with his nearness to a pulsing body part that hasn't pulsed for a long time.

"What are you afraid of?" he asks, softening his tone as his fingers comb through my hair.

My lids lower, and I shake my head again, denying him an answer.

"Are you afraid I'll leave?" My gaze momentarily jolts to his before drawing away. I tug at his collar, my fingers needing something to do. He's hit it on the head. People don't stick. My parents disowned me. Howard left. Friends are gone. Ewell dead. *Hannah will go soon.*

"Everyone leaves," I whisper, hoping he doesn't hear me. It's too difficult to state the truth.

"Not me," he says, cupping my chin so I look up at him. His upper half still leans over me. My knees spread to straddle his broad chest. He's so close to me, overwhelming me.

"Yeah, well, you'll go when you get what you want, or when you realize this isn't what you want anymore." Breeding horses. Borrowed land. It speaks of temporary. My tone returns, gnashing and sarcastic, but his fingers tighten on my chin.

"Not me," he repeats.

"All men disappoint."

Jedd shakes his head, which feels like it's come closer. His lips are within reach, but that's a warning for me. My hand covers his face, palm at his nose and fingertips at his forehead, and I push at him because I need space. He laughs, tugging my hand free and kissing the pad of my palm.

"All men? That's a broad generalization. How many men you been with, Bee?"

"None of your damn business," I snap. One. Came close to another but didn't trust myself. But not this close. Jedd is too close. He's still holding my hand, stroking his thumb over my wrist.

"Besides fictional men like Tripper," he adds.

"Tripper's very real," I defend.

"Oh, yeah. Can he do this?" Jedd's teeth graze the puffy skin under my thumb. I squeak. My mouth gaping with shock.

"Or how about this?" he continues, drawing my wrist to his lips and sucking at the sensitive skin over my vein.

"Or what about this?" Jedd leans forward, and before I know what's happening, his lips brush mine. Tender, soft, quick. He pulls back, staring at me, waiting on my response, but I have nothing. No words form. No thoughts collect. Only my body reacting with flutters in my belly and a thumping at my center. My right leg twitches, and I want to wrap it over his hip and pull him to me.

Instead, I push at his face again, and he retracts a bit, chuckling when I say, "What did you do that for?"

"Because not all men are the same, Bee, and I'm out to prove it." He dips his head but tips a brow. "I can be patient, but not that patient. You'll come around, Bee." With that, he hops up from the floor, agile as a cat, and holds out a hand to help me stand. I shove it away. I'm not going anywhere with him, but as soon as he leaves the room, I twist in the chair for the hallway entrance, realizing Jedd Flemming might see me as a door, but a glass one, and he sees right through me. My heart hammers, and my stomach twists with hope that he really won't disappear.

* * *

A few nights later, I stand in front of the mirror in my room, my robe loosely covering my body. I've just showered, and my hair is damp

and springs to my chin. The white color still shows through the moisture, and the cut hints at the old me. The one with a bounce in her
step and a smile on her lips. I grin in the mirror, but it looks more
like a grimace. My lips lower to their natural pout, and I examine
myself. My skin remains pale as I haven't sat in the sunshine in
years. My eyes appear brighter, sharper even, with the new color
contrast of my hair. A hand comes to my throat and rubs down my
neck, smoothing the large crease around the middle. I recall once
reading an article, stating you can tell a woman's age by looking at
her neck.

*You look so much older than you are. Sort of on the shelf, if you
take my meaning. Spinsterish.* Hazel Cumberstone's unflattering
words come to mind. I've felt older than I am. I'm well over shelf
age, in the terms of historical romances, and as for being a spinster,
well, I've been married. I'm more the scorned woman. I chuckle at
the thought. I don't want to think of Howard, but it's a good
reminder of not being wanted by another human being.

What's wrong with me? I wonder as my hand wanders down my
chest, loosening the already ill-fitting robe to expose the swell of my
smallish breasts. I pause and consider touching myself. My nipples
are already points, highlighting my awareness that it's been a long
time since I've been caressed. Suddenly, a movement reflected in the
mirror alerts me to the outline of someone in the doorway.

My heart leaps to my throat, choking on the scream as my body
freezes with momentary terror. He becomes clearer in the low light
of my room when he shifts forward just a little.

Cheeseoncracker.

"Beverly." The way he says my full name. The ruggedness to his
deep tone. The struggle in his loud voice sets my girly bits pulsing,
and those peaked nipples are so rigid they ache. My hand stills at my
sternum, caught between the fright of him standing just on the edge
of my room and the temptation to cover the needy swell.

"I called out your name, but I guess you didn't hear me."

My eyes remain on Jedd while my heart continues to race. Does
he ever considering knocking? He nearly tore down my door that

149

first meeting, but now he just lets himself into the house. *Into my room*.

"I should…" he starts, motioning over his shoulder with a thumb, hinting he should leave, yet his body remains still, and then he steps forward.

My gaze leaps to his residual limb, the space empty beneath the edge of his classic gray T-shirt. From there, my sight traces over his shoulder and up his neck, thick and solid like the rest of him, to the edge of his jaw, covered in silver stubble.

Jedd clears his throat, and my eyes leap to his.

"Do you have any idea how beautiful you are?" The tone reminds me of rustled covers and sleepy caresses, and shivers whisper over my skin. I can't answer him. I don't see myself in that manner.

His hand comes to the back of my neck, cupping it like he does. He pauses, holding my eyes through the reflection as if he's asking for permission. I'm not certain what I'd be agreeing to, but the way he's questioning me, I can't deny him. I blink, lazy like my lids are heavy. The signal triggers his grip to tighten on my neck. The rough palm moves upward, his fingers delving into the short locks. He spreads those thick digits, and my head nods forward, the sensation sending ripples of calming pleasure down my back.

"Your hair is so soft." With a loud voice, Jedd struggles with volume control. His tone lowers so his eyes meet mine in the mirror to confirm I heard him. My lips curl just the slightest, and Jedd continues to massage the back of my skull, fat fingertips working at the base and moving upward. He gives a little tug, and my head lolls toward him.

"Mmm, Bee. Your skin is just as tender." His mouth whispers along my neck, his lips not yet touching the skin, but his breath is like a kiss. The fine hairs on my body stand at attention, waiting for more, longing for more. Then his mouth brushes the juncture of my neck and shoulder. With fingers wrapped in my hair, he tilts my head, and my lids lower again. His mouth opens, and he sucks at the sweet spot.

My legs give as a hissing cat sound escapes my lips. *Mercy, that feels so good.*

With the collapse of my knees, Jedd quickly releases my hair and wraps his arm around my waist. He holds me against his chest, continuing to nip at my shoulder and nudging the material of my robe farther over the joint. His nose reverses the trail of his lips to the edge of my ear while his hand fists at the knot on the tie of my robe.

"You smell like sunshine and honey."

I swallow against any answer as his hand rises and slips into the opening of my covering. The warmth of his thick palm flattens against my belly, and my abs retract, not from displeasure but surprise at the heat. His fingers gently press on my stomach, holding me still, allowing me to feel the temperateness of him. His mouth continues to work over my neck and shoulder, blazing a trail of kisses only to return to my ear and trace the outer edge with the tip of his nose.

With the rise and fall of my chest, the draping of the robe at my shoulder slips to the crook of my elbow. The material catches on my nipple, barely containing my breast. Enough of my cleavage is on display for Jedd to pause in his kisses.

"How long has it been, Bee, since a man savored you?"

A quick retort rests on my tongue, stopped short by my teeth clenching. *What man would want to savor me?* I think, but the twinkle in the midnight of his eyes tells me this man wants me. At least at the moment.

"Never," I croak because my throat doesn't work, and I can't move my tongue properly to form more words.

His hand moves across my skin, not a smooth stroke but a hesitant skitter until he's just under the weight of an achy breast.

"May I?" he whispers directly at my ear, the question mixing with his breath. May he? *Can I do this?* I must give some sort of affirmative because the thick pad of his hand covers my entire breast, and my knees weaken once again. My head falls back to his shoulder, and my eyes close as I'm experiencing the tenderest touch I've even known. Without hesitation, he pinches the ripe nipple between his forefinger and thumb, tugging forward just enough for the pull to ache, and I whimper in pleasurable pain. In deep lust. In desperate desire.

I want this man's hand to move everywhere on me. Considering he's only using one hand, the only physical hand he has, he's driving me mad. A cyclone of want swirls inside me: Kiss me. Tease me. Please me.

He releases the nipple and returns to massaging the weight of my breast.

They're small, I think, and Jedd speaks as if he heard me. "The fit is perfect. Right in the palm of my hand," he mutters, still rough and scratchy and all Jedd.

Jedd, Jedd, Jedd. Ms. Mabel was correct in her pronunciation of his name. Thrusting and sexual, I want it to grace my lips.

I consider turning toward him because I should return the pleasure. Howard always demanded it be equal—a kiss for me, then one for him—but I don't want to move. I don't want this sensation to end. Selfishly, I feel desired in a way I've never been desired.

Jedd's hand releases my breast, and I softly purr in protest. His lips curl against my neck again, and our eyes lock in the mirror. His palm returns to my belly, pausing while we stare at one another for a long minute.

"Now, I'm the curious one…" His voice drones, reminding us of him catching me snooping through his things. Reality slams into me as I realize I still don't really know Jedd. I mean, I watch him every day. I recognize the gait of his stride, the curve of his shoulder blades, and the shortness of his hair, but I don't *know him* know him. What's his story?

My expression must says something to him, along with another reality check—headlights outside my window. The stream grows brighter, and I'm aware Hannah's pulling up the drive. *What's she doing home so early?* The question doesn't linger as Jedd slowly retracts his hand, and I want to protest. My eyes prickle with liquid, blurring the mirror before us like we're blurring lines.

He lives in the barn. He's borrowing my land. There's nothing between us.

Or there shouldn't be.

Why not? my body cries as he presses a quick kiss to my neck and then moves his hand to right the edge of my robe, returning it to cover my shoulder. He stands for a moment with his one arm crossed over my chest, holding the material in place over my clavicle.

"This doesn't get rid of me, Bee. I'm not going away," he states, his voice a little louder, more Jedd's normally heightened tone but with confident assurance. He's leaving my room but not my home. The loudness startles me, and I flinch against him. Releasing his hold, he takes one step back. His eyes watch me before he nods once and then steps back again, disappearing into the darkness outside my bedroom.

I'm left feeling flushed but chilled from his absence. Flustered as well. *What just happened here?* I hadn't said more than a few words to him, but none of them would equal the three words I feel for this man. Confused. Frustrated. Yearning.

When I finally come to my senses, holding my robe at my shoulder with my arm over my chest in a similar manner to the way Jedd held me, I question if I've dreamed the entire thing. Was he really in my room? Did I just project him into a fantasy? Yet his warmth loiters. His touch lingers. The scent of him remains.

"Momma, did I just see Jedd leaving the house?" Hannah calls out as she enters through the kitchen. I smile to myself, noting I'm not insane. Jedd Flemming just kissed my skin. He touched my breast. He was here. He was real, and I don't know how I should feel about it.

CHAPTER SIXTEEN

[Beverly]

To my surprise, the container I left for my patron's dinner rests in the sink the following morning, along with three flowers in a colored-glass bottle set on the table. My eyes travel to the back door, unable to see through the room-darkening shade covering the glass. I should warn Hannah about our unknown neighbor, the homeless man. She works hard, and I shouldn't be offering extra helpings of dinner to this stranger, but then again, I shouldn't shun a man in need, especially after he helped me. He appears to be thanking me for my generosity with the mini bouquets and his small notes. The singular B on the Post-it has been turned into a bumblebee image, blending the bumps in the letter to the wings of the busy pollinator. The drawing is rustic but whimsical, and it makes me smile to see it next to the bottle holding flowers this morning.

Along with the flowers is a collection of ingredients: lye, distilled water, and coconut, olive and palm oils.

"What's this?" I ask Hannah when she enters the kitchen midmorning.

"Good morning, Momma," she addresses me, a silent reprimand for not greeting her properly.

"Good morning, sunshine. Now, what's this?"

Hannah peers at the table after pouring herself a mug of coffee. She shrugs. "It was on the table last night when I came in. I thought you knew as you mentioned Jedd was dropping something off."

To explain Jedd's late-night presence, I did say something to that effect. This collection of bottles supports it, but it doesn't explain what the collection intends to make.

"I guess I should go ask Jedd to explain himself." Hannah smiles into the coffee mug.

"I guess you should." There hasn't been any mention of the night Jedd tossed me into the tub. I'm grateful as I don't like confrontations and deep conversations, but I'd be open to whatever Hannah needs from me. I hurt her that evening, but I've also had to grapple with my own emotions about what she's done to me over the years. She's enabled me, allowed me to bury myself deeper into needing her instead of forcing me to accept myself and stand on my own two feet. Then again, it wasn't up to her to make me see myself. If there's anything I took from Alcoholics Anonymous years ago, it's that the only way I could get help was to admit I had a problem and then accept that the only means of change was through me.

A brisk, unexpected bath in an outdoor tub can be the same kind of wake-up call. A baptism of sorts. A phoenix rising up from a pool of water instead of the fiery ashes. Maybe I'm another kind of mythological creature.

I lift myself from my seat. "I like your new sweater, Momma."

Is she accusing me of being frugal? Her grin assures me of her compliment. I bought something for myself when I was out with Naomi.

"Thank you," I mutter as I turn for the door. The pale plum sweater dips off my shoulder, exposing a new matching bra. I'd like to think I didn't consciously dress this way today, but I did. Last night lingers in my mind as does the touch of Jedd's hand on my skin. A residual hug is what I consider the haunting embrace I can still feel around me.

As I head to the side of the old barn, I hear the clanging of metal on metal. Rounding the corner, I find Jedd banging on the faded green tractor with a hammer. As I come to a halt, he steps back without appearing to notice me and tosses the hammer into the field.

"Whoa. What did that hammer do to you?" I stammer with a chuckle.

Jedd rounds to face me, hands on his hips as his chest heaves with the exertion of beating the tractor and tossing the hammer.

His head lowers as he laughs. "It's been a rough morning."

"I'm sorry," I offer as my brows pinch in question. Looking off in the distance, I notice the unfinished stable. "What's going on?"

"It's nothing," he mutters, glancing in the same direction as me. "The boys will be back in a few days to finish it up. Nathan works construction by day, so I don't want to abuse his generosity in helping me."

I nod. I'm not concerned, but I am worried about him. Does he regret what he did last night? Should we discuss it? I don't even know how to bring it up other than to beg him to do it all again.

I'm staring at him when his head turns back to me, and our eyes lock for a second. He takes a quick step toward me, and just when I think, hope, pray he's going to kiss me, he stops short.

"Who are those flowers coming from, Bee?"

My mouth drops open and then snaps shut. I'm not certain how to explain the man. Should I mention I'm feeding a homeless guy living somewhere out here? Somehow, I think this act of kindness might upset him more than the misleading crush of Tripper Hanes.

"None of your business," I retort, resorting to the familiarity to push him away. He looks off in the distance once again and chews at his lip. When he turns back to me, his eyes intense, his words nearly take me to my knees.

"You got another beau? One that's real instead of a television sensation?" The bitter mockery to his tone sends up the fine hairs on my neck, but my feathers ruffle as well.

"Not that it's your concern, but no, I do not have a *beau*. And I don't do random hookups either." Another concept I've learned from daytime television. My eyes roam his body, drinking him in. Could I do that with him? Hook up with him. I'd already been a one-time girl, and it resulted in a permanent residence with the man.

"You implying I'd be a hookup?" His eyes narrow at me. "I've already been there, done that. I'm not interested in hooking up anymore."

"Right. Was that during the military or as a rodeo star?" My irritation grows. He's probably been with at least a hundred women, and he's accusing me of being with random men.

"Rodeo star?" he teases. He hasn't mentioned the buckles I saw in his trunk, so I'm caught knowing more than I should about him. "You were a curious cat, weren't you?" He grins, but it isn't softening the edge to his sharp cheeks.

"PAFRA is important to me. I love horses, and I have a competitive spirit. It filled a hole for me. It was a place I needed when I didn't feel like I had any place to go." He shrugs his left shoulder, emphasizing the injury to his arm.

"So why are you here?" I ask when he takes a breath.

"Because now I want a home."

"And taking over mine will be that for you?" I ask, suddenly not liking the direction of this discussion. He's somehow weaseled his way into my barn, building another structure on my land, and letting himself into my house. And none of that compares to what he's doing to my heart.

"I'm not taking over your home, Bee, and you know it. I'm living in your barn." His tone turns condescending as if he's ashamed of his position. "And I'm improving land that's been neglected and needs a purpose, as do you."

His chest rises and falls in his agitation, and I'm shaken. He lowers his head, shaking it side to side again and then he steps back, reaching for another tool in a bin and returning his attention to the tractor. I move forward, leaning against the side of the oversized tire.

"Speaking of purpose, what's the point of the stuff on my kitchen table?"

Jedd pauses in his clanging of the wrench against the metal but keeps his eyes on his work.

"They're ingredients for soapmaking. You said you were interested in making soap, so I bought you the stuff. Some scented oils are on the way."

Soapmaking. Scented oils. I don't know how to make soap. I said soapmaking as a knee-jerk reaction to his question. He asked me my interest while soap cascaded down his body, and all I wanted was to be those suds.

"I don't really know how to make soap," I admit, not unappreciative of the gesture but concerned because I don't have the skills to be grateful for the gift.

"I figured you could just look it up online."

I don't often use computers, so I haven't mastered that skill either. My child definitely surpassed me in this ability, and while I've always been curious about the secondhand desktop we own, I've never taken the steps to learn more about its benefits.

"You watch a lot of television, right?"

How does he know that?

"I see the blue light on in your room."

Does he watch me through the sheers? Instead of freaking me out, it thrills me to consider.

"You could look it up online almost the same as using your television. Watch a video on Youtube."

It sounds easy enough. I could ask Hannah for help, but I pause with the thought. I *could* ask her to teach me how to search for things on the computer, but I don't want to ask Hannah. Considering his gesture—to find me something I might have an interest in—he provided me with the tools, and I want this *for me*. I want to make soap. If I need assistance, I can ask my librarian sister for help with the internet.

"I can do it," I whisper, but his left side faces me, and he doesn't hear my affirmation. Instead, his hand slips, and the wrench knocks against his knee. He stands but immediately bends at the waist, a litany of swear words stringing together like wash on a laundry line.

"Are you okay?" I ask, trying not to chuckle as I know it isn't funny, but it kind of is in the way he's hobbling around, bent over and cursing.

"No. No, I'm not okay." He stands a little straighter, shaking out his knee with a few more expletives and then adds something I'm not expecting. "And tell me what your issue with Vernon is? What happened with him?"

Whoosh goes the air in my lungs. Jedd stands still again, facing me, and suddenly, I understand his frustration might not be just with the stubborn tractor.

"I…" I don't know how to explain Vernon and our past relationship. "We were friends." My eyes pinch in the brightness of a cloudy fall day.

"Friends?" he scoffs. "Yeah, I'm not believing that one."

"Why? What did Vernon say?"

"Nothing. That's just it. He's very tight-lipped about you, but he's obviously familiar. His boys know Hannah. They mentioned spending time here as kids."

I don't think it's my place to mention how Vernon's wife is a raging alcoholic. Raging in that she tries to smack around her husband who's oversized compared to her, and who beat her boys, who were always taught never to retaliate at a woman. Vernon struggled between smacking her back and holding her off from both him and the boys.

"He's married," I state as if that in and of itself should explain things. Vernon Grady *is* married, but we once confided in one another. Howard had left me. Abigail was an abusive addict. My husband slept with his wife.

"Vernon and I were friends. And then we weren't." It's all I'm going to admit to Jedd. The rest goes to the grave with me.

Jedd shakes his head, not believing me, and then returns to slamming the wrench at the tractor.

"Finally, you bastard," he mutters as some gasket comes free. Working on the tractor reminds me Jedd mentioned making an exchange with Vernon to fix it. My brows pinch. Did he respect my wishes? Did he not make a deal after all? Is that why he's sweating, swearing, and struggling with this old machine on his own?

"If you need Vernon's help, you can ask him," I say, making certain I'm louder than his mutters and the hammering of metal against metal.

"I don't need Vernon," he says, standing abruptly once again and then climbing onto the tractor seat. His back is to me. I'm taking his position as a dismissal, especially when he turns the key and the engine grinds to life. His hand slams on the steering wheel, and then he lifts his fist in victory. He twists in the seat.

"Come for a ride with me." He extends his right hand down to me, wiggling his fingers as his demeanor has shifted in the success of starting the machinery.

"I...I don't think it's safe," I yell over the rumble of the engine.

"Just down the path and back. I'll even let you steer. I'll be the legs. You be the hands. Trust me."

I chuckle at the comment looking down at the cuffs around my arms. I remove my hands from the supports and reach for the tire to help me move forward. I've been working my left leg, pressing it on the floor to rock my rocker, hoping any renewed movement helps restore some muscle tone. I do find it's getting easier to maneuver around than it's been in the past. Tossing the crutches off to the side, out of the path of the tractor, I reach up for Jedd's hand. With a strength that surprises me, he tugs me upward. I awkwardly struggle to shift my left side over his lap as I grip the steering wheel. With his hand on my hip, he guides my lame leg over his thick thighs. A tractor seat doesn't really allow for two people, and he tugs me down to his lap.

His head wiggles over one shoulder and then the other.

"Hold the wheel, honey," he yells, as his hand falls to the shift stick and his foot releases the clutch. I squeal from the jerking motion as the tractor lurches forward, but Jedd's quick footwork steadies us, and we chug forward with me on his lap and my hands gripping the steering wheel for dear life.

CHAPTER SEVENTEEN

[Jedd]

Setting Beverly on my lap might have been one of the most idiotic moves of my life. A tractor is a one-person vehicle so she isn't wrong in that driving with someone else is not the safest, but it's for more than one reason this position isn't secure. Bouncing up and down on me with every rut and groove of the ancient path, I have the hard-on of all hard-ons. The ache in my balls digs deep as she starts out with screams and squeals. When she mellows into laughter, it's worth the struggle. Her laugh is a lyric calling to me like a siren to a sailor.

Beverly is tall-ish, so sitting on my thighs sets her higher than me, and I need to rest my chin on her shoulder in order to look around her and guide us.

"Tell me more about yourself, Jedd Flemming," she hollers over the roar of the engine. My right ear rests near her left, and I hear the vibration of her words.

"What do you want to know?"

"Tell me more about those rodeo buckles."

Unable to help myself, my nose rubs along the length of her neck, and I chuckle in her ear. "So curious."

Beverly laughs again, and I love the sound. I'll answer anything she wants as long as she keeps offering me that sweet trill.

"I had a falling out with my stepfather and went into the military." It really wasn't quite so simple, but it's a start. "I didn't think I'd be in for as long as I was. Once I was hurt and recovered, I didn't have a purpose. No place to call home." I look off in the distance to a house we can't see from here. "Then I learned about PAFRA. Although it had been a few years, my love of horses was still strong, and I was a show-off. I might have won a few awards." I chuckle as my chin rests on her shoulder.

Beverly screeches. "A few? That trunk is full of buckles and medals and ribbons."

"Yeah, well." I dismiss the accolades, almost embarrassed by them, although I've never been embarrassed before to claim my fame.

"What exactly is PARFA?"

"PAFRA," I correct. "Professional Armed Forces Rodeo Association." I pause momentarily, recalling how I found the association. "A few good men designed the organization for veterans with a love of horses and a need for stability. A purpose of sorts to those lost when they returned home, and a place to channel competitive energy." Not to mention the anger of missing body parts or a clouded mind or a wounded heart.

"Were you lost, Jedd?" she asks, her voice softer but still loud enough over the drone of the engine. We hit a bump, and she shifts on my lap, coming down on a part that wants to get lost in her. Instead, I run my fingers up and into her hair like I did last night. I love her hair. We're older, but I don't crave a brunette or a blond, especially as the white tones on her locks look sexy as all get-out. Her hair is also thick, which I wouldn't have guessed from the tight knot she kept at her nape when I first met her. The waves float through my fingers like whitecaps over tan knuckles. She lets me play while I process my thoughts.

"I guess I was. But not all who wander are lost. I had wanderlust. I'd been all over the Western states and Texas, not to mention halfway across the world. I love PAFRA for what it offered me, but I'm ready to settle down. Plant my roots in one spot."

Beverly keeps her gaze forward, but her voice tightens. "What if the wanderlust returns? I'd think a man used to being a nomad wouldn't care to be strapped to one place."

"Depends on who's doing the strapping, honey," I tease. She isn't wrong. I'll always want to visit places and have adventures, but there's nothing wrong with making a sedentary spot an adventure as well. "This right here is what I want." I tug gently at her hair, and her brows pinch, not taking my meaning.

"So serious." I chuckle, running my nose over the shell of her ear. She hitches her shoulder to her chin, knocking me out of my pleasure.

"That tickles." She giggles. That spot is more than ticklish, it's her trigger point, and I recall how she responded to me kissing and nipping her there last night. That shoulder of hers, exposed from the sweater continually falling to the side hints at a pale plum bra, and that's my trigger point. I want to kiss her, right now, and I search the distance for a place to give us some privacy. Not that anyone's around, but I don't think Beverly would take kindly to me ravishing her out in the middle of some field. Then again...no one is around. I nip her neck, and she jumps on my lap with another bump. *Dammit.*

"We're gonna have an accident if you do that while I'm driving," she teases, but her tone turns serious. A driving accident is no joke to her.

We're headed toward the property edge where the climb to the mountain begins. In the vast distance to our left, another home can be seen. It stands lonely and sad, too far away to note if anyone lives inside. I already know the answer. I'd love to stop and stare a moment, the thought reminding me of a Robert Frost poem, but I'm worried this old tractor will stall if we pause, so my kissing her is going to have to wait.

"We need to turn around," I bellow over the engine. Beverly nods and gently adjusts our direction, turning in a wide curve to accommodate the lack of agility of the rusty beast beneath us. As we turn, something catches Beverly's eye, and while the tractor curls back to the path, Beverly's attention remains fixed on something off in the woods marking the edge to her property and the start of the mountain.

"What is it?" I ask, shifting my head behind her and squinting at the trees.

"Nothing," she yells. "Just thought I saw a bear."

"A bear?" I twist in the seat as best I can, keeping my hand on Beverly's hip so she doesn't slip off me. I don't see anything but the thickness of trees. My eyes flash over to the house far off, and my stomach pitches a bit. Then we jut forward in the direction of Beverly's.

"Tell me about you, Bee," I ask, hoping to rid my thoughts of the house off yonder.

"Nothing to tell. I live here. Been here most of my life, other than growing up in Cedar Gap."

"Cedar Gap?" I interrupt. "Never heard of the place."

"You aren't missing much. My parents had a church there. They practiced their own religion of sorts, and believed in hell and damnation for things like drinking, smoking, and cavorting."

"Cavorting?" I laugh.

"Sex," she clarifies. Although I know what she meant, hearing her say that word does things to my belly that only adds to the existing tension of her vibrating on my lap from this ride.

"How'd you end up with Howard, then?" I chuckle without humor, hoping I don't insult her but knowing full well that Howard was nothing short of a sex fiend. A philanderer, my momma called him. Sticking his dick where it don't belong was more like it.

"It's textbook really. It only takes once."

See, sticking his pecker where it didn't deserve to populate.

"Sonofabitch."

"Yeah, well, despite that, I have Hannah." Beverly and Hannah are close in a strange mother-daughter dichotomy of parent-child-best-friends. All seems to be forgiven for what Beverly said weeks ago, but I also notice Hannah isn't around much. My sympathy towards Beverly being a homebody has shifted. She's alone too often. And while I'd already had the firm opinion that Beverly was more resourceful than she let on, it's become more evident in the last week or so with the subtle changes in herself. Her clothes. Her hair. Her confidence.

"Howard is the only man I'd ever been with," she admits, and it's me who then needs to grip the tractor seat in hopes of not falling off.

"That was like twenty years ago," I holler over the engine.

"Seventeen, actually." Her voice is loud but not strong.

"And you never considered letting somebody else in your life?" The question has multiple interpretations, and I hold my breath, wondering which way Beverly will take it.

"Hannah's an only child, not by choice," Beverly states, her voice saddening, and I damn Howard again for not doing his husbandly duty and giving her more babies if she wanted them. My hand has slipped around Beverly's hip and settles on her belly, wondering what the swell of her stomach might have felt like, knowing I'll never experience any such thing as getting someone pregnant and having kids of my own. I'd never considered it a loss until I hold Beverly.

But my question isn't about children. I mean a man.

Is she worried someone else might leave her just as Howard did?

"It didn't seem right," she calls out. "I always thought I'd only ever be with the man I married, and seeing as he ran off with another woman, and then the accident...well...I just figured my life plan was to be alone."

She's got to be kidding. *Who wants to be alone all the time?*

We each stay quiet as we travel the remainder of the way back to the main house. My thoughts run rampant with the desire to pull this beast over and kiss the daylights out of this infuriating woman. Her shoulder keeps escaping her shirt and teasing me with the smooth skin over her clavicle. My mouth waters, and I want to nip at her until she screams my name repeatedly. It's a good thing Hannah came home last night, because if Beverly had given me the green light, I wouldn't have been able to stop myself. I wanted to feel her hidden heat, explore her depths, and dive deep inside the mystery of Beverly Townsen.

Currently, my nut sack aches from need with each squirm of her backside against my zipper region. As we near the barn, I'm ready to toss her off me before I do something ridiculous. She steers us close to the back of the barn, hiding us from the main house, and I let up on the accelerator until we rumble to a stop. Not the smoothest transition, but I can't take the pressure any longer, and then Beverly shifts, angling her body so her side leans into my chest.

"Is this place what you need?" she asks, and I swallow back the deep yes. *I need you, over me, naked and willing.* Then she clarifies. "Is this land the place you want to plant your roots?"

"It's good for me to be here," I tell her honestly. It isn't so much the recovery of the land I thought I deserved, but a solid place to set a foundation, and I'm doing that here on her property.

"Then I'm glad you're here if you think this is the place you need," she admits, and the soft timbre makes my insides warm and gooey, which isn't very manly, but I'm cookie dough to her words. Her eyes cast down at our precarious position. Her thigh must feel the thickness bulging at the seam of my jeans. Her breasts rise and fall as her breathing increases, and her arm crosses her body so her fingers can dig into my tee. "That couldn't have been a comfortable ride for you."

Her voice dips sultry and deep, and I swallow. *What is she doing?* my brain screams, while another part of me hollers for her to drift lower with those hands.

Her breathing becomes more rapid, her breasts heaving. Her shoulder rests against mine as her fingers climb up my shirt. Her hand flattens, skimming over my left pec. Her gaze leaps to my arm, the one I've draped over her leg in her twisted position.

"Did it hurt?" she whispers, and I'm thankful I've tilted my head, so my right ear is closer to her lips.

"I don't quite remember. I was just doing my duty, thinking I was doing a good deed for this town we'd destroyed, and then *bam!* I don't recall exactly what happened, but I must have slipped and just reached for the closest thing, which was a downed wire that happened to still be live. I woke with it gone." I wiggle my prosthetic arm. "It hurt after. I'd have a rush of pain. Phantom limb, the doctors called it. When you have the sensation the rest of the appendage is still there, but it isn't."

Her fingers release my tee and caress over my shoulder down to the socket holding the prosthetic in place over the residual limb. My arm.

She stops.

"It freaks you out, doesn't it?"

Her head twists, coming face to face with me. She's so close I can see the spark in those steel-colored eyes.

"I'm afraid of you," she whispers.

"You are?"

"In some ways."

"What scares you?" She swallows and shakes her head, looking away from my face. I don't want to frighten her, but I need her to look at me. I have to do it. I lift my arm, and the claw comes to her cheek, gently prompting her to gaze back at me. Once she looks at me, it isn't enough to hold her in place. My opposite hand reaches for the back of her neck, and with a gentle squeeze, I tug her to me.

Our mouths meet, and while I want to dive into her, all my strength goes into keeping it slow and soft. Beverly hasn't been kissed in a long time. I want her to forget all the kisses before and only think of mine.

Our mouths move like a slow dance, mine leading hers to taste all she wants of me. She pulls back for a second, and I assume she's done with our experiment, but she surprises me by twisting further at the waist and wrapping the arm wedged into my sternum around my shoulder. Her mouth returns to mine, the vigor and intensity growing.

I growl when her tongue comes forward, and she pulls back with a giggle.

"Am I hurting you?"

In the best of ways, my dick screams. Her additional shift presses me firmly into the side of her thigh. There's no mistaking what she's doing to me, but I'm curious what effect I'm having on her. I tug her back to me with a firm hand slipping into her hair, unleashing my tongue to tangle with hers. She squirms on my lap.

Dammit.

I release her mouth, panting heavily as I press my forehead to hers.

"What is it?" she asks all innocent, and I draw away, trying to read if she really doesn't recognize what she's doing to me. Her expression remains stoic, but her eyes—that spark.

"Don't you be teasing me, you little vixen. Or I'll drop you over my knee so I can spank that fine ass of yours." She gasps, but I'll give her proof of my meaning. I remove her hand from my neck and slide it down my chest, forcing it over the bulge in my pants.

"This, honey. You're doing this to me, and we need to slow down before I have a problem."

Beverly sets her foot on the running board of the tractor, and I'm thinking she's about to hop off me. Instead, she stands, balancing her stronger leg on the narrow strip while using my shoulders for support.

"Help me get my leg over you," she commands, and if my dick wasn't already rock hard, it'd petrify at the demanding tone. I'm so turned on I can't breathe, but I assist her weaker leg over my middle, and she lowers herself to straddle me.

"Is that better?" she mutters, leaning in for my right ear. She knows damn well it's not. At that moment, I curse Howard Townsen for not knowing what he had in this woman and then thank the heavens he was fool enough to leave her. Because if he hadn't deserted her, and if he wasn't gone, she wouldn't be straddling me at this time, on this tractor, riding me behind this barn.

I cup the back of her neck, bringing her mouth back to mine, and she adjusts on me, rolling her hips once to get the full effect of what she's done. She's playing me for a fool, being coy and hesitant as she moves over me, but then again, it's been a long time for her. The claw hitches into her belt loop, and I tug, directing her to rock back and forth.

"I'm the tractor, now," I mumble against her lips, a smile breaking along hers with the cheesy tease.

"This your gear stick?" she retorts, her mouth still over mine.

"I like how your mind works, Bee. You're my kind of naughty."

She giggles against my mouth, and I take her lips again; only this time, I don't need to lead her. She rocks back over me until she can't keep up the dual attention.

"I..." She gasps, pulling back and looking down at how she drags her body to and fro over mine. "I don't know what's happening to me." If she admits next that Howard never brought her to orgasm, I'm going to lose it. I'm already set to burst, and it's going to be a mess as I haven't dry-humped like this since I was a teen.

"I want to touch you," I admit. "I want to run my fingers over you and feel how wet you are."

"So..." Her breath catches again.

"I bet you're sweet, Bee, with honey drips and—" Her mouth crashes mine, tasting my naughty thoughts as her body stills. Her thighs clench outside mine, and her breath hitches against my tongue.

That's it, sweet Bee.

Her hands hold my face as her lips pull back. Her forehead rests on mine, breathing deep until I move her over me. I'm not done with her yet. I'm so close. I just need a little shift, and...

"Momma, you still out here?"

Beverly leans away. Her hands slip to my chest. Her head swivels toward the corner of the barn, which hides us from the house.

Nooooooo, my dick screams.

"I..." Beverly begins, turning back to me. Her head tilts up, and her eyelids flutter like it's the first she's noticed there's a bright sky over us, and the brightness blinds her.

"Bee," I say, but she's already trying to extricate herself from my lap. In her scramble, her foot slips from the running board, and she starts to fall. I reach for her thigh, hoping to adjust her balance, but I see that if I don't let her go, she'll be doing the splits standing upright. It would be comical if it weren't for the panic in her face. I release her leg, and her trajectory drags her downward until her backside hits the ground.

"Bee," I bellow, hiking my leg over the steering wheel and jumping down to her, but she's already scrambling back on her hands, using one foot in the mix.

"I just…" Her head glances over her shoulder, and when she sees her crutches, she twists at the waist and lunges for them, laying herself out flat on her belly.

"Bee, please. Let me help you." I hustle over so I'm standing with my legs steepled over hers, but she's already got the crutches in her hands, and she's scooting to one knee. I bend at the waist, wrapping my arm around her.

"I got it," she mutters, but I hoist her up so she can at least get her feet under her. She weighs next to nothing. Her arms slip into the crutches, and she pulls out of my grasp.

"Bee?" *What just happened?*

She doesn't turn back. She hitches herself forward, moving faster than I've ever seen her move with her crutches. Still, I'm worried she'll stumble on the uneven ground, and I step forward.

"Don't," she throws over her shoulder, and I stop. The sting to her voice returns, and I swipe my hand down my face.

At the corner of the barn, she pauses a second, swipes her hand down the front of her sweater, and dusts off her thighs. She turns her head back to me for only a second, and then she's gone around the corner, leaving me with aching balls and a twisted gut because I could love that woman if she'd only give me a chance.

CHAPTER EIGHTEEN

[Beverly]

What have I done? I admonish as I wash off in the shower, scrubbing away the guilt while at the same time, not wanting to remove the memory.

I can't believe I did that.

For some reason, memories of Howard flood me. Unbeknownst to me, Howard was engaged to another woman when he met me at the diner. A little trailer off the highway, which served greasy hamburgers and cold Coca-Cola reminiscent of the 1950s, wasn't a place one would meet a stable man. Most men were passing through town, traveling the treacherous highway famous to motorcyclists known as the Tail of the Dragon. I'd become good at tossing off the come-ons. I had my own collection of kissing boys back in Cedar Gap, but this one man…he came back to see me again, and I fell fast.

Love at first sight, remember?

Only it wasn't love, and I was pregnant the first time we had sex. Howard wasn't hard to trace. He'd already told me he was from

Green Valley, a dip in the highway on the Tennessee side of the mountain. A farmer, he told me, who owned a profitable estate. *Ha.* When I appeared on his doorstep, the surprise on his face was like a sucker punch to my gut. He stepped out on the decking, asking me what I was doing at his house. How did I find him, and who did I think I was. His daddy stepped out next, wondering about the commotion on his front porch, and I just vomited all the truth.

"Your son is the father of my child."

The last to hear those words was an innocent woman with jet black hair and deep eyes behind thin-rimmed glasses. She stood just inside the screen door until she stepped out and looked up at Howard, puzzled and hurt.

"You promised it wouldn't ever happen again." The statement should have tipped me off to Howard's history. I don't know why I thought I'd be the exception. She pulled the ring from her finger and threw it at him right there on the very porch. It bounced off his chest and landed on the wood flooring while the woman raced down the steps and climbed into a car. Howard followed her, but Ewell bent to pick up the ring. He stared at the gold band with a small stone set in the center.

"My Mary would be so ashamed of him," he muttered, staring at the jewelry. After heated words and Howard chasing her vehicle down the drive a bit, he returned to the front steps.

"Is it yours?" his father barked. I remembered standing straighter, crossing my arms, daring Howard to deny he took my virginity. It might have been the last time I stood up to him.

"What do you want me to do with her?" Howard asked, falling sheepish under his father's glare.

"You'll marry her, or you'll get nothing."

Those were the damning words.

I scrub harder at the memories in my head than the ones on my body. The ones where I sat over Jedd, undulating over the unmistakable thick length in his pants. My center pulses like the phantom limb he mentioned: remembering him, aching for him, wanting to feel him again.

I shouldn't have kissed him back. But his kiss? My lips curl, fingers tracing over them to relive the pressure. His kiss was so sweet at first, tentative and tender. I don't think anyone's ever made me feel so precious, like it was a gift to place my mouth to his.

Then I overheated. My body wanted more of him, and desire took control. I slipped over him, and with his permission, I moved in ways I hadn't in years. The rhythm set against an unfamiliar body was surprising, though we moved as if we'd always been together. Even though I was feeling out of practice, my body knew what to do, what it wanted, and how it wanted it.

And I wanted Jedd. *So much Jedd.*

Soap rinses off my skin, spattering to the shower floor as I grip the handrail inside the tub, the desire almost stealing my breath and knocking me over.

Just as I panicked outside.

When Hannah called my voice, it was like a reality check. Like her headlights the night before when Jedd stood in my room. My mother's voice called out to me from the grave: "

What are you doing?" As if I was sinning. A disgrace. A Jezebel.

I fell in front of Jedd, landing right on my backside. Seeing the shock in his eyes, and hearing the plea in his voice, I couldn't get away from him fast enough. I shouldn't have let myself get carried away. I'd done that with Howard. I'd given him everything—every piece of me—and look what I was left with.

Nothing.

Despite the pressure of Jedd's lips, despite the feel of him under me, despite the desire racing in my heart, I must not give in to him.

He'll leave. *I have wanderlust.*

And I'll be left behind once more.

* * *

I crossed a line when I crossed the yard, and I promised myself I wouldn't do it again, so I simply remain in the house and ignore Jedd for the remainder of the day. But true to his MO, he seeks me out, letting himself into my house in the evening.

"Care to explain what happened out there?" He corners me in my hallway.

"Have you no sense of privacy, personal property, or space in general?" I scold as he pins me to the wall, crowding said space.

"You want space?" Jedd questions, and then immediately responds. "No."

I blink up at him.

"No, I'm not letting you push me away. And you aren't running from me either."

"I can't run," I state, and his eyes narrow at me.

"Beverly," he warns.

"I...I shouldn't have done that." I tip my head in the direction of the yard.

His prosthetic arm rests against the wall near my head while his fingers cup my cheek and then curl into my hair.

He's always touching me, my head laments.

You like his touch, my heart argues.

His knee slips between my thighs.

"What was wrong with what we did? We kissed. You got off on me. There's nothing wrong with that."

"Do you need to be so crass?" But he isn't wrong, and normally, I like his naughty thoughts. But dirty thinking is what got me into the mess with Howard...and into the mess earlier today with Jedd.

They aren't the same men, whispers somewhere through my head, but I don't listen. My hands come to his shoulders, ready to force him back.

"Always ready to push me away, only you really want to pull me forward," he teases, his deep, sleepy voice lowering as his fingers trace around and around my ear. I want to lean into his palm, but I hold still, fighting the will to inhale him. I've memorized his scent. I'll hold it in my memory for years to come when he's long gone.

Just like Howard.

Not like Howard.

Howard smelled like cigarette smoke and cheap perfume and the back seat of cars.

Jedd doesn't smell like that.

Fresh air. Wood shavings. Promises.

"What did we do? I kissed you. You kissed me. Did you not like it?"

My eyes close as his fingers pause. He's leaning into me. The heat of his body radiates near mine. The desire to give in to him rises again.

"You don't need to be afraid of me."

"I'm not afraid," I bite as I lie, and my eyes snap open. I'm deathly afraid of Jedd and the way he makes me feel physically—all twisted up and yearning. Yearning when I don't feel the right to yearn.

Seventeen years.

"Then quit fighting me. Or better yet, let's fight. Let's knock down and drag this out, and wrestle until we're so wrapped up in each other we can't draw another breath."

Sweet butter on biscuits.

"I got out of control." My voice lowers as my thumb stretches for the button on his flannel shirt.

"That was nothing, honey. Out of control is how I feel about you, the things I want to do to you, but there's no rush. I want to understand, and I don't want you running off."

Jedd's eyes drift down to my fidgeting fingers, and he brushes aside my sweater, slipping it off my shoulder. My attention focuses on his face as his finger traces the line of my collarbone. His face lowers, and his nose rubs along my neck. My eyes close again, and for a moment, I forget all my reasons for denying him. My fingers spread and grip his shirt. My legs open wider over his thigh.

"Jedd." I intend to hiss, but his name comes out as a plea, and he wraps his hand around my neck. I know what's next. He'll pull me to him, kiss me again, and I'll want it when I shouldn't.

"I like the feel of your skin against mine."

Melting margerine. My core pulses. My heart gallops.

"Jedd, I can't do this," I mutter, tightening my hold on his shirt, fisting my fingers.

"Yes, you can, honey. Nothing's stopping you but your head," he whispers, only the ruggedness in his voice croaks.

I should tell him the truth, but I swallow against the thickness in my throat. The lump is like a wedge of bread, choking me with honesty.

"Want me to marry you?"

My breath hitches as my knuckles turn white with fistfuls of flannel. "Because of what I said earlier, that I thought I'd only ever be with my husband?"

"Is that what you want?" His voice rings with questioning candor. "I'll make you an honest woman. I'll marry you, Bee."

I inhale him, desperate for sincerity in those words, yet knowing marriage isn't really the reason I'm refusing him. At least, not marriage to him.

His fingers at my nape massage and rub in soothing strokes like calming a scared cat.

"Marry me, Beverly." The full use of my name breaks the spell.

"I can't," I choke on the refusal. My heart breaks at rejecting him.

"Why not?" he teases, thinking this is a game, and I'm just pretending to be coy.

"Because I'm already married," I blurt, and everything stills. Jedd doesn't breathe. His fingers on my neck pause. His chest heaves once and freezes. His eyes search mine in disbelief, at first questioning me as though I'm teasing him and then scowling when he sees I'm not joking. I only wish it were a joke.

"I'm still married to Howard."

CHAPTER NINETEEN

[Jedd]

*I*s *she serious?*

This has to go down as the most awful rejection in the history of rejections. How is she still married? Howard has been gone for twenty years. And how did I not know this about her?

"Wha...?" I can't even form the complete word. What in the ever-loving fuck?

Instead of asking myself the more pertinent question, *where did that marriage proposal come from*, I'm stumbling to comprehend the fact she's still married to that asshat. Slowly, I pull back from her, releasing her hair and disentangling my leg from hers. I press my palm flat on the wall, extending my arm, still caging her in, but no longer touching her...and it hurts. It hurts to think she might still be married, still be loving him, after all this fucking time.

"He disappeared. Left without a word." Her fingers weakly spread and swirl like a magician. The sound of her voice is weak as she tries to jest. But my heart plummets to my stomach and my gut turns over, and I want to wrap her in my arms and kiss the pained expression right off her downturned mouth.

But is it the pain of still wanting a missing man or the discomfort of a failed marriage?

"You aren't divorced." The words choke my airway, and I swallow back the internal struggle of wanting to hitch her over my shoulder and run off to Nashville with her—*fuck Howard*—or just run far away from this situation.

"He couldn't be found. People came to the house looking for him. Debt collectors. A motorcycle man. Someone else's husband. But Howard wasn't in Green Valley, and I had no idea where he'd gone. I only knew he went off with some floozy from the Pink Pony."

The Pink Pony? The place her daughter works? That fucking bastard.

"You never filed divorce for yourself?" I question. Why hasn't she let him go? There are ways around his desertion. *Get a fucking lawyer.* Did I say that out loud?

"A lawyer is expensive, and I didn't know where I'd send papers. We didn't have the funds. Every penny we made, we needed. I didn't want to waste the effort on Howard."

My thoughts buck and jolt, ricocheting in all directions. At some point, she did take the effort to find him, though. "What about the night of the accident? You went after him then."

Beverly exhales, her shoulders sagging. "Vernon told me he'd seen Howard at The Watershed. I didn't think I could face Howard without additional courage and—" I raise a hand to stop her. She's already told me this part. She drank too much and drove.

"Did you intend to ask him for a divorce then?"

Beverly pauses, licking at her lips and my brows pinch, the twinge of a headache beginning.

Did she still want him? What about now?

"You would have taken him back," I mutter, answering my own question.

"I..." She swallows again, her eyes lowering for the hem of her sweater where she clenches at the fabric. "I don't know what I would have done."

It doesn't fit. The strength I know in this woman? She would have kicked his ass to the curb. My eyes roam over her thin frame. Her tongue alone could have cut him to pieces. There's something I'm missing here.

"Are you still in love with him?" My voice rises, the volume enough to make her flinch.

"He was my husband," she hisses.

"He still is," I remind her. My anger growing, I press off the wall, putting more space between us. I'm not mad that she's married. I'm not even mad that she didn't tell me. But how the fuck could she still be in love with him? "Being your husband on paper...as he's clearly not here in presence...means nothing. If he isn't here, hasn't been for twenty years, why else would you hold onto him? Unless you still love him."

I'm flabbergasted at the thought. Why do good women love bad men? My sister loved a person who was rotten to her. Beverly has done the same thing. My mama and Hasting. Maybe this is why I've had so many one-night stands myself. I don't trust women. *Women are the ones who can't be trusted as they love the wrong person unconditionally.*

"If Howard Townsen walked in that door right now and said he wanted to come back, what would you do, Beverly?" The volume of my voice doesn't make her flinch, but I'm loud. Louder than I might have a right to be. If she loves him, I can't change her mind, but dammit, I want her to love me.

See, I'm all over the place with her. Marriage proposal. Wanting her love. *What am I doing?* Like being on the back of a horse that's bucking and kicking, trying to shake me, I stick. I take the licks and the beating because I'm holding tight to her when she doesn't want me.

"I'd..." Her shoulders stiffen, but I can't hear her answer. I can't listen to her tell me she loves him. I raise a hand to stop her waste of words. She'd stick to him. She'd return to him. She'd allow him back with his pretty promises and his foolish actions.

Stay away from my sister. I'd cursed him on the very porch attached to this house.

Whatcha gonna do about it?

I'd tell his wife about his infidelities. The ones everyone knew he had.

My wife will never believe you. Besides, she always takes me back.

The thought hits me hard, like my ass meeting dirt after I've lost the wrangle with a horse under me.

"I came to tell you I'm heading to Nashville for a few days. I have some horses to look at, maybe pick one up." This fight still makes adrenaline course through me, but I was done with the subject of Howard. I need to get out of here for a bit.

Beverly stares up at me, her eyes wide and worried. What does she need to worry about? I'm just the horse man, living in her fucking barn, trying to build something on her withering land.

Forget that I can't stop touching her.

Forget that I like to spend time with her.

Forget that I've fallen head over backside for her.

"I'll be back in a few days," I tell her although I'm not certain why I'm telling her. I have an appointment to view horses, and I was hoping to convince Beverly to come with me. I was hoping to take her away from here for a few days and get her out of this godforsaken house for a little bit, but I see there might be a reason she's never left it.

Say something, I want to yell. Explain why you stayed with him. Explain why you aren't divorced yet. But I don't scream, even though my insides eat at me. I take a second glance at her eyes, and my heart begs: *Tell me you want to run away with me.*

But I don't ask her because I already know she won't leave. She hasn't yet. She's been sitting here waiting...*but for what?*

* * *

Grady's Seed and Soil is my first stop even though it's out of the way of Nashville.

"Why the fuck didn't you tell me?" I yell at my best friend, who blinks back at me as he bounces back in his rolling office chair.

"Good afternoon to you, too, Jedd," Vernon says to me. He smirks as he tilts backward, hitching his hands behind his head. "Nice to see you."

"Don't you 'good afternoon' me. How could you not mention Beverly is still married to Howard?" Vernon tips in his seat, reaching for his desk to prevent him from falling off the chair while at the same time his feet hit the floor for stability.

"What the fuck?"

"My sentiments exactly," I reiterate. I swipe a hand down my face and glare at my old friend.

"I had no idea," he states, trying to reassure me as he sits forward and rests his elbows on his thighs.

"How could you not know?" I glare at him as if he holds all the answers.

"I just assumed they were divorced. He left her." Vernon's eyes avoid mine, drifting to the stack of mayhem on his desk. His office is a mess, with receipts littering his desk and file folders askew in a desktop file organizer. His computer is on but flips to the sleep mode, and a tractor slowly crosses the screen with his logo.

"Vernon, did something happen between the two of you?"

His dark, tired eyes turn to mine, and he sighs. "Beverly and I were friends, but I didn't know all the personal stuff about her."

"That's not what I'm asking, Vernon." I pause, narrowing my eyes at him. He hasn't had it easy over the years, sticking with a drunk woman who's abusive in both action and words. "Tell me Vernon's personal stuff. Who was Beverly to you?"

"We were just friends," Vernon repeats, sitting upright and forcing his thick hand into his even thicker hair. He holds the cluster back as though he could manbun it, and I'll throat punch him if he does. *Manbun?* Who came up with that?

"Friends shmemes, Vernon."

His bushy brow hitches, wrinkling exposed his forehead as he continues to hold back his hair. "What are you, five?"

I'm going to act fifteen and go all adolescent crazy on this man if he doesn't share something with me.

"We were just…two lonely adults."

"Did you sleep with her?" My heart falls to the floor, spilling out of me like an oil leak.

"No, man. I'm married. I would never do that to Abi."

"But?" I pause, not suggesting he should have slept with Bee despite his marriage, but there's still something missing.

"Look, she used to come into the store with Ewell, Howard's father. They were tight, and when Howard left Beverly after Ewell died, she came in more often. Working that farm alone with a small girl wasn't easy. The boys liked being over there. There wasn't any screaming at them when boys were boys, running, wrestling and making a ruckus."

He releases his hair and leans his body forward, returning his elbows to his knees and clasping his hands.

"I didn't mean for it to happen."

My breath catches, the air intake stopping my lungs.

"What did you do?"

"One little kiss, man. One innocent, I-forgot-who-I-was kiss."

"Then what?" I demand because there's still something more.

"She felt guilty, and I felt guilty. That's all that happened. When I'd heard Howard was back, I'd told Beverly. I never thought she'd…I didn't ever think she'd…" *Drink and drive.* Vernon scrubs at his face with two hands and then forces them away like he's shaking them dry.

"I'm sorry, man," I mutter.

"Me, too. So very sorry."

And I know he is.

CHAPTER TWENTY

[Beverly]

W hy?
The question haunts me over the next few days.

Why am I still married to Howard?

The simple answer was because of the cost of divorce and the inconvenience of chasing a man who didn't want to be chased. When I was first home after the accident, I watched a ridiculous amount of daytime television and nothing scared me more than divorce court programs. The arguments. The accusations. I shiver with the recollection, but now...I'm wondering why I've let all this time pass without pursuing it. I might lose this farm. I might lose my home. But cutting the final hold Howard has on me is something I can afford to give up, especially if I want wishes of a healthy, happy home like Tripper Hanes states to close each *Nailed* episode.

Ironically, it was during an episode of late-night *Rehab Dad* that spurred the thought to pursue my rights.

"We never know what we'll find when we tear into an old wall.

Sometimes, we have setbacks like a leaking pipe or an insect infestation. But other times, there's a reward, like this." The camera zoomed in on a hidden fireplace, sealed over with plaster wallboards. I could see the potential beauty in it once it was cleaned up and restored.

Potential. Clean. Restore.

All I want is to know I tried.

When Naomi comes to visit on Wednesday, I startle her with my announcement.

"I need you to drive me to an attorney's office."

My sister's eyes, so similar to mine, although more trusting than suspicious, stare at me.

"Which attorney?" she questions after a long pause during which she watched me hunt for my jacket, check my appearance one more time in the mirror, and reach for a manila file folder containing one sheet of paper—my marriage license.

"Julius & Caesar is the name."

Naomi snorts, and I double-check I have a house key, cell phone, and wallet. I'm not a purse person, so I tuck these items into the various pockets of an old barn coat, which is two sizes too big for me.

"You realize there's irony in a name like that for an attorney's office."

I stare back at my sister. I don't have time for her library humor today. Though, on second thought, I'll need it once we return.

"Can you drive me or not?" I ask, falling into the familiar rhythm of snapping out interrogatives. I take a deep breath and mutter an apology under my breath. Naomi blinks, her head flicking back as if I've startled her.

"You okay, Bev?"

"No. I want a divorce," I admit, and Naomi blinks again. Slowly, her face cracks. The grin grows at the corner until finally, a full-wattage, wide-mouthed smile graces her face.

"I'm so proud of you," she says, and tears threaten my eyes. *I won't cry*, I tell myself. No more tears for Howard.

"I just want to be free." *Let love in.* The thought whispers through me, and I recall telling my sister the same words. I want to be free to love again. To love Jedd. I want to say yes if he ever decides to ask me to marry him in earnest, not while flirting up against a wall. But I can't worry about that yet. First, I need this step.

* * *

I'm nervous being at the law offices of Julius & Caesar. Naomi wasn't wrong in suggesting there's an irony to their name, but the irony isn't in their title. With a limited number of attorney offices in Green Valley, I found Janice Julius's name in a pile of papers left behind by Ewell. Her office is in Merryville, and I thought I'd feel more comfortable speaking to a woman about my situation until I see who the woman is.

A beautiful brunette with raven black hair, despite her over forty appearance, and brilliant blue eyes greets us as we sit in the cramped lobby to their offices.

"Hello, I'm Janice Julius." I stare at her, not accepting her offered hand as déjà vu arrests me in my seat. Janice looks at my sister, whose eyes are boring into the side of my face, but I can't look away from the woman.

"You need an injury law attorney?" The thick Hispanic accent of a man in his mid-thirties interrupts my stare down.

"What?" I choke on the question. He points with a dragging finger up and down my leg.

"You need. An injury. Attorney?"

My brows pinch, and Janice turns to the man. "She isn't hard of hearing. She's here for a divorce."

The demeanor of the man shifts as he brushes a hand down his tie. He clears his throat, placing a fist over his lips, and then reaches forward to introduce himself with a handshake.

"Ramirez Caesar, at your service. Number one divorce attorney in Merryville." His voice is miraculously clear of his accent.

"I'm pretty certain you're the only divorce attorney in

Merryville." Janice shakes her head at her partner, and I realize I haven't shaken either hand offered to me. I slowly stand, not liking my position of being lower than either of them as I greet them.

"I'm Beverly Townsen." My eyes narrow in on Janice, but she evidently does not remember me. However, I'll never forget the shocked hurt of her pretty face as she looked out a screen door—now on my porch—and questioned Howard.

You promised it would never happen again.

Howard one-upped that promise. He impregnated the girl.

The reality of who I am was slow to dawn on her professionally polished face. Horn-rimmed glasses that would look nerdish on some looked stylish on her. Bright red lips. A crisp navy-blue suit. She was everything I was not, and Howard gave her up for me.

He didn't have a choice.

"I think I've made a mistake," I say, placing a hand on my belly, willing myself not to vomit in the tight confines of this room.

"You don't want a divorce?" Ramirez Caesar asks.

"She wants a divorce," Naomi speaks up for me.

"I don't think you should represent me," I blurt, looking at the beautiful woman before me. I hate how threatened I feel by her presence even though she did nothing wrong to me. I wronged her, and she's standing here as if nothing ever happened. I repeat my name with emphasis. "I'm Beverly *Townsen.*"

"I know who you are," she says patiently although her brows pinch for a fraction of a second.

"Oh, you know one another. This is good. Good, good," Mr. Caesar states. "But I'm still the divorce attorney in this office." He turns a pinched smile on his partner and turns back to me. "If you'd like to follow me." He waves a hand and steps back for me to lead the way to his office.

Naomi follows me down the short, narrow hall, and Ramirez calls out, "First door."

We enter another small room with an oversized desk with piles of folders on the floor. Mr. Caesar steps over them and collapses into his seat. He swipes a hand through his jet black hair and smiles at me as he folds his hands on the desk, equally cluttered with pens, papers, and more file folders.

"So whose ass do we want to dump?" he begins, and Naomi snorts.

* * *

On the return drive to my home, I mentally review all I've learned after I filled in Naomi on the particulars of my history with Janice Julius. The woman engaged to Howard. Eventually, Ewell's attorney. I don't know the story of how the two connect, but it doesn't matter.

My divorce is considered a fault-based divorce in the state of Tennessee, which is proven by Howard's voluntary desertion of Hannah and myself.

"We need to give public notice in the local paper. *The Valley Chronicle* will suffice, and maybe another notice in Knoxville. In general, it states your claim to divorce," Ram explained, telling me that twenty years of absent Howard should be enough evidence to prove abandonment, but the legality of a formal announcement shows due diligence on my part to officially divorce. I bite my tongue at having to show good faith toward Howard for anything. However, I want everything legal and binding to officially remove Howard from my life. The whole process could take months, but hopefully less if Howard doesn't respond within the court-appointed posting schedule.

The question of property and assets was mentioned but quickly dismissed to be discussed later. I'm assuming Howard and I would split the sale of the land unless I wish to buy him out, which I can't afford. Jedd comes to mind. Maybe I should sell it to him. He's already built a stable and gone to Nashville to purchase horses. The land is more his in spirit in less than two months than it has been mine in decades. I'd be sad to part with my home, but it's time. It's time to move forward, as Naomi reminds me.

"Speaking of time," I begin, swallowing back the next big decision. "I was wondering if you could teach me how to search for something on the computer."

Naomi's head swivels as she drives, but she quickly returns her attention to the road. However, I don't miss the look of shock on her face.

"What do you need help with?"

"I'd like to learn how to make soap."

"Soap?" Naomi questions.

"Yes, soap."

"Soap," she repeats.

"Soap," I state, finding this conversation strangely reminiscent of the one with Jedd when I first mentioned the interest. I have no idea if it really will interest me, but I don't want to dismiss his efforts to help me find something other than Hannah's assigned hobbies.

"Jedd. He...uh...he thought I'd like to learn to make soap, and he bought me the ingredients. He also ordered some essential oils to fragrance the bars, and I'd like to try..." My voice fades. It sounds silly, right? But Naomi smiles, her hands gripping the wheel at a perfect ten and two while she drives.

"Bev, I can teach you how to make soap. I do it all the time."

"You do?" I ask, never having recalled this about my sister. It makes sense that my tree-hugging, book-loving, sews-her-own-clothes sister could also make soap, but as snarky as I sound about my sister's interest, I give her credit for knowing who she is and living by it. I swallow back the difficulty in asking the next question.

"Naomi, could you teach me how to make soap?"

My sister's lip trembles, and she rolls them inward, fighting off some emotion.

"Beverly, there's nothing I'd like more than to teach you how to make soap."

CHAPTER TWENTY-ONE

[Jedd]

It's late when I return to the farm. I should tell Beverly I've returned. Maybe warn is a better word. I was able to get out of my head for a few days, reveling in the thrill of horse purchasing and traveling back to Green Valley with a sense of pride. I owned these horses, my heart pinching only once or twice in memory of the one I last rode.

Damn activists. You want to stand up for a cause, be educated about it.

I dismiss the thoughts of my final buck ride as I drive the horse trailer over the bumpy gravel leading to the new stable. With the help of others, the new building holds stalls from recycled materials. I'd been over to Hasting's on a couple of occasions, never finding Boone present or any evidence he'd been back until my most recent visit. Something struck me as off. I couldn't place my finger on it, but my mind kept drifting back to the kitchen. What was different? What stood out of place?

My mind wondered as I groomed the horses after getting them out of the trailer. Chattering softly to them, I ask them if they liked their new home. The soothing strokes of brushing their flanks, fetching fresh water, feeding them oats and hay, and a final check for the first night gave me untold satisfaction.

Still, something niggled at my brain when I finally rolled myself onto the cot in the darkness after midnight. I'd taken a quick soap-and-rinse shower, which was shockingly frigid in the cold air of the barn. Mid-November was turning down the thermostat, and I didn't know how much longer I could handle sleeping in the drafty, anti-quated structure. I'd built up my room good and solid, but I'd need a little wood stove or something to stay warm, and the thought of adding the necessary chimney stack and flue was just one more thing on my growing list of things to be done.

My mind skittered all over when I first hit the pillow, but my body was tired from another day of hard work. It seemed like a dream to go out on my own. Find land. Purchase horses. Raise them right. But there was a moment on the ride home and more than once while I was strug-gling to get the darn Quarter Horses out of the trailer when I wished I'd had another set of hands. I'd come to terms with the hands I have, and I manage just fine, but I'd been thinking in a more metaphorical sense, like a partner in my pursuit of happiness, and not just the financial sort.

I'd decided this was the reason I'd asked Beverly to marry me—a rash and hasty, spur-of-the-moment suggestion which turned into THE question—and she'd turned me down, with good reason.

She was still in love with her husband. Her missing, deserting, disloyal husband.

I don't understand that kind of love. That selfless, never-ending kind Beverly must hold for a man who clearly did her wrong. My momma was like that with Hasting. Whether I like the idea or not, I'd have to get over myself. Going after a woman whose heart belonged to another, especially one whose heart remained with an absent husband, was not my kind of quest. She rejected the notion of marrying me, plain and simple, and it stung.

However, my dreams were filled of Beverly—so much for the pep talk to let her go—and when a gentle tickle traveled up my arm and my name was whispered, I thought my brain was playing a trick on me.

"Bee?" I hissed, when my eyes flipped open startled at her presence leaning over the cot. "What's wrong?" Like a jack-in-the-box springing upward, I sit up, which startles her, and she stumbles backward. On reflex, I reach for the back of her neck, which almost topples her onto me. Scanning her body for harm, I find her dressed in an extra-large Irish-knit cardigan and what looks like a long slip plus cowboy boots.

"I...I..." She seems to swallow, words escaping her as she stands in the darkness of the cold barn, and it is dark. Too dark. I can only make out the outline of her body, and I want to see more.

"You shouldn't be wandering around outside this late." I have no doubt Beverly can take care of herself, and she's never suggested she was afraid of being out here in the middle of so many acres without a neighbor. Still, that niggling feeling about the old house raises my hackles when I think of Beverly traipsing around on her property after midnight.

"I wanted to make sure you were back okay. Wanted to know if you needed anything."

Needed anything? In the middle of the night? My brows pinch, but she can't see me in the pitch black. My hand slips from her neck to stroke up and down her sweater covered arm.

"I'm okay, Beverly." The words hang in the air, lingering with more but left unsaid.

Are you okay? Are you really still in love with him?

"Okay, well, then..." She pulls back, but I lean forward, following her retreat.

"Whatcha need, honey?" I ask, my voice dropping. Her face lowers toward the bed. Without an answer, I flip open the sleeping bag, which isn't zipped. I'm only dressed in my skivvies and a T-shirt, preferring to sleep with the blanket she made me against my skin, which prickles with the possibility of Beverly climbing on this cot. It's going to be a tight fit, and that's just what I want.

She doesn't speak as she spins herself, removes her arms from the cuffs of her crutches, and lowers toward the taunt mattress. She sits a second, and I'm thinking she'll change her mind. I lower myself to my side and rub my hand up her back, again feeling the intricate pattern of the wool sweater over her. She shifts to straighten her spine. *If she's rejecting me, what's she doing out here?* But I remain patient, silent.

Beverly slips her shoulders from the sweater and tugs the material forward. Underneath, she wears something silky that exposes her shoulders and is fitted to her breasts. Then she shifts to her hip and lowers to her side, settling herself in the narrowness between the piping-edge of the cot and my front.

"Is this okay?" she states, not looking at me but facing out at the black shadows of my room. Her voice is low but loud enough, as she knows I can't hear her if she whispers.

"It's all good," I murmur, slipping my arm around her waist. My nose rubs at the edge of her short hair. The satiny material is cool under my palm, but her skin is warm at my nose.

"The other day…" she begins. "I want to explain."

"No need to say anything." It was my fault. I took it too far.

"I'm sorry about Howard," she continues.

"Me too, honey."

"I don't love him," she says, and I freeze, my position a permanent hold on her. "It isn't that I don't want to remarry."

I notice she doesn't say *you*—she just doesn't want to marry period—and I'm ready to retort that I wasn't really asking, slip of the tongue and all that, but her hand moves, and she swipes at her cheek. I press my nose deeper into her nape.

Don't cry over him. "What did he do to you, Beverly?"

"He wasn't nice," she says, her voice meek mixed with a silent sob. I tighten my arm around her. With a heavy, choking sound, she adds. "And I filed for divorce."

"Bee, don't do anything you don't want to do." *What are you doing?* my heart screams, and my dick echoes with growing enthusiasm as the thinness of Beverly's nightgown isn't much of a match for the cotton of my boxer briefs. "I'm not mad that you're still married or that you didn't tell me. I just don't understand if you still love him."

"I don't love him," she repeats. "And the divorce is long overdue." Her fingers hesitantly rub the hairs of my forearm. The tender, light touch feels nice and reminds me of when I was young. My mother would tickle over my arm when I was a restless boy refusing to take a nap, and I'd be asleep in no time. My lids fall heavy with the weight of the past few days, but I don't want to sleep yet.

"Howard was my first. I was raised thinking he'd be the only one, and I settled for that notion. I thought this was how it was supposed to be. He never struck me, but he was so mean. I know it could have been worse, but some days…it was so hard. Nothing I did pleased him. He ignored everything I said. And then in the bedroom…" Her words drift.

"He was a fool." My nose rubs back and forth at the fine hairs on her neck.

"I felt so dirty. He was with so many others." Her voice chokes, and I tug her tighter.

"Shhh, honey. It doesn't matter now. He's gone. Long gone." *And good riddance.*

"I never thought I'd be in a position where it mattered."

"Where what mattered?" I inhale the hope in my chest.

"Where it mattered that I was married. Where I'd find someone else and being married would be in the way."

"Beverly, what are you saying? Are you thinking I might be that someone?"

"Now, don't be getting a big head, Jedd," she admonishes, no bite in her wet voice as she struggles between tears and a laugh.

"If I had a big head, it wouldn't fit in this bed," I tease. Although there is another head attached, and *it* is getting bigger.

"This is hardly a bed," she retorts. She isn't wrong. It's stiff and tight, and I'd sleep on it every night if it meant she'd rest this close to me. We remain silent a minute, and my lids lower, breathing her in. *Sunshine and honey*. She's also heat, and I grow sleepy and comfortable.

"I'm glad you're back," she says, and I'm surprised I've heard her with her voice so quiet. Snuggling her into my chest, I tell her the truth.

"I'm not going anywhere, Bee."

I wake with a jolt, dreaming once again of Beverly. This time she's riding a horse, racing off for the woods, and somehow, I know it's dangerous. Despite the danger, she looks beautiful. She's dressed in something silky and body clinging, and her sweater slips off her shoulder as it often does. Her head turns so she sees me over her shoulder, and her short hair whips in the wind. She smiles back, laughter ready to escape, and then *bam!* I'm awake and can't quite pinpoint what happens to her in my dream, but I tug her closer to me, thankful she's still on the cot.

Her hand rests on my forearm, squeezing to signify she's awake as well.

"Good mornin'," I mutter into her neck, damp from sleep. It's warm with the two of us under cover of the blanket she made and the subzero-thermal of the sleeping bag, not to mention our bodies spooning together with my knees behind hers and my arm over her waist.

"Morning," she croaks, her voice sleep-rough and adorable. "It's early." She isn't wrong, although how she knows the time is beyond me. My phone is face down on the crate/nightstand, and my alarm hasn't gone off yet.

"I need to get up," I warn, using the excuse for more than one reason. I have an issue pressing long and swollen into her backside, and while I'd love nothing more than to relieve myself deep inside her, I don't know where we stand yet. In addition, I need to feed the horses and start a daily routine of water, feed, and exercise for them.

"My side is asleep." She giggles, and I think she's teasing me that she doesn't want to move until I realize she's on her left side.

"Okay, I'll roll you toward me and then climb over you." Beverly's breath catches, and I realize what I've said, which doesn't help my stiff and achy cause. My other struggle is, I'm on my left side as well, and I can't just perch myself upward with only the stump of my arm and make it over Bee without dragging my body over hers, which has all kinds of danger signs blaring at me. Her satiny nightgown has risen up her thighs in the night, and my cotton boxers aren't enough of a barrier to prevent me from brushing where I want to brush.

I reach for Bee's hip and gently rotate her so that she rolls to her back. Only on the tight confines of the cot, her hip knocks right over my erection. I groan as she lands on her back with my dick projecting into her hip bone. Her eyes lock on mine. I want to kiss her so badly I can taste her lips, but I promised myself I wouldn't do anything she doesn't want. But I want her; there's no denying that.

Reaching over her, I grip the edge of the cot for leverage to hoist myself up, except the leg I intend to hike over hers, slips between her thighs, and I crush Beverly.

"I'm so sorry," I say, pulling back in horror while the weight of my lower body rests on her. I quickly press up on one arm, balancing only as high as I can with my left limb. The pressure wedges me against Beverly, and her eyes close. She swallows, and my nose lowers for her neck, running the tip over the dip in her throat.

"That tickles." She giggles, and I pull back, looking down at her once again.

"A man would be spoiled, waking to that sound every morning."

Her eyes latch back on mine. "What sound?" she questions, her voice still the smoky morning gruff, and my lower appendage jolts against her. I fight back the groan.

"Your laughter in my bed."

"Jedd," she mutters, and I sense her hand fist near her hip.

"I'm getting up," I mumble before I do something stupid like kiss her, which is only going to lead to making love to her.

"I thought you already were," she retorts, and I still. My mouth pops open.

"You're teasing me, aren't you?" I nudge her with the tip, wanting entrance to her, which is warm between her thighs. "You know I like a sense of humor."

"I thought you liked dirty words."

"Ah, she's catching on," I flirt, rubbing my nose against hers, jutting forward once again until she purrs at my ear.

"Jedd," she whispers, breathless and sweet, and I repeat the motion. Her hand slips over my shoulder, fingers tickling the nape of my neck, and her hips press upward. Is she doing what I think?

"Bee," I warn in a voice rough with sleep and restrain. "A man can only take so much. Don't be teasing me." I curl at the pelvis, poking back at her core, which is heating my tip.

"I… I don't think I'm teasing." Her fingers tighten on my neck, and her foot slips over my ankle, running up over my calf to my knee. Fuck, this is where I need two hands—one to balance myself and the other to lift that leg higher, hitching it over my hip.

"Wrap around me," my voice commands and her eyes pop open. In the dim darkness, the steel color sparkles like freshly polished silver. Her leg climbs higher, looping over my hip. "Good girl."

I rock over her, tapping against her as her lids lower once again.

"Look at me. See that it's me." I want no risk of her fantasizing about Howard or any other man.

"You're the only man I see, Jedd." Her other hand comes to my cheek as her hips thrust upward, and she groans. "It's not enough."

She means the friction, so I quickly shift to my side and slip my hands over her belly. Hastily, I tug the silky material upward, exposing her center.

"You're missing panties, honey."

"I don't sleep with them."

Fucking dripping butter. My fingers slide lower and slip into her. Her back arches, and her thighs clench. My thick digit does the work another part of me wants, but I'll give her what she needs first. She wiggles and writhes against me, and I slide another digit into her.

She's tight and tender, unloved but not by me. I love this woman, and I'll do what I can to set her free of doubt.

"That's it, honey. Ride my fingers." She rocks and moans.

"So crass," she mutters.

"I can be a lot crasser, but let's just enjoy this for the morning." Because once I finish this, I'll definitely be visiting her again this afternoon, and maybe this evening too.

"Jedd," she whimpers, and her eyes pop open. Fear and frustration, uncertainty and unpreparedness. "I...it's never been...I can't..." And then she curls upward, her head coming off the bed, and she bites her lip and clamps her knees together.

"Sugar sweet and dripping," I mutter to her ear as she bucks and jolts, purring as she releases what she's been holding onto for too long. She falls back and rolls her head to me. Her hand comes to my belly, stretching lower, and I quickly withdrawal my finger from her to still her hand. She freezes.

"You don't want this?" She struggles a bit under my grip, attempting to wrestle her hand free.

"I want nothing more, but this is going to lead someplace I don't think you're ready yet."

"Ready?" she admonishes, her voice rising. "I've been ready for twenty years. Maybe even longer. That was...I've never..." She sits up, pushing forward, and I release her hand as I join her in a seated position; only the unequal distribution of weight pitches the cot upward. I fall back to right the rising bed, and Beverly crashes against my chest.

"Not like this, Bee. Not in a cold barn where there isn't enough space for us to move because move I will. Up and down that body. Over every curve and curl. I want to explore and discover and drive deep, but not at the risk of this wobbly cot flipping."

Beverly breathes hard, her barely contained breasts heaving and brushing against my side.

"Okay, Jedd," she says, pushing herself upward, and there's another thing a man could get used to—the sight of her over me.

"I want to make love to you. Soon," I tell her, or perhaps it's a warning. *Be ready for me.* Her eyes flicker, and she bites her lip. I smack her backside, and she yelps. "But I have horses to feed." And I need to get out of this bed before I do risk the wobbly legs, the instability of this cot, and the temptation of giving my soul to this woman.

CHAPTER TWENTY-TWO

[Beverly]

By midmorning, I haven't seen Jedd yet and I'm growing anxious, which I shouldn't be. My face heats at how I let him touch me this morning, taking care of me without asking for anything in return. A conflict arises in my heart. What will he eventually want from me? Then I remember how he told me he wants to make love, just not on that cot.

My entire body heats with thought, and I'm grateful for the cooler temperature as I step outside. Making love. *What would that be like?* Howard was more of a sprinter, wanting the race over. After several times of dissatisfaction with him myself, I wanted the dash to be done as well.

"Is there coffee in that thermos for me? If so, you're an angel," Jedd calls out to me as he meets me outside the stable. I smile, looking down at the container clutched between my fingers wrapped around the hand support.

"And if it's filled with something else, what am I?" I smirk.

"Still as pretty as this morning," he replies, and the air swooshes out of me.

"You haven't had breakfast, have you?" I pause, looking around him into the stables.

"You worried about me, Bee?"

I am, so I straighten, preparing to tell him something. Inhaling deeply, I decide to plow ahead. The worst he can do is say no, which might crush me, but I still need to speak.

"I think you should stay in the house."

"You asking me to move in with you?" he sasses, a brow hitching.

Am I? "I ... well...seeing as you let yourself into my home often enough without permission..." I joke, trying to lessen the awkwardness I feel and the possibility of him rejecting the idea.

"I'm teasing, Bee. What exactly are you suggesting?" He's stepped up to me. I miss the heat of him. The way he felt wrapped around me last night. How he nuzzled his nose into my neck. The feel of his fingers buried deep inside me this morning.

Sweet butter on a biscuit.

Jedd gives me a knowing look as I rouse myself from the memories. "It's so cold in that old barn, and we have so many rooms. I'm on the first floor, but I could trade with Hannah if she isn't comfortable with you upstairs." Is this a bad idea? Maybe I shouldn't ask? He's going to say no.

"I don't want to inconvenience anyone," Jedd says, although he's fighting a smile on those damn lips.

"I wouldn't ask if—"

He holds up a hand and finishes for me, "If it was an inconvenience."

He chuckles, and I smile, but I'm holding my breath.

"I'd love to move in with you, honey."

And before I can object that that's not exactly what I asked, he kisses me.

* * *

"Does it hurt them? To be ridden like that?" I followed Jedd into the stable, peppering him with questions as he explains the particulars of a bucking bronco. It sounds dangerous, and I don't know how he did it one-armed. No wonder he was a star. The women must have gone crazy for him. A warrior. A cowboy. And still so physically fit. I'd felt that strength when I sat on his lap while we were riding the tractor the other day, but even more so, I felt it last night as he surrounded me. His strong arm over me was a comfort I'd never known.

"It doesn't hurt," he states, pulling me from my memories of last night, curled into him, his broad chest at my back. "Some animal activists get all up in arms, but it doesn't make any sense for a bronc rider to hurt the horse. It's a game of wills, not destruction. The thrill of trying to tame something untamable." Jedd's eyes focus on the side of my head, but I don't look over at him as I stroke the white patch on the nose of his new Quarter Horse, Lucky One. He's three years old, and a horse trainer tried to get him to race. He's a worker, not a racer, though. He refused to follow rules, and the supplier thought he'd make a better rodeo horse. A little kindred spirit speaks to me with this one; there is mischief in his eyes as though he's daring me to ride him. With my condition, I don't think so.

"You know horses can be very therapeutic," Jedd states as if reading my thoughts. "Even the bucking ones can help a guy out." Jedd reaches over to touch Lucky One, and the horse whinnies and nips, causing Jedd to retract his fingers as he hopes to keep the remaining ones he has.

"You little..." He pauses before cursing at his new steed. "That ornery spirit will make you a winner," he teases the beast. Lucky One has turned his head back to me, and I hesitate as I hold up my hand, the palm forward for him to inhale my scent again before I reach for his patch.

"Dammit, I think he has a soft spot for you, Bee. You seem to have that effect."

"I think ornery just recognizes ornery." I laugh.

Jedd huffs in agreement. "Horses are smart. He senses something in you, but don't you be softening him up. I need him tough."

Maybe that's what the horse senses—a tough spirit that doesn't want to be tied down. I've been down too long. It's time to buck up, as the saying goes.

"Did you own a horse? The one you bucked. Is that the right terminology?" It sounds dirty, and my eyes meet Jedd's with a sly smile. I like how we think alike, even if I won't admit my thoughts. But Jedd isn't smiling in return. He's been leaning on his left shoulder against the stall as we talk. He slides his body so his back supports him on the wall. Looking across the center aisle, he wrestles with a memory before speaking.

"I didn't own him. You get what you get and whoever stays on the longest wins. But a bucking horse has a flank belt strapped to him, like I told you. It doesn't hurt. In fact, if it did, a horse actually won't buck because of the pain. They'd stand still with fear of moving. Some damn activists, as I mentioned, can get their nose in a snit. They hadn't been able to prove PAFRA was hurting any animals, so they went after individuals, stating our spurs weren't meeting standards. All cowboys have spurs on their boots, but when broncing or riding they should be dull, so again, no harm will come to the horses. The spurs are even inspected. A particular...shall we say person...went after me. Had it out for me, I guess, and made a claim I'd harmed a horse by my spurs. I would never, ever do such a thing," Jedd states with heartfelt sincerity. He rolls back to perch on his shoulder and reaches up to the beast to prove his tenderness, only Lucky One snaps at him again.

"Dammit." He chuckles without humor. "Anyway, the evidence proved otherwise. In fact, the evidence proved more damage than any spur could have done to an animal. The horse died. The rodeo blamed me." His sadness fills the entire stable. "They didn't revoke all my titles, but they stripped me of the ones I'd earned last season. PAFRA did what they could to go easy on me, but they didn't want the trouble. I don't fault them. I fault—" He stops short, and I turn my head to him.

"Who?"

"It doesn't matter." He squints at my hand stroking down Lucky One's nose. "What's done is done. PAFRA couldn't take me back. I hung out a bit, working where I could, mostly helping out with animal care and giving advice on broncing. That's when I got the idea to just hang up my boots and assist others in learning the challenge." He smiles with pride. "I'd really like to help veterans once I get up and running a little better."

The thought of more people around the farm worries me, but then again, if they are all like Jedd—even-tempered, tender—and trying to do good for others, a few more bodies might not be a bad thing.

"Can I ask you something?" And I hold my breath, waiting out Jedd's answer.

"Shoot."

"Why here? Why my farm? I know you mentioned you were from these parts, but you never said where specifically."

Jedd rotates to his back again and tips his head against the stall. This makes the ball cap he's wearing tip up a bit on his head.

"Where I'm from doesn't exist anymore. But this Valley is home to me, and I was ready to come home. I just needed a reason." He turns to face me, and his cap falls back into place. "I found my purpose."

I swallow at the intensity of his dark eyes, the sharp edges of his jaw, adding to the earnestness of his comment.

"Why *my* land?"

"Why not? You have lots of unused space. It's beautiful." His eyes zero in on me. "What's not to love? It's perfect."

I have to disagree. It isn't perfect—the rotting barn, the old house, and the overgrown land—but it was beautiful in its own right. However, the gleam to Jedd's eyes hints he doesn't mean my pastures are the beautiful parts.

Can he love it here indefinitely? Will he want to stay? Will he continue to grow and expand his dream, or will he get bored? He's already told me he had a nomad heart. Can his heart allow him to plant roots in one spot? Or will he need to sow his seed, like

Howard? I don't like the thought, and something in my expression must give away my negative feelings.

"What is it, Bee? What's that pretty head thinking?"

"Just wondering what you want for breakfast," I say instead of offering my concerns. The glimmer in his eye turns to a full spark as his gaze roams down my body. I shiver. I want to give in to that look, to the appraising perusal, the hungry stance.

Forgetting what a certificate says regarding my marital status, am I free enough to open myself to Jedd?

"I'll take whatever you give, Bee. Remember that." He leans forward, kissing my neck and nearly getting nipped by Lucky One, and we both laugh. It feels damn good to laugh. His eyes narrow on me as he addresses the feisty horse.

"Damn horse. You might be named Lucky One, but I'm warning you now, I'm the only one getting lucky with this woman."

CHAPTER TWENTY-THREE

[Beverly]

"You did what?" Hannah shrieks, hardly holding back her astonishment.

"I asked Jedd to move into the house." I stand at the kitchen sink washing dishes, fighting the pull to look out the window and search for him. Now that he spends more time in the horse stable, he's harder to view, but when I see him walking toward the house, a solitary man, my heart leaps to my throat with relief. I need to let go of this fear. The one of him leaving us behind. I need to trust him, and I vow I'll try.

"Momma," Hannah drones. "That's another mouth, plus keeping after him. We aren't—" Hannah pauses when I slide a few hundred-dollar bills across the counter to her.

"We don't accept charity," she whispers, the words I've taught her to say at any hint of help.

"It's not charity. It's rent. Room and board, which includes three meals a day."

"Who's going to shop for him?" Not the first question I'd expected, but I explain how Naomi takes me out once a week anyway. Adding the last of the dishes to the drainer, I limp over to a kitchen chair and take a seat.

"And his room?"

"I was thinking he could take Ewell's old bedroom upstairs." I struggle to look at my daughter, holding my tone steady as I speak. This is my decision, but I need to take into consideration she sleeps up there as well.

"That's next to my room," Hannah states.

"I could move upstairs again as well," I suggest, and Hannah's mouth pops open. I thought of shuffling around the rooms. Having Jedd take a guest room and return to my old room as the master of the house, but I don't want reminders of my life with Howard.

"Are you sleeping with him?" The quiet accusation settles like a slap.

"Hannah," I groan as if the thought hadn't occurred to me. It only occurrs about ten times a day, but she doesn't need to know that.

"Sorry. Momma, I'm sorry. I didn't even think you liked Jedd." Hannah's hands wring together, her eyes darting everywhere but at me.

"Well, I..." I should say I don't. It would be the truth. I feel so much more for him, and if I'm not careful, I'll get in over my head, so I'm as honest as I can be at the moment. "I do like him. He's turning out to be a good tenant."

Hannah eyes me suspiciously, and her mouth opens like she has more to say, but then it closes as she thinks better of whatever it was.

"Jedd wants to update the contract. One year on the land, paying us rent with room and board."

"I don't understand," she questions.

"What don't you get, sunshine?" I ask like she's eleven again, and she's struggling with a math problem in her homework.

"Am I not enough?" Hannah stares at me a long moment, gripping the back of the kitchen chair.

"Oh my goodness, girl. You are everything to me, but Jedd …

Jedd just needs a place to plant roots, and he's doing good things out there. It isn't charity he's handing us, but rent, and it's time we put the land back to use."

It's time a few other things got some use as well.

* * *

"I can't believe you fooled me into thinking he was your man," Jedd teases as we sit on the couch after dinner, a rerun of *Nailed* plays on the television in my front room. Hannah has gone to work, and Jedd and I are alone in the house. It's the first night he'll sleep here inside, and I'm nervous, though it makes no sense.

"Why? Was it so strange I'd have a man?" I snap back, but my tone stays sassy instead of spiteful. My energy is like a balloon losing air, and I find my emotions converting to something lighter, like helium.

"Nooooo," he drags. "Just jealous you *had* a man." The comment shuts down all insecurity, at least for a few minutes. It's hard to imagine someone jealous over me, and while jealousy is one of the seven deadly sins, the idea that Jedd would covet me and not want anyone else to have me is empowering. We sit awkwardly on the couch. He took the corner so he could position his body toward the television, which rests at an odd angle for watching from the sofa. Normally, I would take my perch in my rocker diagonal to the view, but I took a seat on the center cushion, leaving space between myself and Jedd, but feeling a great divide between us as well.

My lawyer, Mr. Caesar, tried to tell me that in the eyes of a court, my marriage is a technicality. In the eyes of the world, I'm long since divorced of all responsibility and connection to Howard Townsen. He deserted me.

Left behind.

I shiver at the thought.

"Cold?" Jedd's voice roughens, reminding me of last night when he'd tucked me into his body and flipped the blankets over us. I've never been so warm in my life, overheated in more ways than from

just the covers on my body. I want him with the passion of a thousand blazing suns and the desire of the largest bonfire.

I want to make love to you.

My face flames with the thought, and Jedd's hand runs up my
spine, reminding me I've taken too long to answer him.

"No," I say, too quick, too sharp, and his hand retracts, misunder-
standing my meaning. I'm not declining his touch. There's nothing I
want more than his hands on me, exploring me like he did this morning, but suddenly, I'm nervous. *Is it too much too fast?* This was my
reaction to Howard—short and sweet and too quick—and I don't
want to be caught up again. I don't want to give in to pretty words
and empty promises.

Jedd chuckles beside me, and my lids flip open. I've missed what
Tripper Hanes has done on the screen.

"Have to admit, he is a little funny," Jedd remarks as we both
watch Tripper and his crew demolish a kitchen.

"I find construction invigorating," I blurt out for no reason, then
close my eyes at the admission. My hands have been in my lap, and
one slips to the cushion, gripping it in mortification. As my fingers
curl over the worn fabric, the callused tip of Jedd's finger strokes
down the side of my pinky and the digit flinches. Jedd curls his thick
finger around my smaller one and strokes up and down.

"Yeah. You like a man working with his hands, Bee?"

I nod in answer because I can't find my words. My throat clogs
from the attention his forefinger and thumb are paying to my littlest
finger. He tucks his fingers under my hand, loosening its hold on the
cushion, and slowly spreads his fingertips under my palms. The
rippling effect reminds me of throwing a handful of pebbles into a
puddle and the nerve endings shoot like fireworks up my arm.

How'd he do that?

Whatever he did, it's setting my heart rate higher. I squirm a little
in my jeans, hoping not to draw attention to myself yet wanting his
attention all over me. Jedd turns his blunt nails under the pad of my
hand one more time. His thumb strokes over the top, tracing the
veins to my fingers, and then the tips of his fingers join the thumb in

massaging down each digit. Each rub, each tug, is like a live wire straight to a part of me that wants those fingers strumming something more intimate.

"Every woman's hand is a story," he begins, and I swallow the dryness in my throat. My veins stand out. My skin hosts age spots. My fingers are short. I have no idea what any of that says about me.

He flattens his palm underneath mine again, feeling my warm skin against his.

"You've worked hard at some point," he notes. "Tilled soil. Pulled weeds. Planted flowers."

He has no idea how much I want to see a garden again. Not just pots of tomato plants, but flowers blooming. Golden tickseed, lemon bee balm, black-eyed Susans, an explosion of yellows and purples and pinks.

"These fingers have also loved a child, caressed her cheek, and felt her heartbeat." My eyes prickle with the reminder of my daughter as a younger girl when she allowed me to hold her hand, hold her close, and pray that all her dreams come true.

"But who holds your hand, Bee?" My eyes leap up to his, but he keeps his focus on his fingers, stroking over mine, touching my skin, and caressing the lines in my palm.

"It's been a long time," I state, but Jedd already knows. I can't recall a single time Howard held my hand just for the sake of touching me, supporting me, or encouraging me. Jedd lifts mine, flipping it palm up, and presses a lingering kiss to the center. Something inside me leaps to life, and I want his mouth on other parts of me.

"Jedd," I whisper, the yearning unmistakable, as is the fear. It's been a long time since I've done anything remotely sexual.

"What do you need from me, honey?" he asks, dangling his tongue along the length of a finger and then sucking it into his mouth.

Cheeseoncrackers.

I don't know how to tell him what I want. I don't know how to go about these things. I don't want to recall the way it went with Howard.

"You'll need to tell me." Something in my face must show I'm horrified, or possibly terrified, at explaining to him what I want him to do. "Or you could let me explore on my own."

"Explore," I say. I don't think the words leave my lips, yet somehow, he heard me. He leans forward, cupping my neck and dragging me to meet him in the middle. Lips connect with lips. Tender and sweet but quickly heating to tempting and sinful. Suddenly, I'm pressed into his chest, leaning against him in an effort to be closer. Our mouths move as one, his leading mine, and I'm eager to follow.

He breaks away, lowering for my neck. His nose finds the sweet spot where I want him to nip and suck. My chest heaves with the anticipation, curious and breathless over what he'll do next. He doesn't disappoint as his mouth opens and teeth scrape. I whimper, and the next thing I know, I'm sliding. Jedd shifts our bodies so I'm over him, chest to chest, thighs to thighs as mine straddle his.

He moves my hips until we connect, and he rocks me back and forth as our mouths meet again. My core pulses. My heart races. He's going to make me come undone again without removing any clothing.

"Sweet Jesus, Beverly. I want you so badly."

I agree, but something isn't right. It's the way he said my full name. Not Bev. Not Bee. Not honey. I dismiss the thought as his mouth drags me back to full attention. His lips, hungry and divine. His hands rocking my hips in time. Our parts rubbing at one another.

"Fuck, baby."

I love it, and I hate it that he's used such a term.

"I told you I'm happy with pieces of you, Beverly, but this is one part where I want the whole cookie." Suddenly, hands are roaming, and clothing is moving, and I'm losing my grip on the moment. I'm rocking over him, but the steam is settling for some reason.

"Fuck baby, just like that." And I stop.

Jedd's eyes open. He hasn't been looking at me. He hasn't been watching me in the brightness of my living room. It feels all wrong…and I don't know why.

"What?" he asks, frustration in his tone as my body cools under his hold. It isn't that I don't want to do something with him. I want him to explore me. I want to explore him, but I can't place my finger…

"What's wrong?"

"Nothing," I lie. I can do this. I've done it before, over and over with Howard, when I didn't like it. Didn't like him.

"Stop," Jedd says, his voice shaky as he peers up at me. I shift back, my hands pressing at his chest. I stare down at him, everything hitting me hard.

Fuck baby. Just like that. These words trigger me like I didn't know they would. Technically, I'm still married, but I don't feel guilty. *Should I?* What strikes me is the way Jedd morphed into Howard. He sounded like him, or maybe I projected Howard into Jedd. I glance around the room, feeling like it's all wrong to be here. In this space. On this couch.

"Where'd you go?" Jedd asks, still looking up at me over him, his eyes searching mine.

"I'm sorry. I…" How do I explain myself? How do I tell him what it was like with Howard? How it hadn't ever been tender but rough and crass—too quick, too aggressive, too demanding.

Jedd said he wanted to make love to me, and I'm falling for the prettiness of those words instead of the reality. Making love involves being in love, and that's not how Jedd feels about me. We've moved from enemies to business partners as he had a contract at the ready for me to sign. It was rather convenient.

My brows pinch.

"What are you doing with me, Jedd?" I stammer, holding still in our precarious position, but no longer finding the sensuality in it. What is he doing *to* me? I've come undone by this man: the tractor, his cot, and now almost this, but it doesn't feel right.

I'm not ready, but I am, and I know I'm not making any sense. I swallow as I slip off his lap, and his eyes follow my retreat.

"How did I lose you?" He hikes up to his elbow, the prosthetic supporting him as he looks up at me standing over him.

"I...I think I just got lost in my head." His lips twist in response, and he frowns. "It's not that I don't want you, it's just...I don't know what happened and..."

"I can't fix it if you don't talk to me."

I don't know what to say. How can I explain that the fear of rejection stems deep? I'd try things, and Howard would criticize me. I'd want things, and he'd refuse. It isn't that I don't want Jedd, or he isn't willing. I just want it on my own terms and to be considered an active participant, not passive, in what we're doing. Telling all this to Jedd seems like I'd be opening myself up even more to him, giving him more than just my body.

"I think you should go to your room." The strain in his voice surprises me.

"Excuse me?" I hiss, hands coming to my hips. I realize my sweater has fallen off my shoulder, but I don't right the material. Jedd's eyes fall on the exposed skin. His nostrils flare.

"You need to walk away, so I don't feel like I'm doing the walking."

"What...?"

"I promised I wasn't leaving, and I'm holding to that promise, but right now...I just need...Go." His tone turns gravelly and deep, and for the first time, I see Jedd on the edge. The need in him is as strong as the desire is in me. I want to take advantage, but I've shut down.

I don't want to feel like I'm doing something I shouldn't do. And I don't want to rush into the deep end without wading in the shallow a little. I went too far too fast with Howard, and it's how I got here. Right here, where I waver as I stand. I lower for my arm crutches, slipping my hands to the supports and turn my back on Jedd.

As I move forward, I feel his gaze tickle up my spine. I imagine him undressing me, taking his time, and I realize all I had to do was explain. I only had to tell him to slow down, or how I wanted it, but I'm afraid. If there's one area my courage lacks the most, it's in the bedroom department. The last two times, Jedd's caught me off guard, but this…on my couch…with those words…it felt different. It felt too much like Howard, and my eyes prickle with tears.

Will I never be able to let him go? Will he ever stop haunting my thoughts? Will I ever be free of him?

I pause at my bedroom doorway, looking down the narrow hall to where Jedd is still seated on the couch. He's watching me, and our eyes lock for a second.

Come after me, I want to whisper, feeling silly at the notion. *Chase me*, because just once I'd like a man to follow me and not feel like I'm the one running after him. Tears fill my eyes with the thought.

Jedd doesn't look away, and I realize he's waiting. He won't move until I'm behind my door. With a final nod, I enter, hesitating until I hear the click of the latch, and then place my forehead on the wood and let the tears fall, cursing Howard all over again for ruining my life.

CHAPTER TWENTY-FOUR

[Jedd]

"What's all this?" I ask, standing outside a room with a large wooden desk, an old file cabinet, and a rack containing bars of soap. It's been a difficult couple of days avoiding Beverly, so I hadn't noticed how busy she's been.

"Soap," she states, and I turn to see her standing near my shoulder. Everything in me tells me to lean over and start my day as I wish with a good morning kiss, but I don't. Something set her off the other night, and she hasn't been able to tell me what I did.

"Soap?" I question.

"Soap," she repeats, and I grin, finding the conversation similar to the one when she caught me in my outdoor shower. My mind shifts to taking a shower with Bee, and I'm feeling the twitch of a problem in my jeans. Why can't I just keep it clean for five seconds? Then thinking of cleaning returns me to soap on Beverly's body, and the dirty thoughts start all over again. I scrub a hand down my face and shake my head.

"You gave me the supplies, and it produced a lot."

"I'll say." I laugh. There must be at least fifty bars in the slatted shelf on the table in this office.

"They need to cure. They're sorted by the fragrance oils you purchased for me." Honey. Citrus. Lavender. Lilac. Almond. These are the scents I ordered, not certain which one she'd want. "Naomi helped me. She told me I could add texture to the soap by sprinkling in bits and pieces of the coordinating product, like real lavender. Or make the soap original like lemon lavender, adding lemon zest in the combination. That reminds me, I'll have to remember to pick up dried lavender from Samantha Hill at the winter market."

"What's the winter market?" I ask, noting it sounds like a farmers' market.

"It's a farmers' market in the winter with seasonal items. Vegetables. Sometimes roots and bulbs. Winter fare and holiday crafts. That sort of thing," Beverly offers. I nod as I look back at the soap.

"You should sell your soaps there."

Beverly looks over at the piles and back at me, innocent surprise on her cheeks. "Why?"

"What else you going to do with fifty bars of soap?" I chuckle as I enter the room and reach for one, inhaling the unmarked bar but instantly recognizing the fragrance. Honey. And all Beverly. My eyes close as I recall running my nose along her skin, nipping her neck, and wanting so much more. She said I could explore, and then we stopped. What happened? I've been beating myself up for days, giving her the space I think she wants from me.

"There are sixty-three actually." She pauses, watching me inhale the bar a second time. "You really think people would buy soap from me?"

The way Beverly questions herself makes me want to raze this Valley. Why doesn't she have more confidence? Why haven't people supported her instead of letting her become a shut-in?

"Sure, honey. Ladies like pretty things, right? Maybe make some kind of label for the outside so people know what fragrance each one is."

Beverly stares at the rectangular shapes, and I can't decide if the wheels are turning or if she's thinking I'm crazy.

"Huh." She snorts, turning to glance up at me. "Breakfast is ready." Despite our silent truce, she's been feeding me three times a day. The woman knows the way to a man's heart. Now, if I could only figure out how to get to hers. I'd thought we were all good. Contract signed, making me a tenant, paying her rent so it felt legitimate that I could use the land. But she shut down after that. Is it the contract? Does she think that's all I want? Does she think that's it?

Oh, how so much has changed.

Her movement out of the room returns my thoughts to the office.

Sixty-two bars, I say to myself as I slip the one that smells like her into my pocket. My shower time just got a whole lot dirtier.

* * *

"I think Boone is still in the area," I tell my sister as I lean against the fence, watching Lucky One and his friend, Firecrack, in the pasture after breakfast. The post before me wobbles under my weight, and I add checking fences to my list of things to do.

"Why do you think that?"

"I found a butter tub in the old house."

Janice snorts through the phone. "Case solved, Sherlock. Mr. Crawford with a tub of butter in the kitchen."

"Very funny," I mock. "I hadn't seen it before when I'd been there, and it just stood out. Too new. Too bright." The morning after Bee slept on the cot with me, I noticed a plastic container sitting on her back steps. Not the butter tub, but another disposable bowl with a set of flowers on it, which made me think of the tub. It finally clicked what stood out to me at Hasting's. A recyclable butter tub.

"Maybe he's still at the house, and we're just missing him," Janice suggests, but we both know that's wishful thinking. We've been there at odd hours to check for him, and I'd been there for days at a time removing materials from the old horse barn. He wasn't around.

"I think I have a clue as to where he got it." I take a deep breath and tug my ball cap from my head for a second. "I think Beverly's feeding him."

"Butter?" Janice squawks.

"No, silly. She made me some cookies and left them out on the back steps in the tub. I never got them. I think Boone took them. I keep seeing containers on her back porch. She's leaving food for someone. Then when I saw the butter tub in the old house, I just put two and two together."

"Let me get this straight. Beverly Townsen made you cookies but left them on her porch for you like a dog or something?"

"Janice," I groan. "I was building the stables, and she set them out for a treat." The more I think about the description, the more I realize it does sound like that.

"Let's back up to Beverly making you cookies." A heavy pause follows the statement. "What are you doing?" It's a question my sister has asked almost every time we've spoken lately.

"She was being nice." I brush off the kindness with nonchalance, but a smile creeps across my face.

"You know she filed for divorce, right?"

"How do you know?"

"She came to our offices. Ram is representing her."

"Shit. You didn't mention me, did you?" Guilt immediately knocks at my chest. I should just tell Beverly who I am and how I know her.

"Jedd, I love you, but so help me if you play with that woman's emotions." Another heavy pause follows her threat.

"Why do you care? Don't you hate her for *what she did to you*?" I nearly snarl as I repeat my sister's words from twenty-seven years ago when her fiancé admitted he knocked up some girl he hardly knew, trying to tell my sister the other woman didn't mean anything to him. *"It just happened,"* he'd argued.

"I don't hate her, and she didn't do anything to me. It was all Howard." Janice's voice drops, an edge of sadness and sympathy in her accusation. "Besides, I got my revenge on him."

I'm not certain what she means, but I'm relieved she doesn't blame Beverly. If I had to make assumptions, I'd surmise an innocent girl of seventeen fell for the attention of a twenty-three-year-old man visiting the diner where she worked, and he worked his way into her pants a little too fast.

"Well, you have nothing to worry about. I'm not playing Beverly in any manner. I'm her tenant. I'm using her land. It's all legit and legal." The words taste bitter on my tongue especially when I mix in my thoughts of Howard. *Shit.*

"No side deals?" Janice drawls.

"No side deals." Shit. Shit. *Shit.* Does Beverly think I'm playing her? I've worked hard to assure her the land is all I want, and then suddenly, I'm all eager to get in her pants. Does she think the two are connected? I swipe my hat back onto my head, like knocking some sense into myself.

"How's her divorce going?"

"You know I can't discuss a client with you."

"You know you did once before. You also know I don't want Howard showing back up. Why does there need to be a public notice?"

"This is the legal process. I understand it might feel like she's divorced in the eyes of the community, but in a court of law, she's still married, and she no longer wants to be bound to him."

"And you didn't mention me, right?"

"Jedd, not everything is about you," she sasses me like the older sister she is.

"I know that. I just..." The words fade. If she finds out...If she connects the dots. She'll never want me.

"You just what?" Another weighty pause. "Jedd Hudson Flemming, did you sleep with that poor woman?"

"I did not," I can honestly answer, but I can't say I don't want to. Because I do. I so do. "And Jesus, you sounded like Momma there for a minute." Janice sighs, and the exhale falls on my shoulders. "I miss her, ya know."

"I know," my sister agrees.

"I'm going back over to the house," I tell her.

"Be careful, Jedd. I don't think Boone is stable."

"I will." I'm not afraid of Boone, though. I'm afraid of Beverly finding out who Boone is before I find him.

CHAPTER TWENTY-FIVE

[Beverly]

I t's been a few nights since Jedd moved into the house, and he's gone over to Vernon's for whatever reason. I try not to pry into his personal business, but he's rather forthcoming with his plans for the future and what he's doing with the horses. He still hasn't turned the back pasture like he promised Hannah and me, but the soil can't be turned until spring when the planting will be done as well. His enthusiasm for all projects is infectious—*The Jedd Juncture*—and sometimes I get wrapped up in the possibility of a future with him.

Then I remember Howard and note how Jedd keeps his distance. Since the near miss the other night, Jedd hasn't tried to touch me. That night something in his eyes told me he wasn't going to stop at just a kiss, and something in mine must have told him I wasn't ready. Then he sent me to my room like a rejected child.

On this night, neither Jedd nor Hannah are home, and I'm taking a chance that the stranger-savior I've been feeding will approach my back steps even with me sitting out here. It's a calm night despite the chill of November. Stars fill the sky, and a rare moment of appreciation settles over me. The silent night. The dark calm. The crickets and cicadas and anything else chirping after dark are hibernating by now, and I sit with a blanket over my shoulders, waiting on my nightly visitor.

He visits every evening, evident by the cooled dinner I leave for him in a plastic container and find the next morning empty of every crumb. I wish I could give him a hot meal as the nights dip cooler, but it doesn't seem possible. I've watched for him, but he doesn't appear any earlier than ten o'clock. It's almost as if he waits until I'm asleep before he approaches. Tonight, I'm trying to fool him. The lights are off in the house except for the soft glow over the stove, which I always leave on for Hannah. No television reflections this evening. With making meals for Jedd, plus daily visits out to the stable, I've cut back on the number of times I watch *Nailed* or *Rehab Dad*. I'd say I miss my old friends, but they aren't really friends, and life has become a tad more entertaining than the reality programs.

"Hello," I call out when I hear a rustling on the other side of the garage. "It's safe to come closer." Is it, though? Is it crazy that I'm feeding a stranger every night? Hannah hasn't noticed the missing servings, but Jedd seems suspicious.

Why is there always a plastic container on the steps in the morning?

I leave scraps for the stray cats, I lied, holding my breath waiting on Jedd to remark about lids and how a cat can't use its paws to open the cap, but he didn't comment.

"My name's Beverly," I say into the dark, not knowing for certain if he's out there or if it's just another creature of the night. *Please don't let it be a bear.*

"I hope you've enjoyed the dinners. I appreciate the gifts." Whoever he is, he's brought me little signs of gratitude each morning. First the sunflowers. Then a container full of acorns. One time it was a package of gum, reminding me of Boo Radley from *To Kill a Mockingbird*. All gifts are complete with the letter B printed on a scrap of cardboard along with a drawing, mostly a buzzing honeybee or a larger bumblebee. The images have given me an idea.

"I make soap," I say, feeling foolish speaking into the quiet night, but hoping he's near and listening. "And I need a label for them. I can't draw a straight line to save my life, so I was wondering if I could use your design, seeing as you sign my gifts with the letter B, and it's the appropriate letter for my name. Plus, I like the bees you draw. It sort of represents me. Jedd says I remind him of the pollinator because I sting with my tongue." I chuckle at the comments. First off, how wrong does stinging with my tongue sound? I haven't done any stinging in that manner other than the kisses with Jedd. Second, I don't think I've stung in a figurative manner half as much as I did a month or so ago, working hard at keeping my calm and strangely finding it isn't taking as much work as it used to. The bee reference still fits me, though. Bees work hard. They persist and persevere. By the grace of God, I've done the same thing, working even harder during the past months than I have in years. Third, I'm speaking out to this bear-man as if he knows Jedd, and finally, the fact I'm speaking to this invisible stranger at all is just ridiculous.

Reaching for the railing, I use it to hoist myself upward and stand. Looking out into the vast darkness, I realize I'm just talking to myself, and I shake my head.

"Enjoy your dinner," I say softer, letting the mountain breeze collect the words and draw them out to the mystery man. He'll come for supper when he's ready, I decide, and turn for the kitchen door. Stepping cautiously, one step at a time, I guide myself into the house without the use of the arm crutches. The supports rest just inside the door, and after I've set my arms into the cuffs, I turn back for the outdoor barrier to lock the bolt. Reaching up for the shade, I see a motion in the yard, just inside the shadow cast by the large overhead light on the front of the barn. I pause and notice the outline of something large and shaggy towering near the corner of the garage.

Holding up a hand, I place my palm on the glass as if to wave, and to my surprise, he copies the motion. I'd love to open the door and step back outside, but I understand this is for the best. We shouldn't interact with one another. It's safer that he's out there, and I'm inside. In my heart of hearts, I know he's grateful for his meals, and my chest warms because I'm happy to share them with him.

The next morning, Jedd tells me he has a surprise for me and to meet him in the barn as soon as I'm ready, but he returns almost as quickly as he left out the back door with the empty dinner container in his hand.

"There's a piece of packaging or something with this one." Jedd holds in his hand a panel from a food box, evidently powdered potatoes from the colorful image on one side. He inspects the solid-colored, interior flap and then flips the image, holding it up for my inspection.

"A drawing," he notes. "Since when are cats artistic?"

Not quick enough on my feet with an answer, I reach for the imperfect piece of cardboard, noticing a sculpted capital B and a beautiful butterfly drawn within the letter. My thumb traces over the line drawing, and I slowly grin.

"Who is he?" Jedd asks, startling me as I'd almost forgotten his presence. My hand lands on my chest, my heart racing underneath my skin. The accusatory tone startles me.

I'd like to lie and tell him I don't know who he's talking about, but something in his narrowed eyes warns me to speak the truth, and the old Beverly revives.

"None of your business," I snap.

Jedd's eyes don't shift from their pinched look, but his gaze turns momentarily out the window on the kitchen door.

"What do you know about that house out yonder? The one in the distance from the back pasture," Jedd asks. His words come slow, hesitant as if he's calculating what he asks.

"The old Crawford estate?" I question.

His head whips back in my direction. "Yeah, Crawford," he mutters.

"I don't know much, other than Ewell and the old man had some issues."

Jedd shifts his body, swiping his ball cap off his head while he still holds the food container in his clawed fingers. "Oh yeah, like what?"

"It goes back before I was here. Seems Ewell and Crawford both loved the same woman once. Then there was some business about Crawford marrying Ewell's little sister against Ewell's wishes. Crawford believed he had the right to this land through the marriage. Ewell said over his dead body would he pay a dowry for a sister he considered dead. Then she died, and that added more troubles between the two farmsteads. Old Crawford remarried." My voice lowers. "And then Howard was engaged to the daughter when I got pregnant with Hannah."

My chest aches with the recall of standing on my-now front porch, heart in hand, head filled with hope, to discover it had all been a lie. But I couldn't go back home unwed and with child, and Ewell saw fit that he didn't lose his grandchild.

"I wasn't allowed over there, and I don't think the sister would have wanted me calling anyway after our first encounter."

I can still recall the morphing of her face. Surprise and shock to hurt and heartbreak, then fury at Howard as she stormed off the porch for her car, and Howard chased after her, leaving me to watch.

Left *behind*.

Jedd doesn't ask for clarification about Howard's original fiancée, and I'm grateful not to recount the details for him.

"Howard won the deed in a poker game that got out of hand. He presented it to his father like a fatted calf, but Ewell was upset. I'm not certain what happened after that, other than we owned the property. The sister was gone. The parents died. The boy remained."

"What was the boy's name?" Jedd asks, taking a deep breath that makes his chest rise.

"I don't recall. Bob? Tom?" I pause. "No, something unusual, but I don't remember. I'd never met him, only seen him from afar when I'd wandered to the edge of the property once."

I'd forgotten all about the time I ran as if I could run away. As if leaving Hannah behind was a possibility. I'd just lost a second baby, and Howard and I were fighting endlessly. I sprinted over the field to the farthest corner to hide under my favorite tree before the forest when a man around my age scared the bejesus out of me. He was kicking dirt from the other side of the large oak and swearing at something, which I soon learned was a horse running off in the opposite direction of its rider. I watched him for a while, wondering if he was friend or foe as I'd been warned about the Crawfords. I'd heard the elder had a temper, strengthened by words and an occasional fist. Heard he ran off one of his sons with his selfishness. I could have used a friend and wanted to approach the young neighbor, but Ewell rode up in his beat-up field truck, and both of us froze as if we'd done something wrong when we hadn't even spoken. In fact, the surprised look on his young face told me he hadn't noticed me as I'd noticed him.

When the rusty pickup came to a halt, dust flying in all directions, Ewell hollered for me to get in. My eyes met my unsuspecting companion, who'd been equally surprised by the intrusion of the truck. It was as if Ewell had materialized out of nowhere. As I climbed into Ewell's beater, he cussed at the kid, telling him he wasn't allowed to look at me, and then he turned on me.

You stay away from that Crawford boy. Them Crawfords are never up to any good, always trying to swindle deals with others. They're bad news.

I shiver with the memory and remember thinking back then that Ewell was only looking out for me. He reminded me I was a Townsen, and Townsens and Crawfords didn't mix. I wanted to remind him Howard had been courting their daughter, but I didn't mention it.

"Does the kid still live there?" Jedd asks.

"Again, I don't know. After Ewell died and Howard left, I didn't keep up with the neighbors. I didn't even know Howard had acquired the land until after his father's death."

Jedd's brows pinch before he asks, "What do you mean?"

"Howard wanted to sell it off. Make the kid buy it back or something, but it didn't happen."

"Why not?" Jedd's breath hitches with the question.

"I don't rightly know. Just know Howard wanted to sell, and then he didn't. He left shortly after mentioning it."

Jedd steps up to me, setting the container on the table as he passes it. "Do you know if he sold it? Does it still belong to Townsen or someone else?" Jedd's rapid-fire questions morph his face from edgy to angry and then panic before smoothing over into something like relief. His shoulders fall, and he lets out an exhale as he shakes his head as if he's remembering something he forgot. Then he looks back at me. "He couldn't have sold it."

It's my turn to question him. "What do you mean?"

"Nothing," Jedd mutters. "So you've never seen the boy who's definitely grown into a man by now. Never met him. Never spoken to him. But you were neighbors all this time."

Jedd's accusatory tone returns as if I should have made this forbidden neighbor my concern.

"I had my own issues, Jedd. Raising a daughter single-handedly and working a farm too big for the two of us. Whoever he was, he didn't step over and offer me a hand any more than I reached out to him. Hell, I don't even know if he still lives there."

When I first worked the fields, I only went as far as the fence line, leaving the final half acre to the other home. They'd had horses over there at one time, but I learned the animals were sold to pay off debts. The barn was left to rot, similar to my own, and the house fell into disrepair.

The stories surrounding Ewell, his thwarted love affair, and then his sister running off hinted at something like *Wuthering Heights*, only there isn't any romantic moor separating the two houses. When I learned the details of the gambling trade of deeds for debts and the exchange of land but not the house, I was reminded of historical romance novels with swarming rogues and bodice rippers. None of it seemed real; but I lived in a small mountain community, and anything was possible.

Jedd flips his ball cap back to his head, turning it backward as it settles over his short hair. He glances back at the container he set on the table. "You're feeding more than a stray. Do you think it's him?"

He states the obvious with a touch of hopeful in his tone, but I still can't find words to explain myself.

"I don't know."

Jedd's brows rise. "You don't know him?"

I shake my head. "We haven't spoken."

Jedd's forehead furrows deeper. "What if this person is dangerous? You live alone here with Hannah."

I want to remind him I've lived here for years without this stranger, and I've taken care of Hannah without help. I could throw in that he lives here now and remind him he's stranger as well, but I don't mention it.

"He'd never hurt me," I defend, standing taller, feeling confident in my answer. Whoever he is, he's never come near me other than to offer me assistance, which reminds me of what happened after Jedd tossed me in a tub of water.

"How do you know this? You said he hasn't spoken to you."

Again, I shrug. Jedd doesn't need to know I was talking to myself last night or that the mystery man heard me. I look down at the drawing, fighting the smile wanting to cross my lips. *He was listening.* I swipe my thumb over the penciled image once again.

"He doesn't speak," I say, as if I know this about him, but for all I know, he simply refuses to speak to me. "He leaves me these drawings as his gratitude."

"Is he the one leaving you flowers? He's probably got a crush on you for feeding him and showing his admiration with pretty pictures." Jedd waves out his hand in exasperation and swipes his ball cap from his head.

I'm on the defense again. "And would it be so wrong for someone to be interested in me? Take his time with me? Show me appreciation? Give me gifts?" I don't even know what I'm arguing as I'm not interested in a homeless man wandering on my land. It's the principle of Jedd's accusation that's upsetting me.

Without a response to my question, he reaches around his back and tugs something from his back pocket. I want to ask if the floral arrangement is from him, but I know the answer, and the expression on Jedd's face tells me he knows as well.

It's from *him*.

He holds in his hand the tip of a pine bough and a sprig of boxwood tied together with red twine. Reaching out for the small bouquet, I lift the fragrant conifer branch to my nose and inhale. Pulling back the collection, I smile again as another idea comes to fruition. I glance at the pencil drawing on cardboard in my other hand.

"Bee, what's going on here?"

"I don't know," I honestly answer, no longer able to fight the grin on my lips as my eyes meet Jedd's. "He leaves me these little gifts as a thank you for his dinner. That's all it is."

Jedd closes the distance between us so quickly I almost shrink back from his haste. His hand cups the back of my neck as his claw comes to my waist, looping into my jeans and tugging me to him.

"Honey, you need to be careful. He could be dangerous." His eyes scan my face, but I reassure myself the stranger won't come near me. Last night was the perfect example. He keeps his distance. I lift the heady pine-scented branch for my nose and then tip it up to Jedd.

"It's pretty, isn't it? Holiday-ish."

Jedd cocks a brow at me. "You aren't listening to me, are you? Or are you just ignoring what I've said?"

"Ignoring you," I honestly answer.

"Beverly," he groans, lowering his forehead for mine. "I don't want anything to hurt you."

"Nothing will," I tell him, but instantly other thoughts whisper through my head. *You might.*

Standing this close to me, acting all protective, is sending me mixed signals of Jedd's feelings. I've tossed and turned over the other night. Sure, he said he wants to make love to me, but that's only because of the strong attraction—the inexplicable pull—we feel between one another, but it doesn't mean he wants to *love* me. He's politely labeling baser actions that I won't refute I want as well. But it's more than just a sexual attraction I feel for this man—so much more—when I shouldn't feel anything at all.

"You said you had a surprise for me," I mention by way of distraction.

"You aren't going to tell me more about this mystery person, are you?" he asks, pulling his head back from mine.

"There's nothing else to tell." It's true. I know nothing more about my savior other than he's suddenly become my inspiration. I spoke to the dark, and my words were answered. He's drawn me a second symbol to use on my soap. I just need to find a way to copy the design.

My fingers brush over the spindly branch, releasing the piney scent into the room. Bayberry. It smells like Jedd, and it's the perfect holiday scent for soap. My fingers also note the red twine tied in a haphazard bow. The simplicity of the brown cardboard, the pencil drawing, and a thin strip of colorful twine are all the packaging I need. I decide on the spot I'm going to take Jedd's suggestion and sell some soap at the winter market and dismiss the rest of this conversation as Jedd overreacting.

CHAPTER TWENTY-SIX

[Beverly]

J edd's surprise is another horse, bringing the grand total to
three.

"Her name's Hickory." Jedd pets her nose while patting the
side of her long neck. We're silent a long minute before Jedd
addresses me while staring at the blond beauty. "I think you owe me
an explanation."

"Excuse me?" I snap.

"I've given you space, Bee, but I'm losing my mind over you."

My breath hitches. "What do you mean?"

"I want to be near you. I want to touch you, but I don't know
what I did. I don't know why we stopped."

I squint at Hickory's neck where Jedd's hand strokes the horse. "I
got in my head a little. What you said. Maybe the room." My eyes
lower for the dirt floor under my feet. In my periphery, Jedd's hand
comes to my nape, and it forces me to look up.

"Let's be clear. I want you, anyway I can take you. If it's bits and pieces, I can wait."

"You said you could only be patient for so long."

Jedd huffs with a strained chuckle. "Yeah, well, you were witnessing a man at the end of his rope," he teases. "I'd been wound tight coming here, and you weren't what I expected would unravel me."

"And what did you expect?" I tug back, but Jedd's grip on my neck holds me in place. Does he mean he thought he'd encounter someone young and fit? Someone loose and bubbly? Someone like one of his buckle bunnies?

"I didn't expect you."

I tug back again, adding my hands to the mix and pressing at his shoulders. We've shifted from him petting the horse to my back against the stall. He's caging me in as he does—a trapped animal looking for an escape.

"No running," he warns as if he reads my thoughts. "I didn't expect how I'd feel about you. How badly I'd want you. That sassy mouth. Those steel eyes. That damn fucking shoulder." Without further words, he grips my coat, tugging it to the side, taking my loose sweater with it, and sucks at my skin. My knees buckle, and he wraps his arm around me. He nips and licks, working his way to just under my ear.

"A man changes all his plans for a woman like you."

My mouth gapes, but he doesn't give me time to respond before his lips crash into mine. Rough and ready, he commands me to open to him. This isn't the tender, sweet touch of the man on my couch but a man on fire with need and desire. And I feel the same. I don't want to be wishy-washy or come across inconsistent because there's something he's doing to me. I pull back.

"Don't call me baby." I gasp before his mouth returns to mine.

"Okay…what else?" He doesn't let me respond, coming in for more lips.

"Don't ask me to ride you?" He pulls back, searching my eyes.

"What the fuck?"

"And that too. When you said fuck, baby, I just…" *Shut down.*

"Fucking Howard, that's what I should say," Jedd hisses.

"Yeah, and for good measure, maybe he shouldn't be mentioned either."

Jedd chuckles, wrapping his arm around my neck and tugging me back to him. "The only name I want to hear cross those lips is Jedd."

Jedd. Jedd. *Jedd.*

"I might be persuaded to do that."

"You don't seem like the type to be swayed, Bee." He teases me, but he runs his nose up my neck and nips my earlobe.

"And that's one more thing. My name."

"Bev. Er. Lee," he groans, and I shiver at his teasing tone, but then I still, and he draws back.

"I've never been a fan of nicknames. Never thought I'd want endearments, but there is something about you calling me Bee and honey, and not calling me Beverly when we're…you know."

His expression softens, and his cheeks pink with the cool air of the stable. "You know?" He tips up an eyebrow and then chuckles. "That's a mighty long list. Anything left I can do?" He's still teasing me.

"That list is short." My brow tips back at him. "Unless that's all you got." The innuendo is present and clear, and Jedd's eyes narrow on me.

"You should know by now how long I am, but maybe you need a persuasive reminder."

"I…" His mouth covers mine, and the next thing I know, we're moving. My back hits another stall, and then the door behind me slides. I'm pressed inside, and the door closes. Jedd's mouth comes back to mine, and we lower.

"A roll in the hay," I mock as we collapse rather uncoordinatedly to a pile of straw. He tugs at my coat, slipping it off and sliding it under me, lower than necessary. My butt rests on the padded material. A piece of hay pokes through my sweater, but I'm distracted quickly by Jedd's mouth on mine again and another long minute of corner mouth kisses and sucking my lower lip.

"The only thing rolling is going to be my tongue." With that, he pulls back, shrugs off his jacket and slips it over his head. He looks ridiculous until I understand. My jeans come undone, and he shrugs them to my knees. My backside hits the fabric inside my open coat underneath me.

"Bend," he commands, and I do as I'm told while at the same time, I can't believe what he's about to do. With his jacket draped over his head to keep me covered and warm, the heat of his mouth hits my core, and I buck up.

Sweet butter on biscuits.

"Dripping honey," he moans, holding his forearms over my thighs to keep me in place as his tongue returns to my center, lapping and licking, and I see I was wrong. The list might be short of things Jedd can't say or do, but it's long on the things he can. I squirm, and I moan as he sucks and savors, drawing over me like a favorite treat. Quickly, I relax, giving in to a pleasure I never had in this position. Jedd takes his time until I'm calling out his name like he promised I'd do.

"Jedd. Jedd. *Jedd*." The final cry is a sweet purr in response to the mystery and magic of that wicked tongue. Jedd drags out each lap until I can't take any more. My quivering thighs cease. Dripping honey, indeed. I'm liquid on this pile of scratchy straw.

When Jedd pulls back, he's pleased as punch with himself. He sits back on his haunches, and I sit up, right my pants and then tug him back down to me, kissing him in gratitude.

"You like that, honey?" He chuckles against my lips. I freaking loved it, but I don't tell him. His smug satisfaction spurs me on. I press at his shoulders, flipping him to his back. I slip over him, kissing him like we were on my couch. Maybe that's the trigger. Maybe it's the house. Maybe I can be free as long as it's not inside. My kisses aren't as practiced as his. I'm eager and anxious, but I know what I want to do.

I lower on Jedd's body.

"Bee, honey." His hand comes to the nape of my neck, but I won't be deterred. My fingers fumble and shake as I undo this belt.

His head lifts, and his claw-hand stops my struggle. "We don't need to rush. You don't need to do this."

My eyes meet his. "I need this." For some reason, I want to prove I can do this. I want to give something to him. My expression must tell him what I can't say because he reaches for his jacket, pushed aside after what he did. He drags it under his backside. "Don't need straw where it ain't intended to be."

Dear God. I laugh, the tension easing out of me as I finish unbuckling his heavy belt and then unzip his zipper. I inspect him. I don't mean it to be an assessment, but more inquisitive. I've only ever seen one man's...and Jedd is notably different. Long and thick in my fist. My mouth waters, and I lick my lips.

"Sweet Jesus," Jedd moans, and I look up to see him watching my face. "When you lick your lips..." His head falls back, and I giggle before lowering. Taking him in, I swallow, and Jedd flinches. His hand comes to my head as he swears with a word I warned him against, and then he quickly apologizes before begging me, "Don't stop. Please. Bee. Please."

I like that he's struggling, straining for control like I was under him. My tongue curls up his shaft until I suck the tip. When I lower again, he hisses my name. His nickname for me draws out like the buzzing sound the insect makes, and I'd laugh if I wasn't concentrating. I want him to come. I want to feel the jolt and surprise, and the empowerment of making him unravel.

It doesn't take long before he does what I desire, and I pull back, pleased with myself.

"You've got a satisfied look on your face," he mocks, his voice rumpled sheets and morning-after sounding, and I smile at the sound of satisfaction in his voice. He tugs at his T-shirt to wipe himself off, and then pulls up his jeans but doesn't close them. Instead, he reaches out an arm for me, and I tuck into his side. He grabs my coat and throws it over both of us. Pressing a kiss to my forehead, he moans.

"This is all I ever wanted."

"What?" I chuckle, looking up at him.

"Land. Horses. A beautiful woman."

I smile, nestling back into his chest. It's a pleasant thought.

"Bee, I can't go without you again." He shifts so he can see me better. "No more running. I want you in bed. My bed. Your bed. Nothing needs to happen, but I need to hold you each night. I need to wake with you in my arms. It's killing me that you're downstairs, and I'm up. We need to rectify that."

"Sleeping together?" My voice croaks.

"If sleeping is all I get, I want it. No more separation."

"What about Hannah?"

"She's a big girl, darlin'. She can handle it."

I hope Jedd is right, but can I handle it? Snuggling back into his chest, I close my eyes a second and decide I can. This is all I ever wanted as well.

CHAPTER TWENTY-SEVEN

[Beverly]

It's been a few weeks, and Jedd's been in my bed every night. We haven't had sex, but we've done so much else. Mouths. Tongues. Fingers. *Explore*...and I've never felt so worshipped, so treasured. He holds to his promises, which include not taking me on the couch and not using certain words. The longer I'm with Jedd, though, the more I see it's silly to put these parameters on him. He can be dirty with me in all kinds of ways, and my rocking chair has become a sacred piece of furniture.

Eventually, the winter market arrives, sporting seasonal roots and vegetables, holiday bakery items, and crafts. While I'm used to selling my tomatoes through the summer, I hibernate in the winter, hardly going to town. The community center is packed on this day, and I feel out of my element with my new hairstyle, fresh clothing, and different wares to sell.

"Mrs. Townsen," Ashley Winston-Runous greets me, hardly batting an eye at the changes in me. I have continued to work at improving my strength, and it's nice that someone isn't staring at me as I limp along the table, stronger than I've been in the past. My daughter went to school with Roscoe Winston, Ashley's younger brother, and Bethany, her mother, was a dear friend from the community. Ashley reaches for the green-tinted soap Naomi helped me make and lifts it to her nose. As she inhales, her eyes widen at the scent, and she smiles. "Bayberry." She lowers the soap and inspects the packaging, reading the inscription aloud.

"Bee joyful." She looks back at me, and her smile grows. "That's rather inspiring for the season."

My lip crooks, and my anxiety dissipates a little. Along with the letter B interwoven in the buzzing bee for a logo, Naomi encouraged me to include a play on the concept of the pollinator with each of the various fragrances.

Bee Joyful for bayberry pine.

Bee Courageous for citrus and floral.

Bee Inspired for lemon lavender.

Naomi also helped me copy the logo digitally and then cut the brown paper into strips for the wrapping. Coordinating twine holds the wrapper on the bar. Red and green. Orange and pink. Yellow and purple.

"Such pretty packaging," the only Winston daughter comments. "I'll take six Bee Joyful. One for each of my brothers." She pauses a moment, mentally calculating. "And I need a Bee Inspired for Serena because she loves lemon, plus a Bee Courageous for both Shelly and Jessica." She stops again, running through her list. "Oh, almond and vanilla...Bee Fearless for Jenn and another for Simone." Ashley chuckles to herself.

"I think I got everyone." Then she sighs.

"And a Bee You for Claire." This last one is honey and sunshine as Jedd calls it, but it's mainly honey-scented soap with a hint of a secret ingredient. He tells me it smells like me, and it's the only one without the bee symbol but rather a butterfly instead.

A butterfly is more fitting to describe you, Bee. You're going through a metamorphosis, and you're beautiful.

Gah, that man sometimes.

He isn't here today, and neither is Hannah. I wanted to do this on my own. Naomi helped me with the display of things, arranging the soap as she has practice setting up books at the library. My sister and I have a newness to our relationship, and I'm appreciating the time we spend together, getting to know one another better. Her Nathan has helped her open up herself as well.

"Beverly," a deep masculine voice addresses me after I hand off Ashley's parcel filled with soaps. I'm still riding the high of my first sales when I look up to see Vernon before me. My heart hammers in my throat as I tersely greet him.

"Vernon." I don't have anything else to offer. The loss of his friendship still stings. Taking an obvious swallow, Vernon scans the stacks creatively displayed on my table.

"What's this?" he asks, and I respond with the obvious.

"Soap."

He picks one up, holding it under his nose and inhaling before his eyes leap up to mine. He pulls back the fragrant rectangle to read the inscription on the wrapper and a lump forms in my throat as I realize he's holding a Bee You bar.

"Appropriate," he mutters, and the lump thickens. He sets the bar back on the pyramid.

"How you liking the horses?" he asks.

"I don't have much interaction with them, but I'm enjoying getting to know Hickory." The blonde Quarter Horse filly, pretty and slick with a spirit all her own, was a pleasant surprise.

"You should really stay away from that one. She doesn't want anyone on her back." The hint includes a warning and innuendo, but the horse and I have the same relationship as Lucky One and me. She's calm around me, or maybe I'm the one calmed by her presence. It's strange to think such a large animal can be like therapy, but stroking their coats and rubbing their noses is exactly how I feel about such beasts, and it's what Jedd wants to host with a few of his charges. He has a veteran friend coming to help him tend the stables.

"I warned Jedd about buying that one for you," Vernon adds, and my head shoots up.

"Jedd bought her for me?" I sound like a parrot, repeating what Vernon has said, but I'm also surprised by the comment. Jedd hadn't mentioned Hickory was mine. He just told me he bought her at auction. Untamed and wild, he thought she needed a good home.

Vernon's brows pinch in confusion. "Maybe I have it wrong."

Naomi helps another person while Vernon steps aside.

"I could sell some of these in the store if you'd like. See how it goes on the retail side," he mentions. While Grady Seed and Soil is mainly farm supplies and flowers, they have a small shop with novelty items that his sister Wilhemina runs.

"We don't need a hand—" I don't get to finish my word as a hand rests on my forearm. My younger sister glares at me a moment and then addresses Vernon.

"Mr. Grady, that would be wonderful. How many do you need, and by when?"

I glare back at my sister who's squeezing my arm, cutting off my circulation like when we were children. Her warning is clear. This isn't a handout. Vernon isn't offering charity. He's offering help, business help, and I need to accept it as such if I want to try my hand at selling more soap.

"I'd love to speak with Wilhemina," I suggest. Vernon pulls a card from his pocket and writes down a number.

"You can call her directly. I'll let her know you'll be phoning." With a nod, Vernon steps back from the table, and a heavy pat smacks his shoulder.

"Vernon," Jedd addresses him. I hadn't seen him approach, but something in his sharp tone hijacks my heart. I'm actually happy to see him, but suddenly wonder if others can see the pleasure on my face. Will they know what I've done with him? Will they know he sleeps in my bed each night? We aren't really a secret, but I don't know how I feel about publicizing our relationship. I no longer care what the Valley community thinks of me. They judge, and they moralize, and it's none of their damn business. However, I don't need more rumors about me.

Jedd nods to me, and the two men step aside, chatting as I turn to other potential customers inspecting the soaps. Hazel and Mabel wander past and each purchase a bar. My eye keeps drifting off to Jedd and Vernon, who move off even farther from the table while still remaining within the vicinity.

"My, isn't this something?" The judgmental feminine voice is none other than my oldest sister, Scotia Simmons. Naomi freezes next to me.

"Scotia," Naomi chokes.

"Sissy, how nice to see you," I address her. Scotia cringes at the ancient nickname, and I want to kick myself for falling into a false tone with her. I've always sought the approval of my older sister, wanting her to like me when it felt like she didn't. Naomi had the opposite opinion. She didn't care if the eldest Winters sister liked her or not. Maybe it's because I'm the middle sister. Maybe because I was the second child, but I wanted my sister's acceptance, and I've never had it.

Scotia huffs in response to my greeting. Her eyes scan the soaps like she smells something odiferous. She picks up a bar with two pinched fingers as if the item were garbage and could potentially soil her. Lifting the fragrant rectangle for her nose, she inhales once with a sharp snort. Then her eyes widen and clash with mine.

"Did you make these?"

I struggle for air and force a response. "With Naomi's help, yes." I'm not worldly like my older sister, not as intelligent or socially accepted as her, and I hate the inferiority I feel when I'm around her. She's my sister. Nothing makes her greater than me except the power I've always given her. The power to feel superior to me.

"Huh," she remarks, setting the soap back on the pile, purposely positioning it so that it teeters to the side. My sister is a business entrepreneur in her own right, having inherited quite a bit of money upon the death of her husband. The Fried Pickle Princess made deep-fried phalluses famous. With her perfect skin, erect posture, and trim outfit, I'd be surprised if a greasy delicacy has ever graced her lips, but her claim to fame is coated deliciousness. She's also famous for her superiority complex and her disapproving attitude.

"What do you think?" I ask, hating that I've asked, hating that I'm a grown woman still seeking her approval. Naomi's hand returns to my forearm, not squeezing as hard as it did while speaking to Vernon but more in solidarity with me. Scotia's eyes leap to the movement.

"Always a pair," she snips, reminding us of how Naomi and I were the closer sisters, although really Naomi and Jebediah, our brother, were the closest Winters siblings. Those two had been best friends to the core, pushing our parents to the brink.

"Scotia," Naomi finally speaks, more a warning in her tone than a greeting. Naomi never could understand our sister's lack of attention after my accident. I wrote it off as Scotia's embarrassment—her sister a drunk driver. Naomi considered it just downright mean and rather unchristian for a woman preaching the Good Word like she had a direct line to God himself.

"Another hobby?" Scotia scoffs, forcing me to recall the many hobbies I've had over the years, my dedication to each slowly waning over time. Am I really considering I can make this craft into a habit? A hobby into an income? Who do I think I am?

"Jedd Flemming," his stern voice snaps me out of my pessimism, and I notice his hand outstretched for Scotia, who sneers back at the metal glint of his opposite hand. Her eyes remain on his claw, apparent as his shirt sleeves are rolled up to both elbows, exposing his left arm for what it is.

"Scotia Simmons," she huffs, her nose rising higher as if an additional bad smell wafts in front of her. Jedd snaps his fingers, dismissing her lacking hand.

"Pickles," he replies.

"Fried pickles," she clarifies, lowering her nose and her furrowed brow to morph into a more surprised but pleased expression.

"Yeah, I don't like pickles, but I'm certain the fried stick is decent." The way Jedd drawled the st- made the word sound like something else, more phallic in reference.

Naomi's mouth pops open, and the grip on my forearm tightens. I snort, unable to contain the sound.

"Well, I never..." Scotia states, lifting a hand for her pearls even though they aren't present.

"I bet," Jedd responds, and Scotia's lower lip falls. "Nice to meet you." His salutation is a dismissal, and our sister turns on her heels, tapping away from the table. Naomi begins to snicker as soon as Scotia is out of earshot, but I'm still startled by how Jedd stood up to her.

"Jedd, that wasn't very—"

"The Fried Pickle Princess is more like the abominable biscuit bitch. She's your sister?" His eyes move back and forth between Naomi and me. Naomi's chuckles grow although a hand over her mouth tries to stifle the laughter.

"Jedd, may I see you for a moment?" I shouldn't leave my table. I have soap to sell, but I need a second with him for more reasons than one.

Jedd sheepishly follows me out of the large cafetorium and into an empty classroom. The community center is an old elementary school turned community central for things like the Friday night Jam Session, the annual Halloween party, and the winter market.

"Did you buy me a horse?" I ask the second I've closed the door and pulled the shade for privacy. It's risky slipping into a room. If I don't want gossip, I shouldn't give people something to talk about, but this can't wait for some reason.

Jedd chuckles. "That's not what I expected you to ask. I thought I was in deep horse doodoo for speaking to your sister how I did." Jedd reaches behind his neck, scratching nervously.

"Let's get to that in a second. Vernon told me you bought Hickory for me."

"Well, I... Did he say that?"

"You didn't tell me you bought her *for me*." Jedd's already told me she was a natural buck, and the previous owner tried to beat it out of her. This infuriated Jedd, and he bought her. What use do I have for a bucking bronco, though?

"She reminds me of you. The blond coat is like your hair when you were young, and her fiery spirit...well, she's like your spirit animal. Her owner tried to beat her down, but she still fought back. You've become a fighter, too. Seeing as Lucky One took to you, I figured she'd take to you as well."

My smile is a puzzled one. I'm pleased with his love for an animal and his analysis of her as my spirit creature, but I'm still so confused.

"But a gift?" I pause, wanting to cross my arms, but I hold my crutches instead. "Why would you do that?"

Jedd sighs. "Bee, you remember how we were chatting in your kitchen, and you questioned if it was strange for a man to be interested in you." He pauses, glancing at the old chalkboard and then back at me. "It isn't strange because that's how I am—very interested. You also asked if I thought it wrong for a man to take his time with you, but I think I'm proving I'm giving you all the time you need. And you accused me of thinking it odd if a man appreciates you and gives you gifts, but I appreciate you and the horse is a gift."

"Why didn't you say anything?"

Jedd takes a quick step forward, cupping his hand around the back of my neck and tugging me so our foreheads meet. "Because you weren't listening to me. You were too damn excited about a scrap drawing from some stranger you're feeding, and a horse suddenly seemed inconsequential."

I close my eyes. I'd said all those things, and he'd already bought me a gift. I slammed him with questions about my desirability, and he'd already desired me. I wasn't listening to him, but he was clearly listening to me.

Slipping my arms out of the crutches, I lunge for him, wrapping my arms around his neck. Doing the only thing I can think of to show this man my appreciation, I kiss him with all I have, sweeping my tongue forward, begging him to take me in and allow me to apologize. I'm a fool sometimes. Our mouths clash deliciously, and Jedd slips his hand up into my shorter hair like he does. He tugs, and I moan into his mouth, wanting to take things deeper.

When I finally release Jedd, he looks a little dazed, and I remember we're in the community center.

"What was that?" He chuckles.

"No one's ever stood up to Scotia like that, *for me*, and the horse…it's a freaking horse, Jedd. She's not inconsequential. I love her. I love…" I stop, sucking in air before I say something I don't think I'm ready to admit. "I love everything you do for me." My heart hammers in my chest, and Jedd looks both relieved and disappointed in what I've said. Does he want me to tell him I love him? Are we to that point yet? Am I ready to say such a thing to another man and risk the rejection of him? What Jedd and I have seems innocent enough, perhaps foolish and private and fun, but love? I just don't know if I'll ever love again. Gift horse, or not…

CHAPTER TWENTY-EIGHT

[Beverly]

"Beverly," the harsh whisper of Jedd's voice filters into my dream where I'm curled up in his arms, warm and toasty as the nights have grown rather cold. December is upon us, and I feel like a bear needing to hibernate. It's silly, really, as I don't go out much anyway. I've gone weeks without stepping outdoors in the past. All that has changed with Jedd.

"Bee," another hushed call comes to me, and I nestle into the bed, feeling that phantom hug, wishing Jedd was with me. *Why isn't he in bed with me?* I've been working hard at making soap, turning Ewell's old office into a storehouse. Wilhemina, Vernon's sister, took as much soap as I could offer, stating the bars were flying off the shelf for the holidays, not to mention, people wanted to buy local wares in general. She's suggesting we add the collection to their online store, and I'm appreciative of the help.

Just Bee Bath Bars is making a splash. Naomi thought of the tagline.

"Beverly, honey." When a warm hand touches my shoulder, my eyes spring open. Jedd stands before me in the darkness of my room.

"Jedd, you okay?" I'm slow to sit up, sleep still fogging my movements.

"Come with me," he whispers as low as he can. He pushes back the layers of covers over me and holds out a hand.

"Where we going?" My voice squeaks quietly, although I should be scolding him for waking me. I glance at the digital clock and notice it's after midnight. "Is Hannah home?"

Jedd shakes his head, still holding my hand as I stand.

"I want to show you something. Can you get dressed? Bundle up, though. It's cold outside."

Whatever it is he wants to show me, my sleep-deprived irritation quickly dissipates, and excitement grows.

"Give me a few minutes," I ask, and he leans in, kissing my cheek before pulling back and exiting my room.

I dress as quick as I can in jeans and a thick sweater, and find Jedd waiting for me in the kitchen. He pulls out a chair so I can sit and slide into boots, and then he holds out my coat. Once I slip it on, he haphazardly wraps a scarf about my neck.

"What are you doing?" I giggle as the knit length falls in loose loops around me.

"I don't want you to be cold." He holds out a knit cap for me as well.

"Where are we going?" I ask again, anticipation turning to excitement like a kid on Christmas, which reminds me it almost is. Jedd shakes his head, a sly smile on his lips as he holds out a hand again. Jedd and I will never be your average couple walking down a street holding hands.

I stare at the extension, my enthusiasm fading a bit. I can't link my fingers with his, as I need to clutch my crutch support and he only has one hand that can feel my skin.

"What is it?" he asks.

"I can't hold your hand and follow you," I admit, look up at him with panic. Will he leave me behind if he can't guide me?

"Actually, I was hoping we could just walk together. Lean on me, Bee. I can support us." The simple statement prompts me to set the braces aside and reach out for his extended palm. I hop to him, and he wraps his arms around me.

"We're like a three-legged race," I joke to hide the discomfort of knowing I've put more weight on him.

"There's no race, honey. We have all night."

I shiver with the thought as he opens the door and leads me down the back steps. Immediately, I hear the heavy snort of a horse.

"Hickory?" I question although this one doesn't have a blond mane like my girl.

"This is Jetson." Jedd holds out his hand and pats the side of another new steed. "He isn't a buck like the others. Been through too much, poor guy. I'm using him for other things."

Jedd speaks to the animal in a soft voice. The softest he can muster with the depth of his range and the volume.

"You're gonna be good for Beverly here, right, boy?"

"What?" My delight wains to trepidation, concerned Jedd implies I'm going to ride this thing.

"He's skittish, but I know you have a way with my beasts." Jedd chuckles, but I don't find the humor. He teases me that I'm calming those he needs to stay wild, but I'm not doing anything. I just stand there and pet them, and they turn into me. Sometimes I think Jedd's loud voice is what turns his charges reckless while I never speak to them. Silence is my only vocabulary.

"Put your hand on him, Bee. He'll respond to you."

I do as Jedd asks, noticing the horse quiver. The night is cold, and I can't decide if he's reacting to the temperature or anxious of me.

"It's okay," I whisper as I flatten my palm and stroke over his side, feeling his heart race under his soft coat. A blanket is over him and a bridle over his head. Before I know it, Jedd's behind me, hands at my waist.

"Don't scream," he warns as he lifts me like I'm nothing, and I voluntarily straddle Jetson. The horse stammers and struts, stomping his feet.

"Jedd," I warn, gripping the reins as if I'd know how to use them.

"Just relax. He'll take to you." Jedd continues to stroke the long neck of his new pal and then clicks his tongue. Together, they begin to walk out toward the field as I hang on for dear life. It's been forever since I've been on a horse, and knowing this one doesn't really want a rider makes me as skittish as him.

"What are we doing?" I whisper. The night is so quiet, I'm afraid my voice will fissure the darkness.

"You'll see," he says as we walk until we come to the paddock fence off the stables. Jedd uses the first rung as a step and then hikes himself up behind me.

"Whoa, boy. You're okay," he tells Jetson once again. Jedd's heat surrounds me, and instantly, I feel better, settling into his chest as he sets us off at a slow canter.

We saunter in silence, letting the airiness of the night fall around us. It's dark but bright, and Jedd points out the full moon.

"It's beautiful," I say, keeping my voice so low I'm surprised Jedd heard me.

"Yes, you are," he says, breathing near my ear. I want his nose on me, but I'm bundled up in the warmth of scarf and cap so I settle for his breath instead.

The bright moon casts a bluish glow over everything, and then I notice something else in the sky.

"It's snowing." Sitting up a little straighter, I tip back my head, feeling the faint caress of a flake or two as it drifts slowly to earth. Jedd's had both hands on the reins, but he slips one arm around my waist and squeezes, hinting for me to melt back into him.

The white puffs dance toward the ground like dandelion wisps in the wind. I'd like to make a wish on a snowflake like you can with the seed of the summer weed. I'd hope for this night to never end. The depth of the darkness softened by the blue cast from the falling snow—it's magical.

"It's so pretty," I admit, still speaking low, afraid to disturb the nature around us.

"It's otherworldly, isn't it?" Jedd says, stealing my thoughts. I nod to agree.

"When I was overseas, I'd look at the moon sometimes and know that others were looking at the same moon as me, wishing, waiting on something, wanting more in life. It made me feel lonely and understood all at the same time. Does that make sense?"

"Absolutely," I reply. I've ignored the moon over the years, but once upon a time, I'd do the same thing. Staring at the round light illuminating the dark, I'd feel hopeful someone out there was looking at that same moon, and maybe we were thinking of each other without even knowing it. I used to dream it was Howard missing me, but I'd long since given up on that thought. The longing I felt was for someone else, and maybe I'd finally found him. Or he'd found me.

"One of my favorite history lessons came from learning how on a night like this, actually Christmas Eve, when the north and south were fighting for this country, brothers and cousins crossed the lines to the song of "Silent Night." They greeted each other. Maybe hugged their brethren, missing homes and families, wives and children. Wishing each other a happy holiday before returning to their side of an invisible line and taking up arms again. How can there be so much hate when a night like this speaks only of love and hope and faith?"

A tear trickles down my cheek, and I don't know why, but I begin to hum the Christmas carol until Jedd's deep baritone voice breaks in with the words "silent night." From there, I sing the remainder of the song, out of practice from using my voice in such a manner but remembering times I sang with Hannah when she was in the school choir. Memories of past holidays float through my mind as the words come back. The song grows hollow in my heart as I realize at some point, I let the holidays disappear. I gave up on the cheer and joy as I wallowed in my pain, and I forgot the magic of moments like this night.

I chuckle without humor as I finish the song.

"That was so beautiful," Jedd whispers, his voice choked. I try to turn, but he keeps me facing forward. "Why'd you laugh, though?"

I shake my head. "My sister Naomi believes in the spirit of the moon. It's a feminine power opposite the sun, which is masculine. She'd have much to say about that fullness—make a wish and it will come true."

Jedd's quiet for a moment, his face nuzzled into my scarf, and a heavy breath brushes my cheek.

"My wish would be to propose to you properly, Bee. Maybe on a night like this when it feels hopeful and peaceful and anything is possible. At a time when you feel free and safe enough to be with me."

I shift forward, and he releases me. Looking over my shoulder at him, I watch the lines of his neck as his head tips back, looking up at the sky. His Adam's apple rolls once, and my mouth waters, my tongue wanting to lick up the strain of his throat.

I'd like that, I want to say. Instead, I tell him, "I trust you, Jedd." It's hard to admit, but I don't have doubts about him. Telling him this is almost as risky as admitting my other feelings. My fear of him disappearing and leaving me behind hasn't seemed warranted with this dedication to building up the barn, not to mention adding more and more horses. He's so invested in his animals, and he never hints at wanting anything other than being right here. "*Bloom where you're planted*," he likes to tell me, and his arrival has made me blossom from the stagnant weeds of my life.

"Thank you, honey. That means so much to me."

Jedd leans forward and brushes his lips softly over mine. His are warm, and we quickly heat. Almost as swiftly, he leans back, lingering as he pulls away. I want to follow his retreat, beg him to keep us warm right here on his steed. The kiss felt sad, less hopeful than the peace around us. I turn away and settle into his chest again, blinking away tears of frustration.

Jedd turns the horse back for the house. We've traveled as far as we did on the tractor a while back, and I focus on nothing and every-thing, drinking in the quiet of the night, the somber sense of darkness, the brightness of the moon, and a strange feeling that something bigger exists around us. I can't see the house I know lies off in the distance, the old Crawford place Jedd asked me about, but I wonder about it. There's not a light to be seen, but it's also late. Does someone still live there? What happened to that boy turned man? Maybe I should pay a visit after all and reacquaint the families. Maybe bury the old hatchet that no longer exists. Thinking of this, I see movement near my barn as we near the stable. The two structures aren't close, but I can see around the lower building at this angle. A large body lingers by the corner and then disappears into the shadows on the side. For some reason, I think back to the day I first snooped in Jedd's room. He's since packed up his belongings and moved them inside, even though he accused me of stealing back the blanket I made for him.

Indian giver, he called me, which isn't politically correct any longer, but I know what he meant. He thought I gave him something and then took it back.

"Did you see that?" I ask Jedd, wondering if he noticed the man by the barn. We haven't spoken about the stranger I feed again although I sense Jedd's continued disapproval. *He's only worried about my safety*, I tell myself, but I'm not afraid of the man, whoever he is. Maybe I should talk to Jedd about him after all.

"What?" Jedd questions.

"It looked like a shooting star," I fib with a change of heart at exposing the stranger-savior.

"Huh. I missed it," he mutters, sounding like he's lost in his own thoughts.

Jedd guides us up to the house and slips off Jetson. Lifting his arms, he grips my waist again and helps me off the horse. He doesn't leave much space between the creature and himself, so my body slips against Jedd's. My breasts scrape over his chest despite the thick padding of my coat, and my hands come to his shoulders as my feet hit the ground.

"Thank you for sharing this with me," I tell him.

Jedd leans forward and rubs his nose over mine. "You know I want to share everything with you."

Come inside, I want to tell him. *Let me share myself with you*, I want to say, but I don't. We just stand under the moonlit sky, breathing each other in despite the cold.

"I need to get Jetson back," Jedd says, stepping back to give me more space. Then he slips his arm around my back, and we become the three-legged couple as his knee slides between my thighs. I laugh as we fumble to the steps, and then he releases me, knowing I can handle the stairs on my own.

"I'll be in soon," he says, and I wish he meant it as a suggestion, but I know he's simply stating the passage of time. *Soon?* How much longer do I need to wait? It's been decades of loneliness.

Holding up a hand as a wave, I watch him take a step backward and then another step as if he doesn't want to release his eyes from me. Then he spins and reaches for Jetson's reins to lead him back to the stable.

Knowing sleep will evade me after the burst of crisp, cool air, I decide to make a cup of tea and turn on the coffeemaker for Jedd. It's the middle of the night, closer to early morning, but I'm more awake than I've been in a while. Every part of my body hums with an anxious need to burn energy.

Once the water is set to boil, I hear the latch of the back door open.

"Bee," Jedd addresses me as he enters.

"I'm not ready to sleep," I say. "Thought I'd have some tea. I made some coffee to warm you up."

Jedd chuckles. "If I drink coffee, I'll never sleep tonight."

I hobble over to the refrigerator and tug a chair with me. Standing on the seat, I reach for the cabinet above as Jedd mutters, "What in tarnation are you doing?"

His hands grip my hip, keeping me steady as I search for what I know lingers in the back corner. Once I have it in my hand, I hold it out to Jedd who's right behind me.

"This might help you sleep," I say, holding out the bottle of vodka. Jedd's eyes leap to mine as he takes the bottle from my hands. He questions me about the secret stash, but I laugh. "I was a whiskey woman."

Jedd chuckles. "If only I knew you then…" he teases. "But I think I'll skip this too. How about some tea as well?"

He sets the bottle on the table and helps me off the chair, holding me for a moment like he did outside. Bodies pressed to bodies. Fingers hooked through the loop of my jeans. Our eyes lock until the kettle whistles, and I pat Jedd's chest to release me. I make us each a cup, methodically watching as the steaming water flows over the tea leaves and the water turns dark in the ceramic mugs.

Jedd leans against the counter as he takes his mug. He blows on the hot liquid and then sets it to the side without taking a sip. My eyes travel the outline of Jedd's body. Long legs casually crossed at the ankle. Firm abs and chest under his open flannel. Two bulging biceps despite the one bionic piece. My heart races, and my lungs burn. A flutter takes up residence in my belly.

I set down my cup of tea and step over to Jedd. My fingers shake as they reach out for his shoulder, running down to the cuff over his stump. The mechanism is exposed because Jedd rolls his sleeves to his elbows, liking a balance in his shirt. My fingers trace over the cool material until I reach the metallic claw.

"Whatcha doing, Bee?" he asks, his voice rugged and shallow.

Tapping his metal wrist, I tug the arm forward to loop into my jeans and step between his legs, which spread to allow me entrance between his thighs.

I just want to hold you. I don't say the words, feeling too vulnerable to admit them, so I show him instead, hoping he won't push me away. I slide my palms up over the soft flannel covering his chest, around his shoulders, and then lean against him as I wrap my arms around his neck.

"Bee," he whisper-chokes, but I shake my head in the crook of his neck.

Just give me this minute. My heart continues to race, and other parts of me pulse. My wrist. My neck. My core. My skin is alive. My blood flows. I want to absorb him into me.

And then his nose drags up the side of my neck to just under my ear, and my lips find his skin. His hips nudge forward, and mine press back. My breasts brush against the firmness of his chest, and my nipples peak. My arms tighten around his neck. I can't let him go.

"In my fantasies, I push you up against the wall and take you, but I'm afraid that might be awkward with my arm," he teases, turning me on even more with his thoughts.

"I don't need the wall," I murmur into his warm skin, and his head tips.

"That tickles." He chuckles.

"This is how you torture me," I tease back with another kiss and then a sip, opening to suck at the edge of his scruff.

"Torture?" he questions, slipping his fingers into my hair and tugging my head back to look at him. "You have no idea how hard I work to resist you."

I swallow hard, my eyes closing. I can't face him with my request. "Jedd, for one night, can we not resist?"

CHAPTER TWENTY-NINE

[Jedd]

S he has no idea what she's asking of me. I should deny her, give her more time, but when she nips at my neck a second time, I break.

I'm just a man in need of loving this woman.

I push her back once again, only enough to bring her lips to mine. I'm not lying when I say I want to toss her up against a wall and take her rough and fast. The fridge would work. The counter would be better. But with the deliberate strokes of her palms on my chest and her lips at my throat, I realize Beverly needs it slow.

We kiss for too short a time, sipping at each other's mouth before she leans away, drags her hands down my arms, and threads her fingers through my right hand. She spins with calculation and begins to lead me with one measured step at a time. She should be using her crutches, but the clutch she has on my fingers tells me she isn't letting go. She's not risking I'd run away. Little does she know there's nowhere I want to run to other than wherever she leads.

Following her at a painfully slow pace, we make it to her room, where she shuts the door and then falls into me. Our lips collide, more frenzied than the kitchen exploration. More frantic to be close. She's the air I need to breathe, and I can't draw her in fast enough.

My fingers find the edge of her sweater and lift it. We break long enough for the thick material to slip over her head, and then her lips find mine again. I don't miss the tremble in her fingers as she works the buttons of my flannel. At three buttons, I give up the torture and yank the shirt from the back of my neck, slip it over my head, and expose the holster of my arm.

"Take it off," I suggest, and her eyes narrow in on the contraption.

"Tell me how."

My hand covers hers as I guide her to remove one strap and then the other, slipping the large holster off my back. The sock comes next, and she rolls it down, wiping at the skin as she tugs. Moisture can gather there, and I'm worried I'll offend her somehow, but she's cautious and curious, and then she surprises me by leaning down and pressing a series of kisses over the puckered skin.

I've had women obsessed with this part of me, wanting me to do all kinds of things to them with it. I've also encountered women repelled by the stump but not repelled enough to reject the entirety of me. But I've never met a woman who took such care to caress this piece, and I swallow back the lump in my throat.

"Bee," I warn, worried I'll break even more if she keeps up the attention. She stands to her full height, gripping my T-shirt in her fists and pushing it upward. With her chest uncovered, I unsnap her bra. If we're going to be skin to skin, I want it all. Her breasts are smallish, but as I've told her before, they fill the palm of my hand, and that's all I want from her. Her eyes close as I cover one, tugging taunt the nipple, which is already hard. Lowering for the tip, I swallow her, laving the sharp point.

Her fingers scrape at my scalp, holding my head to her breast. She whimpers when I move to the other one. My fingers find the button of her jeans, and she pushes at my shoulder, so I stand as her hands find the waist of my pants.

"I'm fine if all we do is touch," I tell her, stroking a finger along her waist while it flinches and flexes.

"I want more," she states, keeping her voice steady as her fingers work at my jeans. "I'm going to need to sit to remove these."

My first thought is that she means my pants until she hops to the bed, and I realize she means hers.

"We're quite a pair," I tease, knowing there might be limits to our fantasies of each other, but there won't be any barriers between us. I take down my own pants while she struggles to remove hers. Kicking off my boots, I reach for hers and tug them forward, which makes her fall back on the bed.

She laughs, and I draw in the sound, knowing once again this is how it should always be with her. Laughter in bed. Leaning forward, I climb over her.

"Scoot back." She wiggles up the bed until we both cover most of it, and then I slip a leg between hers. My body blankets most of her as I balance on one arm. Her head rotates to my severed limb and back to my full arm. She's not comparing them but sizing up the situation. Sparing her all thoughts, I kiss her. Within seconds, one leg wraps over mine, and she shifts so that our fronts collide. She's moved me in a way the weight comes off my arm, and we meld into each other as our mouths lead the way.

We've been in this position before, discovering one another, but tonight feels different. The kisses linger, speaking without words. I want this woman more than anything in the world. Only her and this night.

I press her to lay on her back, and then travel down her body, sprinkling kisses on her shoulder, at her neck, and down her chest. I suck each breast once before continuing lower. My teeth find the band of her underwear, and I tug one side while my fingers pull down the other. My nose skims over her hip bone. She's too thin, and I suck at the projection a moment before continuing to lower.

"Honey," I state, knowing she'll be sweet and dripping when I meet her center.

"Oh God," she moans, and I haven't even touched her.

"You ready for this, Bee?" I ask, a smile curling my lips, which latch onto her before she even answers. I delve into her, savoring the nectar and devouring her essence. She whines and whimpers, combing fingers through my barely-there hair. Without cognizant words, she begs me to take her to the edge, but there's no way I'd stop until she reaches it. Her heel presses into my shoulder blade as her thighs tremble and then she cries out my name in a soft, thrusting purr. With a last lick and a final kiss, I rub my nose down her thigh before climbing back up her body. She's melted wax from a hot candle, and her smile says it all.

"Did you enjoy that?" I flirt, knowing the answer. The foot that found my back hooks over my hip, nudging me toward her.

"Condom?" I ask, knowing this is a tricky question. I don't carry them around lately, and I'm assuming Beverly doesn't have them stashed in a drawer.

"It's been too long," she states, her voice low and choked, embarrassed by her lack of practice. My fingers find her chin as I roll to my side, forcing her to look up at me.

"None of that matters." I'm actually thrilled I'll be her first in a long time. "But we need to be safe."

It's been a while for me as well, though not near as long as Beverly.

"I can't get pregnant," she states, her eyes closing with the thought. "After losing a few, the doctors tied my tubes. I didn't want to risk any more failures."

"Not failures, Bee. Angels not ready for this earth."

She nods and swallows thickly.

"I'll need you to trust that I'm clean."

Her eyes pop open, giving me a long look.

"We can stop if you want," I offer. I'll get a test, I'll prove myself, but her eyes tell me there's nothing she wants less than more time.

"I'm good, if you're good. I..." I swallow back my own admission. "I've never done it like this." Never been tempted before, knowing no one would last with a man on the road.

"Let me be your first." She has no idea how many firsts she's already been.

I roll over her, spreading her legs with the width of my hips. Resting just outside of her, I return to kissing her, assuring her with my lips there's no one I've ever wanted more. Her hips roll upward, searching for friction, and I smile at her impatience.

"You're going to need to assist me." I press up on one arm, but I need her to lead me home. Her fingers tentatively wrap around me, and I jolt. She squeezes, and I scowl.

"Bee," I warn. A smile graces her face, knowing what she's doing to me. She brings me to her entrance and then releases me as I work my way in. My breath hitches at her warmth as I slide freely into her depths. Slowly, I press forward, feeling my heart race within my chest, feeling her clench around me. It's too much. She's too much.

"Bee," I strain, wanting to rush but enjoying each minute thrust as she brings me into her. Once sheathed to the hilt, I pause. My arm quivers as all the strength of my body works to resist pulling back and slamming into her. Reckless and wild like the broncos I train, I want to be free with her, but I also want to absorb this pleasure. "You okay?"

"Hmm...." Her head rolls to the side as her fingers dig into my hips. "Move," her lips say although there's no sound.

"Anything for you, honey." I pull back, teasing her to the edge. Her heels dig in just under my ass, hinting to return, and I give in, pushing forward to fill her once again. Her head tips as her back arches. She's a cat in heat, no longer curious but craving. Her fingertips tickle up my back, and I repeat the rhythm of dragging to the end before delving deep. We continue this beat, and I notice Bee's eyes open, staring off to the side of the room.

"Whatcha looking at, honey?" I ask, wanting her attention on me. I'm worried I'm losing her even though her body keeps pace with mine. When I turn my head, I see what she sees. With the moonlight streaming in her room, there's a vision reflected in the floor-length mirror of me over her, entering her. My arm pillars me upward, giving only a hint of her breast near my forearm. Her hip hides my thigh, but there's no doubt where we join, where one body leads and the other accepts. It's a vision, and our eyes meet in the mirror. "Like what you see?"

Her sly smile grows as her eyes spark like polished silver in the sliver of light illuminating the space before the mirror.

"You're so beautiful," I say to her reflection. I turn my head back, so she'll look up at me over her. "You're everything to me."

"Jedd," she quietly moans, and the sound sets me off. I increase the pace, tapping into her with more enthusiasm. "Jedd, Jedd, Jedd," she repeats my name, matching the thrusts as her eyes roll back again.

"I want it all," I demand. "Touch yourself."

Her eyes pop open, hesitation in them.

"Get there. Help me." If I move my arm, I'll collapse over her, putting all my weight on her in this position. I don't want to rotate. I don't want to move. I just want to feel her explode around me.

"I've never...not like this...I just..."

"Do it," I demand, my hips rushing, my heart racing. My back prickles, and I'm getting close. Her fingers skitter down her belly, pausing near the fine hairs before slipping lower. I'm losing control as I watch her hesitate, watch her experiment. Her fingers brush against me entering her, and I can't hold it together any longer.

"Dammit," I hiss, stilling the majority of my body as only two parts pulse: my heart and my dick, both racing out of control. Her fingers are trapped between us, and then she groans. A tightening occurs. A clench. A clasp, and I experience something I've never experienced—utter bliss.

Bee holds me inside, refusing to release me until we both are drained. When I feel her relax, I collapse over her. Pressing my nose to her neck, I give her a brief kiss and then tug us both to our sides.

Her leg hitches over my hip, keeping us attached as I pull her to my chest.

Her lips move near my left ear, and I feel her breath, but I can't hear what she says, if she's even speaking. Her arm tightens around my neck, and she presses to my chest. My brows pinch, sensing I'm losing her to her thoughts while her body continues to hold me.

"Don't let me go," I say, and her lips move on my ear again, but I don't know what she's said.

CHAPTER THIRTY

[Beverly]

Never, I whisper in response, knowing he can't hear me after whispering other things I don't think he's heard.

I love you.

Nothing else will ever be enough.

Don't leave me.

The second we finish, fear consumes me. Will he regret this? Will he change his mind? Will he leave me behind? These are ridiculous thoughts after the passion of the moment, yet my mind can't stop racing as I hold my body tight against his. His fingers trace up my spine, tickling my skin, and I shiver.

"What's this?" he mutters, and I shake my head, blinking back loose tears. I'm overwhelmed by everything. His closeness. His words. What we did. "Beverly, look at me."

Releasing my arms from his neck, I pull back, thankful for the darkness, although the moon still illuminates a sliver of the room. My eyes catch the brightness reflected by the mirror. I'd never done anything like that before, watched myself. Watching Jedd do what we did, it was out of body, otherworldly, and definitely a little dirty, yet I don't feel soiled. I feel liberated, my body loose and relaxed despite my galloping heart and stinging tears.

"Whatcha thinking, Bee?"

I love you.

"Just a little…" I don't know how to explain myself. "Overcome is all." I expect a sarcastic retort. Some joke about coming and such, but his thick thumb brushes my cheek as if he understands.

Then, he says, "I'm not going anywhere," like he's read my thoughts.

I nod to acknowledge I heard him, but he still asks, "Did you hear me, Bee? Are you listening? I'm. Not. Going. Anywhere."

The dam on my tears breaks, and more rebellious drops escape. Jedd pulls me back to him, scooping one leg over his hip and securing me to his chest with his arm around my back. He doesn't speak, and I'm relieved as I can't find the words to talk.

Eventually, Jedd gives in to the embrace, settling slowly into sleep while I remain awake. My body is tired but not my thoughts, so I continue to lie against him. At some point, he slips free of me, and I snuggle to his side, the damaged limb between us. My fingers stroke over his bicep, noting the difference between his two arms. He's still bulky, but I can feel how one is leaner than the other, which isn't noticeable on sight. Cupping my palm over the stump, I outline the tug of skin, the severed bone, and my heart aches for new reasons.

Why do bad things happen to good people?

Jedd works so hard. His thoughts are constantly positive, his outlook carefree. I don't want to question his nomad spirit as he's planted in the stable on my property, but a familiar tug in my chest tells me not to invest in him. Take tonight for what it was—a desperate woman seducing a beautiful man after a romantic gesture.

I sigh as I release his arm, tucking my own to my chest. Still wanting to touch him, I loop my ankle over his leg, and he adjusts his foot in his sleep, allowing us to hook feet, roots entwining.

* * *

I wake when lips brush over my shoulder.

"Good morning," I whisper, though I'm uncertain Jedd hears me. His lips linger on my skin as I clear my throat and try again, but still, the greeting comes out groggy and rough.

"A man could get used to this," he responds, rubbing his hand down my arm before reaching up for my hair and pinching the ends with his fingers. His eyes eventually land on mine, and he smiles, which lights up his face. I reach up to cup his jaw, drawing him to me, and we kiss. I'm not a fan of morning kisses—because morning breath—but I wouldn't dismiss this tender exchange for a tube of toothpaste.

As with previous kisses, we start out slow, taking out time, but something in me snaps, and slow turns to brisk, then a shift of my hips, and the next thing I know I feel like I'm sprinting—over his lips, over his pelvis. Jedd settles to his back as I straddle him, his solid length underneath me.

"Bee." Jedd chuckles through the nickname but doesn't stop me. His hand swipes through my hair before slipping down to my hip, encouraging me to glide over him. After two slow drags, it isn't enough. I tip my hips to find the edge of him and press. Jedd easily slides in.

My eyes roll back as my hips jut forward, drawing Jedd to a new depth. Sitting astride him, he's deeper in a sense, filling me in a different way, and I sit up, holding the position while I adjust. Adjust to his strength, adjust to his look, adjust to this man under me. My heart doesn't race as it did last night but sputters and stops, trying to catch up as I collect images of him to store in my memory. As if reading my mind, Jedd's hand presses over my heart, resting heel to breast as he lingers.

"Watch yourself," he states, but at first, I think he's warning me. *Don't get ahead of yourself, Beverly*. You've done that before. Love at first sight shouldn't exist. Love at twenty-thousand blinks shouldn't either.

After a short minute, I understand what Jedd really means. He nods toward the mirror, and I take in the vision of myself over him. A woman with tussled white hair, looking reckless and wild, sleek to the point of almost too thin. Tiny breasts—one of which is cupped by a large male hand—and eyes filled with determination and desire. The bedcovers haphazardly fold behind my backside, exposing my thigh at Jedd's hip and it's clear from how I sit what we are doing. It's a work of art in an unstructured form.

"Take what you want, honey," Jedd groans, and I rock back, watching the movement in the mirror, watching myself take control. I'm methodical and a bit rigid at first until I've set a rhythm in which I can no longer look. I want to see Jedd's reaction.

Gazing down at him, he locks his eyes on me, and a sly smile grows, hinting he liked watching me watch us.

"It's like riding a bronco," I tease.

"Honey, you on me is nothing like that, but if you want me to buck, I'll give you all I have."

I laugh at his response until he jerks up at the hips, thrusting into me and hitting a spot that forces a yelp.

"Did that hurt?" he asks, but his eyes spark despite their dark color. He knows his way around a woman, but I'm not going to consider how I'm not his first. I shake my head as my hands fall to the sides of him. He lifts one for his chest, and I follow his lead with the other, massaging at the firmness under my palms as I continue to ride him. He bucks upward again, spearing me. My trigger spot presses at his pelvis bone, and something in me takes over. My hips move. My eyes close. My mouth gaps open for air as I enjoy Jedd.

"Take all of me, honey. This is the full cookie." I don't know what he means, and I'd laugh if I wasn't so in my head, so into him, and taking him as if I were possessed, and in a way, I feel like I am. I want every part of him. His body. His mind. His soul.

"Jedd, I—" A sharp inhale cuts off the words, and I gasp.

"That's it, honey." He already knows my body, and the way I'm reacting to him. My knees tighten at his hips. My thighs clench, and then I give in. My head falls back as my channel squeezes, and I praise the moon and all the stars and anyone listening in heaven above.

Jedd responds with his own release, which drums and pulses within me, and my head lolls forward. A giggle escapes as I absorb the jolts and jerks inside me. The movements feel wonderful.

Jedd's eyes meet mine, twinkling in the heavy darkness of dawn. The moon is gone, and somewhere near the horizon, the sun is waking up. The black within my room glows as impending daylight marks the night is coming to an end.

"A man could get used to this," Jedd whispers in his not-so-able-to-whisper voice, rough from disuse through the night. I collapse over him, wrapping an arm around his neck. His heart thumps under my breast as our slick skin presses together.

"A woman could too," I whisper into his left ear, the one nearly deaf, but as if he reads me without the sound, he turns and kisses my neck.

* * *

Jedd asks me to stay out of the yard for the next few days.

"Another surprise," he warns, and I hate to admit the anticipation is killing me. I'm not one for gifts, but I do as he asks, curious when I hear hammering out of sight of my spying eyes. Hannah seems in on this one and only assures me I'll love it. She's become quieter with me but offers small pats of comfort, reminding me of when she was a child and saw too much, heard too much, of the unhappiness between Howard and myself. Her grandpa tried to remove her from scenes, often taking her out to the yard to distract her from the unpleasantries. Ewell himself never intervened.

It's your marriage, he'd say to his son, but what he really meant was, you made your bed and now you have to lie in it.

I suppose I made that bed as well, and I should have checked it first for bed mites before I did. Thoughts of Howard haunt me in a way they haven't for a while. Jedd continues to reassure me he isn't going anywhere with a short kiss or sudden touch. I've been worried about Hannah as well, concerning this new relationship I have with another man. Jedd's been equally reassuring to Hannah of his intentions to be present for the long term. His interest in her life choices warms my heart, and whatever the two of them are doing out in my side yard, I appreciate the effort he's putting into knowing my daughter. Although her life has been fatherless, she hasn't been minus male role models. Ewell. Vernon Grady. Hank Weller, I suppose. A number of friends with decent fathers. But Hannah hasn't had that one man who can guide her, support her, love her.

That's not to say I haven't tried as a single mother to do as best I can. Lord knows, I tried to balance the one-sided scale, but still, I hate thinking Hannah missed out by not having a dad. A girl needs her daddy, and as stern as mine had been, I still worshipped him as a child. It was my mother who strong-armed kicking me out of the house. As a preacher man of sorts, my daddy struggled to forgive but found acceptance eventually. My mother preached forgiveness while passing judgment to the final day. The hypocrisy wasn't lost on me.

It's wishful thinking Jedd might play a fatherly role to Hannah. Nearing thirty years old seems a little late for stepfather wisdom. Still, I hope Hannah can accept him and maybe find a friend in Jedd for his noble characteristics—kind, patient, understanding.

* * *

The mystique of the holidays has dwindled over time. There didn't appear to be anything magical to celebrate, especially about ten years ago when Hannah was off to college, and Howard was rumored to be nearby. Hannah and I had lessened the enthusiasm by only including a small tree cut from somewhere out back, decorated with a popcorn string and a garland of old quilt straps tied together. One set of lights and we called it a day, as we decorated only on Christmas Eve. One night of remembering brotherly love, like Jedd recalled, and then back to the daily fight for life.

This year, I wanted something a little more, and Jedd agrees as he hasn't had a proper Christmas in years. He's told me he has a sister in the area, and while she'd invited him to dinner, he'd like to spend the day with us instead. On December twenty-fourth, I'm awoken by the thud of boots and the stomp of feet along with a set of laughter. Rousing from bed, I slip an afghan over my shoulders, hardly covering my nightgown, and find Jedd and Hannah struggling with a too large evergreen in the living room.

"What in tarnation?" I snap, but there's no bite to my tongue. Instead, I laugh as well, finding their enthusiasm contagious.

"Merry Christmas, Momma," Hannah says, carrying a metal tree stand in hand.

"Merry Christmas, sunshine," I attempt, finding the joyful blessing foreign on my tongue as I witness the warm glow of her rosy cheeks and the smile on her lips. When was the last time I saw such unfiltered happiness on my girl's face? Her expression brings a tear to my eye.

"Bee?" Jedd questions, and I shake my head, hastily wiping at the leaky tear duct. He hesitates, wanting to cross to me and comfort me while knowing Hannah's present. I shake my head to dismiss the sad thoughts and give him a reassuring smile. He winks at me, and I softly laugh.

The next few hours involve setting up the tree, adding lights and Hannah's decision that we must make ornaments out of any scraps we can find: yarn, fabric, construction paper. The made-from-the-heart decorations, as Hannah calls them, give a bit of a preschool look to the tree, yet it's the most beautiful thing I've ever seen.

Virginia Hanes, be jealous.

After a modest dinner of lasagna, Jedd tells me to bundle up again because he's taking me outside. Excited by the prospect of another horse ride through the night and the possibility of what happened afterward, I dress in my best jeans, a thick sweater and boots, hoping the outfit will entice Jedd as it did before. With a thick cap, scarf and gloves, Jedd guides me down the back steps.

He no longer finds food containers on the risers. I had a hint to where my mystery man lives, at least during these colder months, and I've moved the location of the dinners I offer. If Jedd notices I'm no longer leaving out suppers for a stranger, he doesn't mention it.

Anyway, he leads me a few paces toward the garage and then tells me to cover my eyes. This would be near impossible as I need my hands to hold the supports on my crutches. Jedd immediately notes my dilemma and comes up behind me, slipping his gloved palms over my face.

"Jedd, this will be impossible." I laugh at the awkwardness of being bundled and bulky with clothing as his leg slips between mine.

"Nothing's impossible, Bee. We'll just go slow." The drop to his voice does things to me, and he has no idea how slow I want to go with him. Or how fast. We haven't discussed the other night, but it's there between us. The attraction. The pull. The pushback. However, together, we move forward, with his leg between mine as we cautiously step around the back of the garage.

"Merry Christmas," Jedd whispers at my ear, and I smile into his glove-covered hand. Then he removes the blinders, and I blink.

When, what to my wondering eyes should appear...but a greenhouse aglow with tiny white lights.

CHAPTER THIRTY-ONE

[Jedd]

She isn't saying anything, and I worry that I've upset her instead of surprising her. I'd first thought of the greenhouse as a gift a month ago, before her suggestion of soapmaking, when she'd spoken with such longing over her previous gardens.

Buddleia davidii, she'd said, and while I hadn't remembered the full name, I remembered the tone of her voice on the sound. Lust. Love. Longing. Wilhemina Grady helped me order the kit and a few starter sets for flowers. A butterfly bush is one of them. The idea of butterflies floating over this yard makes me smile. It's a better metaphor for my bee who no longer stings. She's been a chrysalis waiting out a too-long winter season to morph into a beautiful butterfly. Beverly's sister has also had a hand in the greenhouse project, and when I mentioned her sister as a butterfly, we had the strangest conversation.

"What color butterfly do you see her as?" Naomi asked me one day when I stopped in the library to ask her thoughts on building the

structure. When I stared at her, Naomi explained how colors have meaning and auras about them.

"A white one," I quickly said, thinking of Beverly's brilliant hair and how I love the unusual color on her. Not that white isn't common among older people, but forty-five is young to be such a solid shade. Then again, the streak and texture of Beverly's hair are unique, and I struggle to keep my fingers out of it.

Naomi dreamily sighs with my response. "A white butterfly has many myths around it, but mainly ones focused on change. A change is coming. A transformation looms. Of course, if you believe in angels, it means they are watching over her." Naomi pauses for a second, clutching her hands at her chest. "Perhaps you're her angel, Jedd. She's definitely changed with your presence."

The sentiment warmed my insides as Beverly has done the same for me—changed me—but it also makes my heart pinch a bit as there are some things I need to tell her.

"It's glorious," Beverly finally says, her voice choked as she breaks into my thoughts. She blinks several times, and I glance at her face, a slight glow on her cheeks from the cold of the night and the dim lights within the greenhouse.

"Do you really like it?" I ask. I fretted over styles, size, and shape until finally designing something classic and mimicking the one from her favorite show, *Nailed*. That Tripper is a character, and I can't believe I thought he was Beverly's boyfriend. However, the man loves his wife, and his kit for a replica of her greenhouse is online.

"I love it," Beverly exhales on the words, her eyes pinned to mine.

I love you, I want to say, but I'm not ready to share such deep feelings until I can say them without any impediments between us.

If anyone knows of any impediments as to why these two should not wed, speak now or forever hold your peace.

I can think of one impediment and something Vernon recently told me regarding him, but I won't let Howard ruin this moment.

"Let's go inside," I say as I escort her the remainder of the steps into the glass and wood structure. For the time being, there's a small electrical heater, but eventually, the nature of solar heat will warm the insides of these walls, allowing Beverly to start the gardening process and pot plants under protection. I open the door for her, and the burst of warmth hits us first. The inside is edged with two levels of potting stands. One allows for Beverly to sit on a stool instead of standing. The back wall holds an array of pots and flats with the collection of seeds. A basket with a large bow holds gardening tools.

"That's Hannah's contribution, along with a few suggestions and some actual support holding up the braces as I built this place." I eye the structure around us, taking in the pointed roofline and see-through walls, glazed over by condensation from the cool air outside and the warmth within. When I look back at Beverly, her eyes aren't looking at anything but me.

"This is the nicest gift anyone has ever given me," she says, her voice breathless and low. Her fingers clutch the edge of my jacket, and I notice she's removed her gloves.

"I thought Hickory was the nicest gift," I tease.

Beverly tilts her head, thoughtful a second, and I think she's about to renege her claim when she says, "*You're* the nicest gift ever given to me, actually."

"I…" I don't see how I'm a gift. I'm a little battered and a bit worn, but the expression on her face makes me feel like the present of all presents, and I want her to unwrap me. As if reading my mind, Beverly speaks.

"Make love to me." Her forward command should startle me, but instead, I'm instantly aroused. I like demanding Bee when she isn't stinging with sass but dripping with desire, and Lord knows, I desire this woman.

"Right here?" I tease.

"Right here," she demands, and now I'm more concerned about the temperature than exposure.

"It's cold out here, honey," I warn, struggling with the hunger in her eyes and the mischievous grin she's giving me. She's daring me to deny her. Dammit, doesn't she already know I can't deny her a thing?

"Then warm me, Jedd." The heavy heat in her voice breaks my resolve, and the next thing I know, Beverly and I are joined on the ground, in a pile of winter clothing, and I believe Naomi was incorrect.

Beverly's been the greatest present given to me. She's *my* angel, and I do believe in them.

Oh, how I do believe.

* * *

I don't want to part from Beverly even though I release her as soon as we enter the house. She needs a shower to warm up, and I need a second to collect my thoughts. I go to my official room on the second floor, but sometime during the night, I find myself sneaking through the dark, wandering into her room, and sitting on the floor. My head rests against the wall behind me as I watch her like a stalker. Asking her to let me sleep with her seems childish in some ways. What am I afraid of that I can't sleep alone? I've never been one to shy away from the dark or worry about made up monsters under the bed, but I feel haunted lately, and it has to do with something Vernon mentioned.

I saw Howard Townsen in Knoxville.

My first response was shock. After all these years, would Howard be so recognizable? Would he really look the same? While some people hardly age, others look considerably different as they approach their fifties, and Howard would be close. I look different. From the scrawny kid to a buff soldier and then a leaner rodeo rider, my body has transformed over the years. Even through suffering the loss of my arm, I've remained broad in shoulder and thick in legs. But Howard?

My second concern is Vernon knows what he shouldn't know. He knows I've slept with Beverly. After the mishap of their kiss, he'd told Beverly about spotting Howard in the area. Is this Vernon's gut reaction? Is this an attack of guilt, of suspicion, of jealousy by telling me he's seen Howard? While Vernon and I go way back, there's been a lapse in friendship. He doesn't necessarily owe me anything, but rather I owe him, after asking him to look out for Boone, who doesn't show any further signs of returning to the old house.

He's out there. I know he is, but where?

As for Vernon, well, I'm holding my breath he's wrong about Howard because if Howard returns, if he finds that newspaper notice and shows up, everything is going to implode, like white light and fissured sparks, and the result will be dismemberment of another body part—my heart. While my first visit to the Townsen property had one intention, my intentions have so greatly changed, and I'm not ready to give up either purpose.

"Jedd?" Beverly's deep, sleepy voice rouses me from my thoughts, and I lift my head to face her, feeling guilty for being caught in the dark, sitting in her room, just to be close to her. "Jedd, you okay?"

I'm not okay, I think as I watch her press upward, angling on one arm while the bedcovers slip down her body to expose another satiny nightgown. I once expected Beverly to be the type to wear something tight at the throat and down to her ankles, covering her arms with a ruffle around the cuffs, but she's a vision in the silky material, cut over her breasts and exposing her thin sternum. She's watching me watch her, and then she shifts, flipping back the blankets. I think she's going to slip from the bed and join me on the floor, but instead, she scoots back, allowing space on the mattress. She softly pats the vacant spot, and I press off the floor, a sailor responding to the siren call.

I stand and remove my shirt and pants. My socks and boots are upstairs in my room. Climbing into the space she's offered, I shift to my side to pull her face to my chest.

"You okay?" she questions again, her lips brushing over my chest, my heart racing underneath, and I settle into her.

"Never been better," I tell her, which is true on a million levels and also a deep lie. "Merry Christmas, honey."

"Merry Christmas, Jedd."

* * *

A pattern develops for the remainder of December, throughout January, and into late February.

I leave Beverly's bed before daylight, not wanting Hannah to discover me there. Although she's a grown woman, I still don't want to scar her. It's uncomfortable to consider your parent *doing it*, so I hike my tired body up the stairs and dress for another day of animal care. Their needs don't stop because it's a holiday or a snowy night.

Secretly, I'm counting down the days of Beverly's six-month public announcement of her intent to divorce. She's checked in with Ram Caesar, her attorney, who assures her there's been no response to the advertisement. I hold my breath each time she mentions Julius & Caesar, surprised my sister has kept our secret.

"I'm not under obligation to tell her you're a family member," she snips as I finally join her for dinner one night in Knoxville in the last days of February. The restaurant is rather nice, though a bit dark and too intimate for my taste. The place reminds me I haven't taken Beverly on a proper date, but she hasn't complained. She loves our midnight horse rides, and we've had a picnic in the greenhouse where her face lights in animation over the flowers she's growing. We even made Valentine's Day special right in her bathtub by scrubbing each other with one of her bath bars. I smile with the memory.

Janice was in the larger city for a case, and I've driven up here to pick up Tower Hudson, a friend from the military rodeo, at the airport. He's a quiet man, with lots in his head, and he could use a place like my stable. I also need help with that back field I promised Beverly I'd plow. *The land she acquired through the Crawford scandal.* It would have been best to burn the land to rejuvenate the soil, but that was something I couldn't get to in autumn. With spring fast approaching, we can turn the soil next week and plant by the end of April. I have another surprise in mind for Beverly.

My thoughts return quickly to my sister. "I appreciate you not mentioning our connection," I tell her. It isn't that I don't want to explain everything to Beverly; it's just that the well of untold tales is getting deeper the farther I fall into her, and the truth holds me back because I'm afraid she'll set me free when she learns it.

"You're still playing with fire, aren't you?" Janice questions, eyes narrowing behind her dark-rimmed glasses. Her pinched expression reminds me of Momma when she knew we'd done wrong.

"A whole forest ablaze," I admit, letting my head fall.

"Jeddy," she whines, reminding me of when we were kids. "What are you doing?"

"I'm falling in love." I sigh, shaking my head as my fingers circle the lip of my beer mug.

"With the land?" Janice gives me a sympathetic exhale. She knows how much I wanted to stay on the farm, raise my own horses, and invest in the future.

"With her," I mumble, and the tension between us builds as steep as a mountain.

"What are you *doing*?" she hisses. "You've nothing to gain from this, Jedd." The warning in her voice is clear, and I know she's right. Beverly is the new end goal, but once she learns who I am, the game might be over.

"I couldn't help myself."

"Jedd." Her hand flattens on the table as if searching for something to grip. "She isn't a horse. You can't ride her and walk away. You don't pet her and then leave her in the cold night. She's a person, a person who has been through a lot over the years." Janice pauses to take a breath, looking across the restaurant. Her eyes narrow a moment and then return to me. "She isn't a deal, Jedd."

Janice hates the idea of dealing, dickering as Hasting called it. *Dicking around*, Janice joked until she'd learned that Hasting wanted her to marry Howard Townsen in hopes to join the two farmsteads. She wanted nothing to do with him. Who arranges a marriage in the 1990s? Yet somehow, Janice met Howard and fell for his charm. She believed his promises, dating him in secret, as they hoped to show up both families when they ran off together. Janice wanted her degree first, and when she went off to college, she never thought Howard would step out on her. I knew better and tried to warn her. She didn't want to believe me, and it put a rift between us before I left home.

It was going to be my pleasure to confront him one final time in her honor, but I'd been too late. She'd been stripped of self-respect, and he'd gotten someone else pregnant.

My sister's compassion for Beverly baffles me, but I also appreciate that she doesn't blame an innocent girl who knew nothing of their secret engagement or their future plans. Beverly was as much a victim of Howard and his false pledges as my sister.

"I'm not making any deals with Beverly. She wasn't part of the bargain. It just sort of happened…" I say, trailing off as I can't really explain myself. Instantly attracted to Beverly, I'd found myself falling more and more for her as she'd transformed into who she is, who she'd always been. She'd been there, inside, but had lain dormant. She tells me I've awakened her from a long sleep, which sounds rather fairy tale-ish. I'm no prince, but I'm not the villain, either. I just want what I think is my right...*and her.*

"This is going to blow up in your face," my sister states, her eyes falling to my arm as if I'm not aware I've lost the appendage.

"She's a live wire," I tease, recalling the spark of Beverly when she's over me, under me, in front of me. There's nothing she hasn't let me do to her, and once again, I wonder how Howard could have let her go. I'm equally appreciative he did. Now, I just need him to never return.

"This isn't a joke," Janice warns, the commanding tone returning to her stern expression.

"I'm not joking," I state, still smiling with thoughts of Beverly in my head. "And I'm not discussing this anymore with you. We need to talk about Boone."

Janice exhales and turns to glance across the restaurant again. It's a nice place, and I should consider bringing Beverly here. Maybe for a special occasion.

"Boone is listed as a missing person, but the investigation doesn't seem very active. There just aren't any leads," Janice states. The responsibility of conversing with the sheriff has fallen to her as she's the one who has some relationship with him as a local attorney.

Sheriff James has already informed us he believes Boone simply left of his own volition. Knowing what he knows of Boone's history with gambling, the sheriff believes Boone packed up what he could and disappeared. Being as the sheriff knows our concerns with Boone's mental ability, he's keeping the case open but handed it over to his son, a deputy. Deputy James hasn't made Boone a priority, though. Lots of small-time crime and unnecessary speeding tickets to write, I guess.

"What are your thoughts? Any more mystery butter tubs? Boone in the dining room with a spoon of margarine?" Janice's voice mocks me, and I scowl. I still believe Beverly fed Boone, at least at one point. As winter began and slowly progressed, I noticed the containers of food no longer appeared on the back step. Whatever she served, to whomever she fed, was no longer being distributed by the back stairs, and while I'd occasionally see a spare butter tub in the sink, I didn't question the mysterious dinners as they appear to have stopped.

"It's like he's disappeared into thin air," I say, which I don't believe any more than I suspect foul play. It's strange, but I feel like I'd know if something happened to Boone. I also think others would have heard something. Gossip at the Pink Pony or rumors at Daisy's Nut House would lend a hint as to what happened. People who do bad deeds like to brag about them eventually. Even Grady's Seed and Soil might have caught a whiff of conversation about Boone, but nothing has been said other than some National Park ranger reporting a mystery man wandering in the woods. They couldn't identify if he was a hiker or homeless but leaned toward homeless and harmless. I'd already taken Jetson into the woods a few times, but only the edge as the deep parts and steeper inclines seem to spook him.

"We might have to accept that he's just gone," Janice admits, lowering her voice, and the tone reminds me of losing our mother. Hasting moved her off to a smaller place in the mountains where they went a bit native until they both passed away. "There's just nothing left."

"What about the house?" I ask. It's fallen into disrepair and needs more than tender loving care, but it still might be an asset.

"I say we burn the motherfucker to the ground."

"Janice." I snort, laughter filling my throat at her aggressive statement.

"I don't have any decent memories of that place, Jedd. It means nothing to me." I'm taken aback by her adamant disgust and apparent secrets as I remember things being bad but not so bad that I'd want to torch a structure and bury its memory.

"What rights do we have to it anyway?" I wonder. It's just a house. Four walls with a roof and nothing more. The land belongs to someone else.

"We have no rights. It was loaned to Boone out of kindness and regret." Janice pauses. "It's worth nothing except whatever the owner wishes to do with it."

My mind races with plans I shouldn't be making and decisions that aren't mine to decide. I nod like a bobblehead as if I understand, as if I hold regrets about the loss of the old place, but my brain waves are galloping with ways to save it.

CHAPTER THIRTY-TWO

[Beverly]

"Momma," Hannah hesitates, standing in the kitchen midmorning. "I saw Jedd at dinner last night...with a woman."

I... "What?"... *don't believe her.*

I don't believe her.

I don't believe her, my brain screams on repeat while my heart thumps once and drops to my belly.

Jedd went to Knoxville to pick up a friend from the military. He needs help tilling that back field he promised Hannah and me. I got a text around ten o'clock that he was staying the night in the city and would be back sometime today.

"Is that so?" I say through clenched teeth, keeping my focus on the soap I'm making. My bath bars are made through a cold process, and I've already mixed the lye and water concoction in the garage since it needs proper ventilation from the fumes. Jedd and I spoke about converting the space into a soap lab of sorts.

Jedd. *Who apparently went on a date.*

"Who was she?" I ask, closing my eyes as I will myself not to believe it. He wouldn't do this to me.

"I don't know, Momma. I didn't speak with him." Her voice softens as an edge returns to my face. My jaw holds firm. My teeth grind. I've always had trouble holding back my feelings in my expression, and the muscles of my cheeks pinch.

"And where were you?" The question falls into familiar tones of accusation with my agitation.

"I went out with Grizz. We went to Chris Roth's." Chris Roth's is one of the highest-reviewed restaurants in Knoxville. I've never been, but I've heard of it. Some famous chef on one of those cooking shows I don't normally watch on HGTV owns the place. They're best known for pricey steak and fancy desserts. It's romantic, from what I understand.

"Well, good for him," I mutter, keeping my head down as the soapy mixture before me blurs. I'm past the point of trace in my process, because I let the stick blender run too long. Removing the handheld blender from the mixture, I set it aside and brace my hands on the table, pushing myself upward. My arms vibrate as my legs shake, and it's taking all my self-control not to throw the pot of spoiled soap across the room. My heart races, galloping at full speed around a never-ending ring—how could this be happening to me *again?*—and I gulp for oxygen like a drowning fish.

"I need some fresh air," I whisper. My body visibly quakes as I swipe the back of my hand over my forehead as if I'm too warn.

"Momma, I didn't mean to upset you, I just thought you should know. Maybe..." She wrings her hands, and I glance up at the nervous motion. "Maybe it wasn't what I thought."

"Maybe," I mutter, although the word is hollow on my tongue. My history with men leads me down the same mental path. *There is always someone else.*

I slip into my crutches and step over to the hook by the back door for my coat.

"It's really cold," Hannah warns me. She wouldn't dare tell me not to go outside with the tension rolling off me.

"I'll be fine. I think I'll just walk down and see Hickory for a few minutes." Jedd and I have discussed horse therapy, where grooming a horse or riding one helps soothe the soul. His friend Tower is an expert in this matter, at least among veterans.

Jedd told me he was going to pick up his friend from the airport yesterday, but I see he had other plans. Perhaps today is the day his friend arrives. I wouldn't know any different. It's how things went with Howard. Always lies. A drink with a friend. A meeting with someone. A night up in Knoxville at a farm convention. That was my favorite. And I never knew any better. *"What friend?"* I'd ask. *"Meeting for what?"* I'd questioned. *"A farm convention? Can I go with you?"* I'd hope for a romantic weekend away. I chuckle bitterly with the memory of Howard and his excuses as I descend the back steps.

Once I hit the hard ground, I decide the stable is the last place I want to visit. Entering Jedd's sacred domain will be an overwhelming reminder of him, so I veer off toward the old barn instead. Jedd still hasn't returned as his truck is absent both from the barn and the stable. He typically parks outside one or the other, but he would have come to the house, right? He'd come to see me after a night without me? I'd like to think the best, but my head suggests the worst. Was I thinking Jedd would want me and only me? He's told me he has a nomad spirit. He's told me about the buckle bunnies and the one-night stands. He's no different than Howard in that regard. What makes me think he'd be a one-woman man with me?

I press open the heavy barn door, recalling the first time I entered and found the ease with which the door slid free. I'd marveled at Jedd and his ability, admired him actually, and all he could do despite his disability. *"Differently abled,"* he'd corrected. He's found a way to work with what he has, and he's forced me to forge a similar path. He's motivated me to move. Make soap. Garden again. I owe all these things to Jedd. I also owe him my sexual reawakening, and the thought is followed by sadness.

Am I not enough for him?

With Howard, I'd always thought it was my fault. I was to blame for what we lacked. But as time had passed, I'd found myself less satisfied by him as well. Maybe Howard and I had been in a vicious circle, unable to please each other. *Never,* my heart whispers. *You never wanted to please him.* There'd been no reward in being nice to Howard. But what about Jedd? Have I satisfied him? He's given me a horse, a greenhouse, and renewed hope. What have I given him in return?

As I stumble into the empty barn, the hollowness within its cracked panels and shards of dull light feels like my heart. The organ has been restored in many ways but is still not fully healed. And now, the cracks begin to pull apart once again. I stand in the barn with my head turning slowly as I look at nothing in particular.

I wonder where he is.

Suddenly, I'm not thinking of Jedd.

As I've spent so much time with Jedd over the winter months, feeding my stranger guest became more difficult. I didn't want Jedd to frighten him off, so when I discovered the man was possibly sleeping in the barn, I began bringing food here instead of leaving it on the back porch. Giving him a warm meal instead of leaving it to cool on the outside steps made me feel better about serving him, even though I had no guarantee he was eating it fresh and hot as intended. I used Jedd's old room as my drop spot although I knew for certain the stranger wasn't sleeping there. The enclosed room would have been warmer than another section of the barn, but he also would have been exposed if Jedd wandered into the barn. He'd be trapped in the small confines of Jedd's original bedroom—a mouse caught.

"Hello?" My voice croaks as I call out. "Are you in here?"

Silence follows my question, but I'd expect nothing less. I could use a friend. I can't talk to Hannah about my feelings. It doesn't seem right to share my confusion, my hurt, or my quandary with my daughter. I could call Naomi, and I will in time, but not yet. Instead, I speak to him as if he were some angel who could listen and offer advice.

Are you there, God? It's me, Beverly. Again.

"What's wrong with me?" I choke, swallowing back the lump threatening to gag me. "I mean, you're a stranger, and you helped me out. You know nothing about me, and you were still kind. What am I missing?" Is it a physical thing? I refuse to accept this, knowing how well Jedd and I fit together. Knowing how we both have physical impairments, and it hasn't made a bit of difference.

"Is it longevity? Is it commitment? Is that the issue? I'm not worthy of sticking around for." The final statement breaks me, and a sob escapes, though I fight the tears, blinking rapidly. Cold seeps through my jacket. It's becoming unseasonably warm for late February, but it's not the external temperature making me shiver.

"Good thing I hadn't married him," I mock, my voice full of sarcasm and self-loathing, which shifts to disappointment. "I thought he was different."

A hiccup-sob breaks free as I mutter things even I can't comprehend. My throat feels as if fingers press against it instead of a comforting hand wrapped around my nape, tugging me forward for kisses. For foreheads resting on one another. For promises made in the dark.

I'm gonna marry you someday, Bee.

He kept a calendar in the tack room of the stable, crossing off the days until the public notice was finished. His fears are the same as mine. If Howard returns, we'll lose everything, but I have faith we wouldn't lose each other. *Had.* Silly, foolish faith.

I shudder and shake my head.

"You obviously aren't there," I whisper, realizing my stranger guest isn't present, and once again, I've been left behind. Tears cascade down my cheeks, and I briskly wipe them away.

I turn as I hear a vehicle drive over the gravel outside the barn. *Jedd*, my heart leaps inside my chest, thrilled and relieved by his return for a brief second until I recall what Hannah told me.

I saw Jedd with another woman.

I want her to be wrong.

Yet history tells me she's right.

I hold my breath until the vehicle passes. It makes sense that Jedd would take Tower to the barn first and acquaint him with his pride and joy—the stable.

It's all he wanted from you, Beverly, my mind reminds me.

Then why'd he take the rest? my body questions.

Because you're a fool, and you always have been when it comes to men, my heart scolds.

Once the crunch of gravel falls silent, and I know Jedd's down at the stable, I exit the barn and head for my second haven, my greenhouse. Inside the warm walls, I remove my coat and busy my hands in hopes to rid my brain of all thoughts.

Idle hands are the devil's tools.

Pulling forth a plastic tray with thirty-six pockets, I fill the flat with potting soil and begin the tedious work of placing one seed at a time in the miniature pots. I already have rows of seedlings. My hope is the annual blue salvia will take, as it's a hardy plant that attracts butterflies. I'm out of practice at growing from seed, but the pods should break and grow into stems, reaching with grabby hands for the sun as filtered warm makes them cozy inside this glass hut. The change will be slow but steady as young plants burst into independent stalks, growing taller each day, stronger as leaves pop. Working upward until the buds appear, blooms will ready for blossoming, and then I'll move them outdoors to the fresh air, free from the confines of a plastic container.

The process reminds me of a child growing older, and my thoughts drift through snapshots of Hannah over the years. Her progression from pink tutus to choir girl to stripper. My eyes well with tears once again for all I haven't given my girl. Independence. Space to reach her full potential. Fresh air. I don't know why she stays with me.

We've both been confined too long, smothered under this farm, and while I don't want to sell and never have, it might be time to reconsider once I'm divorced. Letting go of the property cuts the final cord to Howard, who won't note the absence of the land or sale of the house as he isn't present. I could find some other place, smaller, maybe one level, with only a little bit of a yard instead of acres. Looking up and around the greenhouse, I wonder if it can be moved, how much would it cost, and if I even want the reminder of it.

Another gift from Jedd. *Who was seen with another woman.*

I blink away more tears, cursing my weepiness. "There must be something in the air," I say into the silence around me as I dust off my hands and reach for my jacket. I decide to skip the coat as I'm warm from working under the heated glass. Instead, I drape the heavy material over my arm and slip my hands through the braces. I've gotten better at carrying light loads in this manner.

Stepping out of the warm hut, I freeze when I see a car in the gravel drive and a man standing near it. My heart skips a beat, and I realize I'm not ready to face Jedd. I know we need to talk. I know there's an explanation. There's always an excuse to be had, but I'm not ready for the painful truth that he wants someone else.

As I take a step forward, I realize the man near the sedan isn't Jedd, though.

Despite my recently busy hands, it's the devil himself looking as charming as ever.

"Howard?"

CHAPTER THIRTY-THREE

[Beverly]

"Howard?"

Before me stands my ex-husband. *Husband!* I remind myself. He looks dashing in a suit until closer inspection. His hands are thin. His hair is as well. His skin appears gray, and the wrinkles around his eyes are deep. But his smile is still the same as ever—that damn smile that got me in trouble—because I believed the lies passing through his too-white teeth and the puffy, pink lips that could kiss like the devil.

Howard is the devil in my eyes, and I wonder what the hell he's doing here.

"Beverly?" he questions, and I notice he's holding that smile a little longer than necessary. My appearance surprises him just as much. I'm no longer the sun-streaked brunette but shockingly white and silver. "It's so good to see you, baby."

I want to vomit, and my fingers clutch tighter at the hand supports within my braces. I sway forward, and that's when

Howard's eyes travel south. My jacket has fallen off my arm, landing on the gravel drive, but I don't feel the cold around me. My blood boils.

"What are you doing here?" I question, unable to take my eyes off his pinched grin. I bet he wants to ask what happened to me as if he doesn't know. As if he had no clue I'd ever been in an accident.

"I heard you were looking for me." The tic to his jaw hints at his lie.

"I'm looking for a divorce," I blurt. *Not you, no longer you.*

"I think we should talk," he retorts.

There are plenty of words I want to say to him, but talking really isn't on my list of things to do with Howard Townsen. I've never wanted to beat a man with my crutch more, but at the same time, I'm having a surreal, out-of-body experience, telling myself I must be dreaming this moment. Howard cannot possibly be standing before me.

The silence that surrounds his declaration to talk is broken by the heavy thud of something crunching over the gravel drive behind me. As if I'm underwater, I hear my name called out, but I can't turn away from the snake before me. Howard's eyes shift over my shoulder, and slowly, his forced façade falls.

"Beverly," I hear shouted again.

"Bee," follows as the voice gets closer. The thundering crush of gravel comes to a halt as Jedd rushes up behind me. His hand comes to my lower back, but I flinch away from him.

Jedd. *Who was with another woman.* The devil has a twin, and I refuse to look at him.

I'd never believe in a million years I'd be standing face to face with the two men who've crushed my heart. I only need Vernon to appear, and I'll have a trifecta. Swallowing back the hysterical laughter threatening to escape, I shift my head from Jedd to Howard and back.

"Howard?" Jedd questions.

"Jedd Flemming?" Howard inquires, equally surprised and

giving him a nod as if recognition comes quick. I recall that some-how, Jedd knows Howard.

He wasn't a friend, Jedd assured me, but what he was I don't know. However, the tension between them might be thicker than the air between Howard and me.

"What's he doing here?" Howard asks, running his eyes up and down Jedd.

"He built a stable on the farm," I state, kicking myself for offering Howard any information. The farm is no longer his concern. It hasn't been for twenty years.

"I've heard." Howard turns back to me with a false smile, his teeth showing. "Heard the farm was turning profitable."

I'm slow to register what Howard's said, but Jedd steps forward. "Is that why you're here?"

For a moment, I'm caught in a warp of wonder, and I want to snap, *Maybe Howard's here for me?* Could that be possible? But quickly, I erase the thought. He's here because he's heard of the divorce. It's the only reason he's returned.

"I've heard the farm has horses for rodeo."

My heart stops.

It isn't me.

It isn't us.

Howard's after money.

Every fiber of my being screams to tell him to get out, get off my land, yet I can't find the words. It's like my tongue is swollen, filling my mouth. Like a child with too much food in her cheeks, I can't speak.

"You've got no business here," Jedd defends.

"My business is her," Howard remarks, nodding in my direction.

"Over my dead body," Jedd growls, and for the first time, I notice another man is witness to this farcical pissing match in my driveway. Tower Hudson, I presume, fits his name. Tall and lanky with a wave of rust-colored hair and beard to match, he looks as if he hatched from the Appalachian Mountains around us. Then I see the scar. A gapping gash down the right side of his face from eye to lip. Unable to help myself, I gasp, and intense blue eyes catch mine.

He nods once in recognition of what's startled me, but he doesn't lean forward to introduce himself. His hold is on Jedd, long fingers firmly over each of Jedd's shoulders preventing Jedd from lunging at Howard.

A moment later, another thought clicks into place. Jedd's only here for the horses as well. Protecting his investment.

"What do you want, Howard?" I ask, knowing we don't need to discuss anything. I'd always struggled to come to terms with why Howard had left me, how he could've stepped out on me, and how he could've abandon his child, but now I have an epiphany as he stands before me. I don't care for his answers. I no longer want them. I just want him gone again.

"We have things to discuss, baby," he sweet-talks in that patronizing tone, making my bones rattle.

"You've got nothing to say to her," Jedd interjects, and my head cranes in his direction. My mouth gapes, ready to defend myself when Howard steps forward.

"I have plenty to say, and it doesn't involve you." Howard's head twists from Jedd to me and then back to Jedd. His weaseling eyes narrow, intensifying the crow's feet at the corners. "Unless you're involved with each other."

Howard's tone is so accusatory I want to smack him. *How dare he?* He will not make me feel guilty for something he's done a thousand times over.

Still, a twinge of unwarranted guilt rustles forward. Sensing a shift in me, Jedd reaches over for me again.

"Bee," he whispers, his hand making contact, and even though I twist out of his grasp, he follows the retraction by gripping the back of my shirt. "Bee, you did nothing wrong. *We* did nothing wrong."

"Whatever stunt you're pulling isn't going to work any longer," Howard warns Jedd, but Jedd isn't listening to Howard. His focus is on me. I can feel his eyes watching me as mine are lowered to the dirt at my feet. My body slumps over my crutches. I don't tremble as much as I suddenly feel like all the blood has been drained from my body. I'm too weak to hold myself up, and I'm tired, so very tired.

"Bee, honey," Jedd mutters again, but with his inability to be quiet, the endearment is heard by all of us.

"Honey?" Howard snorts. "Get off my land, Jedd." My gaze flicks from Howard to Jedd and back to the dirt. Jedd straightens, continuing to clutch at my shirt as if he's afraid I'll try to make a break for it, and he won't let me go.

"Go," I'd whispered once to him.

"No," he'd said in return.

How far could I even get in my condition?

He was with another woman.

The reminder makes me stand a little taller.

"I think you should go," I say in a voice scratchy and rough, like little nails crawling within my throat.

"You can't mean that." Jedd's head spins in my direction, his eyes wide as ours clash. His are stormy midnight with questioning and concern. He roams my face, strokes over my lips, and returns to my eyes. "No, Bee."

"I heard about your date," I whisper, despite our audience. "I think you should leave."

Jedd jostles my clutched shirt, stepping forward into the space between my crutches.

"What?" His tone rings angry. "I didn't go on a date."

"Last night. Hannah saw you," I state, exhaling in hopes not to inhale the scent of him. Manly. Woodsy. Horse. My eyes close.

"Where is my daughter?" Howard asks as if he's an English gentleman come to claim his offspring. He has no right to her, and for a moment, I send up a quick prayer of gratitude she's an adult.

"I did *not* have a date," Jedd continues, as we both ignore Howard. "I went to dinner with my sister."

"Your sister?" I question. Jedd's very rarely mentioned his siblings, and it's a reminder he's still a stranger in many ways.

"I..." Jedd stops as he licks his lips.

"Your sister," Howard interjects in a long-drawn-out breath, and a chuckle fills his throat. "How is Janice?"

The pause between Howard's question, and the twitch in Jedd's jaw drags out for an eternity.

Janice is the name of my attorney.

Janice is the name of the girl to whom Howard was engaged.

Janice is the name of Jedd's sister.

"Janice Julius," I mouth to no one in particular, but Jedd reads my lips and closes his eyes. His hand slips from my shirt and swipes down his face.

"Get off my land," Howard repeats with more dominance in his voice along with a touch of excitement, as if he's one-upped Jedd somehow. Only, I'm the one turned upside down. I don't understand the connections.

His sister. Howad's ex-fiancée. My attorney.

"Beverly." My name is a plea in Jedd's voice.

"You should go," I repeat.

"I am not leaving," he states, his voice rising louder than it already is. Actually, I don't want him to leave. I want him to sweep me off my feet, tell me he loves me, and get us out of here. But this isn't a fairy tale, even if Howard is a villain. And I'm so confused. Jedd's sister was Howard's ex-fiancée. He must have known who I was then. The pregnant girl who stole Howard from her.

"What are you doing here?" My eyes narrow. "Is this some kind of joke?" Is he here for retribution for his sister? Is this Ewell and Crawford all over again?

"I told you I wanted to borrow the land."

"The land," Howard scoffs. "Your family forfeited it. You *lost* it."

"You *stole* it." Jedd turns on Howard. "You took advantage of Boone."

Who's Boone? But I don't ask. I'm still reeling between the two men arguing over *stealing* and *taking*.

"None of that matters," Howard states, holding his head higher as he swipes a thin hand down his front, and I notice a stain near the beltline. "It's mine now. So get off it."

"It's hers, and you know it."

The space around us stills to silence.

"Pardon me?" I ask, my voice rings low as I glare at Jedd. His eyes close for a moment.

"Howard holds the rights to the farm," I clarify. I'd like to argue it's ours in deed, collectively as a married couple, but I'm certain Ewell left everything to his son.

"No," Jedd corrects. "He doesn't."

"Jedd," Howard warns, but a question lingers in his tone. Through gritted teeth, Howard hisses, "This is not your concern."

"What do you mean?" I ask, still facing Jedd, whose eyes meet mine once again, but there's a shift in the midnight color. Something I've never seen in the teasing orbs—fear. Fear, because he knows something I don't yet clearly should. My voice fluctuates between a rasp and a groan, "What do you know?"

"He doesn't own the land, Beverly. You do."

The trees in the distance stop rustling. The wind halts in blowing. The barn seems to straighten as the statement swirls around me.

"What?" I ask, the question drawn out like a whistle.

"Jedd, I'm warning you," Howard begins, stepping forward. "Get off my land." Tower shifts, placing his body between my husband and my lover. The pit of my stomach rolls over, and tears prickle in my eyes.

Jedd exhales, wiping down his face one more time. "I was going to tell you."

I shake my head in disbelief.

"Janice Julius was Ewell's attorney when he was sick. She handled his will, and Ewell willed the land to you. Everything is yours, Beverly. Yours and Hannah's."

I can't process what he's saying to me. "Why?"

"I don't know. I guess he loved you more than his own son."

I blink, astonished. "I mean, how do you know this?"

Jedd pauses a beat. "Janice is my sister."

His sister. Howard's love. Ewell's attorney. *My* attorney.

"You need to go." His eyes widen a fraction and then harden. Howard claps his hands together once, so loudly my shoulders flinch and my heart skips.

"I'm not leaving."

Howard interjects, "Yes, you are. And don't think you can hole up at that old house like your retard brother." The next minute happens so quickly, it takes me a moment to register Jedd clocks Howard in the jaw, forcing him back against the hood of his car. He quickly recovers himself, hesitantly moving his lower face side to side.

"That's assault," Howard states as if he's an expert at law.

"You're lucky I don't murder you," Jedd threatens.

Tower shifts between the men again, and Howard retorts, "That's a threat. Beverly is my witness."

"Beverly is nothing to you," Jedd hollers, and I'm not certain how to take his meaning, but I have other questions.

"What house?"

"Baby, there are things you don't need to concern yourself with," Howard mocks me, reminding me of his past opinions. He thinks I'm stupid, worthless, uneducated, and ridiculous. I will away the memories and glare at Jedd.

"Crawfords," Jedd clarifies, and I stare at him, confusion written on my face.

"I don't underst—"

"Jedd is Crawford's son. Janice is his sister," Howard clarifies, the tone patronizing once again as if he needs to draw me a diagram.

"But you said Hasting…" I stare at Jedd, my brows pinch.

"Hasting Crawford, you—" Howard stops, but *ninny* floats unsaid. *"Not like that, you ninny." "Over here, you ninny."* Recall rushes through my head like a file cabinet opening and a gust of wind tossing out the papers.

"Baby," Howard self-corrects. "Hasting Crawford, baby." Howard's voice does nothing to soothe me.

"But you're Jedd *Flemming*," I stress. Did he lie to me? Is he someone who he isn't? I step back from him, swaying on my crutches, and this time, Tower reaches out for me. Long fingers curl over my upper arm to steady me, and I meet the sorrowful eyes of someone trapped in an awkward situation.

"Ma'am," he mutters, and I nod to acknowledge I can stand on my own.

"Hasting Crawford was my *step*father," Jedd clarifies. He reaches for me himself, as if worried I'll fall back.

"But Crawford was..." *the neighbor*. Our neighbor. My neighbor. The land Howard won in a poker game. *You stole it*. The land Ewell coveted after the death of his sister and the loss of his love. *You took advantage of Boone*. My gaze drifts from Howard to Jedd as I slowly piece things together.

"So Janice was..." *the woman he was engaged to when I got pregnant*. The woman he claimed he loved more than anyone. The woman who he planned to run away with.

"But she is your..." *sister*. I've lost control to complete thoughts as I look at Jedd. If Howard had married Janice, Ewell hoped to obtain the land, settling the Townsen-Crawford feud forever. Instead, Janice left Howard because of me, and then Howard won the land from the gambling son.

"You?" Did Jedd gamble away the family land? Did he lose it to Howard?

"Boone," Jedd adds. "My half-brother Boone, who's younger than me, lost the land."

Howard claps again, and the sound echoes. My head turns as if in slow motion as I glance up at him, now perched on the hood of his car.

"Well, now that we've taken a trip down memory lane and drawn the family tree, I repeat, get the fuck off my property," Howard states.

"Beverly's property," Jedd corrects.

My property.

I blink.

I blink again.

Jedd comes into focus, and my eyes widen.

"The house on the edge of the land. Your brother lived there, and that's why you asked about it." I pause, still gathering my thoughts. "Which means the land you lost…"

Where I'm from doesn't exist anymore.

Because it's mine.

"Is this what you wanted?" My voice cracks, the threat of tears no longer a hint but a thundering warning. Jedd doesn't answer me, and to my surprise, Howard holds perfectly still with his arms crossed and his head lowered. "Is this why you wanted to marry me?"

Howard's head shoots up, and he stares at Jedd, but Jedd hasn't moved. Only his nostrils flare, the anger of a wild horse ready to buck. His hand fisted at his side.

"Things changed."

"But you wanted the land," I shout, swallowing back the tears. I will not cry in front of these men. These horrible, despicable, distrustful men. "You wanted the land, and I own it." Reality hits hard. "You knew I owned it."

I pause, gathering the achy thought and the will to hold back tears. "It wasn't never about me. Never me, but the land."

"Bee." His mouth moves, but all I hear is the blood rushing in my ears. A cathartic *thump, thump, thump* reminding me I'm alive when I wish the earth would open and bury me six feet under. He steps up to me, ignoring both Howard and Tower, boxing me in as he does, stroking my hair behind my ear. "Bee, it's me. You know me. I've told you. Only you. This is the life I've always wanted, and I want it with you."

Because he wants my land. And just like Howard, once Jedd has what he wants, he'll be gone.

No, no more.

"You need to leave," I tell him. Straightening my shoulders, I hold my head upright with the final strength remaining in my body. But I close my eyes. I can't look at him.

"No." Jedd holds my upper arms, but Tower's arm crosses the

front of his friend's body. He's taller than Jedd's six feet, and his arm crooks near Jedd's throat.

"It's time to go," he mutters with a smoky voice, but it's enough to warn Jedd.

"I'm not leaving you," he says to me, and my eyes open, quickly meeting his before shifting to Tower. He's witnessed enough as an outsider, and it's time to take someone out of the ring. Tower presses at Jedd, forcing him aside, and Jedd takes the balancing step. He continues to pace with one foot methodically behind the other, but he reaches out for me with his claw. The two tongs snap, and Howard starts beside me. "I am not walking away but giving you space. I am not leaving you." His voice grows louder, determined, willing me to hear him.

He's not leaving me.

"Egad, that's wicked-looking," Howard mutters still focused on Jedd's metal hand, and I shift my gaze to him, my husand. Howard is a *wicked* being. My eyes drift back to Jedd, who is practically dragged backward by Tower. Eventually, he pushes his friend off him. He stops once in the drive, yards away from me, and I brace myself, thinking he'll run back to me. He'll pick me up and run away with me. Then he turns, and my heart shatters as I watch the most beautiful man I've known walk away.

CHAPTER THIRTY-FOUR

[Jedd]

"Fuckity, fuck, fuck, fuck." I've been repeating the sentiment for the past two hours, one hour of which I've laid here, sprawled on Vernon's couch in his office. My right arm covers my eyes. My head hasn't gotten the memo yet that I want to be drunk. I'm on my fourth beer and contemplating switching to the stronger stuff in hopes to numb myself faster.

"You don't know she let Howard stay," Vernon mutters, commiserating with me, but he's only on his second beer. From his seat, Tower silently peels the label off his bottle, lingering with his first. I should take a moment and beg his forgiveness for getting him into this mess, but he's already stopped me twice from apologizing.

"She didn't let me stay," I mutter, adding another fuck in my head. She couldn't mean it. She didn't really want me to go. But that look... "You should have seen how she looked at me." She questioned if I wanted her or the land. I've survived bucking broncs, an invasion overseas, and an electrical wire, but the look on Beverly's face when she learned the truth, when she connected the dots, when she questioned me.

I shake my head, my nose brushing at my elbow. Beverly's eyes said so much—it was the opposite of wanting to douse me in gasoline and set me alight. It was hurt. Pure, unadulterated, kick-her-in-the-gut pain and it gutted me.

And then she told me to leave.

I admit I'd done her wrong. I'd withheld information, but I'd done nothing the likes of Howard who cheated on her, disappeared, abandoned her, and then returned *for the money*.

And she let him stay.

Screw Howard. I've done all I can to show Beverly her worth, and one glance from him strips it away.

"Fuck," I groan, sitting up so I can take a long pull of my beer. "What will I do if she takes him back?" My chest heaves, pressing my ribs inward, and my heart aches like nothing I've felt before.

Why do women do such a thing? Fall for men like Howard? My mother suffered years of verbal abuse from Hasting, and still, she returned to him whenever Janice tried to remove her.

"He loves me," Momma had claimed.

Insulting someone isn't love.

I should have hiked Beverly over my shoulder and not given her a choice. She's the girl who you change your plans for, and I want her to choose me. I'd gone to her land intending to earn it back and ended up handing over my heart. Beverly changed everything. And I didn't fight for her.

"I should have clocked him in the freezer section," I mutter aloud, recalling the first time I saw her. Without looking at them, I sense Vernon and Tower glance at one another. Tower's perched on a crate, elbows on his thighs. He pauses as he lifts the bottle to his mouth

"You got him pretty good," Tower mumbles. His deep voice reminds me of an old Western actor, like he's smoked a few too many cigarettes, but there's pride in his tone. Once you know him, he has plenty to say, but he's reflective before he speaks. The scar was his lesson in keeping his mouth shut. His beard covers a large portion of the gash on his face, but there's no denying the angry red curve just above the facial hair, marring his right side. If Tower hadn't gotten in the way, who knows how far I'd have gone with Howard. I'm not a violent man by nature, but I was in the military, and even though I'm at a disadvantage with one arm, I'd think nothing of clobbering Howard over the head with my prosthetic if it got me Beverly.

Vernon's been leaning back in his rolling office chair. He lunges forward and then tips back again, adjusting his large body in the tight seat. "You don't know that she took Howard back," he states. "She's got nothing to gain from it. The land is hers."

The land is hers.

And I'd known the truth. Ewell Townsen always felt bad about what happened to Janice. He'd thought she was a good girl, or so he'd told Janice when he showed up at her office as she was fresh out of law school. He wanted her to write him a will in which he left everything to his daughter-in-law and his granddaughter.

"At least I can give them something," he'd said to Janice. In turn, she had repeated the words to me. Ewell must have been weak to his son's extramarital activity but dedicated to Beverly. How could he not be? She'd been a good girl as well and taken care of the bastard. Taken care of both bastards, actually.

The timing of everything makes sense. Howard obtained the land from Boone, and Ewell died roughly a year later. He must have known his son had been on the edge of his seat to sell, so he'd willed it all to Beverly. When Howard found out he'd been cut from his inheritance, he'd decided to leave. He'd had nothing to gain by being with his wife. She apparently didn't know she owned it all, and as long as the knowledge remained a secret, Howard could claim it upon her death. He'd just needed to outlive her, contest the will, and steal from his daughter. I'm thankful Howard isn't evil enough to plan Beverly's death or hire someone for the job. Instead, he plans to torture her by returning and claiming his right as her husband. Maybe he'll make her fall in love with him again. Maybe he'll take her to bed again.

"*Fuh*—" I begin, but Tower levels me with his icy eyes. He isn't a prude, but his glare tells me he's heard the word enough. My head hangs.

"What are you going to do?" Vernon asks, and I'm reminded he warned me he'd seen Howard. I shouldn't have left Beverly alone. I should have taken her with me to Knoxville, had her meet my sister, and planned a romantic night out. She'd insisted she didn't want to hold me back. Said I'd need to push her around in a wheelchair as she wouldn't be able to walk long distances through the city. I should have called bullshit, but I didn't. Single-mindedly, I was concerned with picking up Tower and dining with Janice, and I let my guard down about Howard.

We only needed a few more months, and Beverly could have filed free and clear of any push back from Howard. Now, I'm afraid, there will be lots of contesting on Howard's part, if there's anything to contest.

The way she looked at him…

I could see the initial appeal. A man in a suit, although a bit outdated. His shoes were shined to hide scuff marks. His collar was yellowed, but the tips were still starched. He didn't appear as put together as he wanted to look, but he still polished up nicely. A piece of coal spiffed up to masquerade as a diamond. I'd never seen the appeal of a suit before, but some women go for that glitter and gleam. Give me my shit-kickers any day, and I'm happy.

"I need to call Janice," I say. "I don't trust Howard. I have to figure out how to get those horses off the land." This prompts me to think of my business partner. "I need to get over to The Fugitive."

"What you doing at that biker hotel?" Vernon questions.

"My partner is there."

Vernon shakes his head, disapproving but with a chuckle. "Man, you are mixed up in more manure than I can spread."

"It ain't like that," I admit, falling into a drawl to follow his. My partner is legitimate. Rich as a Rockefeller but not as flashy about it. Reaching for my phone, I press the starred contact.

"Janice," I greet her. "Howard's back."

"I know," she states, and my brows rise as I sit up straighter. Vernon falls forward in his seat, his feet hitting the ground as he sits up, and Tower presses off his thighs. "Hannah called about an hour ago."

"Are they okay? What did she say?"

"She didn't offer much other than to say her father had returned."

Her father has returned. The prodigal dad. Will they break out the fatted calf and throw a party for him? My mockery mixes with jealousy. I care about Hannah, even if I'm not her kin.

"What else did she say?"

"She wants to meet with us tomorrow. The conversation was brief as there was lots of yelling in the background." The comment raises the hairs on the back of my neck, but before I can speak, Janice continues. "Jedd, you need to stay away from there. You could do Beverly more harm than good if you show up."

I don't like the sound of that, not one bit. "Are they in danger?" My eyes meet Vernon's, whose hands clutch at the armrest on either side of him. "Should we go back there?"

"Want me to send Grizz and Kerr?" Vernon says, and I miss Janice's response.

"Vernon's offering to send the boys. Should I call the sheriff?"

"Jedd, unfortunately, you can't report domestic violence for verbal altercations. That would be considered domestic disturbance, and who are they disturbing? Plus, Howard doesn't have a history of hurting Beverly, just striking her with hurtful words." Janice pauses, and my heart speeds up.

"If he lays a finger on her—"

"You'll stay away from him or land yourself in jail and be no good to Beverly." The comment sobers me.

"I can't sit here and do nothing." I exhale, swiping at my forehead with the end of my hook.

"You're going to have to, Jedd. Beverly's only choice is to make a choice, and we can't proceed until we see her. Tomorrow."

Twenty-four hours, on top of the twenty-four I've already missed out on by being in Knoxville? I don't think so. I can't be without her for so long, and she needs me to prove I'm there for her.

"Janice, I need you to do me a favor. I need you to go over there. I need you to make sure Beverly is okay." My blood accelerates, flowing like a rapid river through my veins as anxiety grips me. Even if Howard doesn't touch Beverly, he could undo her with a few words. She's got the sword tongue to duel back with him, but will she use it, or will she give in to his crushing comments?

"I'm not going anywhere near Howard, Jedd. And you aren't either. Just give it a day."

"That's too long," I snap, and Tower and Vernon both sit up straighter, eyeing each other before glancing back at me. I shift the phone to my claw and swipe at my face, whipping off my cap and slamming it on my knee.

"You really love her, don't you, Jedd?"

"Yes," I reply, speaking too loud but adamant again. "Yes, I really do."

* * *

Another hour and a half later, I'm sitting in The Watershed. Todd Ryder is present as is his best friend, Big Poppy, whose real name no one speaks, and by the grace of God, Nathan's here, too.

Tower drove despite the fact six beers didn't seem to faze me. The anger coursing through my bloodstream burns off all possibility of copping a heavy buzz. Still, I couldn't sit still at Vernon's while he stayed behind and called Grizz to head to the Townsen's farm.

"I'll just have him play it off like he was stopping by to see Hannah. It isn't so far-fetched," Vernon assured me before I left.

"I have to get those horses out of there." My eyes meet Big Poppy's over the table, and he nods to agree but doesn't offer a solution. For a moment, I feel like we're a strategy planning committee of sorts. Large men, despite the thinness of Tower, hunched around a small table with a bottle of heavy stuff in the center and shot glasses all around. The cavalry without a plan or mounts.

"What do you think he'll do?" Todd asks.

"I have no idea." Howard was raised on a farm, but that doesn't mean he's an animal lover. Dollar signs seem to be his mission. Though it'd be a hard sell since he doesn't hold the papers on those horses.

"I called Naomi," Nathan tells me; his voice hopeful it will make me feel better. "I hate to send her there alone even though I don't know this Howard character. She called me back to tell me she went to get Scotia."

"Scotia *Simmons*?" Todd chuckles after dragging out her name.

"She's their sister," I clarify, and Todd laughs again.

"I'd wondered why she was at your wedding," he addresses Nathan. "Course, she stood at the back and left as it ended." He continues to laugh, but I'm not finding any humor.

"I don't think Scotia's gonna let old Howard get away with anything," Nathan remarks.

"What makes you so certain?" I hadn't seen Scotia more than a handful of times during the months I'd been at the farm, and each interaction had been almost as unpleasant as the previous one. Her disdain for her sisters, as well as most everyone, was apparent in every comment, every glance, and every stance. I don't know why she bothered to remain in Green Valley if she disliked so many people, but then again, her popularity on the food chain keeps her near the top. Anywhere else and she'd be eaten alive. Scotia is as judgmental as they come, and moreover, all that judgment stems from her own insecurity. I've never seen a woman wear so much confidence and use so many layers of makeup to hide the very vulnerable woman underneath.

"Because Scotia Simmons has a serious set of kahunas," Nathan teases, cupping his hand with invisible balls.

"Her husband might have liked that about her," Todd adds, and Big Poppy snorts. I don't have time to question what he means.

"I need to meet this woman," Big Poppy teases, and we all respond with a resounding *no*, but Nathan might be on to something. If Scotia Simmons can find it in her two-sizes-too-small heart to defend her sister, she's a force to be reckoned with.

CHAPTER THIRTY-FIVE

[Beverly]

I have no idea why I've allowed Howard to stay. The moment I lead the way for him to follow me into the house, I know better.

"What's all this?" Howard's question about the ingredients on the kitchen table isn't one of interest but more accusation. As in, what kind of mess have I made.

"It's for soapmaking," I state, although why I'm explaining myself is beyond me.

"Soapmaking," he repeats.

"Yes, soapmaking." The exchange is similar to my first conversation about interests with Jedd, yet it's every bit dissimilar. This is Howard. I should have followed Jedd.

Visions of his extended hand, his eyes pleading as he muttered my name, force my chest to clench again. The pain is real. I feel like I'm having a heart attack.

"And what do you do with all this *soap*?" Howard asks, drawing out the object like it's dirty. I want to respond with the obvious—wash with it—but I don't.

"I sell it."

"Sell it?" he questions, his brows rising as he picks up the spoon I use to fill the soap molds. His nose wrinkles as he smells the concoction, which doesn't have a scent added to it yet. "What an interesting...hobby."

The word is like a sharp slap in the face, and I flinch at the reference. It isn't a hobby. I'm making a business of it. I'm selling soap and making a name for myself. It isn't some fleeting activity, but one I'm working at mastering, and I hope it will take off. Wilhemina can't keep it on the shelf. I have orders through their website. Jedd's going to convert the garage.

Jedd.

He explained it all—*his sister*—but I'm still confused. Jedd made it clear he is from Green Valley, but no one of importance remained. *There's nothing left*, he told me, but that isn't true. His sister is my lawyer's partner, and his brother lived in the house on my back property. He asked me about this brother, but I didn't have any information. I've been a terrible landlord when I didn't realize I had a tenant.

The land is yours.

How could I not know this? I hadn't gone to any formal reading of Ewell's will. Howard told me it wouldn't be necessary, just a straightforward reading of legal jargon I wouldn't understand. He'd been gone for hours that day. As I put two and two together, I realize Janice must have been the one to read the will to Howard. Did he not want me to go because he knew it was her? Did he know I'd inherit it all, or did Ewell pull one over on his son, like he did when he forced Howard to marry me? How could I have never known these things?

I recall receiving official letters in the mail, but Howard had left by then, and I didn't open them. I assumed they were legal notices relating to Ewell, and without Howard present, there was no way to make claims. I'd been so stupid because I didn't know any better.

As my thoughts wander, Hannah appears in the doorway to the kitchen.

"Howar…Dad?" she chokes, and Howard turns to look at her.

"Hannah girl," he cheerfully calls out to her, stepping toward her, but she steps back, her body language clear he's not to touch her. Howard stops and turns to me before looking back at his daughter.

"Is that any way to greet your father?" His voice turns edgier, his tone deeper, rougher.

Hannah blinks before glancing over at me. She's such a good girl, and I see her struggle. She wants to tell him what she feels. *What father?* I can almost read it in her thoughts. Instead, she nods at him and reaches out a hand, offering to shake his like a business transaction.

"I'm not going to shake your damn hand. Give your old man a hug." Frozen, Hannah doesn't respond as Howard steps to her and wraps his arms around her. Hers fall to her sides, her fingers fisting as he traps her within his grasp.

"Where's Jedd?" Hannah asks; it's a reminder we both count on his presence.

"That's enough," I snap, the mother bear in me awakening to Howard's awkward embrace. He pulls back, keeping his arm around Hannah, but her eyes meet mine, clearly uncomfortable with this position.

"She looks just like you did." He turns to her and kisses her temple, and Hannah's eyes close under a shudder. "What happened to you?" He sneers as he looks back at me, his eyes roving up my body as I stand behind a kitchen chair. Hannah uses the attention on me to slip out from under his arm.

"Excuse me," she mutters and leaves the room. While I don't want to be alone with Howard, I don't want Hannah anywhere near him either. She's clearly uncomfortable with him, and he's not getting the fatted-calf celebration he must have expected.

"What did you do?" he barks at me. "Turn my kin against me?"

I snort. "You aren't serious, are you?" I question. "You did that all on your own." I sweep a hand in the direction my daughter retreated.

"You turned her against me," Howard retorts, and I flinch back.

Again, I want to ask him if he's serious, but my lips remain closed, knowing what I have to say will fall on deaf ears.

"What do you want, Howard?" I ask instead. "What are you doing here?"

He sighs as his hands grip the back of a kitchen chair on the other side of the table from me. "I want to come home. I've missed you, baby." The fake smile has returned. Too many teeth. Too tight jaw.

"Where have you been?" I ask next, ignoring his false plea.

"Around."

The word strikes a nerve. *He's been around?* More like playing around, behind my back, and then off who knows where with who knows who. *No, thank you.*

"That's not an answer."

He glares at me, but I glare back, and something in my expression makes him flinch. He exhales and lowers his head, shaking it side to side.

"I saw your post in the paper. Why'd you have to blast it to the world you want a divorce?" His head pops up.

I snort. "Posting it in the local paper isn't the world, Howard. I'm surprised you found it."

"Is that what you hoped? That I wouldn't read the notice."

How easily he's read my mind, but I don't answer him again.

"I want a divorce," I state.

"Because of Jedd."

"Jedd?" I laugh without humor. "Because of the hundreds of women you've been with."

"Not hundreds, baby."

He's kidding me, right? "Get out of here," I whisper, but venom drips from my tone.

"I'm just joking, Beverly. It wasn't that many." Is any number a limit? I'd say *one* outside the marriage is one too many. Obviously, Howard's and my math skills differ.

"I said get out." My voice seethes, a bitter taste mixing with the saliva.

"Bev, don't be like this."

"Get out!" I scream.

Howard flinches, but he doesn't move from the kitchen. He combs his fingers through his thinning hair and holds the back of his neck.

"We aren't getting off to a good start. I'm going to the living room to relax a bit. When you settle down, we can talk."

"We have nothing to talk about," I yell. "And I said get out. Get out of my house."

"Our house," he mutters.

"Mine," I snap, picking up the blender I use for mixing soaps and hurling it at him. It comes nowhere near his body and hits the refrigerator, denting the old mustard color.

"You're going to fix that," he warns and turns for the living room, removing his suit coat jacket as he walks.

I scream at the top of my lungs, more like a roar, and then I turn for the back door, making my way as fast as I can across the drive. My vision blurs. I fumble over larger chunks of rock in the gravel but continue moving forward, pressing at the barn door and closing myself inside. Instead of leaning on the large wood, I hobble to the middle of the barn and scream again.

Anger. Hatred. Grief.

Why is Howard here? Why, why, *why?!*

As the scream subsides to an echo, I hear a thump up above in the loft and recall the first time I heard such a sound. Jedd had just finished building his room in the barn, and I was snooping.

"I know you're up there," I call out. The stillness within the old structure gives away his presence even more, and my thoughts flip through the feedings and finding him outside the garage. And then the night Jedd and I rode out under moonlight, I saw him slip his broad body through the slats and disappear inside this structure.

"And I know who you are," I yell even though I'm not certain. "Boone, you need to come down."

There's still not a response. No movement. No sound. And unfortunately for me, I can't go up. There's no way I'd risk climbing the rusty rungs of the ladder leading upward a full story or more.

"Jedd's been looking for you," I say, lowering my voice just a little. His questions about the house. The Crawford estate. His old home. Tears cloud my vision once again; only this time, I don't blink them back.

"I'm so sorry, Boone," I whisper because I didn't know. There's so much I didn't know. A boy turned to man turned to recluse, alone in a house on my land. I'd never seen him, but I also didn't pay attention. I'd been too absorbed in myself, acting in my own reclusive behavior. "It's time to come home."

The words are no more than a squeak as the sobs fill my throat, and I fall to my knees. With my hands over my face, I rock forward as tears bath me in all the regrets. Hannah. Boone. Jedd.

Even Howard. I've wasted too much time and too much energy on him, and I've lost years because of it, because of him.

No more, I cry. *No more.* But the tears continue to fall, and I let them. I need to let it all out.

* * *

Drained of all emotion, I finally return to the house. I did walk down to the stables, worried about the horses needing food or stalls cleaned as Jedd is gone. Surprisingly, the animal care is done, and I smile despite my mood, thinking my guardian angel has taken care of things again.

The days are slowly creeping longer, and it's dusk as I enter my home. As the back door closes behind me, Hannah comes down the stairs, and Howard makes his way to the kitchen.

"Where are you going?" he questions Hannah in her yoga pants and an oversized sweatshirt, a bag over her arm which holds her makeup kit and skimpy outfits.

"To work," she tells him over her shoulder as she approaches the coat hooks by the back door and grabs her jacket.

"You work a night shift?" His eyes leap to me, accusatory once again.

"I work at the Pink Pony, Daddy. Aren't you proud?" His mouth drops open at the salty words, and she slips her jacket over her arm and reaches for the back door.

"You're a stripper?" His face turns white, and his lips drain of color. A sickening thought crosses my mind that Howard might have seen his own child naked and strutting her stuff without ever recognizing her. I shudder as the color returns to his face, morphing from blanched to pinkened to a deep maroon. "No child of mine will be a stripper."

"Pot meet kettle," Hannah states, pointing from him to her and back. She turns to me. "Come with me." It's a plea of concern because she's afraid to leave me alone with Howard.

"Your...Howard was just leaving," I answer, keeping my voice low. I reach out and pat her arm. I'm more concerned Howard will do something to the house without me present, and I want him gone.

"Grizz knows you're here, and I'm calling Jackson to come check on you as well." The comment surprises me, especially as Hannah has issues with Jackson James, the sheriff's deputy, because he likes to pull her over and issue unnecessary moving violation tickets.

"We don't need no small-time police coming out here," Howard threatens, but Hannah ignores him, giving him a dismissive eye roll before opening the back door.

"I love you, Momma," she says, focusing her eyes on me.

"I love you, too, sunshine." I smile to reassure her.

As soon as Hannah exits, Howard asks, "What's for dinner?" and I turn on him.

"I'm not running a restaurant here. Get out. And then don't return."

"Careful, Beverly," he warns. "Seems entertaining a man has made you smart-mouthed."

At this point, I should be frightened. He's threatening me with his glare, but I know Howard. He's a lover, not a fighter, and I don't mean that in a positive way. He wouldn't touch me. Gazing out the kitchen window, I see a figure, large and broad, in the receding tail-lights of Hannah's car, and I know I'm safe. My savior-angel is out there.

I'm ready to make my way to my room when another set of head-lights illuminates the drive outside the window. Holding my breath, I want to rush to the glass in hopes Jedd has returned. The thought hits me hard. *Will he come back?*

For another second, I consider Hannah has turned around and come back to force me to follow her, returning to her status as the domineering child over the stubborn mother, but I quickly notice the car is not Hannah's, but a smaller vehicle. It's a VW convertible Bug. As the headlights turn off, two doors open at the same time, and I'm shocked to see the outlines of my sisters.

"Now what?" Howard snaps. He's still standing by a kitchen chair, but his arms cross over his thin chest. The sight of him in a threadbare dress shirt strikes me as so opposite of Jedd. Sleeves to his wrists, Howard's skin is pale compared to Jedd, proving he's spent more time indoors than out. I have no idea what he's done for work over the years, and I don't even want to ask.

"Knock, knock," comes the false cheer of my sister Naomi as she helps herself to enter my house through the back door. Flabbergasted, I stare in amazement as my other sister Scotia follows Naomi in a sleek dress suit with a bright red skirt and coordinating blazer. Her lips are red to match. Her dark hair, with a single stripe of white, is perfectly coifed compared to the waves of our other sister, whose untamed riot is wild and long, giving her the appearance of a good-natured witch.

"Well," Scotia drawls immediately, addressing Howard, "look what the cat dragged in."

My mouth pops open.

"Sissy…" For some reason, I relax. I want to hug her for being the demeaning woman she can be. She's going to eat Howard alive, and I almost want to step back and see where my sister goes with this, but this is my fight, and I need to get Howard out of here.

"Howard was actually leaving," I admit, turning to him.

"Now, Beverly, we were about to have dinner. Perhaps your sisters would like to join us." The sugar-sweet tone doesn't settle with me nor does the inviting sentiment.

"You are not joining us," I growl, taking comfort in my sisters' presence. Naomi crosses the room to the refrigerator, leaning against it like a human shield to protect the stock of casseroles and prepared meals.

"We'll not offer you a morsel," Scotia states, holding firm to her spot as if moving might soil her ensemble. While pleasantly shocked, I'm still grateful for her presence. "What do you want, Howard?"

Her condescending tone could make the best of men grovel, but Howard stands tall, attempting to exert status over my sister.

"How's your husband, Scotia?"

"He's dead," she blurts, and Howard's head snaps back. Score one for Scotia. Howard isn't about to tell her anything she doesn't already know about her deceased man.

"Where's your whore, Howard?"

"Scotia," Naomi hisses, and I pinken with shame on his behalf.

"I don't know what you're talking about," Howard states, but a trickle of sweat graces the edge of his brow. I must admit it's growing warm in the suddenly cramped kitchen.

"We can play this game all night, Howard. I can go twenty rounds with you if I need to."

"Oh, I'm scared," Howard mocks, putting up his hands in a mocking boxer's stance as if preparing to go rounds with her. His eyes dance. "What are you, a hundred by now?"

"Bless your heart, Howard. I'm forty-seven, and that means I'm out of fucks for men like you. Now, tell us why you're here."

Still shocked at my sister's rebuttal, I almost miss Howard's next words.

"I don't owe you an explanation," he definitively states, but Scotia doesn't blink.

"Any explanation you offer will be weak, like you, but we'd like to hear it all the same."

"I'm here for my wife."

My mouth falls open, and I meet the eyes of Naomi across the room, who still has a hand on the freezer handle.

"You forfeited your right to your wife when you stepped out on her. Then you left. She's not your concern," Scotia states, and my head turns to my oldest sister. She has always been forceful, but I've never seen this side of her.

"What's between my wife and me is none of your business," Howard states, and I'm tired of being spoken about as if I'm not in the room.

"The *wife* is present and has a name, and no longer wishes to be your wife."

Scotia turns to me for the first time, and her expression softens just a smidge from the Cruella de Vil look she has going. "I've filed for divorce," I tell her.

"Naomi told me," she says, and I wonder when Scotia and Naomi became friends, although something tells me there's more to the story this evening. They've never been friendly, not like this.

"We aren't divorcing," Howard states, and all heads turn to him.

"By the goddess you are," Naomi blurts. I want to chuckle at my sister's outburst but hold the laughter in.

"Right," Howard drawls. "Still up to your kooky ways." Howard wiggles his fingers in the air as though he's spooked.

"That's enough," Scotia snaps in a disciplinarian tone with the addition of a scathing glare. "Get out of here, Howard. Whatever you want, you aren't getting it."

"I own everything," I tell my sister, who turns to me. "The land. The house. It's all mine. Ewell left it to me in his will."

"Which means it's mine by half because we're married."

Naomi's mouth falls open at this statement, and Scotia crosses her arms. "Being as Tennessee is an equitable state, I can see where you think that's your right, but again, you forfeited that right when you left. No judge in his right mind is going to give you half this estate based on several factors."

I'm impressed with my sister's knowledge of Tennessee law concerning divorce, and it makes me wonder if she ever considered leaving her husband, Karl, before his death.

Howard's jaw clenches. He wants to ask questions, but if he does, he'll appear unknowledgable about the battle he's trying to wage.

"I have a meeting with my attorney tomorrow," I announce, and Howard's head swerves to me.

"Janice?" Howard questions, a slow, sly grin crossing his face. He looks like the Grinch who stole Christmas, proud of his evil ways. "I'd love to speak with her again."

"It's not a joint meeting," I tell him. "And officially, my attorney is Ramirez Caeser." Howard blanches a bit again, and it triggers the thought that Howard is familiar with the divorce lawyer.

"I'll be contacting Haywood."

Scotia shakes her head like Howard is a silly boy who doesn't understand the consequences. "You'll be hard-pressed to find someone sympathetic to you around here."

"Haywood and I go way back," Howard argues.

I have no idea if this is true, but something outside the window catches the corner of my eye. A flash or a spark, like lightning. It's not uncommon for a thunderstorm this early in the season. The weather's warming nicely. Spring is on the horizon, but that spark seemed a bit unusual. My eyes narrow, watching out the dark window for another sign. Thunder. Rain. It's not warm enough for only a lightning show.

Naomi's head turns in the direction of my gaze. Finally, she releases her hand from the freezer and crosses to the sink to get a better view. Her head instantly turns back to me.

"Jedd isn't still out there?" she questions, knowing he moved into the house months ago. Panic paints her face.

"No, why?"

"Because your barn's on fire." The statement is made with cool calm, and Scotia steps over to the sink window as well.

"Bless my soul." The higher pitch to Scotia's voice sets Howard in motion, and I reach for the cell phone I left on the table. Punching in the numbers for 911, I make a call I've never had to make and exhale into the phone when the dispatcher Flo McClure answers.

"911. What's your emergency?"

"Townsen farm. Our barn is on fire."

CHAPTER THIRTY-SIX

[Beverly]

With Naomi's assistance, I make it outdoors, frozen in place as the blaze begins in earnest. The structure is old and the wood brittle, so within minutes, the entire backside is engulfed. It won't take long for the remainder of the barn to catch, and fear slowly creeps in.

"There's a tractor inside." Gasoline could be an issue. "And what about the house?" I murmur, noting the distance between the barn and my home. Will it be enough space to ward off the leaping flames?

"The horses," I note, clicking through a mental checklist, but the animals are down the drive a bit and not in any imminent danger of flames.

"Boone," I whisper. *Sweet butter on a biscuit!*

"There's a man in there," I say, the words catching in my throat and not reaching the volume or warning level I intend.

"What?" Howard asks.

"There's a man in the barn," I repeat louder as a hand comes to my chest. *Oh my, Boone!* My heart races faster as a chorus of who, what, and where follows from Scotia, Naomi, and Howard.

"A homeless man," I explain. "He's been using the barn to guard against the weather."

"He's what?" Howard asks.

"How could you?" Scotia scoffs.

"I'm so proud of you," Naomi offers, and I turn my fearful face to her.

"We need to get him out of there." On instinct, I step forward, although I'd be no good at rescue efforts. Naomi reaches a hand for my forearm stopping me, and Scotia glares at me when she asks, "Where do you think you are going?"

I turn to Howard. "He's in there. He might need help."

Howard's forehead wrinkles in disgust. "And what am I supposed to do about it?" If I'd never been disappointed in Howard before, this moment solidifies it. Not that he's trained to rush into a burning building, but his total lack of empathy surprises even me. Thankfully, we hear the fire sirens approaching and see the rotating red lights in the distance.

Within minutes, a fire engine, ladder, and tanker truck have invaded the drive. Carter McClure, the fire chief, is the first to approach us as his men begin the heavy work of lifting hoses.

"Everyone accounted for?" he inquires.

"Yes," Howard answers as if he's an authority, and Chief McClure does a double take at Howard's presence.

"A homeless man was living in my barn. He might still be in there." I step forward, nudging my way around Howard. Carter doesn't blink at my intrusion but begins barking orders about a possible person in the burning structure. I send up a silent prayer that Boone isn't inside or has gotten out at this point. Then I notice the outline of someone who could be Grizzly Grady, and more prayers are sent out like the sparks floating around us.

"Guys, I'm going to need you to step back." Carter holds out his arms in a protective shield, forcing us to move. "Maybe the front yard would be safer for y'all?" he directs, and my stomach falls.

"Is the house in danger?"

"Shouldn't be," he clarifies. "We'll set up a perimeter of water to deter the flames from traveling. At this point, Ms. Townsen, you must know that barn isn't worth saving. There's nothing of value in there, correct?" Some people store old cars or beat-up trucks under cover of their old buildings. Jedd's already removed his bag and the trunk with his buckles and awards.

"The only equipment inside is an old tractor." I'd be sad to see the ancient thing go as it had new life under Jedd's hand, not to mention Jedd and I shared kisses on it, but none of that seems important to mention.

"Possible gasoline!" Carter calls out the additional warning to his men as he steps away from us once he's ushered us to the front lawn. The air around us should be cool under the blackened sky, but the heat generating off the blaze feels like the sun landed in my yard. Tears prickle my eyes at the sight. Naomi's arm comes around my shoulders, and I let her draw me to her.

We watch in a dazed stupor at the beautiful flames dancing against the dark backdrop. At some point, two pickup trucks pull into the yard, releasing more men to gape at the wonderous hazard before us. One man races toward us, and within seconds, I recognize the outline of Jedd.

His name whispers on my lips, and Howard turns to me, reaching an arm out to stop me from moving forward, but I brush past his forearm. Limping, I have never moved me so fast on crutches as Jedd and I draw toward one another. He crushes me to him the second we are within arm's length and buries in my neck. I can't reciprocate the embrace because he's trapped my arms at my sides.

"You weren't hurt?" he questions, mumbling into my skin, and I melt into him.

"I'm fine," I whisper at his ear, the one where he can hear me, and he shudders against me. Slipping me into position, his arm around my waist, and his thigh between my legs, he moves us in the strange manner he likes best as we return to the collected observers. Nathan is here and Tower is present, as is Vernon Grady, whose arms are crossed over his big chest. He's chewing at his lip.

"He knows what he's doing." Carter McClure reassures Vernon of his son's ability as a fireman. Vernon nods without taking his eyes off the raging fire.

Turning to me, Carter says, "We haven't found any evidence of someone inside. Any idea how the fire might have started?"

"Someone inside?" Jedd asks, tightening his arm at my waist.

"Beverly mentioned a homeless man was living in her barn," Carter clarifies for Jedd, and Howard snorts.

"A wha..." Jedd's voice fades as his arm slips from my back.

"Boone," I mutter. "I think Boone might have been staying in there."

Jedd's midnight eyes turn to me, reflective of the blazing flames like a mirror. "He what?"

"Who's Boone?" Naomi asks, and Carter crosses his arms, awaiting an answer.

"That crazy boy of Hasting Crawford?" Scotia interjects in her condescending tone, and my brows pinch at her harsh labeling.

"He isn't crazy," I defend as if I know anything about the man. Jedd remains eerily quiet.

"Well, we'll still check for signs of life, but I'd say he had fair warning to get out. Any chance he started the blaze?"

"He certainly did," Howard interjects. "I'd like to press charges, and you'll be hearing from my insurance company." Howard aims a pointed finger at Jedd.

"Put your finger down before you hurt yourself," Scotia warns as I step out of Jedd's arms.

"Howard, shut up." I glare at my soon-to-be ex-husband.

Mouths gape and snickers happen, but I'm only warming up with him.

"I don't know who you think you are, or where you've been, and frankly, I don't care anymore. You've done more damage than this burning barn, and I'm done with you, Howard. So done. So don't

you think you can come back here after twenty years. Twenty years!"
I yell. "And make statements and claims and accusations. The Lord
teaches us to forgive, Howard. And God above knows I tried and
struggled for years to do so. But you know what, Howard? If I don't
forgive you, I can't forgive myself. Forgive myself for what I've
done to me, to Hannah, to this land. So I forgive you, Howard. I
forgive you for stepping out, but now I want you to get out. For the
twentieth time today, this is *my* home. Get off my property!" I'm
screaming so loud, Carter McClure flinches, and Scotia punctuates
my ire with an audible huff.

"Now, baby," Howard says, reaching for me, but he stops short.
A moment passes before I realize it isn't the horror in my expression—the disgust that he'll touch me—that stops him, but the
horror in his as he doesn't want to be near the crutches at my
arms.

"You bastard," I say as angry tears blur my vision of my
husband. The man who promised to love and honor me, in sickness
and in health, yet has done none of these things.

Carter McClure clears his throat. "As we don't need this kind of
drama right now, might I recommend a room at Donner Lodge,
Howard?"

"This is my house," Howard states, but his declaration has no
strength.

"If you don't get off this land, I'll testify in a court of law you set
that fire yourself," Scotia warns, and once again, I want to hug my
big sister even though I'm confused by her sudden protective nature.

"Now, Ms. Simmons," Chief McClure begins.

"Don't you 'Ms. Simmons' me, sir." Her voice brooks no argument despite the fact it'd be a false accusation against Howard.

"Mr. Townsen," the chief warns.

"I can't get anywhere with your trucks in my way, but I'll go," he
says begrudgingly, and then remains where he stands. I look to my
side, noting Jedd is no longer close. My eyes find him standing only
a few feet away by Vernon.

"Back to the start of the fire," the fire chief states. "We need to decide if we put her out or let her burn?" Carter keeps his eyes on me. "It's your call, Beverly."

It's my call. Watch the old building burn and hope Boone isn't inside, or put out the flames on a building which is already a loss. I didn't know my homeless angel was Jedd's brother until hours ago, but it feels like a lifetime has passed since then. I still don't know if the homeless man and Boone are one and the same, but I have a strong suspicion they are. I want to ask Jedd what he thinks—let the barn go or put it out—so I turn to him to find him watching me, and something in his expression halts my tongue.

"Jedd?" I question, no longer concerned with the barn but his thoughts and the expression on his face, which I can't read. He quickly steps up to me, bracing one large palm over my heart.

"Bee, I have to know."

My eyes search his, still questioning him with only his name. "Jedd?"

He leans forward, kisses me briefly in front of everyone, and then pulls back, keeping his eyes on me a second longer. He's turning his back on me, and it's like watching something move in slow motion. The loss of his eyes. The curve of his shoulder. His back, broad and solid.

"Jedd, you promised you wouldn't leave," I call out, frantic and panicked as he doesn't respond to me. Instead, he breaks into a sprint, heading toward the raging flames.

"Jedd!" I scream as I watch him running away from me.

And then an explosion occurs.

CHAPTER THIRTY-SEVEN

[Beverly]

I wake on my bed. Someone carried me in here as the world went black after the explosion. I remember cursing my legs and watching Jedd disappear. I couldn't chase him, yet Nathan restrained me anyway, my voice screaming louder than the roaring fire.

Gingerly, I move, struggling to make sense of it all, struggling to find a purpose to sit up, but I need to look out the window. Making my way to my rocking chair, I focus on the burning barn, now a pile of rubble, like a ginormous bonfire. The barn where Jedd built a room against my wishes. The place where I snooped through his things. The space where we spent a night together on his cot. All gone.

Jedd.

I have no idea why he thought entering the flaming structure was a good idea, but I also understand his motive.

His brother. *I didn't know.*

I stare at the lulling flames, now settling after the explosion.

Jedd.

Why did you go after him? Why didn't you let the firemen do their job? Why did you need to be a hero?

I can't close my eyes; the vision behind them something I don't want to imagine. I'll never sleep. I don't want to sleep. I want Jedd.

Only Jedd.

A singular pulse.

Voices travel into my room, but I can't make out who says what. Instead, I sit here and watch out the window. I hope Howard is gone. I think my sisters remain.

As I stare throught the glass, the display across the gravel drive looks like something from a television program. Fire people and fire trucks litter the area. It's more realistic than reality television, and while reality television was once the highlight of my days, Jedd had become my reality. He was real.

"It felt like a fantasy," I say to no one. I don't flinch when my bedroom door opens and I see the reflection of light from the hall in the glass. Then the door closes.

"Bee?" My eyes shut. I'm already dreaming of him, hearing his voice in my head. Rumpled sheets and sleepy mornings. Quickly, my eyes open. I can't close them. The visions of Jedd, flames, a fire. There's a movement in my periphery, and I turn with a start.

"Sweet butter on a biscuit," I shriek, but my voice croaks as my hand comes to my throat. "Jedd?"

He collapses before me, kneeling between my knees as I sit on the rocking chair. He smells of smoke and burnt ashes and life.

"Jedd?" My hands cover his face, my sight blurring as tears well up. His mouth crashes against mine, and the fantasy feels so real. His lips on me. His breath mixing with mine. His tongue stroking mine. He groans, and I pull back.

"Jedd." It's as if I still don't believe he's before me. My fingers coast over his face. "You're…You're…" I break, sobs catching in my throat as he tugs me to his chest. I hold onto him, covering my mouth to suppress the fear and relief.

"I'm okay, honey. I'm right here. I didn't go anywhere."

I pull back. "But I saw you run to the barn. You went into the fire." My hands rub over his shoulders and down his arms, both of them.

"I didn't, darlin'. Grizz caught me just before I made it to the door. I'm sorry I scared you, honey. I had to know...I just had to see for myself." His voice cracks.

"I'm so sorry, Jedd. I didn't know. I should have told you I was feeding him. I should have told you he was here in the barn, and all this time..."

"Shh, honey. Shh." So Jedd. He's soothing me when I should be soothing him.

"Thank you for Boone. For feeding him. For taking care of him." We stare at one another a moment before his hand curls around my neck, and he tugs out foreheads together. His gratitude sounds like goodbye.

"You promised you'd never leave me." I close my eyes even though I'm afraid he'll disappear. A new wave of emotion settles over me.

Jedd slowly pulls back. "I'm not going anywhere. Ever. Do you hear me? Because earlier..."

My hands return to his face, stopping his words. Earlier, I told him to leave. There was so much happening at once. Too much information to process. I needed space. I needed to think.

"Howard's gone," I say, and Jedd nods.

"How do you feel about that?"

I stare back at him. He can't possibly think I'd be sad.

"I love you, Jedd," I blurt. He slips back to sit on his ankles, staring up at me. "I know it might be too much and said too fast. I know we're still learning each other, but I just...I have to tell you how I feel. I thought I'd lost you tonight. The fire. I thought you were gone forever. Not even just out there." I wave a hand toward the window. "And I don't want another second to pass without you knowing how I feel. I love—"

The words are swallowed as Jedd leans forward, covering my

mouth with his and kissing me hard. My knees separate, and I press myself as close as I can to him as our tongues tangle. I come to the edge of the seat, legs open, core pressing at his belly. I need to be closer to him. Cupping his face, I slowly draw back.

"I'm so sorry about Boone. I'm sorry I didn't tell you."

His hand covers my mouth.

"I found Boone. He's fine. Well, sort of, but I don't want to talk about Boone. I need you. I need you right now."

His hand coasts down from my neck, slipping lower toward the hem my sweater. I waste no time pulling it over my head and working at his flannel.

"My arm," he exhales between kisses as our mouths only part with the removal of clothing.

"Leave it," I mumble against his lips, reaching for his jeans. He works them himself, down to his knees as I work mine off around his body. His arm scoops me to the edge of the rocker again, and he kneels upward.

"Jedd," I moan, all the emotion pouring out in his name. I need him. I want him. His mouth comes to mine as he guides himself to my entrance.

"I love you," he says against my lips, and I draw back to meet his eyes. "I think I've loved you since the moment I stood on that porch and you were trying to make me leave. But I'm not going anywhere, Bee. I'm here to stay."

"Don't ever scare me like that again. The thought of losing you…" My mouth comes to his, lingering as I savor what he's said to me. He loves me. We kiss and we kiss until we both need more.

"Bee," he groans, and I lean forward, allowing him into me, filling me, completing me. We use the rocking chair as support, gently drawing us together and apart but never separating. We clutch at one another. His hand in my hair. My hand on his shoulder blade. My leg curls over his hips as I slowly rock, and he meets me, tender thrust for tender thrust, until I still, purring his name at his good ear.

"I love you." My voice tremors with emotion. The feel of him inside me. The warmth of him around me. The depth of him in my heart.

"I love you, too, honey." His voice strains. His nose rests in the crook of my neck as he comes apart, filling me. And we hold, and we hold, knowing we'll never let go.

CHAPTER THIRTY-EIGHT

[Beverly]

I postpone my meeting with Ram for a few days in order to deal with the debris and smoking embers of my old barn. Once again, I find the structure a metaphor for me. Old and decrepit yet still structurally sound, the weathered thing had a burst of passion—heat, flames, fire—like my time with Jedd, and then an explosion, where everything implodes because of lies and truths. Finally, the remains of a tarnished land and ashy air could be a symbol of my heart— blackened and irreparable—but it's not damage that I feel. This is another baptism. Another rising. A new Beverly who will be free of Howard someday. Who loves Jedd and is loved by him every day.

An investigation into the fire ruled out foul play.

"Honestly, it could have been anything," Carter McClure tells me. "Best guess is Boone started a fire to keep warm inside the old thing."

This doesn't sit well with me, as there'd never been evidence he'd done it before. No smoky residue in the air. No fire ring. No remaining embers. Then again, I'd never climbed up to the loft where nothing remained to sift through for clues other than a surprising scrap of extra-thick yarn from the blanket I'd made Jedd. He'd told me it had gone missing. He"d actually accused me of taking it back from him. Then he'd teased me he'd just use my warmth to cover him instead.

"Better than some wielded blanket," he'd teased, reminding us both of our first encounter.

I glance back at Chief McClure as he looks out over the smoldering ash. "Mind my asking what was going on in your house when the fire started, though?" His question surprises me. "There's something I can't quite make out from what that spitfire sister of yours has said."

Scotia? She said she'd attest to Howard starting that fire. "I don't understand."

"Scotia mentioned seeing something large and bear-like at the corner of the barn." McClure lifts an eyebrow as he glances down at me. "Claims she saw a light flicker and then die out."

"Did Scotia suggest Boone started the fire?"

"Oh, Scotia didn't say such a thing, and as far as I'm concerned, no one was ever in that barn, causing a potential hazard." Carter winks at me, and I'm slow to take his meaning. "But a little birdie told me you were having words with Howard inside when your sisters arrived, and I'm curious if someone thought the distraction was protection."

"That's pretty far-fetched, even for you, Carter." I laugh without humor.

"It certainly is, which is why I'm going to stick to my report— accidental and unintentional. Pretend we didn't find the remnants of cotton, which looks like pieces of a blanket, dipped in gasoline and set in an empty butter tub."

What?

"You had a guardian angel that night, Ms. Townsen. Let's leave it at that."

He winks again, and I stare back at the blackened ground, still sizzling a bit in the cool morning sunshine.

A guardian angel? I certainly have.

* * *

"You've had a bit of excitement in the last week," Ram teases me in his best broken Hispanic accent when I arrive a week later.

"Why do you do that?" I ask, and his brows rise in question. "Act like you're a hick when you're actually an accomplished attorney."

"Old habit," he says, straightening his tie and sitting upright in his chair behind his desk. "People have a preconceived notion, right? Especially in a small town. I must be some cross-the-border immigrant, coming to pick apples in an orchard. I play the part and *pow!*" He smacks his hands together. "Hit them with my intelligence as well as my comprehension of all they say in English, adding to it my understanding of the law. It's fun to watch people's faces in court. The sheen of sweat. The stunned confusion." He exaggerates, wiping his brow. He reminds me of a guy from *That 70s Show*, but I can't think of his name under pressure.

"Is that what you're going to do with Howard?" I chuckle, but Ram grows serious.

"Howard's already been here."

I sober at the serious look on my attorney's face versus the carefree, teasing one.

"Beverly, you know all about Janice and Howard, right?"

"I do," I admit.

"She didn't want to take you on as a client because of conflict of interest due to her history with him, but you also know she represented Ewell, correct?"

"Surprisingly, I only learned about it the other day."

Ram's eyebrows rise higher, and his smooth tanned forehead wrinkles.

"You never knew you inherited all Ewell's property?"

"I did not. Howard came to the reading of the will, and he never told me what was said. I was young, naïve, and unfortunately, in love with a terrible man. I didn't question him when he told me the will reading was standard procedure and he'd inherited everything."

"That's my fault," a stern feminine voice at my back makes me shift in my seat and face Janice over my shoulder. She closes the door behind her and nods at Ram. *What's going on?* I wonder until I realize I've said it aloud.

"I could be disbarred for all I've done," Janice begins. "Ewell Townsen was a ruthless man, but I liked him." She smiles guiltily as she perches on the corner of Ram's desk. "He encouraged Howard and me to see each together at his home as if we pulling something over on Hasting, and I perpetrated the rivalry. After all, Howard and I were going to show them both when we ran away." She shakes her head.

"But you know what happened." She isn't accusing me of anything, but we don't need a history lesson. "Ewell came to see me when he'd heard I'd become a lawyer. He expressed his concern that his son might sell his land and the land Howard had acquired from my younger brother. He wanted to ensure you and Hannah were taken care of, and this was his contingency plan."

I nod once as I understand the musing of an old man filled with revenge himself, and then fear that it would all be for naught.

"He loved you and Hannah, in his own way." She chuckles, possibly understanding my plight. Ewell was stern, a bit abrasive, but someone you forgave for his harshness. He was just a grumpy old man. "Hannah was his pride and joy."

I smile in appreciation that Ewell and I shared the same love of my child.

"When he died…" Janice turns more somber and closes her eyes. "I did something I never thought I'd do."

She licks her lips, and I swallow in anticipation of bad news.

"I slept with Howard, feeling like I'd really fuck him over." I startle at the brash words and feel sick at the same moment. "Because afterward, I nailed him with the news of the land." The innuendo in her little confession isn't lost on me, and neither is the aggression in her tone. She hated Howard almost as much as me.

"I'm sorry he left you and never told you the truth of the property. Follow-up letters were sent."

My guilt returns at never opening them, but I'm still in shock at her admission she slept with my husband while we were still married. A stronger woman might stand and smack her while I think I want to shake her hand for trying to screw Howard over. Then again...

"Howard was here this week," Janice continues, and she nods to Ram.

"He tried to blackmail Janice into agreeing to be his lawyer. Said he'd tell whoever would listen she should be disbarred"—he clears his throat and acts demure as he states—"*for being with him.* He believes she tricked him out of his rightful inheritance. But I stepped in as your attorney, warning him I'd petition every woman he's been with in this county to testify to his adultery. Then I brought up the gambling debts I've uncovered and unpaid bills in his name. Not to mention trickery in a card game with Boone Crawford. The amount of debt he's incurred doesn't balance his claim for half your property. Those debts are his, and any judge in Tennessee will agree, holding it against his claim for fifty percent. In addition, you're disabled, and this means you haven't been able to work. With the injustice in lack of livelihood *and* the eight years of child support he never paid to you, he might actually owe you more than fifty percent of the estate." Ram pauses, and I note his voice has shifted from immigrant Latino to accomplished attorney. There's the *pow!* moment, and I'm stumped myself.

"I don't think I really want anything from Howard. I mean, I understand that I'm owed, but I just want him to disappear again."

"That's what I figured. I also advised him he could contest the divorce and the will, which would both be additional legal fees, and when he lost, which he would because, let's face it—he's been missing for twenty years and has no just cause as to his disappearance, like kidnapping or incarceration—he'd lose even more. We'd sue him for the additional emotional distress and attorney fees." Ram smiles a full-wattage, white-toothed grin, which I imagine is pure evil when he's up against a testy client, but it makes me laugh.

"So what's next?"

"He signed the papers." Ram flips the blue packet and presents me with Howard's legal name on the line. "If you want the child support and loss of income, we can file a suit."

My head pops up from examining the signature and yellow sticky arrow pointing at where my signature goes under his.

"I think I'm happy to have Howard written out of my life."

"That's understandable," Janice adds.

"Give me the pen, then." The second my name breezes over the line, I feel lighter. I drop the pen on the desk as if it holds germs. *Goodbye, Howard.*

Shifting in my seat once again, I look up at Janice. "There's a world of things I could say to you about what you did, but I've spent years holding onto grudges and losing my patience over things I can't change. I also feel guilty for my behavior with Howard. I never knew he was engaged. Never dreamed other women could exist. And I'm sorry my pregnancy prevented your marriage to him."

"We were both duped by him and hurt, but the emotions have been a waste. He wasn't worth it to either of us," Janice states, and I smile in agreement.

"With that said, I have another legal matter I need your help with. Your brother is very important to me, so I don't want this to be another conflict of interest for you."

Ram nods, and Janice purses her lips in curiosity.

"Could you help me with something regarding the land?" A smile crosses my lips. *My land.* Which I want to share with Jedd.

EPILOGUE

[Jedd]

With all that's happened, I'm a week behind on my promise to till the back pasture, but I start the tractor I borrowed from Vernon and begin the first stretch of the field. It's a glorious mid-March day, and spring has arrived in all its wonder. Butterflies flit. Birds flutter. And my heart is full. I've never been happier than to be here.

Boone was found buried in a haybed of his own making in the stables. Thankfully, he was cleared of any possible charges. I don't know what he was thinking or if he was thinking at all when he started the fire, which I'm not saying he did...but my best guess is he did. He did it for Bee.

She'd agreed to let Boone stay in the old house under the guidance of Tower. His patient temperament is suited for someone like Boone. Boone and I would probably argue as we did when we were kids, but Tower understands him. Janice and I got him some medical attention after months of homelessness, and a psychologist is lined up to help us better understand what happened to him. I'm also hoping Tower can teach my brother a skill and give him something useful to occupy himself. However, it turns out my brother is quite the artist. Beverly already has him sketching larger art pieces for her.

Beverly. My chest warms just thinking of her.

She proposed turning the old house into a veteran's home. A place for warriors wounded in heart and spirit to stay and possibly work with the horses. She's a girl after my own heart. She owns my heart.

I shake my head as I shift gears, tearing up the ground. My thoughts rumble to the purr of the beast beneath me as I reflect on how I got here. Proposing I raise horses on borrowed land and falling in love with an incredible woman seem like opposite ends of a straight line, but I've never lived a straight line. Still am not. My mind fills with the naughty things I've done with Beverly, and how she loves all of it. I love her, and she loves me in return. It's a heady feeling.

I'm turning the corner when I see someone driving toward me. Whoever it is cutting a crooked path across the pasture, heading straight for me. As the other tractor draws near, white hair comes into view, and a sweater slipping off one shoulder gives away the driver.

Beverly. I smile just thinking her name. *My Bee.*

I cut my engine but hold my position a moment, drinking her in as the wind blows her hair. I love to thread my fingers into and tug on those short locks. A healthy glow graces her skin from spending time in the spring sunshine. I can't make out her expression, but she looks like she's laughing.

What is she doing?

Then I see her driving closer at a speed that suggests she's not slowing down.

Holy crap.

I hop off the tractor and wave my arms like she hasn't seen me.

"Brake," I'm yelling as she continues jostling closer. She doesn't appear like she's going to stop, and I eventually step aside so she doesn't get my toes.

"What the hell?" I call after her as she draws up to me and then brakes with a jolting halt.

"My," she blurts. "That was fun." She's laughing as I walk up to the shiny new equipment and place my hands on my hips.

"What are you doing?" I admonish, though there's no bite to my bark. Her laughter is infectious, and I'm reminded of when she giggles in bed.

A man gets used to that sound.

"Jedd Flemming," she yells a little too loud as she swings a leg over the steering wheel but then pauses, perched sideways on the seat.

"I might be partially deaf, but you don't need to yell," I retort, tweaking an eyebrow. Beverly's laughter has died, but her smile remains at the reminder of our first meeting.

"And I might be lame, but I'm not lacking," she replies, her grin growing larger.

"What are you doing out here, and where did you get that thing?"

Beverly runs her hand over the steering wheel. "I might have lost my license, but I can drive this all over my land. The insurance company covered this, and Vernon just dropped it off. 'Course I could be asking you the same thing? What are you doing out here?"

"I'm plowing this field." I'm not certain why she's asking me this as we discussed it just last night before bed, laying out our days before we lay out each other.

A man gets used to that.

"And who told you you could plow my field?" she inquires, her expression trying to draw stern, but it isn't quite working because her lips keep fighting a smile.

"Well, see, I made this promise to a woman, and I intend to keep it."

Beverly's expression does drop a bit, but she keeps her eyes on me. "You've made quite a few promises. Gonna keep all of them?"

My head tips, not quite understanding her meaning.

"I'm not sure I'm getting off on the right foot," she teases, and I recall saying the same thing to her when we met.

My brows rise, and hands come to my thighs, swiping at them. "Well, seeing as you aren't standing on your feet...."

I don't give her a chance to respond before reaching up and dragging her down to stand before me. Her hands come to my shoulders as I press her against the big wheel at her back.

"I have a proposal for you," she mutters, smoothing down my T-shirt.

"What's your proposal, honey?" My mind races with all kinds of things I want to propose, but there's only one thing I really want. *Her*.

"Well, Mr. Flemming, I'm in need of a man to run the stables on my land."

My eyes widen as my mouth slowly curls.

"And I'd like to propose you convert that garage into a mini soapmaking factory for me."

The corner of my mouth lifts higher.

"And then I need this field finished and seeded."

We've already discussed all these things, and she knows I've agreed to complete them, but I'll play along. I chuckle softly, lowering my head for hers. "Doesn't sound like anything on that list is for me?"

"Actually..." She pauses and reaches back for the tractor seat, pulling out an envelope from beneath it. She hands the envelope to me, and I stare down at it.

"What's this?" I ask, swallowing as I take the paper from her.

"Something for you." Her voice lowers, and my eyes lift looking for hers, but she keeps them aimed at the envelope in my hand. "Open it."

I flip the envelope, slide open the flap, and pull out a set of papers. Reading through the first few lines, I look up at her, watching her watch me.

"What's this?" I repeat. Although I'm reading it, I want to confirm this is what I think it is.

The deed to Hasting's property turned over to me.

"I think it's time for the Townsens and Crawfords to draw a truce. It's your land, Jedd. The land you always wanted and deserved. It wasn't right of Howard to poker it out of Boone's hand."

She's getting to know my brother, and it warms me the way he responds to her. She's good for him, but he's been good *to* her, she assures me. Her smile weakens a little, and she glances back at the papers.

"I've been done wrong by Howard as well, and it doesn't seem right to keep living with all this land. I can't work it anyway." She draws a deep breath. "But seeing as how you already built a stable on my property, you could still use it to raise your horses, and seeing as how you're already plowing this plot on your land, maybe you could finish it and plant something for me. We'll share the land even though we each own a section."

I stare at her a long minute before cupping the back of her neck and squeezing.

"Is this what you really want, Bee?"

She nods with a firm expression. "It is."

"Well, I don't."

She pulls back, but I tug her forward, and our lips collide. She fights me off at first, but I follow her. Like working with a bucking bronco, you go with the flow of the beast until you're one in rhythm. Bee gets there with me, and slowly, we fall into line. Eventually, she's kissing me back instead of pushing me off. Just when she melts into me, I pull back, and she blinks up at me.

"I have a different proposal," I say, lowering to one knee although this isn't how I planned it. "I propose we share the land but keep it as one piece of property. And screw the Townsens and the Crawfords. Let's make this the Flemming farm instead. You know I'll do anything for you, Bee, because the one thing on the list for me, Bee, is you. You're my whole list."

Tears well in her eyes, and she blinks rapidly, lifting shaky fingers for her cheeks. The envelope is still in my hand, but I transfer it to my claw and then rip it in half.

347

"I don't need the deed to the land, Bee. I need the deed to your heart."

"Oh Jedd," she says, unable to hold back a smile.

"Marry me, Bee. This proposal is for real. I wanted it to be better, more romantic, but I can't wait anymore. I…" Her hands cover my jaw, and her head lowers to mine.

"Jedd," she moans. "Just kiss me."

"Not before you answer me."

"I love you, Jedd. The answer is yes. Now kiss me." Her command is my will, and I do what she asks. I kiss her, letting her know that with this that kiss, I promise to be a good man, deserving of her, working with her, and never letting her be alone again.

"I love you, too, honey," I say, releasing the kiss but not her lips, letting the words I've only ever said to her vibrate between us. This is a first for me. One of many I hope to have with her.

"There's one more thing I think we should discuss," I say, tugging at her from my kneeling position. Her knees buckle, and she lowers to my level.

"What's that?" She giggles, wrapping her arms around my neck.

"I think we should talk about laying my wood in your pasture."

"Cheeseoncrackers," she mutters, rolling her eyes.

"We can use that too if you'd like."

"Oh my gosh, Jedd. You are so dirty sometimes," she teases.

"You like my dirty thoughts, though, don't you?"

"I love them." She laughs. "I love you. Now about that wood…" She pushes me so I fall back on the earth, taking her down with me. She lands over me.

"I have wood for you, honey. I'll give you all the wood you'll ever need." And that's what I do, right there in the field, on the land where we'll work together, love together, and just be…together.

* * *

Did you enjoy this story?
Have you read Naomi's story yet? *Love in Due Time.*

If you like sexy silver foxes and their feisty vixen love match, you might also enjoy: *Silver Brewer*
Please flip the pages for a preview of *Love in a Pickle* (Scotia Simmons) – coming 2021

* * *

More by L.B. Dunbar

Sexy Silver Foxes/Former Rock Stars
When sexy silver foxes meet the women of their dreams.
After Care
Midlife Crisis
Restored Dreams
Second Chance
Wine&Dine

The Silver Foxes of Blue Ridge
More sexy silver foxes in the mountain community of Blue Ridge
Silver Brewer
Silver Player (2020)
Silver Mayor (2020)
Silver Biker (2020)

Collision novellas
A spin-off from After Care – the younger set/rock stars
Collide
Caught – a short story

Smartypants Romance (an imprint of Penny Reid)
Tales of the Winters sisters set in Penny Reid's Green Valley.
Love in Due Time
Love in Deed (2020)
Love in a Pickle (2021)

Rom-com for the over 40
The Sex Education of M.E.

The Sensations Collection
Small town, sweet and sexy stories of family and love.
Sound Advice
Taste Test
Fragrance Free
Touch Screen
Sight Words

Spin-off Standalone
The History in Us

The Legendary Rock Star Series
Rock star mayhem in the tradition of King Arthur.
A classic tale with a modern twist of romance and suspense
The Legend of Arturo King
The Story of Lansing Lotte

The Quest of Perkins Vale
The Truth of Tristan Lyons
The Trials of Guinevere DeGrance

<u>Paradise Duet</u>
MMA chaos of biblical proportion between two brothers and
the fight for love.
Abel
Cain

The Island Duet
The island knows what you've done.
Redemption Island
Return to the Island

Modern Descendants – writing as elda lore
Modern myths of Greek gods.
Hades
Solis
Heph

ACKNOWLEDGMENTS

(L)ittle (B)lessings of Gratitude

No work of mine is complete without the generous assistance of Melissa Shank, Jenny Simms, and Karen Fischer for reads and re-reads, edits and proofreads. You ladies polish me up nicely. Also, special shout out to Heather Monroe for her assistance once again with all things Pennyverse. In addition, thank you to Fiona Fischer and Brooke Mann Nowiski for all the behind-the-scenes work they do for Smartypants Romance and to the Overlord and creative genius, Penny Reid.

I'd like to thank Penny a second time for collecting a group of woman who are incredible writers, incredibly generous, and just amazing people. The Smartypants Romance author group has been a rare gem and I am so honored to call everyone an author friend. Thank you for your constant support as we triumphed round one and then still held hands to make it through round two. Here's an advance cheers to round three.

Hugs and more hugs to readers—old and new. For my little slice of social media (Loving L.B. on Facebook), you feisty vixens know you are my safe haven, my laughter zone, my vent space, and my sexy silver fox headquarters. Thank you for following me into Smartypants Romance. AND to new readers, for taking a chance on an author you might not have known, or someone you'd heard of but hadn't read yet. I'm so honored.

Last but never least in heart is my own tight-knit community—the Dunbar clan—Mr. Dunbar, MD, MK, JR and A. For going along with Mom trying to make her way over forty (actually over 50!).

ABOUT THE AUTHOR

Love Notes
www.lbdunbar.com

L.B. Dunbar loves the sweeter things in life: cookies, Coca-Cola, and romance. Her reading journey began with a deep love of fairy tales and alpha males. She loves a deep belly laugh and a strong hug. Occasionally, she has the energy of a Jack Russell terrier. Accused—yes, that's the correct word—of having an overactive imagination, to her benefit, such an imagination works well. Author of over two dozen novels, she's created sexy rom-coms for the over 40; intrigue on an island; MMA chaos; rock star mayhem, and sweet small-town romance. In addition, she earned a title as the "myth and legend lady" for her modernizations of mythology as elda lore. Her other duties in life include mother to four children and wife to the one and only.

* * *

www.lbdunbar.com
Stalk Me: https://www.facebook.com/lbdunbarauthor
Instagram Me: @lbdunbarwrites
Read Me:
https://www.goodreads.com/author/show/8195738.L_B_Dunbar
Follow Me: https://www.bookbub.com/profile/l-b-dunbar
Tweet Me: https://twitter.com/lbdunbarwrites
Pin Me: http://www.pinterest.com/lbdunbar/

Get News Here: https://app.mailerlite.com/webforms/landing/j7j2s0
AND more things here
Hang with us: Loving L.B. (reader group): https://www.facebook.com/groups/LovingLB/

Find Smartypants Romance online:
Website: www.smartypantsromance.com
Facebook: www.facebook.com/smartypantsromance/
Goodreads: www.goodreads.com/smartypantsromance
Twitter: @smartypantsrom
Instagram: @smartypantsromance

Read on for:
1. L.B. Dunbar's Booklist
2. Smartypants Romance's Booklist

ALSO BY LB DUNBAR

Sexy Silver Foxes/Former Rock Stars

When sexy silver foxes meet the women of their dreams.

After Care

Midlife Crisis

Restored Dreams

Second Chance

Wine&Dine

Collision novellas

A spin-off from After Care – the younger set/rock stars

Collide

Rom-com for the over 40

The Sex Education of M.E.

The Sensations Collection

Small town, sweet and sexy stories of family and love.

Sound Advice

Taste Test

Fragrance Free

Touch ScreenSight Words

Spin-off Standalone

The History in Us

The Legendary Rock Star Series

Rock star mayhem in the tradition of King Arthur.

A classic tale with a modern twist of romance and suspense

The Legend of Arturo King

The Story of Lansing Lotte

The Quest of Perkins Vale

The Truth of Tristan Lyons

The Trials of Guinevere DeGrance

<u>Paradise Duet</u>

MMA chaos of biblical proportion between two brothers and

the fight for love.

Abel

Cain

The Island Duet

The island knows what you've done.

Redemption Island

Return to the Island

Modern Descendants – writing as elda lore

Modern myths of Greek gods.

Hades

Solis

Heph

CPSIA information can be obtained
at www.ICGtesting.com
Printed in the USA
LVHW011759070820
662641LV00003B/455